RITUALS

Also by Kelley Armstrong

RITUALS

KELLEY
ARMSTRONG

sphere

SPHERE

First published in Great Britain in 2017 by Sphere

1 3 5 7 9 10 8 6 4 2

A CIP catalogue record for this book is
available from the British Library.

HB ISBN 978-0-7515-6128-9
C format ISBN 978-0-7515-6129-6

Printed and bound in Great Britain by Clays Ltd, St Ives plc

Papers used by Sphere are from well-managed
forests and other responsible sources.

Sphere
An imprint of
Little, Brown Book Group
Carmelite House
50 Victoria Embankment
London EC4Y 0DZ

An Hachette UK Company
www.hachette.co.uk

www.littlebrown.co.uk

FOR JEFF

RITUALS

CHAPTER ONE

As Gabriel's Jag tore up the country road, I stared at the house ahead. Flames blazed from every window. An ambulance sat in the driveway, lights flashing. As I saw that, I exhaled. The only witness who could set my father free was in that house, and we'd been terrified we'd finally found her only to lose her again. But the ambulance said otherwise.

That's when they brought out the stretchers. With body bags.

"Maybe it's not Imogen," I said.

Gabriel parked, and as we walked toward the burning house, I surveyed the personnel on duty. I chose my target and picked up speed as Gabriel fell back. We were almost an hour outside Chicago, and these police might be state troopers, but that didn't mean they wouldn't know Gabriel by reputation . . . as one of the city's most notorious defense lawyers.

I approached the young officer left guarding the perimeter and extended my hand. "Liv Jones. We've been looking for one of the women renting this house. Imogen Seale. She's a material witness in a multiple homicide."

The trooper peered at me with a *Don't I know you from somewhere* look. But it was dark and smoky and tonight I was just Liv Jones. Not Olivia Taylor-Jones, former debutante daughter of the Mills & Jones department store owner. Certainly no relation to Eden Larsen, daughter of notorious serial killers Todd and Pamela Larsen.

"Hope she wasn't a valuable witness," the trooper said.

"Kind of," I said with a wry smile. "I'm guessing she didn't survive."

"Dead before we arrived, I'm afraid," she said. "Her mother fell asleep smoking on the sofa. You'd really think people would know better."

"No smoke detector?"

She shook her head. "In old rentals like this, nobody checks until something happens. A fifty-dollar investment could have saved two lives."

"Any chance I can see the bodies?" I asked. "If she's definitely my witness, I need to move fast in another direction."

"I hear you," she said, and waved for me to follow. "And I hate to see a killer walk free. Especially a multiple murderer."

Mmm, yeah, sorry, but actually, if we win this one, we do set a multiple murderer free. It's a package deal—getting my father out of jail means freeing my mother, too.

As we walked, Gabriel fell in beside me. When the trooper glanced at him, I said simply, "My colleague."

"Organized crime?" she said.

I choked on a laugh, and she quickly added, "I mean the case. I can imagine you'd need security for something like that."

It wasn't the first time Gabriel had been mistaken for my bodyguard. When we met, I'd pegged him as hired muscle myself. Even the expensive cut of his suit had only made me amend that to "hired muscle for someone with a lot of money." He was at least six-four and built like a linebacker. It was more than his size, though. He just had a look that made people get out of the way.

The trooper said something to one of the paramedics, who nodded and opened the smaller body bag. It was Imogen's mother. Death seemed to have been from smoke inhalation, with signs of suffocation and minimal burning, mostly to her clothing. Which meant there was no chance we were looking at the badly burned remains of a stranger. And the corpse in the other body bag? Imogen herself, mistress of Marty Tyson, one of my mother's victims. Imogen was the only person who could have testified that Tyson had actually killed the first couple my parents were supposed to have murdered. That was the reasonable doubt we'd needed to overturn the conviction.

And now we'd lost it.

Twenty-two years ago, my mother killed four people so that I could walk again. She'd made a deal with the Wild Hunt—the Cŵn Annwn—to take the lives of four killers. In return, her two-year-old daughter's severe spina bifida would disappear. And it had. I don't even remember having it.

For twenty-two years I didn't remember my parents, either. They'd been in prison, the Cŵn Annwn unable to do more than make incarceration easier for them. Of course, what the Cŵn Annwn never knew was that my father played no role in those murders. He'd gone to jail because he believed my mother did the right thing—the brave and strong thing. He stayed there because freedom would come at the cost of testifying against her, erasing any chance she had of winning an appeal.

Now, with Imogen dead, I wasn't sure either of them had any chance at all.

The next morning, Gabriel drove me to work. He'd spent the night at my house in Cainsville. In the guest room, I hasten to add. We'd been up for hours discussing the case. Now, as he pulled into the laneway of his office greystone, his topic of conversation had nothing to do with work and everything to do with distracting me from fretting over my parents' appeal. Gabriel had put himself through law school with illegal gaming, and he was finally sharing details.

"Blackjack," he said as we got out of the car. "That was my specialty. It's simple and efficient."

"It's also one of the easiest games to cheat in, isn't it? Counting cards?"

"No one counted cards at my table. Not after the first time."

As we walked around the building, the front door swung open, no one behind it. I stopped short. When I blinked, the door was shut.

A door opening on its own. The sign of an unwanted visitor.

"Olivia?"

I shook off the omen. Given what Gabriel did for a living, we got plenty of unwanted visitors.

"Sorry. Missed my cue," I said as we walked through the front door. "So, tell me, Gabriel, what'd you do the first time you caught someone counting cards?"

He studied me.

"Well, are you going to tell me?" I said. "Or is this one of those stories you tease me with and then say *Whoops, looks like we're at the office already. I'll finish later?*"

His lips twitched. "You like it when I do that. It builds suspense."

"I *hate* it when you do that. It's sadistic. You have five seconds—"

"Gabriel?" Lydia stepped out of the office, closing the door behind her.

He bristled at the interruption.

"Client?" I guessed.

Lydia nodded, and we backed farther down the hall. She glanced toward the stairs, but there was no sign of the other tenants. Still, she lowered her voice as she said, "It's a woman. She claims to be a relative."

Gabriel grumbled under his breath. The fact Gabriel had a legit job made him one of the few "white sheep" in the Walsh family. So, yes, I was sure relatives showed up now and then, in need of his services. Which he would happily give, providing they could pay his fees.

"Prospects?" he said to Lydia.

Lydia's look said this one wouldn't be paying her bills anytime soon.

"I'll get rid of her," I said.

Gabriel hesitated. While he hated relinquishing control, this was the efficient solution. Also, listening to some distant relative sob on his sofa was both terribly awkward and a pointless waste of billable hours.

"The sooner we get rid of her, the sooner we can get to work on our appeal strategy," I said. "I'd appreciate that."

He nodded. "All right. I'll go get you a mocha. Lydia?"

"Chai latte, please," she said.

As Lydia opened the office door, I raised my voice and said, "So, yeah, don't expect Gabriel anytime soon. This courthouse issue could take all day. We need to—"

I stopped short, as if Lydia hadn't mentioned a client in the reception area. When I got a look at the woman, though, I didn't need to feign my shock.

I couldn't guess at her age. Maybe sixty, but in a haggard, hard-living way that suggested the truth was about a decade younger. Her coloring matched Gabriel's, what his great-aunt Rose called "black Irish"—pale skin, blue eyes, and wavy black hair. She also had the sturdy Walsh build that Gabriel shared with Rose, along with their square face, widow's peak, and pale blue eyes.

Yet I already knew this woman claimed to be a relative, so it wasn't the resemblance that stopped me in my tracks.

I'd seen her face before. In the photo of a dead woman.

I had to be mistaken, of course. The dead woman had also been a Walsh, so there was a strong resemblance—that's all.

I walked over, hand extended as she rose. "I'm—"

"The infamous Eden Larsen," she said, and my hackles rose. I am Eden Larsen, as much as I'm Olivia Taylor-Jones. But calling me by my birth name is the social equivalent of a smirk and a smackdown. *I know who you really are, Miss Larsen.*

I responded with the kind of smile I learned from my adoptive mother. The smile of a society matron plucking the dagger from her back and calmly wiping off the blood before it stains.

"It's Olivia," I said. "And you are?"

A smile played at her lips, and that smile did more than raise my hackles. My gut twisted, and I wanted to shove her out the door. Just grab her arm and muscle her out before she said another word.

"I'm Seanna Walsh," she said. "Gabriel's mother."

CHAPTER TWO

"Seanna Walsh?" I forced a laugh. "Uh, no. If you're going to impersonate a long-lost relative, I'd suggest you pick one who's actually alive."

"Don't I look alive to you, Eden?"

Behind me, Lydia said, "I believe she asked you to call her Olivia."

Lydia's gaze laser-beamed on the woman, as if ready to throw her out. Gabriel's assistant may be well past retirement age, but I didn't doubt she could do it. When I shook my head, though, Lydia walked stiffly to her desk and lowered herself onto the front of it, perched there, ready for action.

"You are not Seanna Walsh," I said. "I've seen photographs of her, both before and after her death. You may resemble Seanna, but those coroner pics guarantee you are not her."

"And I guarantee I am. The pictures were staged."

"Bullshit," I said, bearing down on her. "You cannot stage—"

"With enough money, you certainly can."

"Which only proves you are not Seanna Walsh, who never had a dime she didn't stick up her arm."

"So it's true, then. You and my son are more than coworkers."

Footsteps sounded in the hallway.

"Get—" I began.

"Get where? Under the desk? Behind the bathroom door? Where exactly are you going to hide me, Eden? And why bother, if I'm not really his mother?"

The footfalls continued past the office door. Just one of Gabriel's upstairs tenants.

I took out my phone and texted him. *Can you stay away longer, pls?*

The *please* would tell Gabriel I was serious. A moment later, he replied saying he was supposed to visit a client at Cook County this morning and should he just do that?

Yes, pls.

I pocketed my phone and turned to the woman.

"Sit down."

She gave that spine-raking smile again. "So you *are* sleeping with my son. I notice you didn't deny it."

"Gabriel and I are friends. Good friends."

"Gabriel doesn't have friends. No one wants to hang out with a freak."

I felt Lydia's hand on my arm before I even realized I was surging forward, my fists clenched.

In that moment, I forgot that this couldn't possibly be Seanna Walsh. That was who I saw, who I heard, and I wanted to wrap my hands around her throat and choke the life out of her. It was only when I realized what I was thinking that I exhaled fast and hard.

"Sit down," I said again.

She started for the door.

I stepped into her path. "I told you—"

"No, Eden. You are adorable, really, but completely out of your league. Go back to painting your nails or picking out a new wardrobe or whatever your type does."

I lifted my hand . . . to point a gun at her forehead. "This is what my type does. Or have you forgotten who my parents are?"

She laughed. "You aren't that girl, Miss Eden. You might carry that gun and call yourself a private investigator, but those blue jeans cost a week's salary. You're a trust-fund baby, and *my* baby is going to fleece you for every penny you have. I hope you realize he's running a long con here. Give the debutante her bad-girl dream, empty her trust fund, and then dump her pretty little ass."

I could have told her Gabriel doesn't need my money. That he owned this building. Owned a million-dollar condo. Kept a hundred grand in cash under his bed for "emergencies." But that would mean giving her some idea exactly how much *her* mark was worth. So I shot her.

The woman fell back, yowling, though the bullet had barely scraped her leg.

I turned to Lydia. "Please call the police and tell them I have been forced to shoot an intruder. It's only a scratch, but they still may want to send an ambulance."

Lydia picked up the phone. The woman lunged to grab it.

I motioned for Lydia to hang up and said calmly, "Are you going to sit down now?"

"You—you shot—"

"I grazed you." I grabbed a tissue box from Lydia's desk and tossed it at the woman. "Wipe up the blood. If you play nice, I'll get you bandages. I might even toss in five bucks to buy a patch for your jeans. Now sit. Lydia? Any chance you could grab me a mocha?"

Gabriel had a rule about not involving Lydia in trouble, and the legality of that bullet graze was already highly questionable. When I mouthed, "Please?" she nodded with reluctance.

"I'll be right around the corner," she said.

I waited until she was gone. The woman still wasn't sitting. She wasn't making any move to leave, either, so I decided not to press the point.

"Seanna Walsh is dead," I said.

"No, Seanna Walsh was *playing* dead." She tossed bloodied tissues aside. "I knew this guy—a police sergeant—who used to make problems disappear for a price. We had an arrangement. One night he brought dope to a party, where he got loaded and told me he nabbed a half kilo of coke from the evidence locker. I saw an opportunity."

"To do what? Steal it?"

She snorted. "That would be stupid. I'm not stupid."

I bit my tongue.

"I was dealing with other shit at the time," she said. "I'd conned a guy who blew it all out of proportion. Put a bounty on my head. A *bounty*." She sounded genuinely insulted. "I cut a deal with this sergeant. I'd keep my mouth shut about the dope if he'd help me disappear—stage my death so no one would come after me."

"No one even realized Seanna Walsh was dead until this spring. Fifteen years after she disappeared."

"He screwed me over. The cops were supposed to find this Jane Doe who OD'd—I knew where her body was. My guy would wait six months and then swap her photos with mine and have someone ID me as the dead woman."

"That is the stupidest scheme I've ever heard," I said. "One, someone could have ID'd the real body, which would have ruined everything. Two, six months isn't enough time for those who actually worked on the dead woman's case to forget what she looked like."

"Do you really think anyone gives a shit about some addict who offs herself in an empty building? She was a white chick with dark hair and blue eyes. Close enough. The problem was that, six months later, I was long gone, so this sergeant decided he could swap the photos and leave it at that. Skip the positive ID. I spent years—*years*—on the run because the asshole who put out the bounty on me figured I bolted. All because that bastard cop couldn't hold up his end of the deal."

"And Gabriel?"

Her face screwed up. "What?"

"His mother left him. At fifteen. She walked away without a word. Without leaving him one penny."

A dismissive eye roll. "Gabriel could look after himself. He'd already been doing it for years. Not that he ever contributed anything. Just made enough for himself."

"He was a *child*," I snarled. "He shouldn't have had to take care of *anyone*."

"Why not? Everyone does, eventually. Better to learn that lesson early. And look where it got him." She waved around the office. "A big-shot lawyer. Drives a fancy car. Lives in a fancy apartment. He wouldn't have all this if I'd coddled him."

"Get out."

"Oh, so now you want me to leave? Make up your mind, girl."

I pulled out the gun and pointed it at her head. "Get out now."

She started to make some sarcastic comment. Then she met my gaze, shut her mouth, and limped out the door.

When Lydia returned, I was in the bathroom, plucking hairs from Gabriel's brush and putting them into a plastic bag. I emerged, and her gaze traveled from the bag in my hand to the bag on her desk, containing the bloodied tissues.

"You really think it could be her?" she said.

"I think I need that answer as fast as I can get it," I said. "I'll pay whatever it takes."

CHAPTER THREE

Cook County Jail was about a mile from the office. My car was at home in Cainsville, so I walked to the prison, after texting Gabriel to say I was coming. He usually left his cell in the car, and I was almost there before he replied.

I met him in the parking lot. "Lydia says your schedule is now appointment-free for the day. Any chance we can work at my place? We need to talk, and I don't want that woman showing up at your office again."

He paused before opening his car door. "May I ask what she wanted?"

"We can talk at my place."

He got in. When my door closed, he cleared his throat and then said, "You're obviously shaken, which means it was more than a stray relative seeking free legal advice. I've mentioned that I faced a false paternity suit before . . ."

I burst out laughing, mostly in relief. The paternity suit had been a scam that backfired spectacularly. Anyone who knew Gabriel wouldn't have attempted it. He'd never be careless about anything that could cost him money.

He continued, "Ah, well, I can assure you, it won't be the first time a relative—real or otherwise—popped from the woodwork hoping for a handout. I'm sure your family has their share of experience with that. And in mine, there are even more empty hands and wild stories intended to fill them. But we can work as well at your house as in the office, and Rose has been asking us to tea. Text, and tell her we'll come at four."

We drove to my house. Well, it's not actually mine. I'm halfway through a two-month trial run. The elders offered me the Carew house for an excellent price, purportedly because it belonged to my great-great-grandmother and has stood empty for years. The truth is that they're desperate for me to put down roots in Cainsville.

It's a gorgeous place. A stately Queen Anne with a half tower, forming a window seat in my bedroom. In the past month, I'd been making the house mine. I'd lived in a Cainsville apartment for six months and never even added a throw pillow. Here, I had pillows, art, garden furniture . . . I still claimed I hadn't made up my mind, but I was feathering this nest as fast as I could.

We walked in the front door. I kicked off my shoes. Gabriel lined his up on the mat, which he'd bought last week. He might counsel me not to make a decision too hastily, but I wasn't the only one adding the little touches that turned this house into a home.

Gabriel headed straight to the kitchen to warm up the coffee machine. Even if we don't have coffee right away, he'll make that detour, as if the front door leads directly to the machine. Then he joined me in the parlor, where I'd curled up on the couch. He took the other end.

I shifted to sit sideways. "There's no easy way to say this. The woman who came to the office claims to be your mother."

His brows shot up. "She claims that my mother isn't Seanna Walsh? That's a first."

"This woman says she *is* Seanna."

He looked at me, those eerily pale blue eyes fixed on mine, and for a moment that's all I could see—those ice-blue irises ringed with a blue so dark it looked black. Then he laughed, and the sound was so unexpected, I jumped.

"I don't mean to laugh," he said. "Obviously, you were concerned about how I might react to this impostor. I appreciate that concern, Olivia. And yes, as much as I'd like to say that I don't care—*never* cared—the truth is that until six months ago this was indeed my greatest fear—that I'd walk into the office one day and Seanna would be sitting there with her hand out. I shouldn't say I was glad to learn she was dead. But I was. It lifted a weight."

"I don't blame you."

"My mother is clearly dead," he said. "Dealing with an impersonator will not rattle me. Nor will it resurrect old memories."

I wanted to leave it at that. Shove it aside until the DNA test came back, and once it was negative, I could breathe a sigh of relief. But Gabriel knew me too well.

When he saw my expression, he said, "You don't honestly believe there's a chance she is Seanna, do you?"

"Of course not. I saw the coroner's photos. Yes, this woman looks like her, but she'd need to, in order to pull it off. And her story is preposterous."

"What *is* her story?"

"Oh, some crap about a bargain with a cop." I rose from the sofa and headed for the kitchen. "Do you want coffee? Rose brought over fresh chocolate chip cookies. Your favorite."

I grabbed two mugs and stuck one under the coffeemaker as I hit the button. I was taking out a plate for the cookies when a form darkened the kitchen doorway, shadow stretching across the sun-dappled floor.

"What exactly was her story?" he asked.

"Like I said, some bullshit—"

"I'd like to hear the whole thing."

I told him. When I finished, he walked to the kitchen table and pulled out a chair. Then he stiffly lowered himself into it.

"It's ridiculous," I said, bringing over the coffees, sloshing slightly. I put them down and crossed my arms to hide my shaking hands. "Fake her death to escape a bounty? Not even *actually* fake it, but only switch photos six months later and expect she'll be legally declared dead? There are a million easier ways to disappear. It's a preposterous scheme."

"Seanna's always were." He took the coffee but only placed it in front of him. "She was a petty thief who fancied herself a con artist. That was her idea of career aspiration. Unfortunately, she lacked the intelligence—or the patience—to carry out a proper con. This is exactly the sort of thing she'd come up with and then be shocked when the officer didn't hold up his end of the bargain."

"It isn't her."

He ran his thumb over the coffee mug handle.

"It's not," I said.

"Of course it isn't," he replied, but a little too slowly, his gaze still fixed on his mug. "It can't be."

He turned the mug. Still didn't take a sip. Just turned it. Then he straightened and took out his phone.

"We're going to need to deal with it, though," he said. "I don't have time to argue with this woman. We'll jump straight to disproving her claim through a DNA analysis. That will mean you'll need to find some way to collect hers." He caught my look. "You already have it?"

I didn't answer.

"You have it, and you've sent it in." He nodded and put his phone away. "Dare I ask how you obtained it?"

"I shot her."

His lips twitched. "You . . ."

"She pissed me off."

He choked on a laugh. "I see."

"She *really* pissed me off."

"Dare I ask what she said?"

He was still smiling, but my cheeks heated, and I walked to the counter to fetch the cookies. "It doesn't matter. She pissed me off, so I shot her in the leg. It was just a graze, but I got enough blood for Lydia to send off for a DNA analysis."

His smile evaporated. "Lydia was there?"

"Yes. I'm sorry. I wasn't thinking clearly or I'd never have shot someone in front of her. I got Lydia out after that, though, before the woman gave her story."

He relaxed. "All right, then. The DNA analysis is under way. While I doubt this woman will return to the office today, I will call Lydia with instructions. We'll also need to tell Rose immediately, should this woman attempt to contact her."

"Do you want to call Rose?"

"It is a complicated situation, as I'm sure you're aware. I'd like to tell her in person."

Seanna was the connection between Rose and Gabriel, yet to him, she was the nightmare who didn't deserve the name of mother, while Rose remembered the beloved niece whose life had gone horribly wrong. For Rose, it had been difficult to see the monster her niece had become and not want to say, "But she isn't really like that, it's the fae blood, the drugs, the alcohol . . ." The one person she can never say that to is Gabriel, because it trivializes his own experience.

Gabriel sipped his coffee, his gaze fixed on a spot across the kitchen.

"I have laundry I could fold," I said.

"If you're offering me time alone, just say so, Olivia. Unless your laundry is in urgent need of folding, I do not require time for myself. In fact, I'd prefer to do just about anything else right now, including laundry."

"Let's work, then."

I fetched my laptop bag from the front hall. TC followed me into the kitchen and hopped onto the table to sit in front of Gabriel. They stared at each other. It wasn't a territorial stare-down. It wasn't even TC hinting he'd like a pat. It was, I think, their version of a greeting.

I see you're back.

Yes, I am.

All right, then.

TC hopped off the table, walked to his bowl, and waited. I filled it, and by the time I was finished, Gabriel had relocated to the parlor. I sat beside him on the sofa, my back resting against his shoulder as I opened my laptop.

"I'm going to put aside my parents' appeal for today and clear a few others," I said. "First up, Monty Miller. I'm stalled at—"

My phone chirped with a text. When I made no movement to answer, Gabriel fished the phone from my pocket and checked. The possibility that might be considered rude never occurs to him.

"Ricky," he said as he passed it over.

Ricky Gallagher is my ex. I don't call him that, though. An ex is someone you've left behind, usually with the associated nasti-ness and pain of a breakup. I won't pretend there wasn't pain in ours. No nastiness, though. Ricky had decided we should step back, for very good and very selfless reasons, and I'd had to agree. Which doesn't mean it was easy. Or that I don't light up, seeing his name on my cell-phone screen, before I remember that things have changed. The fact we texted about twenty times a day meant there were a lot of those little stabs of grief. But that constant contact also meant we were navigating the transition from lovers to friends better than I had dared hope.

He'd texted: *I thought hurricane season was over.*

I chuckled and replied: *No hurricanes here.*

Him: *Rub it in.*

Me: *Florida's a bit windy, I take it?*

He was in Miami doing work for his father. I had no idea exactly what kind of work. That's for the best, considering I work for his family lawyer . . . and Ricky's family business is running a biker gang.

We texted for a few minutes. Gabriel read over my shoulder, presuming if it was private, I'd have moved away. After a few back-and-forths, Ricky said: *Got a favor to ask. You busy?*

When I hesitated, Gabriel leaned over and typed: *No.*

Ricky: *It's Lloe. Ioan says she isn't eating.*

Lloe was short for Lloergan, Ricky's hound. A fae hound. "Cŵn Annwn" literally translates to "Hounds of the Otherworld." Lloergan was a badly damaged *cŵn* Ricky had rescued. She lived with his grandfather, Ioan, who was the leader of the local Cŵn Annwn. Yes, Ricky was descended from the Wild Hunt. He wasn't just any human descendant, either. He was the living embodiment of Arawn, legendary lord of the Otherworld. Which meant Lloergan was absolutely devoted to him. But, being a biker and part-time MBA student, there was no place in his life for a dog right now, so she stayed with Ioan, and Ricky took her when he could.

It had been three days since Ricky left for Miami, and we'd hoped Lloergan would be fine. Obviously not.

Ricky texted: *Can u stop by? Take her 4 a run? That might help. Or if u could dog-sit . . .*

Of course, I had no problem looking after Lloe. Given the circumstances with this Seanna impostor, though . . .

Gabriel took my phone. He typed: *That's fine.* Then he erased and rephrased it in Olivia-speak: *Sure, no problem.*

"Otherwise, you'll worry about her," Gabriel said as he sent the message. "And with this woman coming around, I'm not averse to the idea of you having a supernatural guard dog right now."

Thx! Ricky texted back. *I owe u.*

I signed off with Ricky, and I was putting away my phone when TC slunk past, heading for his spot in the front window.

"Hey, cat," I said. "We're bringing home a friend for you. A doggie big enough to devour you in a single gulp. Is that okay?"

He turned a baleful stare on me, as if he understood. I'm convinced TC isn't just a cat, no more than Llocrgan is just a dog. Maybe someday, when I'm moments from perishing at the hands of an intruder, TC will save me in a sudden and awe-inspiring display of supernatural power. Or maybe he'll decide I haven't given him enough tuna that week and leave me to my fate. He's a cat, so I figure my chances are about fifty-fifty.

When footsteps sounded on the porch, TC hissed. I glanced out the window, saw Ida, and groaned. TC hissed again.

"Excellent instincts," I said to the cat. "Now can you make her disappear?"

He tore off up the stairs.

"That's not what I meant!" I called after him.

Like the other Cainsville elders, Ida is fae. As for why she was on my doorstep . . . Well, it begins with Welsh lore. The story of Mallt-y-Nos. Matilda of the Night. Matilda of the Hunt.

According to the myth, on the eve of her marriage to a fae prince, Matilda begged her betrothed to let her ride with the Cŵn Annwn one last time. He said that if she did, the world of the fae would close to her forever. She still couldn't resist and ran to her old friend, leader of the Cŵn Annwn, and there she was trapped, forced to lead the Wild Hunt for eternity.

The truth was a little more complex. That story starts with two boys and a girl. A Tylwyth Teg prince: Gwynn ap Nudd. A Cŵn Annwn prince: Arawn. And Matilda, a *dynes hysbys* girl, half fae and half Hunt. The three grew up as best friends, and the boys agreed that to preserve their friendship—and peace between their people—they would never court Matilda. Of course, they forgot to tell *her* that. She fell for Gwynn, who promptly abandoned his promise. When Arawn found out, he was furious and the two young men made another pact: if Matilda went to Arawn the night before her wedding, she was his.

Again they didn't inform Matilda because, you know, she might have told them they were idiots. The big night came. When Matilda ran off for one last Hunt with Arawn, the world of the Tylwyth Teg closed in a ring of fire.

As soon as Matilda saw that, she raced back to Gwynn, and both young men tried to save her, only to watch her perish in the flames. Cue centuries of animosity, the princes becoming kings, each blaming the other for the loss of their beloved Matilda.

The story didn't end even on their deaths. The three actors are continually reborn. Not reincarnation exactly, but some essence of the originals living on in new players. It is said that if a new Matilda aligns herself with one side over the other—Tylwyth Teg or Cŵn Annwn—she brings unfettered access to the elemental resources that keep the fae alive. In the modern world, those resources—clean air and water and earth—are in ever-diminishing supply, so for both fae and Huntsman, getting a Matilda meant winning the survival lottery.

As might be obvious, I am the new Matilda. I had yet to declare an alliance. I had no idea how to even *make* that choice.

While there was no reason I couldn't choose Arawn as a lover but support the Tylwyth Teg instead, that's not how anyone presumes it will work, so both sides hope if I choose their "champion," it will seal the deal. And those champions? Ricky as the new Arawn. Gabriel as Gwynn.

Ida banged the knocker. I groaned again. Gabriel shook his head and went to answer the door.

"I thought you were over the fae compulsion thing," I said.

"I am. But either we answer or we remain trapped in this house until Ida and the elders decide to leave town."

"I don't think they ever leave."

"Exactly my point." He opened the door. "Hello, Ida."

"We'd like to speak to Liv."

I walked into the hall and saw that "we" meant Ida and her consort, Walter. There was no sign of Veronica, which suggested they were going behind her back for this visit. Veronica had a habit— terribly annoying to Ida—of insisting I not be treated like a lottery ticket found on their doorstep.

"I know why you're here," Gabriel said. "By contractual agreement, you have one week before you can begin your campaign to win Olivia. You are hoping to open preliminary talks, so on that date you may begin full negotiations. The answer is no. You will wait another week."

"It's a ridiculous contract."

"Then you ought not to have signed it."

Ida glowered at him. The problem with having humans as the living embodiments of Gwynn, Arawn, and Matilda? It's like trying to draft all-star quarterbacks who don't give a shit about football.

"If you'll excuse us . . ." Gabriel said, waving me to the door.

I grabbed things and squeezed past Ida and Walter with a quick, "Hey, how's it going? Sorry to run. Gotta pick up a hound."

"A what?" Ida said, following me down the front steps.

"Hound. Cŵn. Ricky's. With him away in Miami, she's not eating, so I'm bringing her here." I walked backward. "That's okay, right?"

She gave me a look. A *cŵn* in Cainsville meant a spy in enemy territory.

"We could do an exchange," I said. "Make Ioan take one of Cainsville's owls. Or a gargoyle. I could insist that Ioan prop one up by his door to keep an eye on him while I have Lloergan here. They're stonework spies, right?"

"There's no point in fishing regarding the gargoyles," Ida said. "We will be very happy to explain everything . . . as soon as you lift the terms of our agreement."

"Oh, fine. One last thing," I said. "If a woman shows up claiming to be Seanna Walsh, can you give her something to drink? Whatever it is you guys use to send someone into permanent la-la land. That'd be swell."

"Seanna—? Did you say Seanna Walsh?"

"Gotta run," I said, hopping into the car before she could reply.

CHAPTER FOUR

I oan wasn't thrilled when I showed up with Gabriel in tow. He was gracious enough, though, having learned that anything else makes me surly. Gabriel, Ricky, and I fight against our roles as pawns by sticking together. That's where the original three failed. We will not repeat their mistakes.

On the return drive to Cainsville, I sat in the back with Lloergan. *Under* her mostly, given her size. I had a bag of her food, and she was taking pieces from me. As she ate, I rubbed her good ear. The other is little more than a ragged stump, and she's partially blind in one eye, old injuries from an attack that killed the rest of her pack.

After that attack, Lloergan had been found by a twisted bastard who didn't deserve the name of Huntsman. He'd helped her recover from her injuries . . . but only so she could serve him. When we took his hound, he'd fled to parts unknown.

All of that left Lloergan a bit of a mess, maimed from the attack and suffering from years of psychological abuse. She was improving, though. Her coat gleamed. Her ribs no longer showed. Perhaps more importantly, she didn't cower before the Huntsmen and their hounds. Her psychic bond with the Cŵn Annwn had been severed in the attack, but we'd seen hints of it re-forming with both Ricky and me.

Gabriel drove along a back road. Snow had begun to fall, and people hadn't yet remembered how to drive in winter, so it was safer staying off the highway.

As I traced a flake down the side window, I said, "Solstice, right?"

"Hmm?"

"Cainsville celebrates Solstice, not Christmas."

"They acknowledge Christmas. They decorate the trees and whatnot, but yes, Solstice is the big day. Or night, as it were."

"And you'll show me your gargoyle then?"

He gave an uncharacteristic, "What?"

"You found your last gargoyle on Solstice. That's the only time it appears. With that, you won the contest and had a gargoyle made in your likeness. Ergo, you'll show yours to me on Solstice night."

"I fail to follow the logic of that explanation."

"It's Liv-logic. I've decided that's what I want for my Solstice gift. To see your gargoyle."

"I don't believe anyone said anything about a Solstice gift."

Lloergan growled.

"Be nice," I said to Gabriel. "You're upsetting the puppy."

"That 'puppy' is nearly as big as me."

Another growl.

"Careful," I said. "You might be bigger, but her teeth are a lot sharper. You—"

Lloe scrambled up, growling and snapping.

"Whoa, girl! Down!"

A shape darted onto the road ahead.

"Gabri—!" I began.

He'd already hit the brakes. The car went into a slide, the road slick with new snow. I wrapped my arms around Lloergan and braced for impact. A thunk as the car went off the road. Then the clatter of wet gravel hitting the underside. A crack, and a jolt slammed me back in my seat, Lloergan scrambling, her nails digging into my leg.

One moment of absolute silence.

Then, "Olivia?" A pause and the clack of a seat belt. "Olivia?"

"I'm fine," I said, my voice muffled. "Just buried under a hundred and fifty pounds of fur. Lloe? Are you—?"

A very cold nose snuffled my neck, and her nails clawed my legs as she tried to stand on my lap.

"Oww . . ." I said.

More snuffling, now with an edge of worry.

"I'm fine, girl," I said. "You make a wonderful air bag, but can you please get—"

The door opened, and Gabriel tugged Lloe out. I started to follow, but he insisted on a quick once-over—*does anything hurt? how's your neck?*—before setting me free.

I wobbled from the car, and I was sure I'd be stiff in the morning, but otherwise I seemed fine.

The car had slid onto the shoulder and struck a rock. It wasn't a big rock. Just enough to stop the Jag and set off the air bags, which left the car non-drivable.

"You'll need to call for a tow," I said.

He took out his cell phone. "No service."

"Naturally." I checked mine. "Same."

"I should hope so, considering we're with the same provider—the one Ricky set us up with. Which I've noticed has substandard coverage. I'm sure it has unlimited texts and calling, which is a benefit . . . to *you* two."

"Um, the guy replaced our ruined cell phones after we both almost drowned, and you're complaining?"

"No." He looked at his phone again. "Not exactly."

"Get a new provider if you don't like that one. Right now, we have a disabled car in the middle of nowhere. On an empty road. With a winter storm whipping up. Can you see any sign of . . ." I squinted against the endless white. "Anything?"

"No."

"All right. Come on, Lloe. We're going for a walk."

She sat on the roadside.

"Yes, I know," I said. "It's snowing. It's cold. You haven't eaten enough to 'need' a walk. But we really don't have a choice."

She lay down.

"Lloergan," Gabriel said firmly. "We are leaving. If you wish to remain here, you may." He opened the door. "It will be warmer in there. I'll turn on the emergency flashers."

"How much of that do you think she understands?"

His look said it didn't matter—the point was that he had explained, and if she lacked the mental capacity to comprehend, that was hardly his fault.

I waved Lloergan toward the open car door. "Go on. We won't be long."

She laid her head on her paws. Gabriel closed the door and started walking away. Lloe rose, growling.

"I think she's telling us not to leave," I said. "She did warn us that something was about to run across the road. Did you see what it was?"

Gabriel looked around as if—like me—he'd forgotten all about the cause of the accident.

"I presumed a deer," he said, "but I couldn't tell."

"This strikes me as a little too familiar."

"If you mean the last time we were run off the road, I believe you'd swerved to avoid one of those." He waved at Lloergan.

"Yes, but *that* didn't cause me to drive your car off the embankment." The hound had been a warning, one that came too late for me to avoid getting run off the road by a killer.

I continued, "Something darted in front of the car after

Lloergan warned us. It disappeared, but not before we went off the shoulder. Now we're stranded on an empty road in a snowstorm, forced to go looking for help."

"An omen, then. We're supposed to search for something."

"Or it's a trap. But the possibility we're stranded here by accident is about zero."

He peered into the falling snow. Then he turned to the hound. "If there's something out there that bothers you, this car isn't going to protect us. We need to find out what it is."

Lloergan grumbled and glowered at Gabriel. She walked over and nudged his leg, none too gently, as if to say, *Well, get on with it, then. It's your funeral.*

As we headed down the road, I said, "What's the last movie we saw together?"

"We've never seen one together."

"Last one you saw?"

Silence, as he struggled to remember.

"Good enough," I said, and he nodded. He knew I was trying to determine whether this might be a vision, and I was zoned out in the Jag's backseat as it roared along.

I shoved my hands into my pockets. We hadn't officially hit winter yet, so I'd still been dressing for fall, expecting to spend maybe five minutes outside. My cropped leather jacket was more fashionable than practical. Same went for my footwear: Louboutin ankle boots with three-inch heels, which threatened to slide out from under me with each step.

Gabriel kept pulling ahead and then having to slow for me. When I got a particularly severe look, I broke into a jog . . . and landed on my ass.

Gabriel put out his hand to help me up, but I motioned for him to wait, gritting my teeth against the pain throbbing through my tailbone. Lloergan nudged me and whined concern.

Gabriel glanced at my footwear. "Aren't those boots?"

"Technically, yes. But for women, boots do not necessarily mean winter wear."

I took his hand and he tugged me up, saying, "You're freezing."

"I'll be fine."

He started taking off his coat.

"No, seriously, I'm fine and that would just weigh me down. We must be getting close to a farmhouse or something." As if on cue, the snow cleared enough for us to spot a laneway. "There. Now let's just hope someone's home."

His look said that was inconsequential. Locked doors don't stop Gabriel. As a teen, he'd survived on the streets using the only thing Seanna ever gave him: her talent for pickpocketing and burglary.

Gabriel patted his pockets and handed me a pair of gloves, which he apparently hadn't been bothering to wear himself. Then he said, "We'll walk slower," and put his arm around my shoulders. I wasn't sure if that was meant to keep me steady or warm, but I appreciated the gesture. Lloergan moved to my other side, sticking close enough to block the wind.

The snow whipped up, driving hard now, and we had to trudge, our gazes fixed on the gravel driveway, as we walked between twin rows of overgrown shrubs. The lane seemed to go on forever. Then those shrubs vanished, but there was still gravel under our feet, with weeds poking through the dirt and stones.

When something rose in our path, Gabriel yanked me back. It was a car rim with a metal pole sticking out of the center. Coated wire ran from the pole to a destination hidden by the snowfall. I put one gloved hand on the wire and followed it to another car rim and post.

"We're in a parking lot," I said. "These are row markers."

I called, "Hello!" and my voice echoed. "Hmm. Empty parking lot. Weed-choked gravel. That isn't very promising."

I checked my cell again. Still no signal. Lloergan nudged my hand. I crouched beside her.

"Any ideas?" I said.

She stared across the lot. When I squinted, I could make out dark shapes behind the curtain of snow. Lloergan took a deep snuffling breath and snorted, condensation puffing from her nostrils. Then she cautiously started forward. I did the same and nearly bashed into a sign—a wooden one, shaped like an arrow with peeling white paint and multicolored letters reading "Tickets!"

We changed course slightly, and after about a dozen paces we stepped onto concrete. Gardens bordered the walkway, the bushes gnarled, beds blanketed with dead weeds. When a giant rainbow appeared overhead, I stopped short. Then I realized it was a wooden arch, painted as a rainbow.

"Curiouser and curiouser," I said.

At eye level, a crooked sign read, "You're almost there!" Below it, a downward pointing arrow proclaimed, "This way for fun and adventure!"

Gabriel straightened the sign so it pointed forward.

"Well, that makes more sense," I said.

I took another step, and my boot slid on the snow-slick concrete. Lloergan saved me the humiliation of another pratfall, as I fell against her. Gabriel tried to get a grip on my snow-covered jacket. I reached for his hand instead. He didn't hesitate, just took it, his fingers engulfing mine.

I looked up, the midday sun blazing through the light snowfall as it lit the scene ahead.

A row of booths stretched across the walkway. On the asphalt, multicolored painted arrows divided the crowd to funnel it through ticket booths. Each booth had been painted a garish primary color. Now that paint had peeled, leaving tiny speckled buildings, the Plexiglas scratched with hearts and obscenities.

Leering from the top of each booth was what had once been a clown head. But now, between the peeling paint and the vandalism, that row of grinning clowns looked like an army of escapees from a leper colony.

"Oh! It's Funland!" I said. "My dad brought me here once when I was little. It was terrible." I called, "Sorry!" as if to ghosts of employees past. "It was a cute little amusement park, just not really . . ."

"Your speed?" Gabriel said.

"Exactly."

My Cŵn Annwn blood means I have a need for speed. As a child, I'd snuck onto grown-up rides with heeled boots. If I still came up short, most operators ignored it, figuring if I was with my father, it was his call. Dad had indulged me in this, as he indulged all my passions. If roller coasters fed some unfathomable need in my soul, then roller coasters I would have. Funland, though, had been sadly bereft of thrills.

"There's only one coaster," I said. "A wild mouse, with a ridiculous height restriction. But it was— Oh, there it is! See it?"

We could make out the top of the tracks over the buildings.

"It's abandoned," Gabriel said.

"Hmm?"

"The park. It's abandoned."

"Uh, yeah," I said. "This isn't just its 'closed for the season' look. It's been shut down for, oh, nearly ten years? In high school, my friends and I planned to sneak in on prom night. But it closed the year before we graduated. I tried to get my friends to go anyway—it'd be even cooler to break into an *abandoned* amusement park. Two of the guys agreed, but only if I picked one of them as my prom date. So . . . no."

"I mean, it's an abandoned *place*. Which is significant."

"In light of the fact we've been lured by fae to several

abandoned places? Right. Sorry. Frozen brain." I looked up at the park gates. "We weren't actually led here, though. Nothing *compelled* us to come down the laneway."

"Except that it was the first one we reached, after my car broke down."

True. I looked at Lloergan. She stared intently through the park gates. I took another step. She stayed at my side, making no more effort to hold me back.

If we'd been lured, there was little point in ignoring the summons.

CHAPTER FIVE

A massive padlock chained the gates shut. That would have been far more effective if someone hadn't used wire cutters to slice open the fencing.

Once we were in, I had to stop and stare. The park looked . . . magnificent. Nightmare and dream colliding in the most wondrous way. Hulking rides, rusted and broken, creeping vines engulfing them. Snow had hidden most of the decay, every surface a pristine white that glittered in the sun.

Then the sun disappeared, as if in a blink, and two young women raced from behind a building. Long hair streamed behind them as they ran, holding hands and giggling. They were barefoot, and light dresses swirled about their legs, their skin glowing in the moonlight.

The girls raced across unbroken concrete toward a moonlit carousel and swung onto freshly painted horses. Then music sounded, sweet and pure and haunting, and the girls clapped and laughed as a young man appeared, clutching a bottle in one hand.

One of the girls swung off the horse, and he called something, teasing, as he waved the bottle. From this distance, I couldn't make out what he was saying, but it sounded like Gaelic.

A memory of fae past, reveling in the park at night, not unlike my own dream of riding the carousel and sneaking through the fun house and, yes, bringing a bottle of something that would make the adventure even more fun and, perhaps, sharing it with a handsome boy who'd make my *night* even more fun.

The scene flickered, and it was daytime again, Gabriel's hand still gripping mine, face taut.

"Just a garden-variety vision of fae," I said.

They'd have come late at night to take advantage of the empty amusement park. And then, after it closed permanently, and nature began her reclamation, they'd have come whenever they wanted. That was the allure of abandoned places. They are a reflection of fae themselves, pushed from their land by civilization, and then creeping back after the humans have left, retaking what was theirs. I feel the energy in these places and the wonder, too, the park a hundred times more beautiful in its decay than when I'd seen it as a child, gleaming and whole.

As Gabriel's gaze crossed the ruins, he didn't share my grin of excitement, but he watched—keenly watched—surveying the landscape, wary and intrigued.

"Where to?" I asked.

"I'm not the one with the psychic powers," he said.

"Sure you are. You have a sixth sense for trouble."

"Then I should hardly be the one who decides where we go."

I grinned. "But *looking* for trouble is always more fun than avoiding it."

"I believe trouble finds us quite easily enough."

I looked down at Lloergan. "Your vote?"

She was gazing about with a look not unlike Gabriel's. Wary yet intrigued. Like him, she gave no sign that she thought we should go—or *not* go—in any particular direction.

"All right, then," I said.

As I took off for the Tilt-A-Whirl, I swore I heard both man and beast sigh behind me. I climbed into one of the ride cars and looked around.

"It went faster before," I said.

Gabriel definitely sighed now.

"See that booth?" I pointed to the operator's box, the Plexiglas a spider's web of cracks. "The guy in there ran the ride and the tunes, and he'd yell, 'Do you want to go faster?' And I'd scream at the top of my lungs. Even Dad shouted with me. It never went any faster. Dude just cranked up the music to make it seem like it did. Total cheat." I twisted to look around. "You know, if both you and Lloergan grabbed a side and pushed . . ."

Lloergan hopped into the car with me.

"Sure," I said. "We can do that. Only you need to be on the inside so I can fall against you. These seat restraints have seen better days." I waggled the moth-eaten padding.

When I looked at Gabriel, he was still standing there, the very picture of patience.

"Ferris wheel?" I said. "I'll climb up and then you can release the brake."

"I have several important cases going to trial this winter and absolutely no time to replace a dead investigator."

"You're so sweet." I hopped out and shielded my eyes against the sun and the blinding layer of fallen snow. "Oh! There. Perfect!"

I broke into a run.

"Olivia! Watch out. The pavement is still—"

My boot slipped. Gabriel ran to grab me, glancing around as if fearing he'd be spotted. I was about to laugh at his dignity-check when I saw a blur between a concession stand and a dart game booth. Lloergan's head swiveled toward it.

"Did you see that?" I said to Gabriel.

"See what?"

I vaulted over the game booth counter. The rear door was cracked open, and I gave it a shove, hoping to startle whoever lurked behind it. No one was there. And no footprints marred the pristine snow.

Lloergan walked to me, her nose working overtime as if to say, *Huh, could have sworn I saw something.*

I backed into the game booth, where dead balloons still dotted the pockmarked board. I plucked out a dart.

"You ever try this game?" I said to Gabriel. "Yes, they're all rigged, but if you know the tricks, you can pick up some sweet prizes."

"Stuffed animals that aren't even worth the cost of the tickets to win them?"

"Hardly the point. Didn't you ever— "

Didn't you ever bring a girl to a county fair? A girl you wanted to impress by winning her a prize?

No, he hadn't. I knew that without finishing the question. There'd been no time for that in Gabriel's teen life, no point when he could afford game tickets just to make a girl smile. The only reason to win a prize would be if he could pawn it for a profit. And the only reason he'd come to a place like this was if he could pick enough pockets to make it worthwhile, given the cost of admission and transportation.

I heard fake-Seanna's voice again, mocking me for thinking I was a badass. I didn't. But where I came from, I *had* been the wild one, the girl who made "shocking" suggestions, like breaking into an abandoned park. When I compare that to Gabriel's life, I am ashamed. Yes, he'd have broken in. To steal food. To find shelter. To survive. And me? I'd plotted silly rebellions from my Inglewood bedroom, chatting on my cell phone, planning to borrow one of my dad's classic sports cars for the excursion.

When I think of Gabriel's young life, I grieve for what he lost. What he can never get back. For experiences he cannot even imagine, ones the average American teen takes for granted. And it is all Seanna's fault.

"Olivia?" he said.

"Sorry. Where was I? Right!" I leapt over the counter again. "I had a mission, and that mission is . . . this way."

I dashed through the booths, startling a stray cat that had ventured forth. Spotting me, it wheeled to zoom through a hole in a concession booth. Then it saw Lloergan and froze, saucer-eyed. We raced past, and I skidded to a halt beside a two-story building so garishly painted that even on a midway it looked like a hooker in a convent.

In three-foot-high letters, a sign overhead announced that we'd arrived at the fun house. Or, the FUN HOUSE!!! Gabriel's expression suggested he was already prepared to sue for false advertising.

"Hey, at least I didn't propose that." I jabbed a finger toward the haunted house. "Given our track record, we'd probably find actual corpses. Then we'd need to report them and explain, again, that we just have a knack for that sort of thing, and if I was following in my parents' footsteps, I'd hardly be reporting my crimes." I pursed my lips. "Though that might be rather ingenious."

"It's not," Gabriel said. "I had a client who tried it. He killed his wife and called it in, and then after he was charged, he killed his mistress and called that in, too, reasoning it would somehow prove he wasn't guilty of either. Just terribly unlucky in love."

"You're admitting he was guilty? *Bad* defense attorney."

"Hardly. He's the one who admitted it. He insisted on taking a plea bargain."

"Against your advice, I presume."

Gabriel made a noise in his throat, evidently still insulted over the situation. He *would* suggest clients accept the bargains in unwinnable cases. Otherwise, he took it kind of personally when they did.

"Coming?" I said as I climbed the steps to the doorway. "Or are you acting mature and waiting out here?"

His eyes narrowed, offended by the suggestion he *wouldn't* join in my silly adventure.

"Remember how I said you need a pair of jeans?" I said as he glanced down at his pressed and pristine trousers. "I'm serious about that. I'm storing jeans and a T-shirt in your car for all future adventures."

A faint eye roll.

"You've worn jeans before," I said. "Jeans, T-shirt, Saints jacket . . . You make a very convincing biker."

His look said I knew very well it was borrowed emergency clothing.

"Hey, it still happened. I have proof. Ricky forwarded me the photo. Don't worry. I filed it in a secret folder, so no one will see it but me."

Which was true, though that wasn't the real reason I'd filed it away. When I had it in my main photo file, every time I passed it, I'd kind of forget what I was doing. Gabriel in worn jeans, a too-small T-shirt, and a leather jacket, with dark stubble and damp, wavy hair . . . Which was not to say he didn't look good in a suit, but then I kept imagining getting him *out* of it and into something more comfortable. Like a bed. Or couch. Or any conveniently located horizontal surface. Even a vertical one would do. I wasn't picky.

"Olivia?"

"Onward," I said. "Lloergan? Do you want to come in or—"

She plunked down in front of the door. I gave her a pat and then went inside. Beyond the entrance, hanging plastic strips curtained a doorway, like a car wash. When we went through, we found ourselves in darkness. Gabriel turned on his cell phone and shone light down the corridor, with black-painted walls and a ceiling so low he had to duck.

"This doesn't seem safe," he said.

"It's not supposed to." I flicked off his cell phone, took his hand, and pressed it against the wall. "Feel your way. If you hit something soft, it's me, and you probably want to stop feeling around." *Not that I'd object, but only if you did it intentionally, which seems unlikely to happen anytime soon.*

I set out, each hand on a wall as I followed the twists and turns of the dark maze. I kept up a steady stream of chatter. If I'm not talking, Gabriel's going to presume I've been rendered unconscious.

When I paused for a response, silence answered.

"You stopped listening five minutes ago, didn't you?" I said.

I expected a chuckle. He'd say something like, "No, I'm always listening," and he was, even when I blathered like a toddler who'd just learned to speak. But this time, there was no answer.

"Gabriel?"

My switchblade has a penlight, and I fumbled to turn it on and then shone it down the hall. The empty hall.

I hurried back. After a few steps I heard deep, panicked breathing. I tore around the corner and there was Gabriel, his chest heaving. When the light hit him, his head jerked up, the blank look in his eyes evaporating with a blink.

"Are you okay?" I said.

"What?" Another hard blink as he pulled himself up straight. "Yes, of course. I just . . ."

He looked around as if he'd see an answer in neon on the wall. I caught his hand, giving it a light squeeze and saying, "Let's go—"

The room went dark, and suddenly I was crouched in a small, pitch-black space, the walls pressing in from every side. There was one single moment where I realized I'd fallen into a vision, and then that awareness evaporated and I was in the vision, thinking another's thoughts, feeling what another felt.

It's all right. It's all right. She'll be back soon.

But I couldn't hear her anymore—hadn't heard her in a long time—and I could always hear her when I was in the small place. Everything had gone quiet and stayed quiet and now my legs hurt, and I was so hungry and cold and I had to use the bathroom.

Maybe if I knocked—

Remember the last time.

I shivered at the memory. I'd had to go badly, so I'd knocked and been very polite about it.

I need to use the bathroom. Please may I come out?

I'd said it exactly right. I knew I had. Sometimes, when other people took care of me, they'd ask if I had to use the potty, and if my mother heard, she'd sneer and say, "My son doesn't use that baby talk." Which meant that I was not permitted to use it.

I'd made a mistake once, after my mother left me with a neighbor and her children for five days. Later, I'd called my stomach my tummy, and my mother made me sit in the corner and told me not to talk like a baby, and the man we were staying with said, "Geez, Seanna, he *is* a baby," and she'd said, "Then he'd better grow up fast. Because I don't have time for that shit."

After the last time, I knew not to ask to be let out of the small place. I had to wait, and when she was ready, she'd open the hatch. I could come out, and I could have anything I wanted to eat. Then we'd go to the shop down the road—the one that smelled weird—where I'd find a book that didn't have pages falling out, and she'd buy it for me.

I just had to wait. Had to be patient. That was the word. *Patient.*

Except I *had* been patient. I'd sat here, and there'd been noise and talking and laughing and then more noise, and I'd been completely quiet, even though she'd forgotten to give me a blanket and I was cold, and I was getting too big to be here without curling up and that hurt, curling up so small when I was not so small anymore.

I had just turned three years old. For my birthday, I'd gotten a special gift. First, I had to play a game, which was special, too, because my mother did not play games. Those were for babies. But this was a grown-up game. There'd been a man in the apartment—one of her friends—and when they were talking, I had to find his jacket and his wallet and take out one bill marked "20." No more than one.

If the man caught me, I could not say my mother told me to do it. That was the rule. It hadn't been easy, because the man put his jacket on the sofa, and I had to wait until he went into the kitchen and then quickly take the money. But I won, and my mother had been happy, and she'd let me buy all the books I could with a five-dollar bill. Then she bought me a candy bar and said that I could play the game every time a man came over and if I won, I'd get books and a candy bar. If I lost, though—if the man caught me— then my mother would not protect me from a beating. Those were the rules. That was fair, she said. Just like it was fair that if I waited in the small space quietly, I'd get a reward when she let me out.

Be patient.

But I had to pee so bad it hurt. Everything hurt, and I was cold. I was hungry, too, because she'd forgotten to give me lunch again, and I knew not to ask, or she'd cuff me and say she was getting to it, even though I knew she'd forgotten.

What if she'd forgotten *me*? I couldn't hear anything. I hadn't for a long time. For a very, very long time, and what if she'd forgotten? What if—?

"Olivia."

The room lit up, and for a second I couldn't figure out where the light was coming from or why I was standing or why someone was holding my arms and calling me Olivia. That wasn't my name. My name was—

I looked up, blinking, into Gabriel's face, felt his iron grip on my forearms. When he saw me focusing, he exhaled and slapped a hand to my forehead.

"You aren't even warm," he said, frowning—my visions usually came with fever.

No, I'm not warm. I'm cold. I'm very, very—

"It wasn't a vision," I said. "It was . . ."

I looked up at him and mentally tumbled back to that place. I started to shiver, and then I glanced aside, sharply. That was what gave it away, and he let go of my arm so fast I staggered.

"Memories," he said. "You were seeing what I . . ."

"I wasn't trying. I would never   "

"Yes, of course. I know that." His voice snapped with impatience. Then he cleared his throat and straightened. "We should have spoken to the Elders after you accessed memories with the lamiae. We'll do that later today."

He took out his phone and tapped in a note. *Just add it to the list. Nothing personal here.* And if I thought his fingers trembled slightly as he typed, clearly I was distraught and a little wobbly myself.

I swallowed and struggled to reorient, to slough off what it had felt like, being in that tiny space, alone and cold and trying so hard to—

Another hard swallow.

"It's physical contact," I said, working for the same matter-of-fact tone. "I've only had those episodes when I'm touching someone. I don't know what triggers it."

"You access a memory *they're* accessing," Gabriel said. "At that moment of contact."

"How long did Seanna leave you—?" I started without thinking and stopped short. "Okay, so let's mark that down and—"

"You are allowed to ask, Olivia," he said, his voice dropping as the snap slid away. "You did not intrude intentionally. While the thought of sharing that memory is hardly comfortable, the question is understandable. I believe it was several days. There was no way of knowing at that age. It was after Rose tried to take me, and Seanna punished her by moving. There was a storage cubby in the new apartment. Sometimes her men didn't mind me being around, but if she suspected my presence would create tension, she'd put me in the cubby. That particular time, the man invited her to a party. Whether she was too high or drunk to remember me—or simply making too much money to hurry home—I only know that I was unconscious when she returned. The next time she attempted to put me into that cubby, I . . . did not respond well. She began instead taking me to a park and leaving me there, presumably to play, though I could never quite understand the attraction."

"I—"

"I'm explaining to provide context. Nothing more. I understand sharing that memory is awkward for you as well. We can alleviate some of that by me simply saying that it doesn't require a response. So let's . . ."

"Move on?"

He exhaled audibly. "Yes. Please."

I understood what he was saying. For those few minutes, I'd experienced the hell of his early life, and I could not now just brush it off to goof around in a fun house.

"I'll just . . . I'm going to go see Lloergan for a second."

"To give yourself a moment to react privately, knowing I

mishandle emotional responses." That chill seeped back into his voice.

"Gabriel, please? I'm . . ." I clenched and unclenched my fists. "Upset."

"I hate her," I blurted. "I have never hated anyone the way I hate Seanna. And if there's any chance she's . . . No, she isn't." I took a deep breath. "Sorry. No. She isn't. Someone is impersonating her. That's all."

"I agree. But if we're wrong?" He met my gaze and lowered his voice. "I'm quite certain I wouldn't fit in that cubby anymore."

He was trying to lighten the mood. But when he said that, all I could think about was how terrified he'd been, what it must have been like, trapped in there for days.

I burst into tears. They started streaming down my face as I frantically wiped at them, blathering, "Sorry, sorry."

I was still babbling and trying to stop crying when he pulled me into a hug. It was a Gabriel hug—an awkward embrace that feels more like restraint.

I swore he counted to three before letting go. But then he reached out and patted my back, the kind of "there, there" comfort you give a child who has scraped her knee, and I had to bite my cheek to keep from laughing through my tears.

"Thank you," I said when I could manage a straight face, and he nodded, obviously relieved that he'd done the right thing. Also glad it was over.

"If it's her, I'll deal with that," he said. A wry twist of a smile. "She can't hurt me anymore."

I threw my arms around his neck. He stiffened in alarm. I gave him a fierce squeeze, careful to keep my embrace even shorter than his. But when I went to pull away, he hugged me back, and by the time I realized that, it was too late to stop withdrawing. He felt my hands falling away and quickstepped out of my embrace, and by then the moment had passed and . . .

The moment passed. There was nothing more to be said. It always passed.

I took a deep breath and shone my light around. "This is silly. There's obviously not going to be a working phone in the fun house."

Gabriel shook his head. "Something drew you here."

"Did it?" I threw up my hands, penlight beam pinging over the walls. "Maybe I'm using my visions as an excuse to knock off work for a while because . . ."

Because of this morning. Because I don't want that bitch to be Seanna, and I'm afraid, I'm really, really afraid, she might be.

"Between your parents' appeal and our normal workload, you haven't had a day off in weeks," Gabriel said. "You're tired, and you need a break. I propose that we agree—both of us—to take this weekend off."

"Uh, didn't you tell me not to make plans because you needed me?"

"I only asked if you had the weekend clear."

"And then said to *keep* it clear."

"Yes . . ." He seemed to flounder before coming back with, "Because you need to rest. Ricky is away, so you won't have plans with him, and I would suggest you don't make any plans at all. In fact, I insist on it."

"Okay . . ."

"You will rest. All weekend. That's an order."

"Uh-huh . . ."

"For now, though, you will explore this fun house."

"Which is also an order?"

"No, it's a very strong suggestion, backed by the warning that I'm the one with the car keys, and if I stay here, you'll be stranded."

"We're already stranded, remember? You can't drive your car until the air bags are reset."

"Good, then that's settled." He waved down the dark hall. "Onward."

CHAPTER SIX

I left my penlight on as I led us out of the dark maze. It opened into a room that was supposed to have a moving floor. Except the floor, obviously, wasn't moving. Nor was it staying still. With the motor off, the boards slid as soon as I put my foot down.

We crossed slowly and exited into the inevitable mirror maze. Out of the corner of my eye, I caught a glimpse of my adoptive dad. I turned fast and saw myself, at eight, when I'd been here with him, both of us making faces in the mirror. Part of me wanted to look away—even two years after his death, it still hurt too much. Yet a part of me wanted to keep looking, to get my fill of that memory. Then it faded, and I saw only myself, as I was now.

As I turned, I heard a familiar laugh, and there I was again, giggling and goofing around with my father, except this time my father was Todd Larsen. I was a toddler, and he was swinging me around, and even if I couldn't hear what I was saying, I knew exactly what it was—*faster, Daddy, faster!* And he obliged, as my adoptive dad would later.

Two men who'd been so important in my life. Two fathers I'd loved with all my heart. Two very different men, and yet in some ways the memories felt the same, and that was confusing and unsettling. It also felt unfair to both, but what else did I wish for? That one of those relationships had been strained, like with my adoptive mother? Hellishly complicated, like with my birth mother? Or just plain hellish, like Gabriel's with Seanna?

Gabriel caught up, and I saw us both reflected in the mirror. Only it was us at our first meeting, when he'd cornered me in the shortcut behind my Cainsville apartment. In the reflection, I saw my wary expression and his cool one, those ice-blue eyes hidden behind his shades, his shadow stretching out to me, making him seem even larger. He'd had a proposition. My mother had written a memoir, and while she couldn't profit from it, he reasoned I should. I'd shot him down. Then, a few days later, I hired him as an expert on my parents' case, not to help me prove they were innocent but to convince myself they weren't.

As I turned from the mirror, I saw another image of myself, this time at a fundraising party with James. *The* fundraising party—a completely forgettable event that was now emblazoned on my memory. We were in the back hall, whispering after we'd escaped for sex. He told me he was considering running for senator—following in his father's footsteps—and all I could think was "I can't do it." I could not be that wife. I was not that person.

Then the call came from my mother, saying she urgently needed me home. I'd spent the car ride trying to figure out how to tell James I might want to go back for my doctorate, definitely wanted to start a career. I'd arrived home to get the news that I'd been adopted, and my world shattered.

Maybe someone else would see that image and say, "You silly fool—you should have been happy with what you had, not whining that you wanted more." But I didn't.

I'm sorry, James. I loved you. I really did. But that wasn't the life for me. I just wish . . .

Two tears fell before I wiped them away, and I glanced at Gabriel, but he was looking in a mirror. I wanted to ask what he saw, but before I could, I caught another image: me on the back of Ricky's bike, roaring through the hills of the Cabot Trail.

I was holding Ricky tight and grinning and thinking how happy I was, how incredibly happy I was. I had a shitty apartment, a demanding boss, a new job that scared the crap out of me, an adoptive mother who'd abandoned me for Europe and a biological one who was definitely a killer. But my *father* wasn't a killer. I loved that terrifying new job. I loved Cainsville. And I'd been in love with this amazing guy. What more could I want?

What more indeed.

Was I still that girl with my fathers, hungry for excitement, the next big thrill? Was I still the young woman with James, dreaming of a more fulfilling life? Was I really a silly fool, never satisfied with what I had, always aiming for the next rung up the ladder?

I loved Ricky. Still did. Always would. Yet as with James, there would always be that sense that we didn't quite fit, that something was missing, that I could be happier . . .

I looked over at Gabriel. He stood in front of a mirror, staring at his reflection. I reached for his hand. Then I remembered what happened in the dark maze and stopped myself.

He glanced over, his gaze meeting mine. He hesitated. Then he took my hand, squeezing it, and when he did, I saw what he did: endless iterations of Gwynn. I recognized one—the boy, hunting in the forest, following Arawn's representative, Carl. Carl taunted him, and Peter lifted his rifle. As I glanced away quickly, I saw another scene, another Matilda, this one in a Victorian gown, screaming at a Gwynn, who stood stunned and pale, holding a bloodied sabre over the body of a man I knew must be Arawn. The woman dropped beside Arawn's corpse, sobbing as if her heart would break, while Gwynn stood, dazed, as if he couldn't understand how he'd gotten there. And in a blink, I *was* that Matilda, feeling her grief and her rage and her confusion, and it hurt so much, and I wrenched my gaze away, squeezing Gabriel's hand.

"That's enough," I said. "Let's move—"

"No," he said. "This is important."

He released my hand enough that I could let go. His way of saying that I didn't need to watch. But he did. He struggled so much with being Gwynn, in a way I did not struggle with being Matilda nor Ricky with Arawn.

Gwynn is the man who betrayed his friend and mistrusted his lover and brought about her terrible death. I understood why Gabriel wanted nothing to do with that part of himself, but now he watched. Forcing himself to take it in. To understand.

When I met Gabriel and Ricky, I admired the way they were both so comfortable in their own skin. They knew what they were, and they accepted that. They knew what they wanted, and they strove toward that. I hungered for such a life. Now I was finally edging toward it.

I was Eden Larsen and Olivia Taylor-Jones and Matilda and just plain Liv.

Yet, at the same time, Gabriel and Ricky had discovered there was more to them. After a lifetime of knowing who they were, that foundation tilted, throwing them off balance. Ricky plowed forward, determined to find that reconciliation of self. Now Gabriel stood here, trying to do the same.

I looked into another mirror and saw yet another tragedy, another death, this time of a young woman, lying dead on a floor, a young man kneeling beside her, another grabbing him and hauling him to his feet and hitting him. He hit him again and again, while the first young man made no move to defend himself, just stared at the dead girl on the ground.

Show him something better, damn it. I know there's some-thing better.

I squeezed Gabriel's hand and pictured Gwynn—the real Gwynn—in those early days. I found him, at about twelve, laughing as Matilda mimicked someone, Arawn joining in the impersonation and grinning at Gwynn, just as happy as Matilda to hear Gwynn's rare bout of laughter.

That was what it had been like, for so many years—three friends, delighting in each other's company. The kind of children who make a blood bond that they will never be separated, who imagine themselves growing old together, still laughing and talking and happy, endlessly happy.

An image glimmered in another mirror, and I looked with reluctance. It was another iteration of Gwynn and Arawn, as young men at the turn of the century, walking down a street, clearly drunk. I could tell in an instant who was who, Arawn singing some dirty ditty at the top of his lungs and trying to get Gwynn to join in, Gwynn laughing and shaking his head and stumbling. Another picture flickered, a girl and a boy in pioneer clothes, running hand in hand through the woods, exploring. The girl stopped to cough, and fear flashed across the boy's face. I knew she would not live long, but for now, she was happy—Matilda was with her Gwynn and she was happy.

More memories flashed, more Gwynns and Matildas and Arawns, and maybe there was tragedy in their futures, but at that point, they were happy.

Finally, Gabriel said, "That's enough."

"Better?" I said.

"Yes."

"They aren't us," I said. "Their mistakes won't be ours. We see those mistakes. None of them had that advantage."

I pointed to the original three, Arawn and Matilda now

finished their performance, the trio stretched out on the grass, watching clouds pass, completely at peace.

"That's us," I said. "You feel it, don't you? We're the closest to them. And that *is* us. Now. It will stay us."

"Yes," he said, and for once there was conviction there. Conviction and determination.

We exited into another room. I kept my light on, and we'd gone only a few steps when I caught voices. I could tell Gabriel didn't hear them, and I said, "Finally." A few months ago the prospect of a vision would have sent me running the other way. Now, I just wanted to get the damn thing over with.

The next room was a kaleidoscope of color and visual distortion. A group of people stood in the middle, their voices as distorted as the room. Five figures dressed in robes, hoods pulled up. My first thought was *Cŵn Annwn?* but the cloaks were wrong, and two figures seemed female.

My next thought was that I'd walked into a scene from a movie. A D-grade horror flick filmed at an abandoned amusement park, where the wide-eyed young blonde stumbles onto a satanic ritual in progress . . . and becomes the star, taking the role of virginal sacrifice. Yeah, serious miscasting. The only part of the description I fit was "blonde," and my hair was really more of an ash shade.

Yet this particular ritual had already found its sacrifice. A young man lay in the center of the circle. Long dead, the gash across his throat bloodless. A cowled figure crouched unmoving beside him, knife in hand, and I would have thought I was seeing a still image except that I could hear someone talking, the voice too distorted to make out words.

Another figure shifted, as if growing impatient. The one with the knife turned the corpse onto his stomach. Then he positioned the knife over the dead man's shoulder blade, and very carefully, as if paring an apple, he removed a swath of skin.

My gut seized as I imagined a different man under that blade, his face so familiar I could feel the contours of it under my fingertips. I pictured his body, lying on his back, dead eyes staring at the ceiling, Gabriel crouched beside him, me asking him to turn the corpse over. He did, and there, on the shoulder, had been that same missing strip of skin, the one I'd seen in crime-scene photographs from my parents' murders, replicated on the shoulder of a man I'd loved.

"James," I whispered as I backed away.

I hit something solid and jumped to see Gabriel behind me, his face drawn in concern. "You're seeing James?"

"No, just . . ." I looked back at the scene. "It's some kind of ritual. There's a corpse. Someone cut the skin from the shoulder. Like . . ."

"The Tysons did."

I nodded. My parents were convicted of murdering four couples. The last two victims we'd proven to be copycat killings. The first two victims—Amanda Mays and Ken Perkins—had actually been murdered by couple number two, Marty and Lisa Tyson. The Tysons had established the ritual, which a host of professionals had tried to identify, but it seemed to be ritualistic gobbledygook.

"Do you want to stop watching?" Gabriel asked.

Yes. But I couldn't, no more than he could stop watching in the hall of mirrors. I had to know what I'd been brought to see.

"I'm fine. It's just . . ." I shivered and rubbed my arms.

Gabriel put one arm around my waist and pulled me back against him, letting me rest there, exactly as he had at James's funeral.

"Is the body Mays? Perkins?" he murmured, bending to my ear.

I shook my head. "It's a young man I don't recognize. Someone's talking, but I can't make out the words. I can't even tell gender. He or she is instructing the person doing the cutting."

"Instructing him in a ritual."

"Right. Which means . . ." I squeezed Gabriel's hand before tugging it from my waist. "I need a better look."

I approached the figure kneeling beside the corpse and bent to see the face under the cowl.

"Marty Tyson," I said.

Gabriel grunted, as if he'd already presumed this.

I looked up at another face. "Lisa's standing right here. Along with three others."

I rose and followed the voice giving instructions, but under its cowl I saw only a black pit. When I tried to move the hood, my fingers passed through it.

I walked up to the next figure and had to stoop to peer under the hood—she was about six inches shorter than me.

"Stacey Pasolini."

Gabriel's brows lifted. I sidestepped to the last figure, a man only a little taller than me.

"Eddie Hilton," I said. Then I rhymed off their vital stats—approximate height and weight, hair color, eye color—and Gabriel nodded and said, "Yes, that's correct." I knew it was. I'd stared at enough photos to recognize my mother's third and fourth victims.

We already knew Pasolini and Hilton were killers. That's why the Cŵn Annwn made the deal with my mother—in exchange for them curing my spina bifida she would exact justice on four murderers whose crimes fell outside their purview. As for what exactly Pasolini and Hilton had done, Ioan didn't know the details and didn't care. Their prey was guilty, and theirs is absolute justice—no extenuating circumstances considered.

We'd investigated Pasolini and Hilton ourselves, but it seemed impossible to find a victim when you only knew the killers.

I moved back to the figure who was instructing Marty Tyson. "Let's get a look at you."

I shone my penlight under the cowl, but it was like shining it into a black hole, the light disappearing as soon as it left the source.

"Damn it," I said. "I can't see a face at all."

"But you see a figure, correct?"

"Right. Okay. Height is . . ." The figure wobbled, and I cursed under my breath. "Taller than me, shorter than you. An average man or very tall woman. Weight . . ." Again the figure shimmered, and I had to rely on my initial impression. "Slender. That's all I can say. Thin to average. As for build, the cloak hides it, but—"

The figures evaporated.

CAPRICIOUS

The moment Gabriel stepped from the fun house, his phone buzzed with an incoming message. They had cell service again.

"Please tell me it's a complete coincidence that we got service as soon as I received my vision message," Olivia said.

"Given the number of times it's happened, I sincerely doubt it."

"When I say 'please tell me,' I mean 'please lie to me.'"

"Ah. Well, perhaps the cell phone outage was caused by the snowfall, which interfered with the electromagnetic field and thereby disrupted cellular frequency reception."

"Not a science major, were you?"

"No."

"Me neither, so it sounds totally legit."

He called for a tow truck as they walked to where the hound waited. Then he surreptitiously checked that incoming text. When it wasn't the one he was expecting, he grumbled under his breath.

Olivia said he'd told her to keep the weekend clear. He *had* . . . but not for work. He had plans. A weekend away. Together.

He would tell her it was a well-earned vacation. Which it was. However, it also marked an occasion. Six weeks since her breakup with Ricky. Not an occasion she'd want to celebrate. Gabriel, on the other hand . . .

He was loath to say their breakup came as a cause for celebration. Olivia had been happy, and Gabriel wanted that. Yet Ricky was not the only person who could make her happy. Perhaps not even the one who could make her happiest.

No, Gabriel was not displeased by the breakup. "Relieved" was a better word. Suitably un-gleeful. Relieved, because the alternative would have been wooing her away from Ricky, which made him uncomfortable. Immensely, if he was being honest. It came too close to repeating Gwynn's mistake.

Gabriel had decided six weeks was a respectful period. He'd planned this getaway down to the last detail. Rent a cabin with two bedrooms, so as not to set up awkward expectations. Arrange catered dinners, to be followed by a blazing fire, a comfortable couch, and vintage wine. He would drink exactly half a glass, enough to relax without risking actual inebriation. Olivia rarely exceeded her glass-and-a-half personal limit, but if she did, he'd cancel his plans and try again the next night. And by "try again" he meant making the most subtle of moves, escalating incrementally so if he encountered resistance, he could withdraw before she realized his intention. Even if she failed to respond to his overtures, it wouldn't mean *he'd* failed. Not permanently. He would resume his careful wooing, showing her that he could be what she needed.

He knew she cared for him. He knew she wanted to be with him in some way. It was simply a matter of inching toward a destination he was confident they could reach, eventually.

Now he waited for a response to his earlier text, informing the cabin owner that they would be unexpectedly bringing a canine. He was not asking permission—that wasn't how one handled such matters. But he was aware that negotiations—and an extra fee—might be involved. That was fine. While having Lloergan there was hardly ideal, in accommodating that, he would please Olivia. He had encouraged her to "dog-sit," knowing it would impede his secret weekend plans, and thereby honoring his pledge to Ricky that, whatever happened, he wouldn't interfere with their friendship.

Lloergan would join them for the weekend, and that would not disrupt his plans. Nothing would disrupt his plans. Particularly not . . .

At the thought of Seanna, his jaw tightened. All Gabriel's life, he'd refused to hate his mother. She wasn't worth it. Even as a child, he'd tolerated her much as one might tolerate a debilitating condition. Accept that it exists and learn to deal with it, and if it goes away, then count that as a blessing but understand that it might return.

For fifteen years, he'd understood Seanna might return. Then Olivia found proof that she was dead, and Gabriel had finally exhaled. His mother was out of his life forever.

And now, perhaps, she'd come back, and for the first time he felt not just anger, but a lick of something dangerously close to rage. Like a child who wants to stamp his feet and say, "No, no, no!"

You will not come back now, Seanna. You will not. He was inches away from a perfect life, and she would not ruin that. *Would not.*

"Hey, Lloe." It took a moment to realize what Olivia was saying. When she called the dog Lloe, it sounded like Thloy, more of a complex exhalation than an actual word. He still struggled with the hound's full name, which sounded something like Thl-oy-r-gan. When he had to say it, he did so quickly, in hopes speed would cover mispronunciation.

The hound hopped off the fun-house steps. The move was awkward, the *cŵn*'s joints having never quite healed, but that didn't stop her from leaping when she saw them. She walked to Olivia and waited for her ear-scratch. Then she looked at Gabriel, and he was never certain whether that look meant she expected the same from him or she was telling him he'd better not try it. Perhaps she was simply acknowledging—with some chagrin—that he was still there.

They started for the exit. Olivia was talking. He listened—he always listened—but it wasn't the kind of chatter requiring his undivided attention. She wasn't ready to discuss the vision. She'd be processing that while talking about something inconsequential, perhaps to ensure he wouldn't broach the subject until she was ready.

It was in that state, listening to her while processing thoughts of his own, that he became acutely aware they were not alone. He looked about.

"Everything okay?" Olivia asked.

He started to say yes automatically. He might encourage Olivia to pursue her preternatural abilities, but he found it difficult to share his own.

"I had the feeling . . ." He looked around without finishing.

"That someone else is here?"

"You sensed it?"

"I thought I saw someone run behind the kiosks earlier. I figured if you didn't, it was just a vision."

He looked at Lloergan. The hound studied him far too intently and then moved alongside him to lean against his leg. He stopped himself before stepping away, and he laid a tentative hand on her head as she scanned the amusement park, seeing nothing but unable to shake—

Something moved behind the carousel. Lloergan took off. Olivia gave a small cry of alarm—a *cŵn* in pursuit often results in a deadly conclusion—and Gabriel broke into a run to acknowledge her concern. He tore around the carousel booth just as Lloergan leapt onto the back of a fleeing teenage boy, sending him sprawling beneath the front hooves of a prancing wooden horse.

"Lloergan!" Gabriel shouted.

The *cŵn* fixed him with a withering look, clearly insulted by the inference she would kill her target. As Gabriel jogged over, he saw the "boy" was perhaps college aged. A young woman stood flattened against the booth, her dark eyes wide. Both wore jeans, sneakers, and jackets. They had light brown skin and braided dark hair and resembled one another enough that they seemed more likely siblings than lovers.

Lloergan growled and let the boy up, and then growled again, as if to say, *Don't go anywhere.*

"Why were you spying on us?" Gabriel asked.

"Spying? We weren't anywhere *near* you until your dog took me down." The boy eyed Lloergan. "I should call the cops. Or animal control."

"Go ahead. I'll wait."

The young man hesitated. "I would, but I don't have a cell phone."

"Here." Gabriel held out his. "Use mine."

The boy ignored that. "We'll let it go this time, but you need to put that dog on a leash."

"What are you?" Gabriel said.

"I beg your pardon?" the girl said.

"What. Are. You?"

"That's rude," she said. "Possibly racist." She looked at the boy. "Is it racist?"

"I think so."

"Just answer my question," Gabriel said.

"Do you ask everyone that?" the girl said. "Or only those who don't look like you?"

"No," Gabriel said. "Only those who aren't human."

The girl laughed. "You're mad."

"Here." Olivia held out a handkerchief. It fell open to reveal a chunk of cold-forged iron. "Do you mind holding this for a sec?"

"*You* hold it," the boy said.

Olivia dropped the metal into her bare hand and squeezed. When she opened her fingers, her palm was bright red.

"Now you," the girl said to Gabriel.

He took it, ignoring the burn of the metal against his skin.

"Gwynn and Matilda," the boy breathed.

"Didn't I say that?" the girl said. "Do you know any ordinary humans who walk about with a *cŵn*?"

"Just because we've never encountered such a thing doesn't mean it can't exist."

Olivia held out the iron. "So . . . are you going to answer Gabriel's question, or are you going to show us how much worse this burns full-blooded fae?"

The boy shuddered. "No, thank you."

"We admit it," the girl said, climbing onto a painted horse.

"Freely admit it," the boy echoed.

"Then answer Gabriel's question, and tell us what you are. I'd run through the list of overly chatty fae, but we'd be here all day."

"True," the girl said.

The boy nodded. "Very true."

At a glare from Olivia, the girl said, "Dryad."

"So they're not all female?" Olivia said.

The male looked down at himself. "I should hope not. Or Nature has made a very serious mistake."

Olivia turned to Gabriel. "They're Greek fae. Even more capricious than most, which is saying a lot."

"That's rude," the girl said. "Talking in front of us."

"Quite rude," the boy said. "Also, quite true. However, if we are capricious, it isn't through malice, but simply a love of adventure and good fun. There's nothing wrong with that."

"Unless you're the person being *played* in the name of that good fun," the girl said.

"True."

"How did you find us?" Olivia asked. "Did you follow us? Or did you have something to do with our car breaking down?"

They both stared at her.

"We're dryads," the boy said slowly. "Not auto mechanics."

"Not tracking dogs, either," the girl said. "You were here. We were here. A happy coincidence."

The boy looked from Olivia to Gabriel and then back to Olivia. He smiled smugly. "You've dumped Arawn, then? Good." He glanced at Lloergan. "No insult to the Cŵn Annwn, but it makes things easier. Throw over Arawn, take Gwynn, and everyone lives happily ever after. Except Arawn. And the Huntsmen. But we fae live happily ever after, and that's what counts."

"If she threw over Arawn, she wouldn't have his hound," the girl said.

"Maybe she stole it."

The girl lit up as she straightened on the wooden horse. "Ooh, yes." She turned to Olivia. "Did you steal the *cŵn*? Whisk it away from under Arawn's nose?"

"Ricky's in Florida. I'm hound-sitting."

"Oh." The girl slumped over her steed's neck.

"What are you doing here?" the boy asked, twirling around one of the poles. "We couldn't figure it out."

"I told you it's a mystery," the girl said.

"I know, that's why I'm asking."

She leaned over to cuff him. "I mean they're *solving* a mystery. That's what they do. He's the king of the Fae."

"She's the lady of the Hunt."

In unison, they said, "They solve crime!"

The girl looked at the boy. "We're forgetting Arawn."

"Hmm. Let's see . . . He's the king of the Fae. She's the lady of the Hunt. He's the lord of the Otherworld. They solve crime."

The girl wrinkled her nose. "That doesn't work."

"Not at all. She'll have to throw Arawn over."

The hound sighed. Deeply. Undoubtedly thinking that, while her life was dedicated to avenging crimes *against* fae, perhaps such crimes were sometimes understandable.

The girl slid off her horse. "It *is* a mystery, isn't it? Something exciting? A terrible death? *Several* terrible deaths?"

"I don't think deaths are supposed to be exciting," the boy said.

"But they are. Right or wrong, one cannot argue with the excitement value of a good murder, because it leads to a good mystery. Is that it, then? You're solving a mystery? Someone has died here?"

"Yes, but it was about twenty-five years ago," Olivia said. "I don't suppose you were around then."

"Of course. We've been around for a very long time."

"But not here," the boy said.

"No, not here. Not for that long. We can help, though."

"Uh, no," Olivia said.

"Why not?"

"Well, let's see. What experiences have we had with helpful fae? First there was Tristan, who left a young woman's head in my bed and then tried to convince me he wanted peace for the Tylwyth Teg and Cŵn Annwn, while attempting to sow strife by killing my ex-fiancé and blaming Gabriel."

"He was a *spriggan*," the girl said. "They're nasty. Not like us."

"Not at all."

"We're . . ." The girl pursed her lips. "What's the word you used?"

"Capricious," the boy said.

The girl swung onto another horse and leaned backward over it. "Yes, that's us. Capricious."

"It isn't a compliment," Olivia said.

"But it sounds like one. It's a lovely word. Innocent and fun. Like dryads. We never intend to hurt anyone."

"The operative word being 'intend,'" Olivia murmured. "And then, after Tristan, there was Melanie, a lamia who tricked us into investigating deaths of other lamiae . . . whom she'd had killed herself, hoping the danger would get her into Cainsville."

"Cainsville?" The girl scrunched her nose. "Who'd want to live there? It hardly has any trees at all. I don't understand lamiae. Never have, even when we lived together back in the old country."

"Tricksy," the boy said, climbing onto the horse behind the girl.

"Yes, that's the word for them. Tricksy. Not nearly as nice as capricious."

"A much different word. As we are much different fae."

"But we'd say that anyway, wouldn't we?"

"True." The boy stood on the horse's saddle. "I wouldn't believe us, either, if I were you. However, being me, and knowing me, I believe us."

"That doesn't help," the girl said.

"I suppose not." He jumped from the carousel horse, landing hard enough to make Olivia wince. "So we'll prove ourselves. We'll solve your crime and prove dryads are not tricksy like lamiae."

"Unless we only do it to ingratiate ourselves with them and *then* be tricksy, like lamiae."

"Look, guys. I love your enthusiasm," Olivia said, in a tone that suggested she'd love *less* of it even more. "But this murder doesn't concern you. The victim wasn't fae."

"A clue!" the boy crowed.

"If it's not fae, though, it isn't that interesting," Olivia said.

"True."

"Which is why you don't have to investigate."

"But we will!"

"We'll be detectives," the girl said.

"I have a hat," the boy said.

"And I have a notepad."

"He's a dryad. She's a dryad. They solve crimes!" The boy looked at the girl. "That doesn't really work."

"It doesn't," Olivia said. "Which is why you shouldn't—"

"But we will!"

They took off, weaving through the rides. Once they were out of sight, Olivia turned to Gabriel. "So that's an example of the fae I'm supposed to save? Score one for the Cŵn Annwn."

"We heard that!" the boy called back.

"But we'll prove ourselves!" the girl shouted. "Just wait."

Olivia shook her head. Gabriel glanced back, but the dryads were already scampering away.

CHAPTER SEVEN

It was late afternoon by the time we made it back to Cainsville, the Jag headed to the auto shop. We went straight to Rose's and told her about the woman claiming to be Seanna. She took the news quietly and then excused herself to go make tea.

"Should we leave?" I whispered when she was in the kitchen. "Give her time alone?"

"If she wanted us to go, she'd make an excuse. She just needs a moment to herself."

"Then maybe *I* should go. This is a family matter and—"

"I would rather you didn't," he said, with a touch of alarm. "We don't—" He cleared his throat. "About Seanna. We don't . . ."

"Talk about her?"

"Yes. We just . . . we don't. Ever."

"Would *you* like to leave?" I asked. "Let me handle it?"

He glanced toward the front door and Lloergan lifted her head, sensing it might be time to go, but he said, "No, I want to stay for Rose."

When I checked my phone, Gabriel said, "The DNA results won't come that quickly, Olivia."

"I'm not—"

His look stopped me.

I put my phone away. "It doesn't matter. I'm sure this woman isn't your mother."

"As tempting as it is to presume that, I need to consider the possibility, and prepare a plan to deal with that."

He took out his notepad and pen, and I realized he was literally going to plan this, as if she were a potential client he wanted to avoid. That was how he would cope.

"Okay," I said. "So if the DNA is a match—"

"I'll handle it," Rose said as she came in with the tea tray. "If the DNA is a match, I'll meet with her. I will handle the situation without Gabriel getting involved."

"I don't see how that's possible," Gabriel said.

"It is. It will be. I . . . I failed to—" She cleared her throat. "I'll handle it."

She failed to handle it twenty years ago. That's what she started to say—that she hadn't realized how dire the situation had been and therefore failed to save Gabriel from Seanna.

It didn't matter if Gabriel had purposely hid Seanna's neglect and abuse. Rose still blamed herself for not seeing through the lies. Nothing anyone could say would change that.

As we sipped tea and nibbled cookies, Rose distracted us with the tale of her latest client—a woman who wanted the cards to tell her if she'd ever lose weight, rather than, you know, *try* losing it. It hadn't taken Rose long to determine that the woman was indeed carrying an extra two hundred pounds that could be lost with no change in diet or exercise. Namely her husband, whose constant bullying and haranguing only made the woman eat more as she sunk deeper into depression.

What the client needed was a therapist. What she wanted was magic. So Rose would give her both, gradually convincing her that a future as a single woman might be the way to both health and happiness.

We were still talking when Lydia called. I scrambled off my chair fast enough to wake Lloergan. I motioned that I'd take the call in the next room.

"Is that Lydia?" Gabriel asked.

When I hesitated, he prized the phone from my clenched hand and set it on the desk. Then he poised one finger over the speaker button and looked at me.

I swallowed and nodded. He hit it.

"Lydia? It's Gabriel," he said. "I'm with Olivia."

After a moment's silence, she said, "I need to speak to Liv on a personal matter."

"Gabriel knows," I said. "He's on speaker. So is his aunt. You have the DNA test results?"

Another pause. Then, "They've run the tests, but . . . they had a problem processing Gabriel's DNA. They think the sample may be degraded. I said no, it's fresh, and we provided plenty of it. I'm going to send the samples to another facility. That may take a few days."

"The results were inconclusive?"

"Yes."

"It's Gabriel's sample that's the problem?"

"Yes. I've let them know exactly how unhappy I am with their explanation. They had the nerve to suggest we'd supplied a manufactured sample, one that wasn't entirely human. We won't be using their services in the future. Gabriel? Could you provide a more direct sample for the second test?"

He shook his head at me.

"I think we're going to drop it for now, Lydia," I said. "Maybe science isn't the best way to handle this."

I thanked her and signed off. When I looked over at Gabriel, he didn't meet my gaze, just pushed his chair back, stood, and walked from the room. The front door opened and then shut.

I tore my gaze back to Rose and tried to say something, but when Gabriel's silhouette passed the front window sheers, I turned to follow it.

"Go," Rose said.

"I shouldn't."

"Yes, you should. Go after him, Liv. Please."

Gabriel was already halfway up the street and moving fast. He'd put on his boots but left his jacket at Rose's, and he didn't appear to notice the cold. It seemed clear that he didn't want company. I slowed far enough back to give him space. He stopped and turned.

"I'm not trying—" I began.

"I know."

"You have the keys to my place. If you want to just go there and be by yourself for a while, I can work at Rose's."

He motioned for me to catch up, and we continued on to my house. Gabriel walked straight through while I took off my boots inside the door and shook the snow from them.

"Do you want—?" I began.

The back door shut with a click. I looked out the rear kitchen window to see Gabriel in the garden, heading for my new wicker set.

I hurried upstairs and grabbed towels. When I got onto the back porch, Gabriel was already sitting on the love seat.

I walked out, towels in hand. "Use these. Those cushions are soaked from that snow. We really need to put them in storage for the winter."

He said nothing. Didn't even look up.

"I'll go back in," I said. "I'll leave the towels here."

"Do you want to go back in?" he asked.

"No, I just . . ." I shifted my weight. "Let's not do this. It always escalates into a fight and hurt feelings. I'm fine with doing whatever you need right now. Just tell me."

He gave me this look, as if I should know the answer and he was confused that I didn't. He lifted his hand. I tossed him the towel and he laid it, folded, on the seat beside him. That's when I understood what he meant—if he wanted to be alone, he wouldn't have chosen the love seat.

I sat beside him.

"I don't want to care," he said after a moment.

"Whether it's her?"

"If it is, I don't want to care that she's back. I'm not . . ."

He trailed off, and I heard his words from earlier, that he wasn't a child anymore, couldn't be shoved into a cubbyhole anymore.

"It's not—" He bit off the sentence so hard his teeth clicked. Then he sat upright. "I'll deal with it."

"Of course you will. But you were going to say . . ."

An abrupt shake of his head.

I let the silence stretch for a minute, and then said, "That it's not fair?"

He rubbed his hands over his face. "*Fair* doesn't matter. *Fair* is an excuse. Expecting *fair* is pointless." He inhaled and took out his notebook. "We need a plan. Whoever she is, she'll come back, and feeling sorry for myself won't fix that."

"But you're allowed to feel sorry for yourself, Gabriel. To be angry. To be frustrated. It *isn't* fair. She was gone, and now, if she's back, you're allowed—"

"It's not productive."

I took the pen and pad from his hands, and set them on my lap. "You don't need to be productive for the next thirty seconds. Tell me how you feel."

Panic sparked in his eyes, sheer and wild panic, and I was about to give back his pen and paper, return his security blankets, and let him do whatever he needed to get past this. But then he blurted, "It feels like punishment. My life is almost— It's everything I wanted and more, and this feels like punishment. Like someone is saying I don't deserve this, certainly don't deserve more, and . . ." A shake of his head. "I'm babbling."

"You're allowed to."

"When clients whine that the charges against them aren't fair, I lose patience. The charges are a problem, which we must focus on fixing. Complaining about the unfairness of it is counterproductive."

"There's nothing wrong with taking a *moment* to whine before you focus on the problem."

"When Rose said she'd handle it, I was glad. I wanted that. I wanted to just say yes, please, do that. And it felt like cowardice."

I reached to take his hand and then stopped, remembering what had happened in the fun house. But he looked over, meeting my gaze, and then took my hand, firmly and deliberately, wrapping his fingers around it as he said, "It's all right."

He didn't mean it was all right to hold his hand. He meant that whatever I saw—whatever memories this might drag back to the surface—*that* was all right.

He leaned over, his lips going to my ear as he said, "Thank you. For everything." He shifted until his face was right in front of mine and again said, "Thank you, Olivia."

I moved to kiss him, just kiss him, don't think about it, can't think about it, brush my lips against his. If it was quick, I could say it was nothing, just a peck between friends. I leaned in, and he moved forward and—

The gate squealed open. Gabriel only eased back and let out a low growl of annoyance.

"Yes, Ida," he said. "We've returned. However—"

He stopped, and I looked over to see the woman from this morning.

Gabriel's lips parted. "Sea—"

He stopped himself. But I knew. Seeing his expression, I knew.

"Oh, am I interrupting something?" She looked up at the house. "I'm guessing this is *your* place, Eden?"

"Her name is Olivia."

Seanna continued as if he hadn't spoken. "I remember this house from when I was a kid. We'd dare each other to sneak back here, with all the weird statues." She glanced toward the pond, surrounded by fae and cryptid statuary. "Huh, they're still here. Nice."

Her nose wrinkled, like a sullen teenager's, making sure everyone knew she was *not impressed.*

"They used to call it the witch's house," she said as she walked toward us. "Kids said Old Lady Carew's ghost still haunted it, and if you saw her, she'd burn your eyes out. They'd dare each other five bucks to come back. I made a lot of money off those morons. Never saw a ghost, though. Old Lady Carew wasn't a witch. Just a crazy old bat muttering and ranting about omens and portents." She looked at me. "You're a Carew, right, Eden?"

"I am," I said evenly.

"So she's a relative of yours. Did you buy the place for sentimental value? Or because you belong here, in your crazy relative's house?"

I laughed. I couldn't help it. Gabriel glanced over, alarmed.

"Seriously, Seanna?" I said. "Is that the best you can do? Try again."

She slowed her approach.

"No, really," I said. "Give me a real zinger. You can do it."

Her mouth set in a way that reminded me of her son's . . . and yet it didn't. Gabriel's lips would compress only for a moment, an involuntary show of emotion. Hers stayed pressed together until she was scowling.

Gabriel had suggested Seanna wasn't the brightest bulb. That hers was only a feral intelligence—the Walsh survival instinct cranked to eleven. I saw the truth of that as her scowl deepened.

After a moment, she said, "So how are your parents, Eden? Rotting away in prison for butchering eight people?"

I burst into a peal of laughter. Beside me, Gabriel snorted, and Seanna's head jerked up, as if this was a sound she'd never heard from her son. When I looked over, he wasn't quite smiling, but his eyes had warmed and he'd relaxed back in the love seat.

"The conviction was recently amended to six," he said. "And Olivia has heard that particular insult before. After the hundredth time, it does start to lose its sting."

He pushed to his feet. Seanna looked up, and something gratifyingly like consternation flashed over her face as she realized exactly how big her son had gotten.

As Gabriel advanced, Seanna steeled herself not to step back.

See? He's not a child anymore. I'd love to see you try shoving him into a cubbyhole now, Seanna. Love to see you try shoving him at all.

"I presume you want something, Seanna?" he said, and there was no edge of warning there, just a matter-of-fact tone, as if she hadn't been gone for fifteen years, but only headed out for cigarettes last week.

He stopped far enough away that he wasn't looming or menacing, letting her look up into his eyes and see no fear to feed on.

"I need—" she began.

"Money?" he finished. "Yes, I'm sure you do." He took out

his cell phone. "If I can get your bank account number, I'll transfer you some right now. Before you leave." He paused. "No, you don't have a bank account, do you?"

"I don't trust banks."

"Yes, yes. I don't have checks on me. Olivia, would you mind writing one for Seanna? Ten thousand, please. I'll wire you the money immediately."

"Ten thousand?" Seanna said. "Did you really think it would be that easy?"

His cheek twitched. He'd hoped it would be. I know he did.

But he only said, "I'm offering you ten thousand to leave and allow me to continue with my life. If you walk away without that check, don't expect it to increase."

"I need a place to stay."

"Ten thousand will more than pay for a hotel room."

"I was thinking more of a high-rise condo. Maybe one just north of the Loop."

Another twitch.

She held out her hand. "Just give me the keys, Gabriel. You'll get them back after we've come to an agreement. Until then, I'm sure your girlfriend won't mind you staying here."

"You are not staying—"

"I'll stay wherever I want, Gabriel."

"No, Seanna," said a voice behind her, the gate half open. "You won't."

The gate opened, and Patrick strolled in.

Seanna stared at him—her son's father . . . looking even younger than her son.

"You," Seanna breathed. "No, it . . ." A sharp shake of her head before she regrouped, demanding, "Who are you?"

"Really? You've forgotten me? After all the fun times we had together? I've held up pretty good, haven't I? Which is more than I can say for you. *Really* more than I can say for you." He shuddered.

I shot Patrick a look, but he only tossed me his usual devil-may-care grin.

"Come along, Seanna," he said. "We're going to leave the kids alone."

"You—you can't be—"

"But I am. You know I am. Either that or you're the one going crazy, not Liv. Yes, I was eavesdropping. I do that. I thought I'd let the kids have some fun. Good show, Liv. You seem to have discovered Seanna's fatal flaw. She's a fucking idiot."

I wasn't sure what shocked me more—the profanity or the undiluted venom behind it. Hate shone from Patrick's eyes, the kind that chilled the marrow in my bones and reminded me that, however charming Patrick might seem, a bòcan wasn't a fae you wanted to cross.

There's more to this story than I thought.

"Come along, Seanna. Let's go chat. Catch up. It's been so long."

He said those last words with a bite that sparked genuine fear in Seanna's eyes. I'd always presumed Patrick had seduced Seanna. He'd suggested as much, happily taking credit for impregnating a teenaged girl. Now I saw the looks on their faces and knew that wasn't the story. Not at all.

As he took her arm, she said, "I won't go anywhere with—"

"Yes, actually, you will." His grip tightened, and he met her gaze and said slowly, "You are coming with me, Seanna," as he worked his fae compulsion.

When he started leading her to the gate, she didn't resist. Patrick tossed back a jaunty, "Ciao, kids," and escorted her out.

CHAPTER EIGHT

The gate had closed behind Patrick at least ninety seconds ago, and Gabriel and I were still exactly where we'd been when he walked out. We stood there waiting for that gate to swing open and Seanna to march back in. Finally, I checked the latch, as if I could somehow bar re-entry.

Talk to Gabriel.

Don't talk to Gabriel—find him something to do.

Help him compose his plan to deal with Seanna.

No, avoid the topic of Seanna, and get him doing work instead.

I turned to see him on his phone, typing something in. As I walked back, he looked up.

"Can I trouble you for a coffee?" he asked.

"A . . . ?"

"Coffee. Please."

"Sure . . ."

"Thank you. I'll be in momentarily."

It might seem that Gabriel was so traumatized by this reunion with his mother that he wanted me to go into the house so he could break down in private. Yet it was also possible that having seen the mother he thought was dead, the most pressing thing on his mind really was rectifying a late afternoon caffeine slump.

As I stepped onto the porch, I snuck a glance back at him. He was still typing, but his face was relaxed, no sign of tension in his shoulders. Yep, he might actually just want coffee.

I went inside, and I'd just begun filling a mug when the back door opened.

Gabriel stepped in and said, "Do you have travel mugs?"

"Uh, sure. Are you . . . leaving?"

"*We* are. The trunk on the Maserati is quite small, as I recall. Correct?"

Again, I thought I couldn't possibly have heard right, but said, just to clarify, "Yes, the Spyder has a very small trunk."

"And not enough space behind the front seats for both Lloergan and luggage."

"Umm . . ."

"Do you mind letting Rose borrow your car for a few days?"

"Uh, no, but Lloergan will fit behind the Spyder's seats fine, and I don't need to put anything in the trunk—"

"I'll switch cars now," he said, taking my keys from the rack. "I'll bring Lloergan back with me. That should give you time to pack a bag. Three days' worth. Casual clothing, the sort for hiking and whatnot."

"Umm . . ."

"Yes, I know. You've pointed out that I lack such clothing myself. However, I have rectified that. It's at my condo, which we'll need to stop by on the way."

"On the way *where* exactly?"

"It's a surprise. Put my coffee into a travel mug, please. We'll stop by that place you like in the city and get you a mocha for the drive."

And with that, he strode through the parlor and out the front door before I could say another word.

———

We'd stopped at Gabriel's condo for his bag, which was already packed, suggesting this wasn't a spur-of-the-moment trip. After we got my mocha, he finally explained that this was why he'd asked me to keep the weekend free—he'd planned a weekend get-away. A surprise for me, because I'd been working so hard lately.

Under any other circumstances, I'd have been thrilled. But as it was, I sat in the passenger seat, my mocha untouched, Lloergan in the back seat giving the occasional whimper, as if picking up my unease.

"I'm not running away from her," Gabriel said when we were outside the city.

"Even if you were, I wouldn't blame—"

"I'd already made plans."

"I know."

"What I'm doing, Olivia, is ensuring Seanna does not interfere with my plans. I had no appointments tomorrow that could not be easily rescheduled, so I am beginning our trip early, knowing that if I stay, this situation will deteriorate and come tomorrow night, when we were supposed to leave, we won't be able to get away." His hands tightened on the steering wheel. "You need a break. We *both* need a break." He paused. "I want this."

He blurted the last part, as if getting the words out before he could decide against them.

I want this.

Three words that most people have no problem saying. Gabriel himself practically lives by those words.

No, that's not true. He's lived by the words "I need this." *I require this*, first for survival and then for security, a series of goals he needed to achieve to relax, secure in the knowledge that nothing could send him back where he'd been.

In the six months I'd been at the law firm, I'd gone on two vacations with Ricky. Gabriel rarely took a day off, and I suspect he's never actually been on a holiday. I know he doesn't own a passport. Maybe now, seeing me take vacations, he thought, *You know, I could do with some of that.* But one of the reasons I suspect he'd never done it before was that he had no one to travel with. So now, having decided he'd like a weekend trip, he framed it as a surprise getaway for me. This wasn't Gabriel fleeing Seanna—it was Gabriel safeguarding his weekend away.

"You're right," I said. "I could use a break. Rest and refocus."

"Exactly."

He drove another couple of miles in silence and then said, "That shot to the leg doesn't seem to have slowed Seanna down."

"So should I aim higher next time?"

He chuckled and relaxed his grip on the wheel. "No. I was only raising the subject to say that, while I'm not averse to the thought of her being shot, I'd rather you didn't do it again. She'll be quick to press charges next time, and I don't want you dealing with that."

"I won't. She just pissed me off."

"Something she said?"

I made a noise in my throat.

"She insulted you?"

"Not—" I stopped myself, but it was too late. He'd laid the trap and I'd fallen straight into it.

"She insulted *me*," he said.

"She pissed me off."

"I won't pretend that I don't find that more gratifying than I should, but I will ask you not to let her get to you. I'm quite accustomed to her insults." He handed me my mocha. "Drink up. We'll be there soon."

When we arrived at our destination, I was out of the car before it even stopped, Lloergan shoving through the seat gap to follow me, alarmed by my haste. I gave her a quick pat and then dashed up the steps and around to the back porch, and when Gabriel found me, I was leaning on the railing, gazing out at the lake.

I grinned over at him. "Does it only get cell phone reception on Tuesdays, if I hold my phone just right?"

"With any luck, it doesn't get cell phone reception at all."

"I can make sure of that." I took mine out, shut it off, and then raced down the back steps and started crossing the rocks.

"Careful, Olivia. It's slippery."

"Then you'll have to come and keep me safe," I called back. "After you change into those jeans you claim to have bought. Come on, Lloe. Time to explore."

CHAPTER NINE

A few months ago, Gabriel and I had sat on the shores of Lake Michigan and talked about our dream vacation homes, places we'd go to get away from the city and Cainsville and all they entailed. Mine had been a cabin on the lake, where I could read and relax on the deck. That's what Gabriel had found for me.

After dinner, we sat on the back deck, watching the waves. The sun had dropped, taking any warmth with it. We had a fire roaring inside and the chalet radiators jacked up, with the rear windows and door wide open to let that heat flood out. We sat right on the deck, in a nest of every blanket and pillow we could find. And we had wine. An amazing—and very expensive—Bordeaux, probably another untouched gift from a client.

Between the fire and the blankets and the wine, we kept warm through the first hour of conversation, but as we entered the second, Lloergan had retreated indoors to lie by the fire, and I could no longer hide my chattering teeth.

"Let's go in," Gabriel said.

"I don't want to."

"If you're—"

"I'll be fine," I said as I tugged the blanket higher. I managed to stop my teeth from chattering . . . only to start shivering convulsively.

"Here," he said, and held out the blanket he was using.

I shook my head and shifted closer to pull it over both of us. He put his arm out, motioning for me to come closer still, and I didn't need a second invitation. I sat beside him. Then I inched closer, as casually as I could, chatting and sipping wine. He put his arm around me, and a few minutes later I was snuggled up against his side, his arm around me.

"Better?" he said.

The pile of blankets trapped our body heat and made it very toasty. But if I admitted I was fine, he might shift aside. So I nodded, chattering my teeth a little, which gave me the excuse to snuggle closer still. He tugged me over until I was curled up in his lap, his arms around me, and I decided I heartily approved of this "lakeside cabin in December" plan.

If I gave another shiver, it wasn't the cold, but the fact I was snuggled up with Gabriel, feeling the heat of his body, smelling the scent—his scent—that permeated his bed when he would insist I sleep there, and I'd wake from dreams I didn't want to have, not while I'd been with Ricky. Dreams that I *was* allowed to have now, even if they left me aching and torn between hoping that one day they'd no longer be dreams and fearing they always would.

When I shivered, he mistook it for a lingering chill. His arms tightened around me, and he lowered his face to my hair, and I could feel his breath and the pound of his heart, and all I could think was *this.*

This, this, this.

This is what I want. This is more than I ever thought I could have with him, and I want to stay just like this for as long as I

*can, not breathe, not move a muscle in case the buzz of the
wine passes and he pulls away.*

I closed my eyes and listened to the sound of his breathing,
and then I smelled wildflowers. Smelled wildflowers and felt the
heat of the sun and arms around me, and I was thinking the
same things. *Don't breathe, don't move, or you'll spook. He'll
realize what he's doing and it'll be over.*

"You're certain you're all right?" It was Gwynn's voice, young.
"You scared the life out of me, Mati, seeing you tumble like that."

No. I squeezed my eyes shut and pushed the vision aside.

*I like you just fine, Gwynn. I like those little glimpses into
what was, those touchstones with the past. But right now, I
want Gabriel.*

One last mental shove, and I smelled the lake and Gabriel.
There. That's better.

I snuggled in, and he rubbed his thumb over my cheek.

"Still cold," he said, and tugged the blanket higher.

"At least I didn't fall in the water again," I said. "Now *that*
was cold."

He went still, and I replayed my words, wondering if there
was any other way to interpret them.

"The river, I mean," I said. "When we fell in the river."

I shivered for dramatic effect, but he stayed tense, his breathing slowed, his arms stiff around me.

Damn it. What did I do now?

"I . . . have a question," he said.

Now I was the one tensing. "Okay."

"If a thing occurred, and one party was not aware that it
occurred, and the other party did not intend for it to occur,
should the second party admit that it did? If the thing is a thing
that may cause discomfort? The answer, I believe, should be
no, that the second party should not admit to it. But if the

second party worries that somehow the first party will find out, and in keeping the secret, the second party will seem complicit in the action, which will cause additional discomfort . . ."

I twisted to look up at him. "I have no idea what you're saying, Gabriel."

He nodded, a little curtly, and started to pull away.

Goddamn it, no. What was I supposed to say?

He stopped withdrawing and stayed still for a moment. Then he settled in, awkwardly now, as if he wasn't quite sure how he'd done it before.

"Let me simplify that," he said. "I'm going to tell you something you may not want to hear, and I hope I'm not doing it merely to assuage a guilty conscience, but if I am, I apologize."

"Noted."

"It's about your fall into the river. When I rescued you, you were cold, as you say. Very cold. Also unconscious, and as I was trying to warm you up, you—" He cut himself off and shook his head. "No. Not you. It was me. I may have . . ." Another head shake, sharper now. "There's no *may* about it. No equivocating. I did. That is to say, I . . ."

He trailed off.

"I kissed you, didn't I?" I said. "I was dreaming of swimming with Gwynn, to this place he had with Matilda, a cavern under the lake. I dreamed of that, and I kissed you."

After a moment, he said, carefully, "You may have started it, but that's no excuse. I did not . . . I didn't stop you. I . . ." He cleared his throat. "I thought you had regained consciousness, and I was having difficulty organizing my thoughts."

"Hypothermia causes mental confusion. I wasn't the only one freezing in that water."

"Yes." A pause. "I mean, no. While there may have been some of that, I'm not making excuses, Olivia. Once I was certain you were not conscious enough to know what you were doing, I stopped. But I let it proceed longer than I should have. I thought you knew what you were doing and I wasn't thinking straight and . . ."

He squeezed his eyes shut. "And that's more excuses, which dull an apology. Which is what this is. An apology. You were very clearly not aware of what you were doing, and I took advantage of that, however inadvertently, and I want to apologize."

"There's no need."

"Yes, there—"

"No." I twisted on his lap and looked him square in the face. "I'm not trying to deny you an apology, Gabriel. I'm saying it honestly isn't necessary."

Because the dream may have started with Gwynn and Matilda, but when I was kissing Gabriel, I'd been dreaming of kissing *him*.

Now I just needed to say that. One tiny step.

It should be so easy. He'd admitted to returning my kiss, therefore my advance, however unintentional, had not been unwelcome. Yet I'd spent so long analyzing that I couldn't help doing it even here.

Screw it. Just screw it. If I waited for every damn omen to align, I'd grow old and gray.

"I actually wasn't—" I began.

Gabriel's phone sounded. We both jumped.

"So . . . apparently we have cell service," I said.

He went to hit a button—Ignore, I hoped—but the phone stopped before he could.

"All right," I said. "Full speed ahead. It wasn't Gwynn I was—"

The phone rang again. Gabriel went to hit it again, harder, and then he stopped. I saw the screen, showing a division of the Chicago Police Department. He moved his finger over Ignore, slower now.

"You need to answer that," I said. "Or we're both going to spend the night wondering which client has gotten himself in trouble."

"I'll be quick."

He rose to take the call inside, away from the pounding surf. I followed and stoked the fire, hearing only the crackle and snap of that as he talked. Then there was a crash behind me, and I leapt up to see Gabriel's cell phone at the foot of the wall . . . where he'd thrown it.

He unclenched his fists, blinked, and stared at the phone as if not knowing how it got there. When he saw me watching, he looked down at his hand.

"It . . ." he began, and then trailed off, as if he'd been about to say it had slipped before realizing that was logistically impossible. "I'm sorry," he said.

"For what? Getting angry and throwing your phone? Not an indictable offense, Gabriel." I walked over and bent to pick up his cell. "It's an inanimate object, easily replaced. It doesn't even look that badly damaged. Try harder next time."

I quirked a smile at him, but he didn't seem to notice, just stood there, frozen and wide-eyed. In his face, I saw a much younger Gabriel, a boy who'd let his roiling anger spill over, instantly regretting it, terrified of the consequences.

I set the phone on the table. "Was the call about Seanna?"

"Yes."

I winced. "She's in trouble."

"The detective wouldn't tell me over the phone. She only said I need to go there. And I . . ." Gabriel swallowed. "I don't want to."

"You don't have to. I'll handle this. Lloe? Time for a ride."

Gabriel shook his head. "You can't—"

"Yep, I absolutely can. Let me do this for you. I'll gather the data as if Seanna were any other potential client. Then she can sit in a jail cell until morning. Hell, with a little help from Lydia, we can make sure she sits there until *Monday*, meaning you and I can continue our weekend away."

He hesitated.

"There's no reason you need to do this," I said.

"And what should I do instead? Pace the floor? Wait for you to come back and tell me what happened?" He lowered his voice. "That doesn't help, Olivia. I know you mean well, but the best way for me to take this weekend off is to tackle this first. Get it out of the way. We'll come back tomorrow night and start again."

"Promise?"

"Yes. No matter what she's done, we'll be back."

CHAPTER TEN

When Gabriel phoned the detective to say we'd reached the city, he was directed to an address. It was not a police station address. The detective still refused to explain, and Gabriel's grumbling protests didn't change anything. She was giving him the runaround for purely sadistic fun, and Gabriel threatening to complain to her superior was like the brattiest kid in school threatening to tell the principal that a teacher was being mean to him.

"Any chance we're being set up?" I said as Gabriel drove through the city. "Some fae pretending to be a Chicago detective, luring you to an out-of-the-way location?"

"I know Detective Fahy. We've had dealings before."

"Uh-huh. What'd you do to her?"

He glanced over. "Is it not possible I simply mean she worked a case I defended?"

"Nope. Spill."

"I may have inadvertently prevented her from getting a promotion."

"Inadvertently?"

"I had evidence thrown out in a case, on the grounds she'd contaminated it at the scene. At the time, she'd been up for promotion, and when the judge ruled in my favor, she lost that promotion. I could hardly foresee the repercussions."

"Did she contaminate evidence?"

"The judge thought it was a strong possibility, given the persuasiveness of my argument."

"In other words, no."

"I could not have been expected to foresee—"

"If you'd known it would cost her a promotion, would you have done differently?"

"Of course not. My job is to defend my client to the best of my ability. It is the responsibility of the police and prosecution to protect their case. Any repercussions from their failure to do so cannot be laid at my feet, as I told Detective Fahy when she complained. She must simply do a better job next time, and if she cannot, then perhaps she didn't deserve the promotion."

"And you're surprised she's giving you a hassle now?"

"Yes, I am. A strike within the realm of the professional never justifies retribution in the realm of the personal."

He slowed at the address, an upscale chain hotel. As we walked in, an anxious-looking manager was waiting.

"Can you tell me what this is about?" Gabriel asked as the manager led us along the main hall.

"Nothing," he said. "Nothing at all. A misunderstanding. An accident. An unfortunate accident. These things happen." He cast a nervous glance at a middle-aged couple and steered us away, saying, "This way, please. The service elevator is quicker."

He whisked us up to the fourth floor, and we passed a member of a crime scene team heading for the main elevator.

"The stairs," the manager said to her. "Please use the stairs. And if you could be more discreet . . ."

The young woman kept walking. Two hotel guests peered out of their doors to watch her pass, forensics kit in hand.

"An accident," the manager whimpered, as if to himself. "They happen. We can't help that."

When we reached the room, he asked us to "Please hurry," and then shut the door behind us.

We walked in and . . . saw blood. Droplets dappled the hall. In the bedroom, an arc drenched the wall like a red rainbow.

Arterial spray.

I glanced at Gabriel. He processed the spray, no expression on his face. Then he stepped into the bedroom, where a blond woman in her late thirties looked up from her phone.

"Where's the manager?" she asked.

"Left us and fled," I replied, and walked in, my hand extended. "Liv Jones."

She ignored my hand, her gaze fixed on Gabriel. She had a gleam in her eye, like she was watching an enemy run a gauntlet of spears, praying one of them sliced through him.

While I'd understood Gabriel's reasoning for not feeling any remorse over "inadvertently" costing Detective Fahy a promotion, I'd sympathized with her. It would be tough enough to rise through the ranks as a female detective. You sure as hell didn't need an arrogant defense attorney shredding your credibility. Seeing that look on her face, though, I decided I didn't feel bad for her after all. She'd brought Gabriel to a blood-drenched scene, telling him only that it involved his mother. That went beyond petty personal retaliation.

"May I ask what this is about, Detective Fahy?" Gabriel said. "You mentioned my mother, but I fail to see the connection."

"This is her hotel room."

His brow furrowed. "Are you quite certain? It seems beyond her budget."

She paused, as if unsure where to go with that. "I think the question of how she afforded it should be the least of your concerns, Walsh. Your mother is missing, and her hotel room is covered in blood."

"Missing?" More furrowing. "If this is your idea of a joke, Detective, it is in very poor taste. I thought you meant she'd once rented this room. My mother has been dead for fifteen years."

Another pause. "If someone told you that, they're mistaken. She's—"

"Dead. Very much so, according to the Chicago Police Department. She died of a drug overdose and was discovered in an abandoned building fifteen years ago. She'd been buried as a Jane Doe because the CPD failed to do the most basic investigation and discover she had both a name and a teenaged son. That's not surprising. A drug addict—particularly a woman—is never worth the department's notice, a fact which I am still considering bringing to the attention of the taxpayers by way of a lawsuit. However, that aside, it was my investigator here, Ms. Taylor-Jones, who discovered the autopsy photos. I confirmed six months ago that the deceased was indeed my mother. The case is closed."

Fahy stared at him. Then she lifted her phone and looked down at it.

"Yes," Gabriel said. "Please check on that. I'll wait."

She pocketed her phone. "I don't know what bullshit you two tried to pull, but your mother was alive a few hours ago. She had a drink with a guy in the lounge downstairs, where she mentioned that she was your mother. She seemed very proud of you, God only knows why. She gave the guest her room key. When he followed her up a half hour later, he found this."

"And?" Gabriel said.

"And what?"

"I'm sure you have more than a woman in a bar trying to impress a man by claiming kinship with a known local figure. I'm guessing she also registered as Seanna Walsh?"

"Another guy paid for her room. He managed to convince the clerk to let him pay cash for a two-night stay, despite that being very clearly against the hotel's policies. The guy was in his mid-twenties. Dark-haired. Handsome. Charming and manipulative." Fahy shot Gabriel a look. "Sound familiar?"

"Dark-haired, yes. Manipulative? I'll accept that. While I'm more often mistaken for being *older* than my age, I suppose someone could mistake me for younger. But I'm hardly attractive enough to persuade a woman to risk her job. Nor has anyone ever accused me of being charming. However, I'm quite happy to speak to this employee and see whether she recognizes me. I'm certain you'll agree that if any adjective might be aptly applied to me, it is *memorable*."

"Is that really all you've got, Detective?" I asked. "The word of some dude in a hotel bar? I doubt you'll even get a proper statement from him. By now he's deeply regretting taking that woman's keycard and has already formulated a bizarre and implausible story for his wife."

She scowled at me. Good guess, apparently.

"A blood test will clear this up," Fahy said. "And we have plenty to use. Walsh? You can provide a sample."

"Yes, I will. When I am court-ordered to do so."

"About the blood on the walls," I said. "I'm sure you've already asked your crime techs to do a wide sampling, to ensure it all comes from a single and fresh source."

One of the techs looked over, his expression saying he'd been told to do no such thing.

"Fresh?" Fahy said.

"The scene could be faked, right?" I said. "Multiple sources or stored blood used to provide enough to make you suspect a fatal incident. You've got a woman who was checked in with no ID, and told some random dude in the hotel bar that she was Gabriel Walsh's mother. Then she invites this guy up, presumably telling him to wait a half hour before following her. And he just happens to walk into an apparent crime scene? It screams setup."

"To what purpose?"

I waited a moment, to be sure she was serious. "What's the first thing you did? Called Gabriel. The next thing you'd have done, I'm sure, is blame him. Six months ago Gabriel Walsh was charged with the murder of my fiancé. Now he's investigated in the suspicious disappearance of his long-lost drug addict mother? Once that hit the news, he'd undoubtedly get a phone call from his supposed mother, offering to rectify this terrible misunderstanding . . . for a price."

"I'll take multiple samples of the blood," the tech called over. "And I'll make a note to check for freshness."

"Thank you," I said.

"Olivia's theory is almost certainly the answer to your puzzle, Detective," Gabriel said. "She shouldn't have needed to reach it first. You're a seasoned investigator. She's only had her license for a few months."

"Might also explain why you got passed over for that promotion," I said.

Gabriel's look of mild reproach said I didn't need to bring that into it.

"Do you drive a red Maserati, Ms. Jones?" Fahy asked.

"One of my dad's old cars, yes."

"Do you know what was seen parked on the street out front earlier this evening? After Ms. Walsh checked in?"

"Let me guess . . . a red Maserati? What time was that?"

She checked her notes. "Seven p.m."

"At which time I was an hour outside the city, picking up dinner with Gabriel. I'll give you the details. The guy at the restaurant will remember us—he recognized me from newspaper photos and said he never thought my parents were guilty."

"A Maserati is not terribly rare in a city the size of Chicago," Gabriel said. "And red must be the most common color. You have a license number, I'm sure?"

Her silence said she didn't.

"If that's all . . ." Gabriel said.

"This stinks, Walsh. It really stinks."

"I would agree, and I believe Olivia is correct that I am about to be the victim of extortion. I'll expect to have the full support of the CPD in countering this attack."

CHAPTER ELEVEN

The manager, understandably eager not to let guests know they had a potential murder scene, didn't object when Gabriel said we wanted to speak to him. He scooted us into an office and answered everything we asked. Then he produced the employee who'd checked Seanna in, and she gave enough detail to confirm our suspicion on who'd been responsible for that. Next the manager brought the man Seanna picked up in the bar, who'd been told by the police not to leave and was anxiously awaiting the go-ahead to escape. If he spoke to us because he mistakenly thought we could grant his reprieve, that was hardly our fault.

As we left the hotel, Lloergan appeared and fell in at my side. Our first stop was the presumed point of egress: the fourth-floor window.

Despite what I'd said to Detective Fahy, we weren't absolutely convinced this was a setup. It seemed likely. The scheme was classic Seanna—clever enough, but overly complicated. Yet we couldn't rule out the possibility she *had* been murdered. There was certainly no shortage of suspects. I was only glad Gabriel and I had been an hour's drive up the lake.

We found blood below the window. It was a small pool, as if

the person climbed down to the second floor and then hung off the balcony before dropping to the ground. A partial shoe print marred the edge. I took a photo of the imprint, but there wasn't enough to identify the shoe size.

The blood dripped for a few yards south, headed into an alley, and then stopped, as if the person had paused to bind the wound. We were examining the blood trail when Lloergan gave a jowl-shuddering sigh.

"Getting bored, girl?" I said. "You can go wander if you like."

Her look oozed reproach, and she glanced to the side just as two figures rounded the corner. It was the dryads from the abandoned amusement park.

"Blood!" the boy said.

"A clue!" the girl said, jogging over to us.

"Wrong crime," I said.

"You have more than one?" she said. "That's hardly fair. You ought to share."

"They are," he said. "They're sharing with us. Even if they don't want to."

"Can we switch mysteries?" she asked. "Please?"

Lloergan sighed again and lowered herself to the ground, as if to wait out what was sure to be a long conversation.

"How did you find us?" I asked.

The girl lifted a brow in what was probably meant to be a crafty look, but she managed it as well as a three-year-old trying to be mysterious. "We have our ways."

"Secret fae ways," the boy said.

"We came to speak to you because we have a problem," she said. "A lack of clues."

"Complete lack."

"Utter lack." She held out a notebook. "We've tried. See? We went through the fun house with a fine-toothed comb."

"We did?" the boy said.

"It's an expression."

"It makes no sense."

"They never do," she said. "But we searched and searched and found no trace of a crime. I know you said it was long ago, so we asked other fae. We'll keep asking, but so far?"

"Nothing," the boy said.

"So we came to find you. Even if it meant traveling to the city." She shuddered.

"Not fond of the city, I take it?" I said.

"We can't hide here." She walked to a wooden fence surrounding the trash bins. When she pressed her hand to it, her skin changed to tree bark. "And this . . . ?" She put her hand against the hotel wall, which made it look like a tree limb growing up the brick. "Even worse. The best we can do is try to blend in with the humans. Fortunately, we're good at that."

"Uh-huh."

She waggled her finger at me. "Don't mock. We are. Watch." She turned to the boy. "OMG, Mrs. Phipps is a total bitch. Did you see what she gave me on that English essay? I worked for, like, a whole hour on it."

"Yeah, and Chem is totally kicking my ass this year. If I don't pull up my mark, Dad'll take away my car keys."

"That sucks. Poor baby. Here, let me make it better."

She kissed him, just a quick kiss at first, but he pulled her into a deep one that left her laughing and catching her breath.

"So . . . you're not brother and sister?" I said.

"What?" they said in unison.

"I thought you were siblings."

"Eww," she said.

"That's gross," he said. "And unsanitary."

"I don't think that's the word for it," she said.

"It should be." He looked at us. "We're mated. Married, as humans might say. Have been for a very long time."

"Very, very long," the girl said. "We're old."

"Incredibly old."

"Almost dead," she said. "But not yet. Which is why we're always looking for fun. Fill in our twilight years with excitement."

"That's where you come in. We're stuck—temporarily—on your other mystery, so we'll take this one. What do you need?"

"Ooh, let me guess," she said. "You want to find the person who left that blood trail. We can do that."

I eased back. "I'd say go for it, but she's almost certainly in the city, which you hate."

"We'll survive. Can we use the *cûn*?"

The boy frowned. "Why don't *they* use the *cûn*?"

"Good question."

Both looked at us expectantly. I glanced at Lloergan. I'd been considering asking her for help, but the rogue Huntsman who'd enslaved her had forced her to track humans and fae, and not for the reasons a *cûn* is supposed to track.

"Lloergan?" Gabriel said. "Could you help?"

"Is that her name?" the boy asked.

"It means moonlight," the girl said.

"You know Welsh?" I said.

"We know many things." Again, she tried—and failed—to look suitably crafty and mysterious. Then she added, "It is a lovely name."

"An excellent name," the boy said.

"If nearly impossible to pronounce. Much harder than ours."

She gave us another expectant look. We hadn't asked their names. I'd been avoiding that, actually. It implied a future relationship.

"What are your names?" Gabriel asked, surprising me.

"He's Alexios. I'm Helia."

Gabriel nodded and turned to the *cŵn*. "Lloergan?" He crouched before her and pulled a sock from his inside pocket, one he must have snagged from the hotel room. "This belongs to the person we're looking for. Can you follow her trail from here? It's up to you, of course."

She sniffed the sock gingerly, as if it didn't smell very good. Then she snuffled the ground and headed into the alley. We followed.

"We can come along?" Alexios called after us.

"Shhh," Helia said. "Don't ask. Just follow until they make us leave."

Gabriel turned, and Helia fell back with a yelp.

"Let me make this clear," he said. "If you wish to help us, we will not stop you. Nor will we set you on tasks or give you any information that might be used against us. If we seem paranoid, understand that we have cause. Outside Cainsville, fae who have asked for help or offered it have been uniformly—"

"Nasty," Helia said.

"Horrid," Alexios said.

"Don't interrupt him."

"I'm not the one who—"

"Yes," Gabriel said. "They betrayed us, which has taught us a few things about dealing with fae. It has also, I hope, taught them a few things about dealing with us. Namely, that we are enough fae ourselves to understand the concept of quid pro quo. Help us and we help you. Hinder or harm us . . ."

"We have heard the fates of those who crossed you," Helia said, going serious. "We might seem foolish, but we did not live to this age by being foolhardy. Our help is offered freely. In return, we hope for a bit of fun and, yes, the favor of Matilda and Gwynn, which is no small thing. *The* favor, not *a* favor."

"Not a specific thing or a chit," Alexios said. "Just to—in the colloquial—get on your good side, because it seems a fine place to be."

"All right, then," Gabriel said, and we returned to following Lloergan.

The trail didn't go more than a mile before Lloergan lost it. *Cŵn* aren't tracking hounds. They can pursue prey in the forest, and they can find them in the city, but the latter requires preternatural abilities, some of which her injuries stole from her.

It was equally likely that, after that first mile, Seanna got into a vehicle and the trail legitimately ended. Either way, Gabriel only wanted to see how far the trail went because it told him that we weren't following someone disposing of Seanna's body. It was her. On foot. And not so badly injured that she couldn't walk a mile.

As we'd tracked Seanna, I'd given the dryads what information I could to help them find her. Not that I expected they actually would, but it would keep them occupied.

"If you go after Seanna, you need to be careful," I said after we'd hit the end of the trail and turned back.

"We will not harm her," Helia said. "She is the mother of Gwynn. She deserves our respect and our care."

"Actually, I meant be careful *of* her. She's a career criminal. She wouldn't have any problem leading you to your doom."

"She's part fae," Alexios said. "We'd expect no less."

"True, but even for fae, she's . . ." I glanced at Gabriel, not sure how much farther I should go.

He said, "Seanna Walsh is a drug addict, an alcoholic, a part-time prostitute, and a full-time con artist. She cares nothing for anyone except herself."

"And you," Helia said.

"No, I am not the exception to that rule."

"Oh." She frowned. "Are you sure you want us to find her?"

"Not particularly, but it seems prudent."

We walked in silence for a few steps. Then Helia said, "I hope you do not feel obligated to find her, Gwynn."

"I prefer Gabriel," he said, but his tone was soft.

She nodded. "We will remember that. But you don't feel obligated, do you? Even among fae, there are two exceptions to our selfishness. One is our mate." She caught Alexios's hand and squeezed it. "You cannot be a partner to someone you do not respect and care for. The other exception is our children. For fae, reproduction is not easy. Alexios and I were never blessed, but we knew if we were, we'd have to change. Be less . . ." She smiled at her mate. "Less capricious."

"Less dryad," he said.

"Exactly." Her voice lilted, a touch of that lightheartedness seeping back in. Then she sobered again as she said, "You don't feel obliged to your mother, do you, Gw—Gabriel?"

"Not one single bit."

"Excellent. We shall be careful, then, for our own sakes and not for hers."

"We could get rid of her if you like," Alexios said.

Helia rolled her eyes. "Again, *agori mou*, one does not ask these questions. Gabriel will say no and then we cannot do it, or we will have disobeyed him."

"Uh, no," I cut in. "Whatever the situation, killing Seanna isn't the answer."

"Oh, we didn't mean kill. We don't do that. But we have ways to make her disappear." That crafty look again. "The secrets of trees."

"No, please," I said. "General rule? Don't harm anyone while completing a task for us unless your own lives are in danger. Okay?"

"No," Alexios said.

I turned to him. "Then you aren't working for us. Either you do as we ask—"

"We will," Helia said. "But you asked if it was okay. It is not. We will do it, though. You need to be more specific in your questions, Matilda. Or do you prefer Eden?"

"Liv or Olivia."

She scrunched her nose. "Olivia is for olives, and in the old country we saw far too many of those. We had to live in a field of them once, when they cut down our forest." She shuddered. "Olives stink. But we will call you Liv, if you insist."

I sighed. "Call me whatever you want. Now, since Lloergan lost Seanna's trail so—"

"It isn't her fault."

"I didn't mean it like that." I rubbed the *cûn*'s neck. "It's hardly her fault that Seanna got into a car."

"I meant that the *cûn* cannot perform as well as she'd like as long as she still suffers from her injuries."

"We're working on that."

"They're deep wounds." Helia moved to Lloergan and reached to touch her torn ear.

"Rude," Alexios said.

"Quite right." Helia crouched in front of the *cûn*. "May I examine you, Lloergan?"

Lloergan turned her head, offering her injured ear. Helia checked it and fingered a few scars. The she settled in front of the hound and gazed into her eyes—the clouded one and the good one—before rising.

"Someone has done well with the ear," she said. "But more scar tissue can be removed to unblock the canal. For the eye, I would suggest a tincture of coleus. But most importantly, consider small doses of nightshade mixed with kanna and skullcap."

"Isn't nightshade toxic?"

"Not to fae. Mixed with other ingredients, it creates a potion that helps dull old memories. Traumatic ones. That's her greatest problem. Not the physical injuries, but the ones in here." She tapped Lloergan's skull and then patted her head.

"Speak to the Tylwyth Teg," Helia continued. "They'll know the recipe. It's a common one for fae." She offered me a half-sad smile as she gave Lloergan one last pat. "In such a long life, there is always something we'd rather not remember."

CHAPTER TWELVE

t was nearly 3 a.m. when we knocked on Patrick's door. It took a while for him to open it, and when he did, he sighed and shook his head.

"I knew you'd be by eventually," he said. "I just expected it at a decent hour. Silly me." He looked at Lloergan, standing at my side. "Protection against Scanna's return? Sadly, whatever her crimes, I don't think she's killed any fac. Otherwise, I'd say setting a hound on her is a lovely idea."

"Ricky's out of town."

"Ah, *cŵn*-sitting."

We walked past him into the house. When I noticed Lloergan wasn't at my side, I looked out to see her on the front stoop.

"Staying out there?" I asked.

She grunted and laid her head on her paws.

"Good call."

We continued through the old house into the largest room, where Patrick had knocked down a wall to make an area that was half old-fashioned library and half modern entertainment center. An odd mix, one that embraced the different sides of the bòcan himself: the scholar, the novelist, and the fae who refused to act—or look—his age.

I settled in on the couch. Gabriel sat at my side.

"We know you paid for Seanna's hotel. But she's gone. And she left a hell of a mess."

He sighed. "Figuratively or literally? No, wait. Both. Stripped the hotel room of everything of value, and management is threatening a lawsuit. Just give me the bill."

"Is that how you intend to handle Seanna's return? A trail of money leading her away?"

"It's worked before," he murmured, low enough that I suspected I wasn't supposed to hear.

Gabriel cut in. "You are correct that she left both a literal and a figurative mess. You are incorrect as to the nature of both. She appears to have feigned her murder . . . after conveniently telling another guest that she was my mother."

"*Cach*," Patrick spat. "Trashing the room just wasn't good enough, was it, Seanna?" He looked over at Gabriel and when he spoke, his voice was tight. "I presume the point of that stunt was to frame you and then magically reappear after you paid her off?"

"We expect so, but I was lakeside, with an ironclad alibi. Yet it doesn't appear that the police will be quick to drop the investigation, and you were the one who checked her into that hotel. Also, someone in a red Maserati parked outside the hotel shortly before Seanna disappeared."

Patrick's gaze shot to me.

"Olivia was with me," Gabriel said. "We exchanged cars with Rose so we could take Lloergan."

"*Cach*."

"That woman is Seanna, isn't she?" I said. "There's no way she's an impostor? Maybe a fae using her face as a glamour?"

"Glamours don't work like that. It's her. I know you'd love to hear otherwise, but going down that path is dangerous. That is Seanna Walsh."

"Because she said something that proved it?"

"No," Gabriel said. "Because Patrick already knew she was alive."

I could swear Patrick flinched.

"You paid her off," I said, remembering his earlier words. "She came back before, and you paid her to go away."

"Any business between myself and Seanna Walsh is personal and private—"

"Uh, no," I said. "Given that the 'business' between you resulted in the man sitting across from you, I think there's a third party involved."

"Thank you for the clarification, Olivia." Patrick's tone cooled, and he used my full name the way my adoptive father used it on those rare occasions when he was displeased, and I went from Livy to O-liv-i-a, each syllable pronounced in full.

"If you had let me finish," Patrick continued, "I'd have said that, in general, I do not wish to speak about my business with Seanna Walsh, but on this topic—and this one alone—I will, because I do not wish either of you to think this might be an impostor. Also, I want to clear up a misunderstanding regarding what you think I did and did *not* do for Gabriel."

"Misunderstanding? When I accused you of letting him go through hell as a child, what did you say to me?"

"I have no idea—"

"Oh, I do. Because I will never forget the words. Here's a hint: steel."

Do you know how they temper steel, Olivia? The application of controlled heat. As strong as the metal will withstand. That produces the most resilient steel. Too much and it will break. It must be tough, yet slightly malleable. Adaptable to the greatest number of situations. That's Gabriel.

"You take liberties, Olivia," Patrick said, his voice heavy with warning.

"Because you allow it . . . except when it inconveniences you. You're like the parent who wants to be all buddy-buddy until the kid disrespects him and then, suddenly, it's off to your room until dinner. Oh, sorry. Wrong analogy. You don't know anything about parenting."

"Patrick?" Gabriel said. "You were confirming that, yes, you did know Seanna was alive."

Patrick took a moment to compose himself and then said, "She contacted me about ten years ago. Ordered me to meet her, or she'd tell the world I was a deadbeat dad. After *she* abandoned you."

A roll of his eyes, more himself now as he settled into his story. "I aged my glamour, and we met. I told her that I thought it convenient she returned when you reached the age of majority and could no longer legally expect anything from her. I managed to convince her that she would owe you compensation for those lost years of care. Then I gave her some money and, as I expected, she went away again. Then, a few years ago, she saw your name in the paper and realized you were far more successful than the average twenty-something. So I had to pay her more."

He looked at Gabriel as if expecting a thank-you.

"I would have appreciated the warning," Gabriel said, his voice deceptively soft.

Patrick only said, "I meant to," and then shrugged and added, "I just didn't get to it," as if explaining why he'd failed to warn a visitor that the front stoop was slippery.

"Perhaps I have misstepped," Gabriel said, those pale blue eyes now as chill as his voice. "I have failed to complain or express any displeasure at the fact you hid my paternity from me. It was unproductive. That has led you to believe that I harbor no ill feelings over the situation."

"I kept her away, Gabriel."

"I beg your pardon?"

Again, Patrick missed Gabriel's tone entirely and turned to face him, as if he only needed to explain more clearly. "When she came back, you were in college and well on your way to a successful life. I wouldn't allow her to interfere with that. So I helped you."

"The time to help me was when I was a child," Gabriel enunciated slowly. "Locked in a cubby while she screwed men for drug money."

Now Patrick really did flinch. "I had no idea—"

"Of course you didn't. You'd washed your hands of me. I don't believe you actively ignored the abuse—you simply didn't open your eyes and look. If you had, you might have seen something inconvenient."

"It wasn't like that."

"Then tell me what it was like."

"I kept an eye on you. Remember I gave you that hint for finding the last gargoyle?"

"You—you gave him the *hint*—" I sputtered.

Gabriel's hand on my knee stopped me. "If you paid Seanna to stay away, then I suspect that was to save yourself further inconvenience."

"It wasn't like that," Patrick said.

"Then, again, please explain."

Patrick walked to the bookcase and began re-shelving a stack.

"I'm not asking you to explain why you seduced a seventeen-year-old drug addict," Gabriel said. "You're fae. It doesn't mean the same."

"I didn't—" Patrick stopped himself and fussed with a book, straightening loose pages in the old tome.

"All right," Gabriel said. "There was likely little seduction required. Perhaps she convinced you she was older. Perhaps she was clean at the time. Whatever the case, I'll accept that she was a willing participant in the affair."

"There was no—" Again, Patrick cut himself short. He took a book from the shelf and scanned, as if looking for the proper spot.

After a moment, Gabriel's hands clenched, ever so slightly, and he drew in a small breath. "I would like to understand the circumstances regarding my conception, and why you left me with a teenaged addict for a mother."

"I did, all right? I take the blame. I made mistakes. I apologize. Is that what you want?"

"What I want is an explanation. I believe I'm entitled to one."

"No, you're not."

I bristled and rose. "Gabriel is—"

"I have never asked you for anything, Patrick," Gabriel said, his voice low. "Even as a child, when you offered to tell me where to find the last gargoyle, I refused. Now I am asking for something."

Patrick shook his head and took out a small stack of books, laying them on the table.

"Damn you," I said, shoving the books aside as I planted myself in front of him. "Your son is asking for words. That's it. *Words*. You'll damn well find the basic civility to answer—"

"Stay out of this, Liv," Patrick said. "It isn't your concern."

"If it's about him, then it is my concern. Isn't that what you once told me?"

"Please lock the door on your way out. It's late, and I'm going back to bed."

He started to leave. I grabbed his arm.

The room went dark. Then flashes. Images. Still pictures coming so fast it took me a moment to realize they were memories of Gwynn and Matilda.

Images flipped past, mostly of that fateful night when Matilda died. A few others I didn't recognize. Then the one I'd seen in

Gabriel's memories—a Gwynn standing dumbfounded over the body of an Arawn, bloodied sword in hand.

"You love games." A woman's voice pierced the darkness. "Just not when they're foisted on you. We could have avoided that if you'd spoken to me sooner. I presume you got my message."

"Matilda is returning," Patrick's voice answered. "Here. To this region."

The woman again. "Yes."

"Has she been born?"

"Not yet."

"When?"

"Eventually. That is all I know, bòcan, so do not press me for more."

"But you know more about Gwynn, don't you? That's who I saw. What's my connection to him?"

"I'm sure you've figured it out."

"I have no idea."

"You lie so well, bòcan. All right. Let me spell it out for you. Gwynn is returning, and you will be his sire."

The voiced faded. Then I saw light. I blinked hard and opened my eyes to find myself staring at an open window, sunlight streaming through.

I always close the curtains. Basic security. Particularly when borrowing a house not your own.

I lifted my head and—

"*Cach!*" Pain stabbed through my skull.

I'm hungover.

How was that possible? The last time I'd been hungover was nearly a century ago, after drinking four bottles of fae wine. Last night I'd only had half a glass.

No, wait. Seanna had brought more.

"Only for you," she'd said. "I know I've had enough."

Seanna had dosed the damned wine. And then what . . . ?

I looked down to see I was fully dressed, and exhaled in relief. Then I glanced at the nightstand, where I'd left my wallet and watch. Watch gone. Wallet . . . I checked. Empty.

I shook my head. That was a fine thanks for rescuing her from a beating and giving her a place to spend the night, but I'd known what Seanna was, and theft, sadly, was exactly what I should have expected.

The scene faded. When it surged again, I was home in Cainsville. Veronica had summoned me, urgently, and I knew that meant trouble, but as I entered the hall, I slowed and pushed back my worry and then swung through into the living room, casually saying, "All right, where's the fire?"

Veronica pointed to the couch. There was Seanna Walsh.

"She was looking for you rather desperately," Veronica said. "I can't imagine why." She cast a pointed look at the girl's protruding stomach.

"No, that's— It can't . . ." I trailed off as I flashed back to the night Seanna had drugged me. The night I couldn't remember. Waking up fully dressed suggested I hadn't done anything to Seanna. It did not mean she hadn't done anything to me.

The scene went dark again and . . .

I woke in Gabriel's lap. He was crouched, as if he'd caught me mid-fall. Patrick stood over us, his face colder than I'd ever seen it.

"Discovered a new power, Olivia?" Patrick said.

"You didn't seduce Seanna," I said. "You didn't even have a fling. You rescued her, and she repaid you by robbing you blind. But your watch and money wasn't all she took. She drugged you and had sex with you. Without your consent."

His face went even colder, and behind his eyes I saw a rage that made me want to take his advice, to get out as fast as I could.

I looked him in the eye. "It was blackmail, wasn't it? She

knew you had money. Another of her half-baked schemes. Only this one worked. She did get pregnant."

"Get out. Now."

I rose. "I will. But you—"

"Stop talking," Patrick said.

Gabriel shouldered between us. "Don't tell her—"

"Get out of my house, Olivia, and if you ever invade my privacy again—"

"Do not threaten her," Gabriel cut in, his voice quiet. "If you want to blame someone, blame me for pressing. I asked because I needed to understand, even if I would love to say it doesn't matter and I'm quite over it. I asked, and you refused."

"I—"

"You refused—to protect your ego and your pride. You were conned and assaulted by a teenager. That did not fit the image you wish to project. So you refused the one thing I asked of you. I will not forget that."

Gabriel ushered me through the house and out the front door.

Lloergan fell in at my side. We'd walked to Patrick's, leaving Rose's car at her house. I had to nearly jog to keep up with Gabriel's long strides as he headed back there. Lloergan whined and pushed at my hand.

In rejecting the overture, Patrick rejected him. It was a reminder that Patrick had left him with Seanna, turned his back, and then said, "Hey, kid, I helped you with the gargoyles. What more do you want?"

What happened to Patrick was horrible, and if it was possible to hate Seanna more, I did. But Gabriel had nothing to do with that. If the admission was too shameful for Patrick to share, he could have made up a story. *She got me drunk and . . . I guess we had sex.*

He refused to answer for exactly the reason Gabriel said. To protect himself. To protect his ego and his reputation.

I would not forget that, either.

IN THE CARDS

It was nearly 5 a.m. and Rose was in her parlor, flipping cards onto the polished wood of her desk. She could say she'd gotten up early, but the ice-cold tea at her elbow told another story.

She stared at the cards. With a soft growl of frustration, she gathered them up and reshuffled, as she'd done so often in the last few hours that she could feel the cardboard edges dig in, tender spots forming as her hands begged for a break.

Give me something. Just give me something, damn it.

Finally, the cards obeyed. The four of cups. Reversed. Seanna's card.

Rose reached to turn it upright and stopped herself. She'd done that for so many years. Tried to fix the card. Tried to fix Seanna.

The four of cups was a card of love in all its forms. Reverse the card, and it tells of too much love, too much forgiveness, little of it earned, none of it returned.

Rose did see love in her niece. Seanna was the product of love between her parents. The recipient of love from her family. But did Seanna *give* love? To anyone? Rose used to say yes, but it was like squinting through a peephole into a shadowy room and telling yourself monsters couldn't possibly lurk in the corners.

You saw what you wanted to, and you knew the deception for what it was.

As Rose fingered the deck, she pictured Seanna in her grand-parents' home, a rambling Victorian only a few houses from where Liv now lived. Seanna's parents had lived in a smaller house right next door, and they'd taken out the fence so Seanna could come and go between her home and her grandparents'.

No excuse there, Seanna. You had a good life, just as I did. A family who loved you. Adored you.

One could blame the tragedy that killed Seanna's parents—a car crash when she was sixteen. But Seanna had left home a few months before the crash, and her parents died while on yet another endless drive through the city, searching for their lost daughter. Years later, Seanna admitted she'd heard of her parents' deaths and just hadn't bothered showing up for the funeral.

I was busy, okay?

Rose squeezed her eyes shut. *Where did we go wrong, Seanna?*

She imagined Seanna at six, standing on her tiptoes to watch her teenaged aunt deal tarot cards.

"Teach me, Rose," she said.

Rose smiled and lifted a card. "See this one? It's yours. Four of cups. That means you're very much loved—"

"No, not that. Teach me to use the cards."

"I am, Seanna. If you understand the meanings, you can pre-tend to tell the future."

"I don't want to pretend. I want to do it. Like you."

"Here's a secret." Rose bent and pushed a dark curl behind Seanna's ear to whisper. "Most of the time I do pretend."

Seanna didn't giggle the way most little girls would have, pleased to be told a scandalous secret. Instead, she said, "But you can really do it. You have the Sight."

Rose's smile fell away as she nodded gravely. "Yes, Seanna, I do. And do you want to know another secret?"

"No." Seanna's small face screwed up. "I don't want your stupid secrets. I want the Sight."

There had been, deep inside Rose, the urge to snap at Seanna. To tell her not to talk to her aunt that way, not to talk to *anyone* that way. When someone offers a secret, it's a gift and an honor. You don't spit on it.

Rose reflected maybe that was where they'd gone wrong with Seanna. In Cainsville, children were cherished and loved and, yes, sometimes coddled. The same went in her family. The Walshes might steal and con outsiders, but family was family, and no family was more precious than children. Instead, they'd tried gently to guide Seanna to better behavior.

That day long ago, Rose had just taken a deep breath, pushed aside her own temper, and said, in a firmer voice, "Well, you're going to listen to this secret, because it's an important one, Seanna. Gifts are curses, too. They give you something special, but that makes you different, and different isn't always good. Even the gift itself isn't always good. Do you know why I usually pretend with others? Sometimes it's because the Sight won't work. Other times it's because what I see is bad, so I tell them something nicer while trying to help them avoid the bad thing. Does that make sense?"

Seanna scowled. "You just want the Sight all for yourself."

That was all her niece heard. Embedded deep in that explanation was the word "no," and it was all that mattered.

"I *can't* give the Sight to you, Seanna. Either you have it or you don't."

Rose remembered her niece's scowl again, and it brought to mind another face. A face she tried to forget. Bobby Sheehan. A boy who lived in the city and had family in Cainsville. A boy, she now realized, who'd been a changeling, taken from a dys-functional fae blood family and placed into a normal one with Cainsville ties. A boy who always knew that he didn't belong—a cuckoo in the nest of very ordinary sparrows.

That realization had driven Bobby to murder while barely in his teens. Murder and then madness, condemned to a psychiatric ward. He'd given Rose the same look Seanna had, when Hannah had told him their secrets: that Rose had the Sight and Hannah could understand animals in a way ordinary people could not.

Hannah.

My, my, you're really piling on the punishment today, aren't you, Rose? Why not add Gabriel to the heap of mistakes you've made, people you've failed to help, failed to save.

But Gabriel was already on the list, wasn't he? Right at the top, and that was what had her up all night, begging the cards for answers. Rose Walsh, who never begged for anything. Now she was. Yet the cards stayed silent, taunting her instead with a never-ending parade of people she'd wronged and mistakes she'd made.

Hannah.

Her best friend from the day they'd met, too far back in memory for Rose to recall, though Hannah's mother always told the story of two toddlers fighting over a toy at a town picnic. Except they hadn't been fighting to take it from the other; they'd been trying to give it to the other. *You want it, so you take it. No, you take it.* True or not, Rose supposed it said a lot about them, and why they'd become such good friends.

Best friends as toddlers, as schoolchildren, as teens. Then Hannah went off to college. Rose had visited her on campus, where they'd gone to a party and had too much to drink. Ducking the advances of frat boys, they'd stumbled, laughing, into an empty bedroom and locked the door. Drunk and sleepy, they'd decided to take advantage of the bed and lie down, and they'd curled up together, as they'd always done, and then . . .

Rose never could quite remember how it started. Or who started it. They'd been cuddling, with the alcohol buzzing, and the cuddling felt so good, not quite like it did with boys, slower and sweeter and not necessarily better but not worse, either. And then the cuddling turned to nuzzling, and the hugging to touching, soft strokes on an arm or a back, fingers searching and then lips searching and a kiss. That first kiss answered all Rose's uncomfortable questions about boys and sex, and why she liked it—really liked it—but there was an itch it didn't quite scratch.

That kiss had seemed to go on forever, and somewhere in the middle of it, hands slid under clothing and then clothing fell to the side of the bed, and then hands on skin and hands everywhere, touching, exploring, and Hannah gasping. Rose had been alarmed until she saw her friend's face, eyes closed, lips parted, panting softly as she moaned, that gasp clearly not telling her to stop. So she didn't, and afterward Hannah whispered that'd been the first time *that* happened. Her first climax. So Rose did it again, and then Hannah did it for her, and that night, that perfect, endless night . . .

Then came morning, when the frat boys picked the lock, expecting to sneak in on one of their confederates, and instead finding the girls in bed, curled up together, naked.

Rose hadn't cared. Rose never cared. That was the Walsh way. *Take your judgment and your so-called morality and shove it up your ass. I'll live as I want. I'll be happy however I want.*

But that wasn't Hannah. It had never been Hannah. Even if today's society had not yet progressed quite as far as Rose would like, it had been so much worse for two girls caught together in bed forty years ago.

Rose sometimes felt the temptation to give Liv a shake and say, "Just go for it with Gabriel." But that impulse never lasted long because Rose understood, better than anyone, that even the strongest friendship could shatter, and the move from friend to lover was exactly the sort of pressure that could do it. Sometimes, you can't go back. You might wish it with all your heart, but you can't, because, sometimes, that isn't up to you.

Rose stared at Seanna's card. Then she went to flip another one, and it sliced the edge of her finger. A drop of blood fell onto the card. Rose quickly grabbed a tissue to wipe it off—these were the cards she didn't use with clients. It was a rare Victorian deck. Gabriel had bought them for her when he was a boy—a Solstice gift that had required both great thought and great expense. These cards reminded her of how important she was to him, even if he was unlikely to ever say the words.

When she wiped the blood, it only smeared on the plastic-coated card, and she started to wipe again. She ran her finger along the edge. Too worn to cause a paper cut. It was a message, then.

Or a wish.

She looked at the card, Seanna under a wash of blood.

I wish you'd stayed dead. It kills me to even think that, but it's true. If there was any good in your life, it's all in that son of yours. You're hell-bent on destroying him, and I won't let you do that. I just won't.

Rose's phone chirped with an incoming text. She picked up the card, cleaning it as she walked. When she found her phone, there was a message from her nephew.

We need to talk. Please let me know when you're up and ready to receive visitors.

Receive visitors. She smiled. That made her sound like a character in one of Liv's Victorian novels. Great-aunt Rose receiving visitors over tea in her parlor. Not exactly the image she liked to project, even if the component parts were accurate.

She tapped back, *I'm up. Come anytime,* and then she went to start the kettle for tea.

CHAPTER THIRTEEN

I t was barely five-thirty, and Rose was already dressed, with tea and fresh biscuits and jam waiting. I was going to say, "You're up early." Then I saw the hollow circles under her eyes.

We settled in at the desk in the parlor. As I spread homemade raspberry jam on a warm biscuit, Gabriel said, "We wouldn't have come so early if it wasn't a matter of some urgency. Seanna disappeared from the hotel where Patrick put her, having faked her death again. There was a great deal of blood, but Lloergan"— he glanced at the hound, eating meat from a china plate on the Oriental carpet—"confirmed that a trail outside the window was indeed hers, meaning she was not seriously injured."

Before Rose could respond, Gabriel continued, "Olivia's car was spotted shortly before the incident. Pending analysis of the crime scene, the police insist on treating this as a possible homicide, which means if they manage to obtain identifying details on the vehicle, they'll know it's Olivia's. That will make you a suspect."

"I—"

"I'm not seriously concerned that you'd be arrested, and even if you were, there's no body, but I still need to obtain the details of your visit."

Rose said, "May I speak?"

"Yes."

"Seanna called my business number and demanded to see me. I went to the hotel. I can confirm it seems to be her."

"It is," I said. "Patrick knew she was alive. He's been paying her to stay away for years."

"And he never imagined she'd come home once she realized how much her son is worth?" Rose shook her head. "I'm sure Patrick thought she'd take the guaranteed payout rather than risk un-faking her death, but Seanna only sees dollar signs."

"And she presumes whatever trouble she gets into, she can get out of."

Rose refreshed my tea, her gaze on the cup. "Yes, I'm afraid early experience taught her that. Police bought her tears and fell for her sob stories. Family bought her lies and gave in to her tantrums. Plenty of blame to go around."

"No," Gabriel said quietly. "The only blame falls on her own shoulders. Mistakes may have been made, but help was offered. Endlessly offered."

That was the hard truth—that the biggest mistake people made with Seanna was not realizing she'd find a way to turn your kindness against you. Even Patrick's rescue had been repaid with the worst betrayal. I wouldn't be surprised if she'd orchestrated the beating herself.

"Back to the visit . . ." Gabriel prompted.

"It was exactly what you might expect," Rose said. "She wanted money, and she said if I gave her some, she'd leave you alone. As tempting as that is, unlike Patrick, I know better."

"And then?"

"And then I left."

Silence fell, stretching until it became uncomfortable, and Rose said, "If you have a point to make, Gabriel . . ."

"I'm deciding how to delicately accuse you of lying. I'm not accustomed to being delicate, but the situation seems to warrant it. Seanna would never let you walk away. I need the full truth from you, Rose, in case this ever turns into an indictment."

"She threatened you. Said she'd ruin you. Which is ridiculous. So I walked out."

Gabriel nodded, but I said, "I suspect she said more than 'I'll ruin him,' but either way, you didn't just walk out. What else happened?"

When her eyes flashed, I said, "Yes, I'm sticking my nose in where it doesn't belong. Family business when I'm not family. But this isn't idle curiosity."

"If it becomes a legal matter, I need to defend you," Gabriel said, "and I need to be fully prepared to do that."

Rose dipped her chin. "It wasn't only a vague threat to ruin you. Seanna has an instinct for weak points, and she's already discovered yours."

Gabriel's gaze flicked my way.

"Yes. Liv," Rose said. "She threatened. Not with physical harm. I'd have warned you about that right away. Seanna says she has something that can guarantee the Larsens don't get out of prison. She's already been to see them."

"She spoke to my parents?" I said.

"Not Todd. He heard who it was and refused, undoubtedly presuming it was a prank. Pamela spoke to her. That was the point where I told Seanna I was sick of her machinations, and I *did* walk out. I needed leverage if I wanted details."

"Whatever her scheme, I'm sure it's as stupid as the others," I said. "But we'll need to pay Pamela a visit."

CHAPTER FOURTEEN

Gabriel suggested we leave Lloergan with Rose. As we left Rose's house, I noticed the front stoop of Grace's building was still unoccupied, it being too cold and early even for her watchful eyes. We turned the corner to my street and—

Ida and Walter's car sat in front of my house.

"Well, apparently it's not too early for everyone," I muttered. "We can shower at my apartment. I have clothes there, too."

While I hadn't been to my apartment in a month, it was still mine. Grace wasn't going to let me out of my sublet early.

We returned to the building and climbed the stairs. I went to unlock my deadbolt and—

My key wouldn't turn. I jiggled it, took it out, and then put it back in. After another try, I handed Gabriel the key.

He tried with the same result.

"Grace changed my locks?" I said. "Seriously?"

"At the very least, I'll threaten to sue her. Which doesn't help us at this moment."

He handed back my key and took picks from his inside pocket. When he fiddled with the locks for longer than ten seconds, I knew there was a problem.

"Fae locked," I said.

He arched his brow.

"No," I said, "I've never heard of such a thing, either, but if you can't open it, there must be a supernatural explanation."

He tried again, but it was obvious from his expression he was making no progress.

"Okay, now I'm curious." I looked along the hall and then pointed to the door next to mine. "That one's definitely unoccupied."

I suspected most of the apartments were empty, having never caught more than whispers in the hall.

I tried the handle of the neighboring door. Locked. No dead-bolt, though, which should make it easy to open, but once again Gabriel's picks failed to work their mojo.

"Fae locked," I said. "Another apartment mystery we need to investigate."

A couple of months earlier, Ricky had opened a door on the first floor, looking for TC, and gotten a blast of arctic air. When Grace caught him, though, the door had been locked. We hadn't had a chance to check it out since—Grace kept it guarded, and I wasn't of a mind to piss her off.

"We can either go talk to Ida or shower at your place," I said.

Gabriel studied the door, and I could tell he wasn't really listening, too intent on this challenge. He tried his picks again. As he was positioning them, he gripped the knob and . . .

The door creaked open.

I laughed under my breath. "How does one open a fae-locked door? With a fae-blood hand. Seems you've got the touch after all. We'll see if that works with my apartment, but first, I'm curious about what's in this one."

I slipped through into a pitch-black hall. I could see the apartment beyond, furnished as mine had been.

The blinds were pulled, and as soon as Gabriel closed the

door behind us, the apartment went dark. He reopened the door enough to find the light switch. He flicked it. Nothing happened.

A thump sounded in the hall . . . and the door slammed shut . . . without Gabriel touching it.

"Okay," I said as I looked around the darkness. "I think that's a sign to get out now."

I felt my way along the wall, knowing the door should be right behind us. Except it wasn't. The wall just kept going.

I hit the penlight button on my switchblade. The light flickered, oddly dim, and I could see only Gabriel and the wall.

No, I saw Gabriel and *a* wall. An unfamiliar wall with peeling and faded wallpaper. The door was ten feet behind him. A thick wooden door that didn't belong here any more than that wallpaper.

"Do you remember I told you I stole a Dr Pepper when I was twelve?" I said.

Gabriel didn't ask what that had to do with the current situation. I was telling him a secret. That's how we handled my random visions—how we proved we were still *us*.

"That's not the only thing I ever stole," I said. "In high school, I liked a friend's boyfriend. I was fifteen and stupid, and I thought if he decided he liked me better, that wasn't my fault. We went out once, while he was still dating my friend. Afterward, I felt like shit. I'd disrespected her. Disrespected our friendship. And for what? A guy I kind of liked? It was never the same again, her and me. So *that's* the worst thing I ever stole."

"I stole fifty dollars from Rose," Gabriel said, and then let that hang there as he tensed, waiting for my reaction. The Walshes had a rule that friends are not marks, which went double for family.

When I didn't react, he said, "It was after Seanna left. I stayed in our apartment until the landlord realized he wasn't getting his rent. After that I spent a couple of weeks on the street. I was fifteen, and it seemed as if I could never get enough to eat. I wasn't sleeping, either, which meant my hands weren't steady enough to pickpocket. I hitchhiked to Cainsville. Rose wasn't there. I stayed the night, and she didn't come home, and by then I'd realized I couldn't put her in that position—having to care for a teenager. So I left. But . . . I took fifty dollars. I knew where she kept extra money, and I told myself I was just borrowing it. I snuck back a few months later and returned it, with an extra ten for interest. But that doesn't matter. I stole. From family."

"You borrowed out of necessity—"

"No, I stole."

"She'd never have begrudged you—"

"That doesn't matter." His face wavered in the dim glow of the penlight. Then he ran a hand through his hair and sighed. "And that wasn't the little secret you needed. Sorry. I'm . . ."

He made a face, and I knew what he meant. With Seanna's return, he felt off-kilter. Exposed. Vulnerable.

I stepped toward him, careful, watching for his wall to fly up. When it didn't, I put my arms around his neck and rose onto my tiptoes to hug him as tight as I could. "You need to tell Rose," I whispered.

He stiffened, but only for a moment, and then he nodded against my shoulder and said, "I do."

When he pulled away, I was ready to step back, but he was only breaking the embrace enough to kiss the top of my head. When something thumped again in the distance, he sighed, softly, the exhalation tickling my hair.

"Yes," I said. "Back to the terribly inconvenient reality that we're mysteriously trapped with a monster in the next room waiting to devour us."

"There is never a monster."

"True. Just bad plumbing, then."

Another thump. Another sigh from Gabriel.

We checked the door first. That was almost incidental, as if we knew it would be pointless. It was. The door wouldn't open, and there was no sign of a lock.

"You're seeing this, right?" I said. "A long hallway with old wallpaper? A wooden door?"

He reached out, peeled off a strip of wallpaper, and rubbed it between his fingers. "Yes."

"That's not normal." I rubbed down the hairs on my neck. "It feels . . . wrong."

He tried the door again, but even wrenching with all of his not-insubstantial strength didn't budge it.

"I'm overreacting," I said.

"No, something isn't right. We'll get this over with and leave. And then, as much as I'd like that shower, I'm going to suggest we skip it. We'll visit Pamela to see what Seanna told her, and visit Todd to warn him about her. Check on the police investigation. And then return to the cabin and turn off our phones."

"A plan. I like it. Now let's get past stage one."

We started down the hall. After about twelve paces, it opened into a room with a sweeping staircase. Cobwebs festooned the wrought-iron railings. More hung from the chandelier. The stink of must filled the dead air. At a squeak, I turned to see a mouse dive between cracks in the rotted floorboards.

I looked up the stairs. "I believe Miss Havisham will be joining us for tea."

"Hmmm."

I glanced over to see him scanning the stairwell.

"Sensing anything?" I asked.

"I . . . don't know." He rolled his shoulders as if to shrug off the uncertainty. "There's no clear sense of danger, but . . ." Another roll. "I can't say."

"Proceed with caution, as always."

"Yes."

We walked around the steps, but there was nothing to see. No other rooms or halls joined this one. I even ran my hands over the semicircular wall behind the stairs, looking for a hidden doorway.

"Serious architectural flaw," I said lightly, but Gabriel didn't even favor me with a nod. This impossible layout told us we weren't in a real house, and that bothered him.

The hairs on my neck prickled again.

"Up, then?" I said.

At the top of the stairs, we reached a landing that stretched in every direction. I took three steps . . . and the floor disappeared, leaving us on a platform, the stairs behind us, the rest darkness.

"Go back down," Gabriel said. "Quickly."

He hauled me toward the stairs. We made it down one riser and then the rest vanished, the next step a drop into nothingness. Gabriel yanked me back, and his arms wrapped around me as if I'd been about to tumble over the edge. I felt his heart slamming against his ribs, as that sixth sense kicked in, and whatever it detected—

"We need to get out of here," he said. "*Now.*"

I could point out the obvious—that there was no apparent exit. But his pounding heart warned that if I couldn't say something useful, I'd best not say anything at all. When I twisted to look up at him, he was scanning the darkness, every muscle taut.

"Something is wrong," he said. "Something is *very* wrong. We shouldn't be here."

He took my hand again, his fingers wrapping around mine tight enough to make me wince. Then he stepped carefully toward the edge, leaning, as he turned on his cell phone light.

"I don't see any—"

The floor fell away.

No warning. No time to do more than let out a yelp before I plummeted through darkness, scrabbling for a hold, none to be found. Yet I hit the floor no harder than if I'd slipped on ice.

Darkness swirled. When it cleared, I sat on a wooden floor, staring at a wooden wall. A hand landed on my shoulder, and I jumped to see Gabriel on all fours.

"I wouldn't have stayed," he said. "At Evans's house. I wouldn't have stayed."

It took me a moment to realize what he was talking about. Our first "case." Trapped in the basement by a killer, Gabriel injured, telling me to just go, leave him behind, that he wouldn't stay for me.

"That's not much of a secret," I said. "You told me then you wouldn't have stayed."

"But I meant it. I wasn't saying it to make you leave. I would have found you a safe place and brought help, but I still would have left."

"Okay."

"No, you don't understand. I would have *left*. I've told myself I wasn't sure, maybe I *was* just saying that, but that's a lie. I would have left you there."

"The fact you'd have taken time to find me a safe place meant I was making progress. Hell, finding me a safe place and going for help would have been the smart move, the logical move. That's how you do things. I jump in with both feet and end up . . ."

I looked around. We were in a small timber-framed building, with a fire in the hearth and the smell of cooked meat ingrained in the wood. Simple furniture, all wooden, with cured skins and a homespun blanket.

"A peasant's home, maybe?" I said.

Gabriel said nothing in response, and I turned to see him on his feet. Lighting lamps. Oil lamps. He'd grabbed a stick from the fire and was lighting the lamps as if that was the most natural thing to do.

"Gabriel?"

"We need light," he said. "Quickly."

"Okay . . ."

"Leave him be," whispered a voice, and I jumped to see a child wearing a peasant's dress. It was the blond girl, another manifestation of Matilda, the one who'd been my early guide in this new life.

"Haven't seen you in a while," I murmured.

Gabriel turned. "Hmmm?"

"Nothing." I watched as he resumed lighting the lamps.

"Gwynn is fine," she said.

"He's not—"

"Right now he's Gwynn. Let him do what he needs to do. Trust him."

The scene faded into another cottage, the one in that terribly *wrong* forest where the rogue Huntsman had been keeping Lloergan. I'd been walking through those woods with Ricky and caught a snatch of a vision, peasants bolting up the house against the falling dark, rushing about, terrified of that darkness and the horrors it held. A primal fear of the unknown, from a time where one couldn't simply switch on a porch light to see what lay beyond.

Something's out there.

Darkness was falling fast. One window had a glass pane, a luxury to allow light in cold weather. The rest had only shutters, wide open, the night air blowing through, bringing a smell that made the hairs on my neck prickle again.

"Darkness is coming," the girl murmured.

"I see that."

"No, you feel it."

Gabriel spun to me. "We need to close the shutters. *Quickly.*"

I ran for one, but he caught my shoulder. "Always start with the west. They come from . . ." He trailed off and blinked hard, as if waking from a trance. "What was I . . . ?"

"The shutters," I said. "We need to close the west shutters."

He jogged over and pulled them shut as I latched them. One resisted when he yanked and I saw it was latched on the outside. I started to reach through, but he beat me to it. As he fumbled to undo the latch, darkness rolled through the trees.

"*Sluagh,*" he whispered.

"What?" I said.

"I—" He stopped and rubbed a hand over his face. "I don't know." Gabriel looked around. "Why are we—?"

"We need to close the shutters," I said.

He didn't argue. When we finished closing the shutters, I turned to him. "You said it was sluagh. What's that?"

"I don't know."

"You *do*. It's like me with omens. Hereditary memories. Trust them."

"Very good," the girl said as she began to fade. "You understand. Finally."

"Sluagh," Gabriel said uncertainly. "They're *sidhe*. The darkness. The unforgiven. That's all I remember. Just that we need to close the shutters and turn up the lights and—"

The roar of wind drowned him out. A wind that set the shutters clattering and the very cottage shaking. A driving, beating wind that tickled at my own memory.

I turned to the lone glass window. Dark clouds whipped past it, and I could make out forms in those clouds, shapes that my brain couldn't latch onto before they disappeared in the maelstrom.

Gabriel's fingers closed around my arm. "Stay back from—"

Something hit the window. Struck it with a shriek that sent me backing into Gabriel, his arms going around me.

Another thump. Another shriek. Then a dark red bird appeared, the size of a sparrow, with empty white eyes and wormlike white legs. It beat its wings against the glass and shrieked, beak opening to reveal rows of pin-sharp teeth.

The bird hammered wings and claws and beak against the glass. Then another joined it, and another, swarming the window like locusts, until all I could see was a blur of dark red feathers and white eyes and white legs and claws and teeth, battering the window and scraping the glass.

I looked up at the ceiling, hearing that wind whipping around the cottage.

Not wind. Wings. The thunder of a thousand beating wings.

"Sluagh," I whispered.

Somewhere in the distance, a howl sounded—a *cŵn*'s howl—the noise swallowed by the roar of wings. The birds continued to beat at the window. A tiny crack formed in one corner, and two birds rammed into one another to get to that spot. Then they both began pecking feverishly, their wings beating like hummingbirds, too fast to see more than a blur.

"Go away," I whispered. "*Ewch i ffwrdd.*"

The birds stopped their mad pecking long enough for those white eyes to find me. Tiny beaks opened, jagged teeth glistening. They let out a hiss and then resumed their pecking.

"*Ewch i ffwrdd,*" I said, moving toward the window.

Gabriel's hand tightened on mine, as if to pull me back, but he only followed, his feet dragging, slowing my pace as I crossed to the window.

I pressed my hand against the glass. It was like hitting Pause. Every single bird stopped its frantic beating and hovered there. Then they went back at it, slamming their wings and beaks against the glass.

Gabriel reached out, tentatively. His figure flickered in the glow of the oil lamps, and an older man appeared, one with graying blond hair and tired blue eyes. It was Gwynn as I'd seen him before—the aging Gwynn, the weary Gwynn, the broken Gwynn.

"*Ewch i ffwrdd*," Gwynn said, his voice firm, his body straightening, the exhaustion evaporating into resolve. "*Fynd nawr!*"

His form flickered, Gabriel reappearing and then Gwynn and then Gabriel again, fingers splayed as he pressed them to the glass.

"*Fynd nawr!*"

Again the birds stopped, for longer now, and then, as a body, they began to hiss and shriek as they hovered. Then they swooped away as one, disappearing into the blur of darkness beyond the cottage.

"Those are the sluagh?" I whispered.

"No, they're the harbingers of the sluagh. The sluagh is still coming. We need to get—"

A tremendous, deafening roar, and I doubled over, hands to my ears. The sound seemed to come from everywhere. The beating of a thousand wings, amplified a thousand times, rising to a frenzy.

The cottage quaked. The shutters cracked against their latches. The door warped inward, boards groaning. And then . . .

Silence.

Everything stopped at once—the roar and the quaking and the groaning—and the silence was, for a moment, almost painful, like coming out of darkness into the light.

"They're gone." I turned to Gabriel. "You did it. You got rid—"

"No," he whispered, his eyes widening, filling with a look that wasn't quite Gabriel, wasn't quite Gwynn, somewhere between the two. "No!"

He slammed into me. Hit me square in the back, taking me down so fast I didn't have time to brace as I fell face-first to the floor with Gabriel overtop of me. Then I heard the barest whine, like a single mosquito. I lifted my head, tasting blood trickling from my lip. Gabriel's hand went to the back of my head, ready to push me down and—

The cottage exploded.

It shattered, a million slivers of wood shooting into the night, darkness billowing in, black clouds that writhed and whipped about us.

I heard a distant bark. Frantic barking.

Lloergan.

Gabriel pushed me down, his body on mine, shielding me as the black smoke wound around us. Fingers clutched my arm. I flew to my feet, Gabriel suddenly gone, and when I turned, I saw a woman in the writhing blackness. A woman with long blond hair and flashing brown eyes.

"Out!" she snarled. "Get out now!"

I knew that voice. Knew it well. But my brain wouldn't make the connection, and I found myself being dragged through the black smoke as I yelled, "Gabriel!" and twisted to look for him, seeing only . . .

Light. A blinding flash of light, and then I was in an apartment. An ordinary apartment, almost exactly like mine, with an old sofa and chairs and—

"Olivia!" Gabriel called.

A familiar voice snapped, "She's right here," and I saw who was holding me. It was Grace, now back in her old-crone glamour, her ugly face contorted in a scowl, one bony hand wrapped around my arm, the other around Gabriel's, as she hauled us toward the hall.

Something bashed against the apartment door, and I stumbled back, saying, "No!" as I imagined the birds again, but Grace only muttered under her breath and released us.

She threw open the door and was nearly bowled over by Lloergan. The hound ran straight to me and then looked around wildly before seeing Gabriel and exhaling, her flanks quivering.

"Yes, they're fine," Grace muttered. "Now get the hell out of my—"

Lloergan spun on Grace and growled, her fur rising as she pressed against my leg.

"Don't you growl at me, *ciûn*," Grace said.

Lloergan kept rumbling but turned her attention to the room, peering about it. When I laid my hand on her head, darkness hit me, a sudden breathtaking wave of it.

I saw the birds again, that dark whirl of them, heard the roar, felt the wind from those wings battering me as terror, absolute terror, washed through me, my legs locking, the growl in my throat turning to a whimper, my tail sliding between my legs, my only thought to flee, to run, to get out.

I snapped back to myself, Lloergan still pressed against my leg, Gabriel's fingers wrapped around my arm. "Are you all right?" he asked.

I nodded, and we passed Grace as we headed for the door.

CHAPTER FIFTEEN

Grace ushered us into the hallway and then locked the apartment door behind us.

"What the hell were you two doing in there?" Grace snapped.

I opened my mouth, but Gabriel beat me to it.

"You changed the lock on Olivia's apartment," he said.

"So you randomly started opening doors?"

"No," I said. "When the lock on mine didn't work, I was checking whether the one next door looked new, if maybe you'd changed all the locks. When Gabriel turned the knob, it opened."

Her gaze met mine. "Just like that. It popped open."

"Yes," Gabriel said.

"As if you *left* it open," I said. "Left it for us to find."

"I would never—" She cut herself short. "If that door opened for Gabriel . . ."

She trailed off, as if realizing that his fae blood must have undone whatever magic she'd placed on it.

"What did you see in there?" she said.

"A crappy apartment," I said. "Just like mine."

"Don't you bullshit me, girl. You—"

"Give Olivia the new key for her door," Gabriel said. "Now. We will return to clear the last of her things, and you will refund all her unused rent money. If you do not, I will sue you for unlawful eviction."

"I didn't change her locks."

"Then undo whatever magic you put on my door to keep me out," I said.

"It's not to keep—" Again, she broke off. Then she said, "I want to know what you saw in there. *Exactly* what you saw."

"You tell us," Gabriel said, his voice deceptively soft. "It's your building."

Her glamour rippled, her true form shimmering through. "Don't play games, Gabriel Walsh. Not with me."

"Nor you with me." He moved closer, towering above her. "Tell me what we saw in there."

"Do you honestly think you can intimidate me, Gwynn?"

"Don't—"

"Oh, yes, don't call you that. You *hate* to be called that. You flee from the reminder. Squeeze your eyes shut and pray it all goes away."

That note of contempt—of outright mockery—had me bristling and moving forward, Lloergan growling at my side.

Gabriel only turned cool eyes on Grace and said, "If you'd let me finish, I was merely going to tell you not to play that game."

"What game?"

"The one where you try to distract me by calling me Gwynn. I was going to warn that it won't work. I am learning to accept what I am. It's hardly productive to deny that part of me is indeed Gwynn ap Nudd. Just don't use that name in hopes of distracting me. And perhaps, if you do use it, you'd do well to remember what it means. What Gwynn was. What I am."

"And what do you think you are, Gabriel Walsh? King of the Tylwyth Teg?" she snorted. "You're a boy. A child. I remember the true Gwynn and—"

"And I remember you." Gabriel's voice held a note of Gwynn's, stopping Grace short. "Is that not what I have of him? His memories? One could argue that is the essence of a person. Not DNA, but memories. I have his, and it only takes a trigger—such as seeing your true form—to bring them back. To remind me of who you are." He looked her in the eye. "And what you did, bogart."

She flinched at that, and then recovered and said, "I've done many things, Gabriel. You'll have to be more specific."

"Do I?" he murmured. "No, I don't think so. When you're ready to tell us what we saw in there—and *why* we saw it here—you know where to find us. Olivia?"

Grace stayed where she was as we walked away.

Only once we were on Rose's front steps did I say, "Okay, I have to ask. What did she do?"

"I have no idea."

"You were bluffing?"

"Hardly. Everyone has something to hide. One only needs to suggest one knows it, and let guilt fill in the blanks."

"Sluagh," Rose mused as she scanned her bookshelf. "I don't suppose you have any idea how to spell that?"

"Gabriel said they were *sidhe*." I glanced at him, and he nodded.

"Which makes them Irish rather than Welsh," Rose said. "That's a start."

Ideally, for the best answers on this, we'd have gone to Patrick. While Rose was an excellent researcher, she was human and relied on human retellings, which often bore only a glancing acquaintance with the truth. Patrick's books—coming from the fae themselves—made for far more reliable reading, but we were persona non grata with him right now.

We'd royally pissed off two elders in a few hours. That had to be a record, even for us overachievers.

Rose pulled a tome of Celtic folklore from her shelf.

"Here it is," she said as she flipped through one and showed us that the book devoted a single page to the lore . . . and half that page was an illustration of a giant bird beating at a window.

"The birds are smaller," I said. "*Much* smaller. Which would make them far less scary . . . if there weren't thousands."

"You called them harbingers," Rose said to Gabriel. "Here, they're the sluagh itself in manifested form. In post-Roman-invasion lore, the sluagh steal the souls of those who haven't received last rites."

"The unforgiven," I murmured.

"Yes. Pre-Christian, it's a more general form of unforgiven. Those who cannot be forgiven, who do not belong in the proper afterlife—the Otherworld. They are trapped between the worlds of the living and the dead, in the form of birds who claim the souls of the unwary. They come at night, through open windows, from the west."

I nodded. "Which matches with Gabriel's memories—close the windows, particularly on the west side. Anything else?"

"They're associated with the Wild Hunt."

"The Cŵn Annwn?"

"The Irish version of it. The lore is divided on whether they *are* the Wild Hunt or just another form."

"Another type of fetch," I said. "Taking souls. Okay, so the question is, why did we see that in Grace's apartment? She didn't seem too surprised."

"No," Gabriel said. "She did not."

"Then I suggest we let her stew on it," I said, "while we pay some visits."

Gabriel advised we start with Todd. He made up some excuse about needing to warn Todd, in case Seanna took another run at him, but the real reason was simply that I'd be in a much better mood for Todd if I hadn't seen Pamela first.

When they brought my father in, he looked as he always did—healthy and grounded and a whole lot more cheerful than one would expect from a guy who has spent half his life in prison. I suspected I wasn't the only one who took a moment to put on a game face before we met.

As always, Todd walked out smiling. Before he sat, he tapped his knuckles against the glass. I tapped mine back. Then he nodded at Gabriel and lowered himself onto the stool.

"You're a day early," he said. "Guess you heard I had a visitation from the dead."

"Actually . . ." I explained that the woman who'd tried to visit him really was Seanna.

"So, not an entirely welcome resurrection," he said when I finished.

"To put it mildly," I murmured.

Todd looked over at Gabriel. He didn't offer any sympathetic comment, but he nodded, as if to say he understood this *wasn't* welcome. Then he turned back to me with, "Well, if she tries to see me again, I'll keep on refusing. I can't imagine what she'd want anyway."

"She says she knows something about your case."

"How—?" He paused. "Right, she's from Cainsville. She knows about the fae, then."

"Actually, she doesn't," I said. "Whatever she's coming here for, it's bullshit. If she tries again, we'd appreciate it if you'd alert the prison authorities, so we can clear up her latest death hoax. But otherwise . . ."

"Steer clear," he said. "I will. I'm not interested in whatever game she's playing. Pam might be, though. You know how she is."

Oh, I know exactly how she is.

"She's already talked to Seanna," I said. "She couldn't resist that. We'll speak to her next, and see what happened."

"I wouldn't worry too much." Todd gave me a half smile. "Your mother can take care of herself. It's Seanna you should be concerned about."

"I'm not," Gabriel said.

"Maybe so, but we know how Pam feels about you, Gabriel. If she sees Seanna as a way to hurt you . . ." Todd shrugged. "Just don't ever tell yourselves that Pam can't do much from behind bars."

"I think she's already proven she can," I said.

He winced. "Sorry, sweetheart. I didn't mean to remind you. I know you're a match for her. Just . . . be careful. Both of you."

We'd just left the visiting room when someone called, "Mr. Walsh?"

It was a guard—a young one I'd seen before, maybe twenty-one. He looked as if he'd come straight from the army with his crew cut, ramrod spine, and manner that was a little too deferential for my tastes.

He hurried over and said, "Thank-you for waiting, sir."

Gabriel grunted, as if he was more comfortable with rudeness. Civilities meant someone wanted something from him.

"It's about that lady who came to see Todd Larsen? Said she was your mother?" The guard inflected his sentences, adding invisible question marks to the ends.

Gabriel nodded curtly, hurrying him along.

"She asked me to give Todd something," the guard said. "I told her we can't do that, but she said it was only a piece of paper, and she was real insistent. So I took it." *Along with a twenty-dollar bill, I bet.* "While I'm sure it's nothing—Todd's a good guy, never any trouble—I can't break the rules. I figured I'd give it to you, and you can pass it along, since you're his lawyer."

The guard held out a church offering envelope. Which could mean Seanna was being clever, gift-wrapping her message in the most innocuous package possible, but it had probably just been the easiest place to steal an envelope.

Gabriel took it and passed an expertly folded fifty, saying, "Thank you, and I apologize if she placed you in an awkward position."

"No, sir. It's fine, sir. Happy to help."

"If she comes back, I would very much appreciate a phone call. She has dropped out of contact, and I'm concerned. My mother has . . ." He dropped his voice and said, "Substance abuse issues."

The guard nodded, a little too puppy-eager.

"I'd like to get her the help she needs," Gabriel said.

"Absolutely, sir. I'll keep my eye out. And good luck with Todd. It seems you have a decent case."

"I hope so," I said. "Anything you can do for him, I personally would appreciate."

"We both would," Gabriel added.

"Yes, ma'am. Thank you, sir."

He backed away, bumping into the wall as he went. I waited until he was gone to roll my eyes at Gabriel.

He lifted the envelope. "May I?"

I nodded. He opened it and pulled out a piece of paper. I watched over his shoulder as he unfolded it to reveal a name: Greg Kirkman.

"Does that mean anything to you?" I said.

Gabriel shook his head and handed me the paper, and I pock-eted it for future research.

CHAPTER SIXTEEN

Pamela Larsen. My mother. Convicted killer. Guilty of murdering four people by her own hand, and a fifth by her command. Except those four were also killers, whom she'd executed to heal me. She'd spent half her life in prison for that. And her fifth victim? Also killed to protect me. Or that was her excuse. In truth, she'd conspired to kill a man I'd loved, a crime intended to separate me from Gabriel by condemning him to life in prison for murder.

How do I reconcile that? The woman who gave up her freedom so I could walk and the woman who took away one man I loved and tried to do the same to a second?

It cannot be reconciled. Instead, we have come to an understanding. Gabriel will handle her appeal because that helps with Todd's. I will visit her when she has something useful for me, through the network of fae who curry the favor of Matilda's fearsome mother.

With Pamela, I got a private visiting room, no glass, no speaker. Ironic, considering she was the actual killer. Also frustrating, when she'd been convicted of the exact same crimes as Todd, given the exact same sentence, and yet she was seen as less of a threat. Women always are.

When we reached the visiting room door, I asked Gabriel, "Have you ever seen *Silence of the Lambs*?"

"No, but I've read the book."

I had to laugh at that, a soft whoosh of a laugh, relief at breaking the tension. "Touché. But that's what this feels like sometimes. My deal with the devil."

"Except Pamela hasn't eaten anyone."

"Allegedly."

I opened the door. Pamela was already waiting at the table. Anyone overhearing me compare her to Hannibal Lecter would laugh on seeing her there, a very ordinary woman with graying dark hair, thirty extra pounds, and a face unadorned by makeup, showing every one of her forty-six years. The type of woman who has settled comfortably into middle age and begun the transition to grandmother-hood, ready to start dandling babies on one plump knee while sneaking them candies from her overflowing purse.

When I first started visiting, Pamela would give me a look not dissimilar to what I get from Todd—unalloyed pleasure, the doting parent happy to see me whatever the circumstances. With Todd, that was genuine. With Pamela . . . I would like to say it was a false front, but it was more a half mask, one that puts a pretty sparkle on uncomfortable truth. Now, when I walk in, I get my real mother, and in her face I see pride.

I don't need to wear a mask for my daughter—she'll see right through it. She's tough and she's smart, and she's a little bit ruthless, a little bit arrogant, a little bit cold. As she should be.

In Pamela's pride, I see the best of myself and the worst, and it is as discomforting as dealing with Pamela herself.

"Gabriel," she said, and others might hear a purr in that voice, but my ear heard a snake's warning rattle. "I met your mother yesterday. Lovely woman. Drug addict. Petty criminal.

Con artist. Has a much higher opinion of her intelligence—and herself—than is warranted. I can see the resemblance."

"Hardly," Gabriel said. "I've never done drugs."

I laughed under my breath and pulled out a chair. "Now you understand why Gabriel and I get along so well. The common ground of maternal criminality."

"Seanna Walsh is hardly on my level," Pamela said.

"True," I said. "She's smart enough not to get caught."

Pamela's eyes narrowed.

"I'd have a higher opinion of *your* intelligence, Pamela," I said, "if you didn't insist on starting every visit by insulting Gabriel, knowing the only person you piss off is me."

And for that, she smiled. Smiled and nodded, pride shining again as she conceded the point.

"You've come to find out what Seanna wanted," she said. "I only wish I knew. She's a tiresome woman. All I could guess was that she was trying to get a better handle on you, Eden. And by you, I mean your financial situation. She wasn't exactly cagey about it, though I'm sure she thought she was."

"What was she asking?"

"How did I meet Gabriel? How was my appeal progressing? Her version of small talk, into which she not-so-subtly inter-jected two primary questions. One, what is the exact nature of your relationship with her son? Two, what are the terms of your trust fund from your adoptive parents?"

"And you said?"

"The truth. I know nothing about your trust fund except that you are financially secure, which is all that matters to me. As for Gabriel, that is also primarily a financial matter—a profitable relationship for both of you. He provides employment for you and gets to handle our appeal because of you."

The last part was bullshit. She just liked to put my relationship

with Gabriel in a business perspective. That was how *she* reconciled things.

We talked for a few more minutes, but there wasn't any more.
Given what Seanna had told Rose, I suspected those questions
about Pamela's appeal weren't as pointless as they seemed, but
whatever Seanna's angle there, she hadn't tipped her hand to Pamela.

As we neared the end of our time, I said, "Greg Kirkman."

No sign of recognition sparked in Pamela's dark eyes. "Who?"

"Greg Kirkman," I repeated. "Do you know him?"

"Not that I'm aware of. In what context?"

"Seanna went to see Todd. He refused."

"Smart man," she murmured. "Watching paint dry is more
interesting than talking to that woman. I hope you told him to
continue refusing."

"I did, and he will."

"Good. But what does this have to do with . . . what's the
name again?"

"Kirkman. Before Seanna left, she bribed a guard to pass
Todd an envelope. The guard gave it to Gabriel instead. Inside
was a slip of paper with that name on it. Nothing more."

Pamela's brows rose. "What did your father say about it?"

"We got the envelope after I met with him. I'll ask him next
time."

"Don't, Eden. Please. If I didn't recognize the name, neither
will he. But he'll worry that he *should* know it, and fret over
why Seanna gave it to him, and then he'll decide he should speak
to her. Which is likely her entire goal. Intriguing him into meeting her."

She was right. I would investigate Kirkman myself and leave
my father out of it.

CHAPTER SEVENTEEN

"The cabin has wi-fi," Gabriel said as we passed through prison security. When I glanced over, he said, "You're thinking of stopping at a coffee shop to research Greg Kirkman before we go to the cabin."

"Actually, given that it's an hour drive, I planned to do it on the way. Tether my laptop to my phone. But I'll take you up on that offer of a mocha."

His lips twitched. "I don't believe I actually offered—"

"You implied it. Close enough."

"Your mocha will be on me, Liv," said a voice behind us. "I need to talk to you before you leave."

The man approaching looked to be in his sixties, handsome, average height, with a build that belonged on a man half his age and a smooth charm that came from decades of experience. Or, in his case, centuries.

Ioan, leader of the local Cŵn Annwn. Also Ricky's grandfather, though the only role he'd played in his son's life was making sure Ricky's father and grandmother never wanted for anything.

"Did you not get my message?" I said. I'd texted to say we'd changed our minds about speaking to him today and would meet up Monday.

"He did," Gabriel murmured. "Or he wouldn't be here. I presume you told him where we were?"

Damn. Yes, I said we had to visit Pamela before we headed out of town for the weekend.

"I won't take much of your time," Ioan said. "But you said it was about the sluagh, and that's not something I can ignore. We need to speak and—" He looked around. "Where's Llocrgan?"

"With Rose. We were picking her up. Running errands with her in the backseat isn't exactly respectful."

"She wouldn't mind, and in fact I'd suggest that she would prefer that. Gabriel? Why don't you go fetch her, while I take Liv for coffee?"

"Fetch her?" I lifted my brows.

"A poor choice of words. I didn't mean any offense. But the most efficient course of action—"

"—would *not* be to have him drive northwest to Cainsville, return to the city, and then drive northeast to our destination. Nice try, though."

"I wasn't . . ." Ioan didn't finish. Unlike normal fae, the Huntsmen aren't fond of lies and subterfuge, preferring old-fashioned charm and manipulation.

"We can spare an hour," I said. "Then we're taking the weekend off."

"I'm not sure it will be that simple."

"Talk fast."

"I don't mean the conversation, but rather the seriousness of—"

"These days, everything is serious. Everything is critically important and demands our immediate and complete attention. You know what's critically important right now? Taking some time off."

Ioan opened his mouth and then wisely shut it. We walked outside . . . to see Patrick crossing the parking lot toward us.

"Pamela's had her quota of visitors for the day," I said. "Come back tomorrow."

"It's not Pamela I'm here to see."

"Jailbird romance?"

His voice cooled, not unlike his son's, as he said, "Given how we parted last night, Olivia, I think a little less sarcasm might be in order. I came here to help you. While I know better than to expect gratitude, you can at least do me the courtesy of being polite."

I snorted.

Patrick looked at Ioan. "I need to speak to them. Go curry your horse."

"Speaking of polite . . ." I turned to Ioan. "Yep, Patrick's pissy. Not a side of him you've probably seen, but you may like it better than the snide comments and subtle mockery. I know I do."

"I do not mock you, Olivia," Patrick said. "Nor do I make snide comments. Please take a moment, unleash your worst, and get it over with. We have important matters to discuss."

"See? No snide comments *at all*. Whatever you have to discuss with us, Patrick, it can wait. We need to speak to Ioan about something."

"The folklore issue you took to Rose this morning? In trying to find you, I spoke to Rose. She asked me . . ." He glanced at Ioan.

"Ioan knows about sluagh," I said.

Patrick's lips tightened. "A waste of time. The Cŵn Annwn don't have my resources. Moreover, you can't trust him."

Ioan's brows rose. "And they can trust you, bòcan?"

"No, they can trust my books."

"And since I cannot enter Cainsville, sadly, you must take Liv back with you, while I go 'curry my horse.' I actually have a business to run, Patrick. Unlike the Tylwyth Teg, we work for a living. And not by jotting down fanciful tales and calling it gainful employment."

Patrick looked at me. "And you accuse me of snide comments?" He turned to Ioan. "If my job is so easy, I'd suggest you give it a shot. I bet it pays at least as well as yours. And it's fun. Which is more than I can say for any 'gainful'—and tedious— job you do, chained to your desk like a common office grunt."

"Did I mention I run—?"

"Enough," I said. "Let's all find someplace to discuss this."

"You said you had a vision, Liv." Ioan sat with his coffee and pastry. "Where exactly did you have it?"

"Unimportant," Patrick said.

Ioan bristled. "I understand that you delight in being contrary, bòcan. Even for a fae, you're difficult, argumentative, and whimsical."

"Whimsical? You take that back."

"You are prone to following your whims, wherever they may lead. That is the definition of whimsical. Also the definition of a bòcan."

"If I soured the cream in that coffee, as bòcan are wont to do, it is not on a whim, but because you would have, to use Liv's colorful vernacular, pissed me off. I am not disagreeing about the importance of her vision. But she did not stumble over sluagh in the real world, so *where* her vision occurred is unimportant."

"I beg to differ and don't see why I can't ask the question."

Because it happened in Cainsville, and Patrick didn't want Ioan to know that.

"The vision took me into an old house," I said.

Ioan's mouth opened as if to say that wasn't what he meant, but I pushed on, leading him through the vision and ending with, "It was getting dark and Gabriel said we had to turn on the lights and close the shutters, starting from the west. I think that's significant."

"It is," Ioan said. "That's the traditional way to fight the sluagh."

"Good call," Patrick said to Gabriel.

"It's just hereditary memory," Ioan said.

"Moving right along," I said. "We shut the windows. One was glass, so we could see out. A swarm of birds started flying around the cottage. Dark red birds, the size of sparrows, with white eyes and teeth. Gabriel managed to banish them. Then something else came and the cottage exploded. That's when we snapped out of the vision."

"How did you banish the harbingers?" Patrick asked.

"He didn't," Ioan said. "The melltithiwyd withdrew in advance of the sluagh."

"Mellti—"

"It means the cursed, the damned. It's our name for the harbinger birds."

"Is that what they usually do?" I asked. "Withdraw when the sluagh come?"

"Well, no, but—"

"Gabriel put his hand on the window. He told them—in Welsh—to go away. When he demanded it, they left."

Patrick nodded. "Given who you are, Gabriel, that would work. With the melltithiwyd, though. Not the actual sluagh."

"Because the melltithiwyd are harbingers," I said. "They foretell the coming of the sluagh."

"Exactly," Patrick said. "They are, in their way, the parallel to the Tylwyth Teg's owls and Cŵn Annwn's ravens. Avian spies. However, our owls and ravens are relatively harmless. They *will* attack each other, as you saw when one of Ioan's black scavengers came snooping around Cainsville."

"That was shortly after Liv's arrival," Ioan said. "Under the circumstances, you can't blame us. And may I point out that owls are as likely to scavenge as ravens?"

"But the melltithiwyd are *not* harmless?" Gabriel cut in.

"Definitely not." Ioan turned to me. "If you ever see them, even in a vision, do what Gabriel did. Hopefully, it will frighten them off."

"Otherwise . . . ?" I said.

"You mentioned the teeth," Patrick said. "Did they remind you of anything? Another beast that normally lacks dentition?"

"Piranha," I said.

"Exactly. A single one won't do more than nip. But in a swarm?"

I shivered. "Feeding frenzy."

"They're like the Cŵn Annwn's hounds," Patrick said.

"Our hounds do not eat—" Ioan began.

"I mean the killing part. The sluagh take souls. But to take a soul, you need to kill the host. *Cŵn* kill. Melltithiwyd *devour*."

"Lovely." I looked at Ioan. "And to take that comparison further . . . Rose's folklore says the sluagh are a form of the Irish Wild Hunt. True?"

"That is a complete misunderstanding and misinterpretation." Patrick cleared his throat.

Ioan glared at him. "If you suggest that those *things* are the same as Cŵn Annwn—"

"No, but the misunderstanding is *understandable*. You both serve a similar purpose."

"We do not—"

Patrick raised his hand and turned to me. "Let's back up a step, and tackle the basic question. What are the sluagh? The word is Irish Celtic, but they exist in our lore as well, the same as the fae or the Hunt exist in other cultures. Think of it as the difference between the Welsh, the Irish, the Scottish, the French, the Germans . . . They're all humans, but with their own cultural identity, heritage, language, regional variations, and so on. Historically, our term for the sluagh is *heb edifeirwch*, which roughly translates to 'remorseless.' But we avoid saying it. Even fae can be superstitious, and some believe that to name them is to summon them. So we use the Celtic term instead."

"But what *are* the sluagh?"

"It's been said they're the third major branch of the fae. I say they're not, but for the sake of argument I'll admit they exist in the same basic realm. We are three types of supernatural beings, then. The first, which the Welsh call the Tylwyth Teg, encompasses all ordinary fae. The Cŵn Annwn is one of the variations on the Wild Hunt. And finally, the *heb edifeirwch*, known as the sluagh."

"So why haven't I met a sluagh? Or have I, and just didn't realize it?"

Ioan shook his head. "You wouldn't have. While the Tylwyth Teg and Cŵn Annwn use glamours to fit in with humans, you've seen their true forms, yes?"

I tried not to glance at Patrick. I'd seen his true form, but I knew better than to bring that up, so I just said, "They're humanoid."

"Exactly. The sluagh are different. They can appear human, but it's a manifestation, not a glamour."

Patrick said, "What you saw in your vision? That thing that looked like smoke or fog? That's the sluagh. The darkness. Which is why I don't consider them fae. Only the most powerful of the sluagh can manifest, so no, they just won't come around to chat you up."

"Would they have any reason to chat me up?" I said.

Gabriel added, "What is Matilda to them?"

Ioan looked at Patrick.

"I don't know if she's *anything* to them," Patrick said after a moment of silence. "But the fact you've had the vision must be significant."

"And the nature of the sluagh?" I said. "Are they confused with the Cŵn Annwn because they also take souls?"

"We'd better leave that answer to my books," Patrick said. "On this case the truth comes best from the source. So you can be sure neither of us is misleading you."

"I would never—" Ioan began.

"Which includes unintentionally misleading you, through our own misunderstandings. Finish your mocha, Liv. You can read my books when you pick up the hound. I know you're both eager to get on the road for your vacation."

"They can't go on vacation," Ioan said. "If the sluagh have made contact—"

"Through a vision," Patrick said.

"Which is the *realm* of the sluagh. To them, it's no different from making contact in this plane. And it's just as dangerous. If they'd attacked Liv and Gabriel there . . ."

"We'd be a pile of bird-gnawed bones?" I said.

"Unfortunately, yes, which means as much as you want this vacation, you cannot leave until we've figured out why the sluagh made contact. And no, I'm not saying that because I want to stop the two of you from spending time together, though I suspect that's why Patrick is being a little less cautious than he ought to be."

I glanced at Gabriel. His lips pressed in a thin line, but he said nothing.

Patrick stayed silent for a moment and then said, with obvious reluctance, "Ioan's right. You should stay close until we figure out what's going on."

CHAPTER EIGHTEEN

I dropped Gabriel off at the dealership. His car was fixed, so he was driving that back to Cainsville. He would pick up Lloergan at Rose's, giving me time with Patrick.

As Patrick led me into his living room, I said, "I didn't try to tap into your personal memories. But, yes, I knew there was a chance I might. Had I known *what* I'd access, I wouldn't have done it."

"Is that an apology?"

"It's a Gabriel-apology. Which means that I'm acknowledging having done something that upset you and regretting that outcome, while not completely agreeing that I did something wrong or that I won't do it again."

"That's sort of like an apology."

"Which is what I always say to Gabriel." I sat. "We needed that information. Gabriel asked for it, and we both know how hard that was for him to do. You owed him an answer. Not necessarily the full story, but some form of an answer."

"Is that why he isn't here? He's upset with me?"

"No, he's coming. He's disappointed that he put himself out there and you rejected him, but that's what he's used to, parentally."

"Can't resist the low blows, can you."

"It's the truth. Gabriel doesn't need a daddy, Patrick. In fact, I'd strongly suggest you don't try to be one, or he *will* find reasons to not come by. But understand that he has zero expectations of you, and maybe try to do more than exceed them."

"In anything else, I would have."

"Not good enough. He asked you for that."

When Gabriel arrived, I stepped out to pet Lloergan, giving Patrick a minute with his son. It really was no more than sixty seconds. Just long enough, I'm sure, for Patrick to apologize and Gabriel to brush it off as "hardly necessary," and then escape the awkward conversation by bringing me inside.

Patrick had the book ready. When I started to open it, Gabriel said, "One moment, please. Patrick, Ioan said that visions are the same as reality with the sluagh. If you're about to send Olivia into a vision of them, you need to clarify exactly what that means."

"This isn't a vision. It's a replay, which doesn't count."

"You're certain of that?"

"I wouldn't send her in if I wasn't, Gabriel. When Ioan said visions are the same as reality for sluagh, he means visions that are the equivalent of human dreams. What do you see when you dream?"

Gabriel's expression closed. "I don't."

"I'm not asking for specifics. In general, when you dream—"

"I know what a dream is; I do not have them. I experience replays of memories, not unlike what I see with Gwynn. It's all factual, though. I do not imagine things that haven't happened to me." He snuck a look my way, his eyes wary. "I do not and have never dreamed."

"Is that his fae blood?" I asked.

Patrick didn't seem to hear me. He was frowning at Gabriel.

"Would his fae blood repress dreaming?" I prodded. "You called them *human* dreams."

Patrick tore his gaze from Gabriel. "Yes. Fae don't dream. Some of us have visions, like yours, but our 'dreams' are the replay of memories. I've never heard of it extending to our off-spring, though." He looked at Gabriel. "I'm sorry."

"I can't miss something I've never had," Gabriel said. "Do *you* regret the lack of them?"

"I'm not sure I'd say *regret*. I envy the ability. That sense of the fanciful. I've often wondered if it's why I write. I'm creating my own dreams."

"Then that is a gene I did *not* inherit. I prefer to apply my imagination to the waking world, where I can use it to solve problems. It seems wasted in sleep."

Patrick smiled. "All right, then. I regret that you missed out on that, but I'll accept that any regret is mine alone. Back to the point. I'm sure *you* dream, Liv. If they aren't replays of memory, what are they?"

"Sometimes fantasy, like my brain amusing itself by telling stories. Sometimes working through problems. Sometimes dealing with anxiety." I looked at Gabriel. "Believe me, you aren't missing anything with those."

"That is where the sluagh come in," Patrick said. "Their world is that of nightmare and anxiety and fear and all those things you repress in the daytime. When we say sluagh can hurt you in visions, we mean visions that are like dreams, the sort you had earlier today. The reenactments you get from my lore books are a whole different thing. Those are dead memories, with no way for the sluagh to get in."

"Can I accompany her?" Gabriel asked.

Patrick looked over in surprise.

"Yes, I've refused before," Gabriel said. "But this time . . ."

He paused, and then pushed on. "I would feel better going with her."

"I won't guarantee it will work, but you can certainly try."

I opened the book. Gabriel moved closer, and I took his hand. Patrick flipped to the right page, and I began to translate aloud for Gabriel's sake.

"Meditations on the nature of the *sidhe* known as the sluagh. The sluagh—also called the darkness or the unforgiven—should not even be termed fae, but rather spirits. Dark and twisted spirits. It is said that they share a mission with the Cŵn Annwn, that the Huntsmen are tasked with claiming the souls of those who've wronged the fae, while the sluagh do the same for those who've wronged humans. That is an egregious misunderstanding, and any fae who indulges in it ought to be corrected before further spreading false information. The Cŵn Annwn send souls to the Otherworld. The punishment, then, is not one of eternal damnation—as the Christians have willfully misinterpreted—but the premature end of mortal life. On rare occasions, the Cŵn Annwn will allow the sluagh to take a soul instead, but only if the crime is so great that it warrants extreme punishment, because the sluagh devour both body and soul. Any remaining consciousness is trapped in the melltithiwyd, doomed to serve the sluagh. In some cases, as when the Cŵn Annwn allow the sluagh to take their prey, it is a fitting and just punishment for a terrible crime . . ."

The words began to swim, and I clutched Gabriel's hand tighter. The ink parted, words falling through, me falling with them, tumbling through space until I landed in the forest.

I looked around for Gabriel. There was no sign of him.

"Damn it," I muttered.

I rose and peered around the night-dark forest. Beyond the trees, a bonfire burned. I climbed a small rise for a better view.

Below lay a temporary settlement, with tents and a single bon-fire guarded by a man in rough clothing.

"The Dark Ages?" murmured a voice beside me, and I turned to see Gabriel, squinting at the camp. "I landed over there." He pointed. "Holding hands, it seems, doesn't help with the drop. Would this be the Dark Ages?"

"Mmm, before that. I'm guessing pre-Roman."

"—know where to find their water source?" asked a man.

We both turned. Behind us stood a small group of men car-rying swords and cudgels. While I knew they weren't speaking modern English, that's what I heard.

"Can they see us?" Gabriel asked.

I shook my head. "As Patrick said, it's a dead memory. Like a virtual reality replay."

I walked toward the men, and Gabriel followed.

"Dump this into their water," the man said to a younger one.

"Won't that poison it?"

One of the other men snickered, and the leader said, "That would be the idea, boy."

"But . . . but that camp isn't a war party. It's their whole clan, including women and children."

"Women can still fight. Children grow into warriors. We'll no longer share the same land with these trespassers."

"Weren't they here first?"

"Who told you such lies?" the man snarled. "Go back to your momma, boy. You aren't ready to act with men." He turned to the man who'd snickered. "Pour it in their water. Can you do that?"

The man grunted his assent, took a water skin from the leader, and loped off.

The scene flickered, like a movie reel hitting a glitch. Then I was lying in a field, looking up at the bright sun.

"Gabriel?"

He didn't answer. I blinked hard and reached out. I'd fallen on something soft, and when my hand touched down, I felt fur, yet no movement or warmth underneath. A skin? I hoped so, though with my luck I'd landed on a dead animal. I blinked again and turned and . . .

I let out a shriek, cut short as I clamped a hand over my mouth and scrambled to my feet.

I was lying on the fur-cloaked body of a woman, twisted and contorted, her eyes bulging, dried blood crusting her mouth, both hands clutching her stomach.

A drinking cup lay at her side, next to a plate of half-eaten food. More food lay spilled by her hand.

The water.

They poisoned the water.

Another body lay beside me. A man, hands wrapped around his throat. I turned to look around me and . . .

Bodies. That's all I saw. The dead. Everywhere.

I closed my eyes, and I heard screams and moans, and a child calling "Mommy!" voice pitched impossibly high with pain. I quickly opened my eyes, and the scene went quiet.

As I looked around, I noticed gaps in those groups of the dead. Untouched and spilled water cups. Those who hadn't been as quick to drink with their morning meal. Those who'd seen what happened. And then . . .

To my left, the body of a man lay over a woman's, his head nearly cut off by a hatchet blade, his arm still around her. Beyond them, another man lay halfway to the tents, a child in his arms, taken down by a blow from the rear. To my right, a woman had been killed trying to drag a dying man to shelter, her hands still wrapped in his tunic.

That was when I saw Gabriel, standing between the forest and the camp. His gaze was fixed on a body near his feet. It was a girl, no more than eight or nine, who'd been running for the forest. An unarmed child. Cut down by a blow so hard it nearly sliced her in two. And under her? A baby, clutched in her arms.

Gabriel's gaze went from me to the girl and the baby, and though he didn't say a word, I saw them in his eyes.

I don't understand.

Gabriel knew death. He'd defended killers, and he conducted that job with cold detachment. But now he looked at these two victims, and he saw no defense. No way to even attempt one.

"Evil," I said. "This is evil."

He nodded and squinted at the camp. Two ravens circled overhead. For a moment I thought they were scavenging. Crows already worked on a body at the periphery, as if they weren't yet convinced it was safe to move in, all the humans gone.

The ravens flew at the crows, croaking, and the smaller cor-vids winged off, cawing indignantly. The ravens didn't take over the feast, though. They kept circling the camp, swooping to take a closer look at the carnage and then flying up again, let-ting out croaks that sounded frustrated, angry.

"Looking for fae," Gabriel murmured.

The ravens were from the Cŵn Annwn, seeking evidence of fae-blood victims among the dead so the Huntsmen could exact vengeance for the massacre. Those croaks meant they weren't finding what they needed.

"Then let the sluagh take the killers," I muttered.

The words were no sooner out of my lips than I fell into darkness again, this time landing near a small encampment. Hide tents in a forest. A smoldering fire pit. Snores from inside the tents.

"The perpetrators," Gabriel said.

An odd choice of word. Very clinical, very legal, and it might seem as if that let Gabriel put this horror into a perspective he understood. But what he understood were killers, while these men had *perpetrated* something far worse.

In the tents, the men snored and mumbled in sleep. Then came the distant sound of a thousand wings beating the night air.

"They deserve it," I said.

"Yes." Simple. Direct. Unequivocal.

The melltithiwyd came. They beat at the tents until they found a way in and drove the men out, and the men ran, pursued by the birds, who swooped and dove and seemed to delight in the chase as the *cŵn* hounds did not.

Then came the sluagh. The darkness. The unforgiven. The smoke wound through the flock of melltithiwyd, and the birds swarmed, engulfing the men.

The screams followed.

Whatever these men had done, it was impossible to enjoy those screams. It sounded as if they were being torn apart, slowly, their shrieks of agony turning to an animal howling that made me stop up my ears. Even Gabriel turned away until, as one body, the melltithiwyd flew up, the sluagh buffeting them into the sky.

And on the forest floor? Bone. Nothing left but bones.

When that wind rose again, I looked to see that the swarm of sluagh and melltithiwyd had changed direction. It plummeted like a black and red cyclone. A scream sounded, and I took off into the forest, Gabriel at my heels.

Through the trees, I saw the young man who'd refused to slaughter the camp—the one who'd been sent away. He must have been camping close to his kinsmen, as if hoping to follow them home.

Now he ran. Ran from the melltithiwyd as they swooped at him, drove him, toyed with him. They weren't waiting for the sluagh. That smoke still hovered above. So there was no excuse for the torment. The melltithiwyd were amusing themselves.

"I didn't do it," the boy shouted. "I wouldn't have."

"He must be lying," I said to Gabriel. "The sluagh wouldn't target him if he wasn't involved."

Gabriel shook his head. "I know the sound of false protests. He's telling the truth."

"Then they're just scaring him. Teaching him a lesson."

We watched the boy scale a tree to escape his tormenters.

"The exact wording of the book was 'some,'" Gabriel said.

"What?"

"'In *some* cases, it is a fitting and just punishment.'"

"But . . ."

The boy screamed. I looked to see the melltithiwyd diving at him. Biting at him. Swooping down and taking tiny mouthfuls and then flying away again.

"Hey!" I shouted. "No!"

Gabriel didn't point out that this was a reenactment, that the melltithiwyd couldn't hear me. I ran to the tree and looked up at the boy, his face and arms covered in tiny red spots, each dripping blood.

"If you're going to do it, do it!" I yelled at the melltithiwyd. "He's the least to blame. Why torment him?"

"Because they can," Gabriel murmured behind me, his voice taking on Gwynn's tenor. "They've eaten their fill, and he's the last, and they don't care if he's innocent or guilty, deserving or not."

The birds continued to dive and snatch bites of flesh, until the boy was covered in blood, and he'd stopped screaming and started to cry. That was all he could do. Lie against the branch and cry, sobbing deep sobs that were more terrible to hear than all the agonized screams of the guilty men.

"Just hurry," he said between sobs. "Please. I've done nothing wrong, but if you must take me, at least show mercy."

"They don't know what that is," Gabriel said.

I turned away and felt his arms go around me, wrapping tight around my head as if he could block the sound of the boy crying as I pressed my face to his chest.

"It's not fair," I said. "It's just—"

The scene disappeared, and in the darkness I heard a voice saying, "It's not fair!" A man's voice, echoing as if through an empty room. A clang followed, like chains. Then the thump of a fist on wood and a low laugh as a woman's voice said, "Do you think fair has anything to do with it, Duncan? It wasn't fair that you left me to care for our son, abandoned me—"

"He is not my son. You already admitted that, and there's no one here to lie for, Mary, so don't bother. You married me because I had a good trade, made a bit of money, and I was too besotted to wonder what a girl like you saw in an old man like me."

The scene cleared. We were in a room that stunk of old stone, with water weeping through the cracks. The man sat at a table, chained hand and foot. He wasn't "old"—maybe mid-thirties—but the woman across from him was little more than a girl. She wore a beautiful dress and bonnet, and it might seem as if she'd put on a pretty frock to brighten the day of her imprisoned husband, but the contrast between his filthy rags and her spotless gown seemed a deliberate slap in the face.

"You left us, Duncan," she said.

"With money," he said between gritted teeth. "My child or not, the boy doesn't deserve to suffer for his mother's sins."

"I need more."

"And you killed my *family* to get it?"

"So you would inherit your due."

"No, so *you* would inherit. I'm in here, framed for their murders. Does it amuse you, seeing me in chains, bound for the next ship to Australia? My only consolation is that you didn't get to see me hang from a noose. That the judge wasn't certain enough to sentence me to that."

"Oh, but I made sure he didn't. I bribed him."

Silence.

Mary smiled. "Do you know why I spared you, Duncan? Give me your right arm, and I'll show you."

He slowly stretched out his arm, gaze on hers. She reached down and brushed aside the thick black hairs.

"I did this while you slept, helped along by a sleeping draft."

As he stared at his arm, I leaned in to see a small red symbol, carefully incised in the skin as if by a razor-thin blade.

"No," he whispered.

"You've been marked for the sluagh." Her lips curved in a smile. "They'll come, and they'll find you convicted of murdering your entire family."

"But I didn't."

She leaned forward in her chair. "The sluagh don't care."

Duncan scrambled back so fast he toppled out of his chair as he clawed at the mark on his arm, clawed so hard his skin ran red with blood, as Mary's laughter echoed through the tiny room.

I turned toward Gabriel and caught only a flash of him before we were pitched into darkness again. When I landed, I heard Duncan screaming. It was the scream of a man running for his life. Except when I looked around, I wasn't in a forest . . . or any setting I recognized. I stood on the roof of an impossible house, with a castle balcony and yawning darkness below and spires behind me, jutting at all angles like spikes. Below, the landscape was equally impossible—a river running straight up a perpendicular mountainside, with twisted trees growing at ninety-degree angles. Duncan was trying to climb those trunks as if they were a ladder. Overhead, a rainbow of moons arched across the sky.

"We're in his dream," I said.

"This is a dream?"

Duncan screamed anew as a swarm of melltithiwyd dove at him.

"He didn't do anything," I said. "He absolutely, beyond a doubt, did not do anything."

"But he's marked," Gabriel said, and I could hear Gwynn's voice weaving through his again. "If he is marked and the sluagh discover he has been found guilty of crimes, that's the only excuse they need."

"Even if they knew he *wasn't* guilty?"

"That's the difference between the Cŵn Annwn and the sluagh. The Huntsmen may not take all factors into consideration, but they know guilt beyond a shadow of a doubt. The sluagh don't care about truth. This isn't a mission to them."

"It's a hunger."

"And a joy, particularly for the melltithiwyd. They were taken themselves by the sluagh, and the only satisfaction they have in their afterlife . . ."

"Is condemning others to the same fate." I shuddered and turned away. "I don't need to see this."

"Agreed." Gabriel put a hand against my shoulder, turning me away as he called, "Patrick? We're done here."

"No," a voice whispered behind us. "I don't think you are, Gwynn."

I spun, and that twisting darkness was right there, wrapping around the balcony.

Gabriel's arms went around me. "They can't—"

"Oh, yes, we can," the sluagh hissed. "You wanted to know more. You reached out. We accept the invitation, Matilda."

"*Find nawr,*" Gabriel snarled.

A wheezing laugh from the sluagh. "Oh, that won't work anymore, Gwynn. We're coming for what is ours. Not now, but we will come. For our Matilda."

"I'm not yours," I said.

A tendril of the smoke caressed my face. I batted it away as Gabriel yanked me back.

"But you are," the sluagh said. "Bought and paid for."

The sluagh swooped, enveloping us, and I lashed out, but it truly was fighting smoke, and then . . .

And then the sluagh was gone, and we were sitting on Patrick's sofa.

CHAPTER NINETEEN

"It spoke to us," Gabriel said, getting to his feet and stepping toward Patrick. "The sluagh addressed us directly. Inside your book."

"That's not possible," Patrick said. "I would never have sent you in there otherwise."

"It called us Matilda and Gwynn," I said.

I told him what we'd seen.

When I finished, Patrick said, "I think it was a dream. A self-produced vision. Liv, you were thinking how unfair it was that the sluagh target innocents. You then projected your outrage and made it personal—what if they came for you? Or it could have been Gabriel projecting fear from the part of him that is Gwynn. He lost Matilda. What remains of him has been searching for her ever since, and now he has her—through you."

"And Gwynn fears history is doomed to repeat itself," I said. "Fine, either is a possibility, but—for the sake of not dismissing a potential threat—let's say we really did see the sluagh. That it does believe it has some claim to me."

"How? You're not a killer, Liv."

"It never said that. It said I'd been bought and paid for. As if someone made a deal. Bargained away my soul."

"Pamela," Gabriel said.

Patrick shook his head. "Pamela dealt with the Cŵn Annwn. Ioan has confirmed that."

"But the Cŵn Annwn made a deal of their own," I said. "They negotiated with some mysterious power to heal me in exchange for the souls of human killers. Like those the sluagh target. According to your own book, the Cŵn Annwn sometimes give those souls to the sluagh."

"There is no possible way Ioan would have promised Matilda to the sluagh."

"You know where I had that first vision of it, right?"

"In Grace's apartment."

"When I saw the sluagh in your book, it said it accepted my invitation. That it was welcome to make contact because of that. Which I suspect means it can't just swoop into Cainsville uninvited."

"Of course not." Patrick got to his feet, taking the book from me and putting it back. "But if you're suggesting—"

"What exactly *is* Grace's building? It seems mostly vacant. Ricky opened a door to an apartment earlier this fall and got a blast of cold air that wasn't from an overworked air-conditioner. When Grace reopened that door, it was an ordinary apartment. So what is going on there? What's the big secret?"

"I can't tell you."

I glowered at him.

"I *can't*," he said. "I've been warned that if I break your contract with the elders, I lose my place on the council, which means you lose an ally when you're going to need one most."

"If I don't understand what her building really is, how do I come up with explanations for why the sluagh were in it?"

"You ask Ida. Just don't expect answers. You need a theory—with evidence—for her to confirm."

"If that theory is in your books, Patrick, say so," Gabriel said. "This is not the time for riddles."

"The answers are in that apartment building. Where Grace currently is *not*, being locked in a meeting with Ida to discuss what happened this morning. Which means you can go there and see what you find."

"In Grace's apartment building?" Gabriel said.

"This is the one we're talking about, is it not?"

"I'm clarifying, because I'm sure you cannot mean the building where Olivia already encountered the sluagh."

"Don't go in that particular room."

Gabriel's look was cold enough to make even Patrick inch back.

"Go in the apartment Ricky saw," Patrick said. "The sluagh won't appear there."

"As they did not appear in the visions created by your book?"

"I still think that was a self-induced vision . . ." He trailed off as Gabriel's look froze a few degrees more. "Stay in the hall. Take the hound. You'll be fine."

We stood outside the apartment where Ricky got that arctic blast. Lloergan sat beside us. Patrick perched on the front porch, after saying loudly, "I'll just wait out here while you kids get Liv's stuff from her apartment."

As expected, the door was locked. As also expected, Gabriel's touch *unlocked* it. I opened the door and then staggered back, hit by a blast of icy air.

Gabriel caught my arm as I surged forward.

"I'm not going to race past you," I said.

"No, but you'll get as close as you can, which will eventually be too close."

Lloergan grunted.

"Thanks for the support," I said to her.

She nosed the door lintel then lifted her head, sniffed, and made a noise in her throat, more rumble than growl, as if she wasn't quite sure what lay beyond, either, but she wasn't dead set against further exploration.

I eased the door open more and . . .

Snow.

A drift of snow blocked the hall. I walked in and bent to touch it, to be sure of what I was seeing. I scooped up a handful and squeezed it into a snowball. I could feel the icy cold, but it didn't melt.

Lloergan moved past me and snuffled the snow, snorting when she got a noseful. Then she pushed through the drift and continued on into the living room.

"Safe enough?" I said.

"I suppose so," Gabriel murmured.

We walked into the next room and . . .

Ice. Snow and ice. That's all I saw at first. A room decorated with snow and ice. A room *made* of snow and ice.

Walls of ice with what looked like a blue sky and bright sun above, the sunlight making the snow glitter and gleam. Snow drifted into every corner, waves of it, like a white desert. And in the center, an Arctic oasis—sheer ice over a water hole.

As I watched, a seal swam beneath the hole. A white seal. I raced out for a better look and nearly face-planted on the ice. I thudded onto one knee as Gabriel caught me.

Under the ice, the seal looked up. Huge brown eyes met mine. Then it gave a start, and I pulled back.

"I think we should go," I said.

Lloergan and Gabriel both made noises of agreement. As I turned to leave, a crackle sounded behind me.

Then, "Matilda?"

I turned to see a woman rising from a hole in the ice. She had long, graying blond hair, and she was naked from the waist up, her lower half still seal.

When Gabriel turned away quickly, she chuckled. "Is this better, Gwynn?" A cloak of sealskin appeared over her shoulders as she rose. Her voice had a rasp to it, and while she didn't look much older than my mother, she moved carefully, like a senior citizen worried about slipping.

"I'm sorry to disturb you," I said.

The selkie smiled. "You're curious. You're fae. I suspect you aren't supposed to be here, but you're quite welcome—"

The room stuttered. Snow swirled, and the selkie vanished behind it. When I blinked against the wind, I opened my eyes to find myself in an empty apartment. An ordinary apartment.

"Mmm, I don't think this is your place, Liv," Patrick said. "Has it really been that long?"

I looked over to see him in the doorway, with Ida glowering behind him.

"I'm sure you find this very amusing, bòcan," Ida said, "but I'll strongly suggest you attempt the impossible and keep your mouth shut before it gets you in more trouble. Now get out of there. Both of you." She looked at Lloergan. "All three of you."

"It's not Patrick's fault," I said. "After what happened this morning, we needed answers."

"You're not allowed them until you open negoti—"

Gabriel cut in. "The terms of the contract do not prohibit Olivia from obtaining answers on her own. You cannot punish her—or claim contractual violation—if she does. We needed to determine the nature of Grace's building in order to better understand what we experienced this morning."

"It's a nursing home, isn't it?" I said. "A place for old fae to live in their natural environments and make them comfortable at the end of their lives."

"Are you ready to tear up our contract, Olivia?" Ida asked.

Gabriel's voice lowered, words enunciated carefully. "I hope I'm misinterpreting, Ida. Otherwise it might sound as if you are using what happened this morning as leverage. Allowing Olivia's life to be endangered, so that she must terminate the contract for answers. May I remind you that the end of the contract means the beginning of Olivia's choice. Between the Tylwyth Teg—who have blocked and manipulated and lied to her—and the Cŵn Annwn—who have been as honest and forthright and helpful as they can be. You have a serious misunderstanding of human nature if you believe this is the proper time to hasten her decision."

"She doesn't," Grace said, walking in and fixing Ida with a beady-eyed glare before turning to me. "Yes, Liv, this is where we give sanctuary to fae at the end of their lives."

I glanced at Patrick, who confirmed it with a discreet nod.

"But that doesn't explain my vision this morning," I said.

"We're going to ask you to tell us exactly what you saw," Grace said. "But not here. You've poked around my home, Liv. It's time to show me yours."

"I'm tired," Gabriel announced as we walked into my parlor.

Ida turned to him. "I realize you didn't sleep last night, and for humans that is difficult. But I'm also well aware that as someone who is less than half human, one night without sleep hardly impedes you, Gabriel, so if you are using that excuse—"

"It is not physical exhaustion. It is mental. Psychological. Emotional. I am tired. Beyond tired. Tired of your bullshit, Ida. I don't use that word lightly. Olivia is your Matilda—the woman who can save your town—and you treat her like a nosy and meddlesome child."

Ida's mouth opened.

Gabriel cut her off. "If you dare to say she brought this on herself—with the contract—then I swear, Ida, I will do everything in my power to convince Olivia that the Cŵn Annwn are the proper choice, and you—and all of Cainsville—can go to hell."

Patrick slow clapped. When Ida spun on him, he said, "Oh, but you deserved that. You've deserved it for a very long time."

"You aren't helping, bòcan."

"And neither are you, Ida," Grace said. "Gabriel has had enough. And he's finally found the guts to stand up to you and say so. You'll do well to remember who he is and listen."

"Sluagh," Patrick said.. "Gabriel and Liv saw the sluagh, so let's cut straight to that and leave the do-si-do'ing to the local square dance chapter."

"We have a square dance chapter?" I said.

"No, but we should. Maybe I'll start one."

He shot me a smile for helping him break the tension. We moved to sit, Gabriel and I taking the davenport.

"Sluagh?" Ida stayed standing where she'd been.

"Yes, and don't pretend you're shocked, Ida," Patrick said.

"If you're suggesting—"

"That you knew they were here? Of course not. I'm suggesting that Grace saw enough to know what it was."

"I'm surprised Olivia still runs to you for help, Patrick, after she learned who you really are, what you did."

"Round and round we go, getting nowhere. Liv and Gabriel went to Rose for sluagh folklore. When I spoke to Rose, she told me about it. I sought them out to correct the folklore. Now, *moving along . . .*"

"The sluagh," I said. "No matter how old they might be, I don't think they warrant a room in Grace's Home for Aged Fae."

"Absolutely not," Ida said.

"Then what the hell were they doing there?"

"That's what Veronica is trying to find out. Walter is assisting. At this point, we don't wish to involve the other elders, and we'll ask you to respect that. For fae, sluagh are . . ."

"The bogeyman." Patrick met Ida's glower with a level look. "The darkness. The unforgiven. The thing we cannot name. What else is that if not the bogeyman? Unfortunately, in this case, it's not an imaginary monster concocted by parents to frighten children. But yes, Liv, I'll agree you should keep this quiet until we know more. And stay in Cainsville until we know more."

"Even if the sluagh are *here*?" I said.

"Veronica has applied wards as a precautionary measure," Ida said. "We'll ask you not to return to Grace's building, because we can't use the wards there—they would affect the elderly fae."

"So we need to stay in Cainsville?"

"Just don't venture anyplace you might both fall asleep. Also, avoid intentionally triggering visions anywhere except in this house. The sluagh can't simply swoop down Main Street, but they can attack through dreams and visions."

"And possibly through Patrick's books." I summarized our experience and then looked at Patrick. "Yes, I know. You believe we caused the visions ourselves. I'm not disagreeing. I just think we need to consider the possibility that isn't the explanation."

"Tell us the *full* story," Ida said.

"We were watching the sluagh attack someone who'd been falsely convicted of a crime and marked for the sluagh. Then the sluagh was there, with us. It said I belonged to them."

"What?" Genuine alarm spiked Ida's voice.

"It said I'd been bought and paid for. Exact wording."

Ida shook her head. "No, absolutely not."

"It called us Gwynn and Matilda, but it clearly wasn't mistaking us for the originals."

Ida looked sick.

Startled, I glanced at Grace, who seemed to be shimmering between the old woman and the fae.

"It's a mistake," Grace said finally. "A trick. No, a lie. It must be a lie."

"And if it's not?" Gabriel said.

"Stay here," Ida said. "In this house, please. With the hound. Lock the doors. Allow no one in but Grace or myself. We'll bring you dinner and anything else you need."

Patrick cleared his throat.

"What?" Ida snapped.

"Perhaps you should let *them* decide who brings their meals."

"Now, bòcan?" Ida's voice rose. "You still need to prove you are their favorite?"

"No," he said evenly. "I was going to suggest Rose."

"Yes," Gabriel said. "We would prefer Rose. We will stay here until morning, but no longer. We are not children. If this isn't resolved by then, you will need to tell us how to stay safe."

CHAPTER TWENTY

"No, apparently not," Gabriel said as he stood at my front window, watching the elders leave.

"No to what?" I said from the couch.

"You were about to say, 'So, I guess no cabin tonight,' and then you realized I might not appreciate the reminder."

His phone rang. Lydia's ring tone. He took it out but only looked down at the screen.

I was about to comment when my own phone blipped.

"Ricky," I said. "I should bring him up to speed. How about you go upstairs and call Lydia back. I'll update Ricky, and then I'll make us a snack. You must be hungry."

He looked vaguely confused, as if I was asking whether he felt like roller-blading. Then he said, in his normally brisk tone, "Yes, thank you. Food would be wise. I'll speak to Lydia upstairs."

Fifteen minutes later, Gabriel's footfalls thumped down the steps as he called, "Olivia?" with fear lacing his voice. "I smell—"

"Fire?" I leaned out the parlor door. "That would be me, trying to be sneaky and forgetting to open the flue. Apparently, closing the door didn't block the smell as much as I'd hoped. So, having ruined my surprise, ummm . . ." I threw open the door. "Ta-da?"

He walked over, still looking not entirely convinced that the house wasn't about to go up in smoke. Then he stopped in the entrance and blinked.

"Can't actually see anything, can you?" I said. "Between the lingering smoke and the fact that I tried to make the room as dark as possible. Simulated nighttime." I waved at the drawn shades. "I even taped them down. So, having ruined the presentation twice . . . third time's the charm?"

I flicked on a lamp. His gaze had been fixed on the roaring fire. Now it moved to the space before the fireplace, where I'd pushed aside the table and laid out as many blankets and pillows as I could quietly scrounge up. On the relocated table, I'd set out a tray of finger food and an ice bucket with Krug vintage champagne, one of the many birthday gifts I'd gotten from old friends who hadn't made actual contact since my life exploded.

"Oh, wait, final touch."

I scampered to a side table, flipped through my phone apps, and hit Start on one. The sound of the crashing surf filled the room.

"Uh, sorry, hold on." I flipped through the playlist and the storm was replaced by gentle waves lapping at a shore. "There. Now we won't feel as if we're on a ship that's about to go down."

Gabriel laughed. Not a quiet chuckle, but an actual laugh. He looked around the parlor and shook his head. "So, if we can't go to lakeside cabin . . ."

"It'll come to us."

"You are . . ." He seemed to struggle for a word, and I could have teased him about that, but it was an honest struggle as panic lit his eyes.

"You're something," he said at last, and I couldn't help sputtering a laugh. His eyes widened in horror. "That's not what I—I mean, you're something else. Something good. Something . . ."

He rubbed his hands over his face. "I'm not making sense. I'm sorry. I'm tired and . . ."

"Let me help," I said. "The problem is, as smooth as we might be in everyday life, when it comes to each other, all that glibness gets zapped from our brains. We can't seem to get it right, and when we try, it's like when you lean in to kiss someone and end up stomping on their foot while elbowing them in the ribs."

His lips curved, just a little. "Yes, exactly like that."

"Right now, what I *should* do is pour the champagne. Then we'd get comfortable in front of the fire and make small talk, relaxing and moving past this awkward moment. Then—and only then—I'd tell you what I want to say. *That's* smooth. But if I attempt that? The phone will ring. Someone will pound on the door. I'll have a vision. And Lloergan will develop a terrible case of gas."

The hound glowered from her spot by the fire.

"Even if none of that happens, I'll screw it up," I said. "I won't find the right words. Or I'll get cold feet and change my mind. So forget smooth." I took a deep breath. "This is what it sounded like, that night in the tunnel."

Gabriel frowned, these clearly not being the words he expected.

"The river lapping against that platform." I nodded toward my phone, playing the wave effect. "It sounded like that, but it echoed, too. Everything echoed. And I was cold. Colder than I've ever been. I couldn't stop shivering. My teeth wouldn't stop chattering. And you were warm. So amazingly warm, and all I wanted was to get closer to you. When I got closer, I realized that was just an excuse to cuddle up against you and then, yes, to kiss you."

I looked up at him. "I might not have been fully conscious, and I might have been slipping into memories of Gwynn, but I knew *exactly* who I was kissing."

I stood there, heart pounding. I should kiss him. That was the proper way to end my declaration. But I couldn't budge. And then I realized I shouldn't. I had made my move. The next step was his.

Gabriel stood frozen to the spot, his eyes slightly wide, in that way I'd come to interpret as panic.

I'd made a mistake. Somehow I'd misinterpreted.

How the hell could I have misinterpreted?

No, I wasn't falling back on that, would not blame myself. If he couldn't make this next move, then he was never going to make it. However he might feel, he was never going to be able to open himself up, accept the risk. Nothing in his life had prepared him to do that.

I squeezed my eyes shut so he wouldn't see my disappointment. No, my *devastation.* Tears welled behind my lids as I struggled to think of what I could blurt before running past him and—

His fingers touched my cheek and slowly moved down to my chin, tilting it up and . . .

I remembered the kiss in the river. I may have told myself it had gotten a little blurry, but that was bullshit. Even if I'd been certain it was just my subconscious conjuring Gabriel for me, I'd clung to that memory, pulled it out and replayed it and polished it so I could not possibly forget, because, real or not, I didn't want to forget.

Even when Gabriel admitted it *had* been real, I'd been afraid to trust my memory. The kiss may have happened, but not as I remembered.

What I remembered was the kind of kiss I would read about in books and chuckle over, and think the author was making a mountain out of a molehill. It was a very nice molehill, to be sure, but the over-the-top description belonged farther along that path, when the fireworks really started.

But that kiss in the river? It *was* the fireworks.

Even as I'd cherished that memory, part of me had wanted to forget it. That kiss was a false promise. It said that kissing should be like that, and if it wasn't with Ricky, then I was doing it wrong. Worse, it said that if I really ever kissed Gabriel and it wasn't exactly like that, I would forever be disappointed.

Now his fingers were on my chin, and he was tilting my face up, and I knew what was coming, and I was the one panicking.

All that lasted about 2.5 seconds, just long enough for him to tilt my face up and his lips to touch mine, and then it didn't matter, because I forgot why I'd been panicking. I forgot everything. Every last damned thing. Because this . . .

This was *not* that kiss. It was better. The last time, I'd known it wasn't quite real, and now it was.

This kiss felt like finding the one thing I'd been unconsciously searching for all my life. With that kiss, I remembered other Matildas, girls and women forever feeling as if they were missing something and never figuring out what it was. That had been me, my gnawing dissatisfaction like a trapped animal ready to chew off a limb. What I'd thought was only discontent with my sheltered life had been a symptom of what I'd been missing—Matilda and Cainsville and the Cŵn Annwn and everything that I could not believe hadn't been part of my life until a few months ago. When I kissed Gabriel, the last missing piece fell into place, and all I could think was, *Yes, this is it.*

He started kissing me with one hand on my chin. And then both hands were on my cheeks and then in my hair, and my arms were around his neck, my body against his, and for once there was no destination in mind. This kiss was not only the first step along the path. It was the destination.

When something thumped beside us, I broke away just enough for Gabriel to murmur, "Hmm?" in a way that sounded like I'd woken him from a deep sleep.

We turned as Lloergan made her way out of the room.

"Good call," I said, and Gabriel smiled.

And that's when, from deep in the house, his phone started to ring.

"Next time you throw it at the wall?" I said. "Harder, please. That was a poor effort."

"I don't hear a thing."

"I would *love* to go with that, but it's Rose's ring tone. Wait here, and I'll get the message."

I ran up to the office, where he'd been working. Five minutes later, I came back down. When he saw his cell phone in my hand, he tensed.

"No worries," I said. "She was just asking about dinner. I said we'll be fine. And your phone is now off."

I laid it beside mine, and he handed me a glass of champagne. We settled in front of the fire, me resting against his leg, but no closer than that, the old tension strumming between us, the one that said we couldn't just slide back to where we'd been, that it was still too new, too uncertain.

I sipped my champagne and watched the flames. Then I glanced at him and said, "For the record, you're an amazing kisser," and he laughed—a spray-his-mouthful-of-champagne laugh.

"No one's ever told you that?" I said.

"I believe the only time any opinion was given on the matter, it was to inform me that I was wretched at it. Which only gave me the excuse to not do it."

"You just had a bad partner."

His eyes sparkled. "That's the answer, is it?"

"Obviously." I took another sip of my champagne. "Or maybe it was an anomaly."

"No, I'm quite certain everyone I've kissed has had the same opinion."

"I mean it might have been an anomaly with *me*. I was never very good at science, but I remember a teacher pounding into me the need for a significant sample size before drawing a scientific conclusion."

"Are you asking me to kiss you again?"

"Normally, I'd be fine with taking the initiative, but with you, it seems best to double-check my invitation. Maybe triple-check. Which leaves me doing that thing where I hint for a kiss instead of just trying my luck."

"It seemed like more than a hint."

"I'm no good at subtle."

"Well, as you rightly pointed out, we have a very poor track record with this. I believe the only way to circumvent that is to be clear." He set down his champagne flute. "You do not need to second-guess the invitation, Olivia. It is as open as it is unequivocal. Any advances you make are welcome."

"In that case . . ." I put down my glass beside his. Then I knelt, leaned over, and gave him a peck on the cheek before starting to rise. "Now, I believe we have work to do and—"

He tugged me back down and pulled me into a kiss. And while my old teacher would insist that a sample set of two was not the basis for a scientific conclusion, I felt very confident in theorizing—based on that second kiss—that the first was definitely not an anomaly.

We kissed, me straddling him as he leaned back against the sofa. We kept it slow as I enjoyed this, just this, feeling his hands in my hair, feeling his heartbeat. Reveling in a moment of being close to someone I never thought I could ever be close to. Being intimate with someone I never thought would allow that intimacy.

So we took our time. There were breaks, for that necessary little thing called oxygen, and even then there was nuzzling and kissing, as if the goal was to touch as much of each other as we could, to get as close to each other as we could.

Even when it went further, it wasn't obvious at first. It was his hands circling my waist under my shirt. It was my hands pushing up his shirt. It was shirts off and more kissing, skin to skin. His hands on the sides of my breasts and then his hands wedged between us, cupping my breasts, and my hands on him, everywhere on him.

More kissing. More touching. More exploring. And then, finally, down onto the blankets and the pillows, belts and buttons undone and zippers pulled and trousers pushed over hips. More touching. More exploring. That last bit of clothing following the rest. Soft sighs and whispers turning to moans and gasps, and occasionally a hand on another hand, no words spoken but the meaning clear. *Slower, just a little slower. I want this to last.* Even that seemed to stretch to infinity, the tease and the exploration and those hands of wordless warning.

Then came the point where *slower* was pointless. Where even a touch was too much, and I arched back with, "Gabriel, oh God, Gabriel," and I was still riding those waves when he pushed into me, and that was . . .

Beyond words. Beyond thought. Beyond everything.

LOVE

abriel was dreaming. Perhaps that is not entirely accurate. It was certainly nothing like the bizarre landscape he'd seen in the mind of the condemned man. Nor was it even what Olivia said dreams were, the mind conjuring up places and people and events that never existed. This was, instead, a swirl of memories, his own interwoven with Gwynn's.

He started by replaying those hours downstairs in the parlor. Feeling Olivia's fingertips on his skin. Hearing the sigh of her breath against his cheek. The arch of her body under his hands. The way she said his name. And how he'd felt—that most of all, the indescribable way he'd felt at having won her. Torn between "Why the hell didn't I make a move sooner?" and knowing that it had proceeded at exactly the pace it had needed to proceed.

Then he realized he was dreaming, and it was like a slap in the face, that cold rush of fear that he really *had* dreamed it all. He woke with a start, reaching out, certain he'd touch empty space. Then he felt her there, naked and nestled against him, and he lowered his head to the crook of her neck and inhaled, his arms tightening around her before he drifted off again.

When it happened again—the memories and then the fear— Gabriel woke a little more forcefully, a little more afraid, and he tightened his grip too much. Olivia half woke, enough to kiss him and touch him, her fingers running over his chest. They made love again, both still drowsy with sleep, not a word exchanged, as if this too was part of the dream.

After Olivia fell back to sleep, Gabriel lay there, reflecting on his own choice of words. *Making love.* He'd never thought of sex that way. It wasn't deliberate avoidance of the term—it just seemed to him that "making love" was a euphemism not unlike "passed away." A term used when one wanted to avoid acknowledging a biological fact of life by adorning it with a fancy bow. It was simply filling a biological need that was little different from eating or sleeping, but you didn't call it sex or, worse, fucking, but "making love," despite the fact that love was rarely involved. In his experience, the act required no emotion at all. It was pleasurable enough, but not unlike the need for food and sleep, something that had to be gotten out of the way lest it interfere with the forward motion of life.

With Olivia, he finally understood why they called it lovemaking, and he used the term automatically. It was the correct one. That was all.

When he slid back into sleep, he found what really did seem like an actual dream. He was kissing Olivia, and despite the darkness, he knew it must be her because he felt all the things he felt when he kissed her. It was a lovely kiss, sweet and deep, and yet while sparks of it reminded him of Olivia, it did not feel exactly the same. That was what made him think he might be having one of those anxiety dreams she'd mentioned.

But even when he mentally hesitated, his body kept kissing her as fervently as it had before, responding as quickly as it had before, that animal part of his brain urging haste before the logical part pushed it back, wanting to enjoy the lead-up. Except here, too, it was different. It felt as if he was struggling to squelch that physical arousal, *needing* to squelch it rather than enjoy the build.

"I think we should . . ." he began, his voice ragged. Except it wasn't his voice at all, but the one he'd come to know as Gwynn's. He blinked hard, and as the darkness cleared, he found himself lying in a meadow with Matilda looking up at him, her arms around his neck.

"You think we should do what?" she asked with a teasing lilt.

"Go riding," he blurted. "I think we should go riding."

Matilda laughed, her eyes dancing with amusement and mischief, and that was when Gabriel saw Olivia in her, her laugh echoing Olivia's when he'd clumsily told her she was "something."

"I would very much like to go riding," she said. "But I suspect it's not the same sort you're offering."

Gabriel felt Gwynn's cheeks burn. And it was not the only part of him that burned as she said that, a white-hot flame of desire licking through him.

"Whenever you're ready to go further, Gwynn, so am I. I just don't want to rush you."

"Rush *me*? No. I—"

I'm fine with anything. It's you I'm taking it slow for.

That was what Gwynn wanted to say. Except it was a lie. They were fae. They did not see sexuality as humans did, as something to avoid until marriage and then do behind closed doors, under the sheets, in the dark.

Gwynn didn't hold back for Matilda. He held back for himself. Because he was terrified that he'd be less than she expected. That he was not Arawn.

In this regard, as in so many others, Gwynn was outmatched. Arawn's lovers saw no reason to keep silent, singing his praises loudly enough that Matilda heard and teased Arawn about it. No one talked that way about Gwynn. There was nothing to say.

He'd spent his youth pining for Matilda, losing himself in his studies and his duties. Once they got together, he realized his lack of experience might prove problematic. So he proceeded as slowly as possible. Building his skills, he told himself, though he hadn't progressed much beyond kissing, telling himself he hadn't fully mastered that yet. Which was a lie. He was just afraid.

As Gwynn fretted and worried, Gabriel saw more of himself than he liked in the fae prince. Gwynn wasn't more than a few years younger than Gabriel, but listening to his stammering made Gabriel feel like an old man watching a boy and thinking, *Was I ever that young?* The answer was no—Gabriel had never been that young. And yet it was, in a way, as if he was looking back on a younger version of himself, from a time so distant that he couldn't quite believe this *had* been him.

Gabriel might not have fumbled and stammered and blushed with Olivia, but he still understood how Gwynn felt, that terror of losing what he had if he took the next step. While he had not been so acutely anxious about Olivia and Ricky, he had to admit that he found a patch of common ground with Gwynn here, too. Ricky was younger, more charming, better-looking, and much easier to get on with. The only clear advantage Gabriel had was his bank account . . . which Olivia did not need and would not have wanted even if she did.

As for sex . . . yes, he would be honest there. That was where he feared Ricky had him beat. Gabriel knew Olivia liked sex, and he knew it was not his area of expertise, having never been a skill he'd cared to improve. If he was better at it, women might not be so willing to let him slip out before morning.

And yet, that worrying had been for naught. The key, it seemed, was simply to care. To care that she enjoyed herself, to care enough to pay attention. To watch and listen and feel her responses and use them as a guide, and those responses were their own reward, the satisfaction of knowing he pleased her, and the more he pleased her, the more she responded in kind.

Quid pro quo, he thought with a chuckle.

If Gabriel could give Gwynn any advice, that would be it. *You love her. You care about her. You want her to be happy. Keep all that in mind, and you'll do fine.*

Of course, he could say no such thing, not to a memory of events long past, and all that passed in a heartbeat anyway—Gwynn's anxieties and Gabriel's reflections. Matilda was still lying there, awaiting a response as Gwynn stammered.

"Do you want to stop?" she asked carefully. "I'd never push . . ."

"No, I just . . . I . . ."

She touched his shirtfront. "May I take this off?"

Gwynn nodded mutely, and Matilda sat up and pushed the shirt over his head, her hands running up his chest as he shivered, desire igniting again.

"You're so beautiful," she said, her own voice taking that husky note of Olivia's. "Can I just . . . ?" She bit her lip and ran her fingertips over his chest, and when he nodded, she said, "Would you lie back? So I can . . ."

Her cheeks flushed, and she didn't finish, but Gwynn lay on his back and she straddled him, her fingers running up his stomach, touching and exploring as she leaned down to kiss him, her hair tickling.

That was when Gabriel woke up. Or, more accurately, when he decided it was time to wake up, pushing himself out of the memory until he could feel the cool sheets of Olivia's bed and smell her shampoo on the pillow and hear the soft exhale of her breathing . . .

No, that wasn't *her* breathing. And there was another smell, one that was oddly comforting, in its way, but not nearly as welcoming as Olivia's. Gabriel opened one eye to find himself on the edge of the bed, looking down at Lloergan. The hound lifted her shaggy head and gave him what he presumed was a good morning grunt. He returned it and flipped over, reaching for Olivia, to pull her into his arms and bury his face in her hair and replace the smell of dog with—

His hands touched down on empty sheets. He patted them. And then bolted up. He looked in the direction of the hall bath-room, listening for the flush of the toilet or the pad of her feet on the hardwood. When he heard nothing, he patted the bed again, finding her spot cold, and a chill seeped through him.

She left. She woke up in the night and realized she'd made a mistake, and she went to sleep somewhere else.

I've lost her.

I always lose her.

Gabriel pressed his palms to his eyelids. *Stop that. Just stop that.* He knew who he was talking to. Yes, it was partly Gwynn, but it was partly himself, too, that equally endless doubt.

I won't keep her. Can't keep her. Never could, and I was a fool to think I could change that.

I was so pleased with myself in that dream, wishing I could give Gwynn some advice. Like the fifteen-year-old boy who has sex for the first time and fancies himself an authority.

Stop. Now.

If Lloergan was here, then Olivia hadn't gone far. Perhaps the room got too light. Perhaps he'd taken up too much of the bed. Perhaps she'd simply gone downstairs to read. All perfectly rational explanations, but he was still disappointed, as if he'd failed to do something that would have kept her here despite the light or the discomfort or the boredom.

He sat up and looked for his clothing, only to remember they'd shed their clothes in front of the fire. He walked into the hall. The bathroom door stood open, as did the office, both dark inside. He grabbed a pair of shorts from his dresser, pulled them on, and hurried downstairs.

The main level was as silent as the upstairs.

Had Olivia gone for a walk? A jog? He'd have joined her for either, and the fact she'd go alone only bolstered his fear that she needed time to herself. Time to reconsider.

He glanced into the parlor. It was as they'd left it—a tangle of blankets and clothing in front of the now-smoldering fire. He was looking for his shirt when he caught a creak from the kitchen and noticed that the door was closed. He jogged down the hall to throw it open.

The smell of fresh-brewed coffee and sizzling bacon rushed out to greet him. Olivia stood in front of the stove, spatula in hand. Her dark blond hair was tousled, as if she'd just rolled out of bed. Her feet were bare, her long legs equally bare, and he realized where his shirt had gone. She wore it. Unbuttoned. With nothing underneath.

As she turned, he stopped to stare. Olivia, fresh out of bed, naked but for his shirt. There was a moment where he was quite certain he really was dreaming, conjuring up a favorite fantasy image, the memory of the first morning he'd woken in her apartment and seen her like this.

"The smell didn't disturb you, did it?" she asked. "I shut the door and tried to keep quiet."

He said nothing.

"So . . . breakfast?" she said. "Even if it's the opposite of actual breakfast time."

He checked the clock on the microwave. Dim light filtered through the window, and he realized the sun was setting, not rising.

"Is everything okay?" she asked, concern creeping in.

He turned and saw her again. Olivia naked, wearing his

shirt. She'd said something about breakfast, but he hadn't quite caught it. He nodded and walked toward her. She set down the spatula with a growing frown.

"Is everything okay?" she asked.

He put his hands on her hips and boosted her onto the counter. Then he stepped between her knees, his fingers going to her hair, murmuring, "Everything's fine," before showing her how fine it was.

CHAPTER TWENTY-ONE

After breakfast, we went outside. Yes, it was a December evening, and in Illinois that is not "take your coffee into the garden" weather. We didn't care. We had blankets and a garden fireplace, and the fenced yard kept the wind at bay.

It also gave me the excuse to get close to Gabriel, followed by the realization I didn't *need* an excuse. Whenever I'd thought of a relationship with him, I'd always presumed there'd still be a barrier, that he'd be the kind of guy who didn't encourage intimacy outside the bedroom. Yet even before tonight, I'd seen signs that maybe his general distaste for physical contact no longer extended to me. Now, he was the one settling in on the ground with the blanket, his arm lifting for me to curl up beside him, his arm around my waist, holding me close.

I buried my feet under Lloergan's warm bulk. "If I buy this place, I might replace the deck with a conservatory. It would give me winter sun and semi-outdoor living space. What do you think?"

As usual, he didn't point out that it was *my* house and I could do as I pleased. It was like when we went shopping for his new living room suite and after we chose one, the clerk handed *me* the paperwork, presuming we were a couple. Which we had been, in our way, long before tonight.

"A conservatory *would* be a better use of the space," he said.

"We could—" I bit off the words. "And I should stop there, or it'll make it that much harder to say no to the Tylwyth Teg."

"I've been compiling a list of alternatives."

"Ways to keep the house if I turn down the Tylwyth Teg? That won't work. For them, it'd be like having your future executioner living down the street."

"I don't believe it would be quite so dramatic, but I meant a list of alternative houses, in Chicago and the surrounding area. The same basic style, with the elements you like. I have three possibilities so far."

"Let's just hope they're still on the market when I make my decision."

"They aren't on the market. In one case, the current homeowner is elderly and finding upkeep difficult. In another, a young couple took on too heavy a mortgage and are struggling with payments. The third has recently suffered a serious financial blow. With a generous offer, any of the three would likely sell."

Because all three were in a position where, even though they might not *want* to move, a good offer would be too tempting to refuse. One might say that was predatory. To Gabriel, it was simple practicality. He'd done his research and found me these alternatives. It was another gift. If he proposed *cheating* these people out of their homes, I would argue. But he wouldn't. He'd suggest a fair—if cold—bargain that would push the homeowners to a choice they'd have to make eventually.

So I said, sincerely, "Thank you. That helps. But I do need to make that choice soon. The problem is that I don't even know how to *begin*."

"You shouldn't have to."

I shifted under his arm. "I keep thinking that, and then I feel like a two-year-old stomping her feet and shouting that it isn't fair. Why me? Why *Matilda*? What did she do to deserve this?"

"Gwynn caused the problem, and Matilda is forced to resolve it."

"I don't mean—"

"The schism began when he made the pact with Arawn and then broke it, only to worsen matters by not confessing to either wronged party."

"They all shoulder their share of the blame."

"But not equal shares. By far the smallest portion goes to Matilda, whose only fault seems to lie in the fact she chose a lover. Which is her right."

"Maybe it's not that she was wrong to choose—it's that she did choose and so she needs to do it again. Not a punishment but a responsibility. I—"

Lloergan leapt up and raced to the gate.

I rose as she whined. "I'll open it for you," I said as I walked over. "But if there's someone—or something—out there . . ."

She whined again, her whole body trembling, tail thumping. Not fear—excitement.

That's when I caught the faint yet unmistakable sound of a Harley.

CHAPTER TWENTY-TWO

heard that motor and, like Lloergan, I felt a spark of joy. Ricky was back.

Then I looked at Gabriel, walking toward me, his gaze turned toward the driveway, hearing the same sound I did.

"We—" I began, and there was this moment where I almost said we should go inside. Leave Lloergan and go inside and turn out the lights and maybe Ricky would think we'd gone to sleep. Forget the fact that it was only eight-thirty at night. Forget that he had a key. Most of all, forget that we had done nothing wrong.

As Lloergan took off, Gabriel held the gate open and turned to me.

"Go on inside," he said. "I'll speak to him."

I shook my head. "No, I should—"

"Yes, you're the one who should break it to him, and to have me do it smacks of chauvinism—as if I've 'taken' you from him. Under any other circumstances, I would agree. But this isn't any circumstances, and I . . ." He swallowed, the slightest bob of his Adam's apple. "I need to do this."

He meant he needed to be the one to tell Ricky because Gwynn hadn't told Arawn. We'd vowed not to repeat those mistakes.

"Tell him I—" I began.

Then Ricky turned into the drive, Lloergan racing behind him. He saw me and raised a hand in greeting, and to run inside without saying hello would have meant something was wrong. That I was ashamed and had to flee.

"Say hello," Gabriel murmured. "And then tell him you're going to make coffee."

"Right. Coffee to the rescue." I tried for a smile, and then realized I *had* to find one—not just for Ricky, but for Gabriel, who kept sneaking looks my way, every one of them asking if my unease might be regret.

"I want things to be okay," I said, and I wasn't sure if that meant anything at all, but he nodded and said, "They will be. Nothing will change. Ricky's not going anywhere."

I feared he would, no matter how clear he'd been that our separation wasn't a test, that he understood how I felt about Gabriel. Despite that, implicit in our breakup had been the unspoken understanding that if Gabriel never became an option, Ricky was still there.

Ricky swung from his bike, petting Lloergan with one hand as he pulled off his helmet with the other.

As I walked toward him, I remembered all the other times he'd come home from business. I'd see him and feel a rush of desire, reminded of exactly how good he looked. Today, though, what I thought wasn't how good he looked, but how familiar. A shot not of lust but of joy.

Ricky's home, and I can't wait to talk to him.

Because that had always been the most important thing. Our friendship. The ease and comfort of that friendship. With Gabriel, I could have deep and challenging and infuriating conversations. Ricky was the guy I could just kick back with, relax and chatter and never tire of it.

"Didn't I just talk to you in Miami a few hours ago?" I said.

He checked his watch. "Six hours ago. I raced to catch a flight home right after we talked. I know it was tough, managing the current crises without me."

"Uh . . ."

He turned to Gabriel. "She's dumbstruck with gratitude. And I'm sure that complete lack of expression on your face masks incredible relief that I'm here to save the day."

"I appreciate . . ." Gabriel began slowly.

Ricky thumped Gabriel on the back as he passed. "I'm kidding, obviously. Liv's trying to think of a comeback that's suitably sarcastic but not actually cruel. I know you guys didn't need me. But I can help, so I want to. Plus Lloe needs me home. Don't you, girl?"

He scratched the *cŵn*'s head as she accompanied him up the front steps.

"I need to speak to you," Gabriel said.

"Yep, we all need to talk. Liv's update was kinda succinct. Can we do that someplace that's a little warmer? I could also really use a drink, too."

"Right," I said. "Let me do that. You and Gabriel can talk upstairs."

"Sure . . ." Ricky said. "Or we could talk in the parlor, while you pour the menfolk their drink."

"I'd rather speak in private," Gabriel said.

"Ah, let me guess. It's about Liv."

Gabriel went still.

Ricky glanced at me. "It's one of those conversations where Gabriel and I discuss how worried we are for your safety, which we know better than to say in front of you because it makes us sound like overprotective cavemen." He opened the door. "Let's talk in the parlor. Riding in December is *not* warm. I'm going to get a fire—"

He stopped in the parlor doorway. That's when I saw the champagne glasses, the tangle of blankets and scattered pillows. And the clothing. My shirt and jeans. Gabriel's trousers. My bra. My panties. His boxers.

"Okay, then," Ricky said. "Well . . ." He turned to Gabriel. "I guess I know what you were going to talk to me about."

"I'm sor—"

"No, it's fine. I said it was fine, right? Told you both it was absolutely fine. So it is." He shoved his hands in his pockets, still staring at the discarded clothing. "Yep, just fine."

I pulled the parlor door shut. "The last time we spoke, Gabriel and I hadn't—"

"No, I get it. There was nothing to tell six hours ago. And now there is."

"I'll get you a beer. We do have things we need to talk about. I could really use your help getting answers from Ioan, especially about the sluagh. I think he might have—"

"Actually, you know what? I'm going to skip the drink. It's been a long day. Long flight, too. I should have just driven out in the morning. I'll get some sleep, come back in the morning, and we can talk."

He didn't give us time to respond. Just turned on his heel and walked out the front door. Lloergan gave a sharp bark of alarm and raced to the door. I put my hand on the knob, but Gabriel laid his on mine, and when I looked over, he shook his head and then nodded at the hound. Open the door and Lloergan would take off after him, and I wasn't even sure Ricky would notice.

"Distract her, please," I said. "I'll go out the back—"

The roar of the Harley's motor cut me short. I hurried into the parlor, but before I could get to the window, tires squealed as the bike tore off.

———

I stood at the parlor window, listening until I couldn't hear the motorcycle, until I was sure it was gone, sure Ricky was gone. Lloergan whined beside me. I laid my hand on her head.

"I'm sorry, girl. We'll take you home as soon as we can. He's just . . . busy."

She lumbered off to lie by the fireplace. I turned to Gabriel, standing behind me.

"It wasn't ever going to work, was it?" I didn't wait for an answer, just thumped down on the sofa. "We were fooling ourselves. Thinking we were better than them, smarter than them. Bullshit. The truth is that it can't work. Someone's going to get hurt."

Gabriel lowered himself beside me. "Not just someone. Everyone."

"But mostly him."

"Yes, mostly him."

Tears welled. "He doesn't deserve it. He did absolutely nothing wrong."

Silence stretched through long minutes. Then Gabriel said, his voice low, "If you realize you've made a mistake, I'm not going to pretend I'm fine with that. But I would understand. This was the only way for you to know."

"The only mistake I made was in thinking we might be able to work past it. And now . . ."

"He needs time."

More silence. Then Gabriel said, "He needs privacy to react, Olivia. He thought he'd be fine with it. He is not fine with it. He realizes that now, and he doesn't want to get angry in front of us when he promised otherwise."

I said nothing.

"If he isn't ready to face us tomorrow, he'll call," Gabriel said. "Then he'll come around as soon as he's ready. He knows we need him."

"But that's what I *don't* want. If he's hurt and angry, and he's not okay with this, yet he feels obligated to stick around because of Arawn and the Cŵn Annwn? That's even crueler."

"No, it's a reason to come back and focus. And doing that will give him the chance to see whether we can get past this."

I was doing the records search for a case when Lloergan's nails scrabbled against the linoleum. She didn't race to the door but stood in place, whining and shifting from paw to paw, looking anxiously back at me. A moment later, a headlight lit up the front window and the sound of Ricky's Harley vibrated through the house.

I glanced at Gabriel. He'd looked up from his laptop and turned to listen. He motioned for me to go to the door. I did, but I waited behind it until the knocker sounded.

When I pulled the door open, Ricky stood there, hands in his pockets.

"I'm an ass," he said.

"No, you—"

"Nope, I was an ass. Don't rob me of my moment. I shouldn't have taken off." He looked down at Lloergan at my side. "On you, either. I'm sorry."

"I should have warned you."

A wan smile. "How? Text me a heads-up the moment you realized something was going to happen between you and Gabriel? Or right after it did? Pretty sure that wasn't exactly a priority. I'm the one who showed up unannounced. Gabriel tried to take me aside right away. Even if he'd managed that, I'm not sure I'd have reacted any better. It's like seeing a right hook coming. You think you're prepared for it, but you're just not. You can't be." He paused and made a face. "My analogies don't ever get better, do they?"

"They make sense to me."

The smile touched his eyes. "That's what matters." He pulled his hands from his pockets. "Can we talk? You and me? Go for a walk or something?"

"I'm kind of under house arrest," I said. "Until the elders figure out what's up with the sluagh."

"Go on," Gabriel said, walking up behind me. "Don't go far and don't be long, please, but you'll be fine."

I nodded, and as I stepped out, Lloergan looked from Ricky and me to Gabriel.

"Better stay there," Ricky said to the hound. "I'll be back. I promise."

She grunted and returned to Gabriel.

As we walked down the drive, Ricky looked at his bike. "Could we . . . ? Just outside town."

I was about to say that was fine. Then I had a flash of the night Matilda died, of her running to Arawn, Gwynn left behind as Matilda rode off with Arawn.

I glanced back.

Gabriel stood in the doorway. He nodded toward the bike. "Go on. Just not far, please."

"Twenty minutes tops," Ricky called. "And we'll be just outside the town limits, with our phones on."

CHAPTER TWENTY-THREE

We turned down the first country road and rode only until Ricky could pull over. Then we walked into the forest. We didn't go out of sight of the road. Just found a fallen tree and sat on it.

"I'm not going to say that was easy," he said after a moment. "Looking through that doorway. Seeing . . ."

"I'd completely forgotten that was—"

"I know. And I knew it was coming. I've always known it was coming, no matter how much you doubted it. But I wasn't ever going to be ready. I see that now."

"I'm sorry."

"Don't, Liv. Please. You have nothing to apologize for, and it only makes me feel bad, knowing you feel the need to say it. You don't. So I'm just going to talk for a few minutes, okay?"

I nodded.

"You and I . . ." He shifted on the log. "I don't know where we were going. Nowhere, if I'm being honest. If I look ten years down the road, where would we have been? Me as leader of the Saints, and you as the wife of a motorcycle gang leader, with the stigma of that, the danger of that?" He shook his head. "It isn't the life for you, and you'd be miserable. So what's the alternative?

I quit the club? You'd never let me do that because then *I'd* be miserable. Where we were? It was fucking fantastic. But it didn't have a future."

He looked at me. "What we have now is just as good, and it *has* a future. I'm gonna miss what we had. I do miss it, every damn day. But I'd miss not having you in my life a hell of a lot more."

"Ditto."

He smiled. "Good." A quiet moment. Then he glanced over. "Do you regret it? Us being together?"

"Never. We had to try. We had to know."

"That's what Arawn never got. He knew Matilda loved him, and he knew it wasn't in the same way she loved Gwynn, yet he couldn't help thinking it was only different because Gwynn got his chance, and if Arawn had, things would have been different. He was wrong. Matilda wanted to be with Gwynn. You want to be with Gabriel. You aren't her, and he's not him, but what you each are *feels* the same way. If that makes any sense."

"It does."

"So . . ." His gaze dropped to my ankle and I knew he was thinking of the tattoo there, the moon for Arawn, for him. "I'll understand if you want that removed."

I looked at his forearm, where he had a small tattoo of the sun and moon entwined. Matilda's symbol. "Do you want yours removed?"

"Course not. I knew when I got it that I almost certainly wasn't going to keep you. It's a marker in my life, for something significant. You were. You still are. I hope you always will be. The tattoo stays."

"Ditto," I said. "To all of that."

Gabriel had cleaned the parlor while we were gone. We were in there now, with coffee and Rose's cookies, talking about the sluagh and Seanna and where we'd go from here. It wasn't until it began snowing—in the parlor—that I realized I'd drifted off to sleep.

In my dream, we were still on the sofa, me sitting sideways with my back against Gabriel, Ricky in the opposite corner, sprawled with his head propped on a pillow as he talked. And it was snowing. Not pretty little flakes but huge gobs of snow, and I was getting annoyed because it was piling up, and then I couldn't hear Ricky because, well, snow.

When I reached out to brush the flakes away, my fingers touched paper instead. Small scrolls rained down like clumps of snow. I unrolled one to see a name.

"Greg Kirkman?" I said. "Who's Greg Kirkman?"

"That's the question, isn't it?" Gabriel said, almost muffled by the paper piling around him.

"Um, yeah, that's what I said." I took another scroll, opened it, and read the same two words. And then another and another.

"Who the hell is Greg Kirkman?" I said.

Gabriel sighed, setting the paper fluttering. "Yes, exactly."

"No, really, I'm asking you guys."

Ricky brushed the drift of papers away from his face. "Um, no. That's your job, right? You were supposed to—"

"Shit!"

I jolted awake, my hands brushing aside imaginary papers. "I forgot to research Greg Kirkman."

In answer, I got Ricky's snores. He was where he'd been in the dream, slouched in the corner of the sofa. I was curled against Gabriel, his arm around my waist.

I slid out of Gabriel's grip just enough to rise and press my lips against his. I couldn't help it. I'd often wondered what it'd be like to wake up and lean over and kiss him. To watch those inky lashes flutter against his pale cheek and see the first sliver of those insanely blue eyes and know that he wouldn't jump up in horror, which was kinda important for a proper morning kiss fantasy.

So I kissed him. And those lashes never even fluttered. But his lips did part, just a little, kissing me back, still deep in sleep. I moved against him—

That's when Ricky snored, and I remembered we weren't alone.

I slid out and headed for the kitchen, Lloergan padding after me.

I'd barely opened my laptop browser when I sensed Gabriel behind me. I was about to say something, but he continued to the counter and silently started the coffee machine. I slipped from my chair, eased the kitchen door shut, and crept over behind him. Then I slid between him and the coffee machine, put my arms around his neck, and gave him a proper kiss.

"Sorry," I murmured. "I had to finish that."

"I was hoping you would."

"So you *weren't* sleeping?"

"I was. But the advantage to not dreaming is that if I wake thinking you were kissing me, I can be quite certain you actually were."

"I couldn't resist. You're very kissable."

He chuckled, shaking his head.

"Let me guess," I said. "No one's ever told you that, either?"

"Certainly not. But I'm glad you think so, and I'll make every effort not to disillusion you."

"Good." I gave him a peck on the cheek and then headed for the table. "I woke up realizing we'd forgotten to research the name Seanna gave my father."

"Greg Kirkman. He disappeared twenty years ago."

"Uh, okay. So only one of us forgot."

He handed me the first cup of coffee. "I did a quick search during a spare moment, found that much, and then promptly forgot about him. Which might be even more grievous than your oversight, considering that I discovered he disappeared under mysterious circumstances and *then* forgot."

"We've been busy."

His lips twitched.

"I meant with the sluagh and all the associated drama. But, yes, *that* too. It's very distracting. We might have to stop until the case is solved."

He snorted, not even glancing over to see if I might be serious.

I sipped my coffee and typed one-handed while he brewed himself a cup. When he sat across from me, I glanced up. His eyes were half lidded, that drowsy, unfocused look I'd only seen when he'd been drinking. Or after sex.

"Too sleepy to even read over my shoulder?" I said.

A glimmer of a smile. "I'll enjoy my coffee. I know you'll tell me when you have something."

That, too, was a milestone, not just that he didn't feel the need to watch over my shoulder, but that he wanted to relax with his coffee, not gulp it down as a mere vehicle for the caffeine required to jump-start his day. In that moment, Gabriel seemed happy in a perfectly average way, pleased by nothing more than a quiet morning, fine coffee, and agreeable companionship. It looked good on him. It really did.

It only took a moment to confirm that he was right about Kirkman. The man had gone missing almost twenty years ago.

"A month before the Tysons killed Amanda Mays and Ken Perkins," I said. "I don't like the timing of that."

"It may only mean that Seanna was clever enough to find an open missing person case from the same time period. That would allow her to suggest she had evidence to wrongly accuse your parents of killing Kirkman. Which is exactly the sort of scheme she'd attempt."

"Clever enough to find a case fitting the time frame. Yet not clever enough to realize that Kirkman doesn't fit the pattern. They were convicted for killing couples."

"She could suggest he was murdered with a *secret* lover. It's a ridiculous stretch, but . . ." He shrugged.

"Typical for Seanna."

"Yes." No hint of anxiety or discomfort touched his eyes, as if that coffee contained a generous shot of Irish whiskey. He took my cup and rose to make another, saying, "Keep looking."

"Yes, boss."

I searched while he fixed me a second coffee and added chocolate chip cookies.

"Little early for sweets, isn't it?" I said.

"Carpe diem."

I had to sputter a laugh. For Gabriel, eating cookies for breakfast was indeed seizing the day.

"So, Greg Kirkman," I said, "Thirty-two years old when he disappeared. Never married. Last seen in Chicago. He went out drinking with friends, got in his car, and disappeared."

"Did his route cross any bridges or inconveniently located steep embankments?"

In other words, after that night of drinking and then getting behind the wheel, had the police thought to check anyplace where Kirkman's car might have plunged off the road?

"Actually, that is a possibility," I said. "Kirkman lived outside the city. He was a construction worker and had built his own house in the forest." I ran searches as I spoke. "Which was apparently about five miles from here."

That had Gabriel's coffee cup lowering, his eyes focusing. "Any connection to Cainsville?"

After a few minutes of searching, I shook my head. "Nothing's jumping out. It seems he'd built the place only a few years before he vanished, and he hadn't made any local ties. Only one of the regional papers even mentioned his disappearance."

"City business."

I nodded. Even growing up in the suburbs, there'd been some of that mindset. What happened in the city stayed in the city—that foreign and vaguely sinister place best suited for quick visits to take advantage of the superior shopping and dining. Even after a few years in this region, Kirkman would still have been considered a Chicagoan.

I kept searching, both casting my net wider and zooming in on specifics.

"Lived alone, never married, no local connections," I said. "No known girlfriend or boyfriend. Something of a loner, but sociable enough if he was drinking with friends." More keystrokes. "Or maybe not. Got a longer article here. I missed it because they misspelled his name as Kirkson."

Gabriel rolled his eyes.

"Yes, not exactly fine journalism. It's the archive of a local crime magazine. I use the term loosely. It was one of those mimeographed newsletters mailed out to a couple hundred subscribers. The guy writing it might not have been professional enough to fact-check names, but he fancied himself an investigative reporter and seems to have done some serious digging on this case. He interviewed the guys Kirkman had been drinking with. They were coworkers from a construction job, and they said Kirkman didn't usually join them, but he had that night."

"Hmm."

"Yep, anytime someone acts out of character—and that action leads to trouble—it could be significant. Which may only mean that it's significant in the sense he decided to be more sociable and paid for it with his life, because he wasn't accustomed to driving after a few drinks."

"True."

"It's also possible that this amateur sleuth, in his zeal to tell a good story for his subscribers, made shit up."

"Also true."

"The guy wrote a couple more articles on Kirkman's disappearance. I'll need to double-check them against more reliable . . ." When I trailed off, gaze still fixed on my screen, Gabriel walked behind me to read over my shoulder.

"Hmm," he said.

"Exactly."

It was a quote from Kirkman's neighbor, who said she'd seen a police car in Kirkman's drive twice in the weeks before his disappearance. When the intrepid reporter contacted the state police, they refused to comment, saying it was part of an ongoing investigation.

"And of course it's Saturday," I said. "Which means contacting our police sources will cost extra."

"Do it anyway."

CHAPTER TWENTY-FOUR

I was just about to start making a proper breakfast when the doorbell rang. Veronica stood on the porch, holding a paper bag from the diner.

"Perfect timing," I said.

She brought the bag into the kitchen. When I hovered, she said, "Sit. I might be a terrible cook, but I'm perfectly capable of serving food from boxes." She glanced around. "I saw Ricky's motorcycle. Are the boys around?"

"Ricky's upstairs talking to his dad. Gabriel is taking a shower and . . ."

Footfalls sounded on the steps.

"And he's done." I leaned out of the kitchen. "Can you call Ricky down? Veronica's here with breakfast."

Gabriel's steps reversed.

"I hate secrets," Veronica said, still emptying the bag. "Odd for fae, but my kind simply don't see the point of them."

"Your kind being *coblynau*."

She smiled. "Nice try, but that's one secret I'm forbidden to share."

"I think you kind of did."

"Did I mention I'm terrible at secrets?" She took plates from the cupboard. "Other fae find them delightful. To me, they're just tedious. Dangerous, too. You get knotted up in lies and misdirection until you can't find your way out. That's what's happening here. The elders spent the night in a meeting. Well, all except Patrick, who wasn't in on the original secret, and when he finds out, he'll be rightfully furious, mostly with me, as the one elder he can count on to keep him informed."

She set out a plate stacked with flapjacks. "Disagreeing with secrets in principle does not mean one is exempt from keeping them . . . or from suffering the consequences."

"And this secret concerns the sluagh," Gabriel said as he walked in.

She smiled at him. "Yes, Gabriel, I'll get to the point. I was waiting because it concerns you. Patrick as well, and I considered having him here, but I suspect that's a conversation best had in private, where he can properly tell me what he thinks of me for keeping it from him."

She tried for a wry smile, but the sadness behind it made me curse Ida all the more. Veronica was right. Nothing good comes of secrets. People get hurt, often those who least deserve it.

"And Ricky," she said as he walked in. "Good to see you." There was no sarcasm in her voice—unlike some elders, she treated Ricky like an actual person. "Sit. Eat. You may have little stomach for it by the time I'm through."

"That sounds ominous," I murmured.

"Anything concerning the sluagh is ominous," she said as she pulled out a chair.

"Before you begin," Gabriel said. "As much as I want the truth, I need to ask how much trouble it will cause you to tell us. If you'll suffer for it, I'd rather confront Ida. I do have leverage. I'm quite prepared to use it."

She smiled. "They know I'm here and what I'm doing. I may have lost my temper at about four a.m. Blame a low tolerance for endless meetings and endless bickering. I informed them that I was telling you the truth, and if they had an issue with that, they could banish me." Her smile grew, her sunken eyes twinkling, and I caught a hint of a much younger fae behind them. "Let's just say that's not an option."

"Ida didn't insist on coming along?" I said.

That glint in her eyes sharpened. "She insisted. I told her I'd lock her in the closet and bind her there if she kept insisting. She knows better than to test me. So it's just me, which means we'll get through this much faster." She looked at Gabriel. "Once I actually start saying something useful, right?"

"I believe I was the one who stopped you."

"Which is never wise. Derail a fae in conversation and you'll spend an hour herding her back on track. So, in the interest of *staying* on track, I'll get straight to the point. Thirty-five years ago, we made a bargain with the sluagh. We . . ." Her voice quivered, and her glamour wavered. She took a moment to pull it back. "This is difficult for me. I'm shaken by what happened yesterday morning, and angry at the role we played in it. At our lack of foresight. This will be easier if I don't need to maintain my glamour. I realize that may be disconcerting for you . . ."

"Whatever makes you comfortable," I said.

"Thank you."

Her body shimmered. A pop of light, like a low-voltage flashbulb. Not enough to make me blink but just to lose visual focus for a split second, and when my sight cleared, she sat in her true form.

Veronica looked about Gabriel's age, with curling black hair, tan skin, and green eyes, brighter than usual. She bore little resemblance to the *coblynau* statue in my garden—a squat, ugly gnome. Yet I could see where the caricature might have come from. As in her human form, she was small, particularly for a fae, maybe barely topping five feet. Sturdier than others I'd seen, with a fifties pinup-model figure. Beautiful for a human, perhaps not by fae standards.

She settled in and said, "Back to my story . . . You were not a surprise to us, Olivia, as you may have realized. We knew a Matilda was coming. The signs were there long before you were born. There would be a Matilda for Cainsville. The question that concerned us most was . . ." She looked at Gabriel. "Would there be a Gwynn? While we could still win over a Matilda without one, it introduces an obstacle. Particularly if there is an Arawn for the Cŵn Annwn."

"It would slant the odds."

"Yes. So we called in favors. We made bargains. We gave up some of our already dwindling power to get an answer from those who could give it. Would there be a Gwynn? Would there be an Arawn? The response was exactly what we most dreaded hearing."

"An Arawn but no Gwynn."

She nodded.

"That was the deal you made with the sluagh," I said. "Somehow they were able to guarantee Cainsville a Gwynn."

"They have powers beyond our own. Dark magics. They heard of our dilemma and offered us a deal. They could promise us a Gwynn. In return for a favor."

"That you give them Olivia," Gabriel said, barely able to force the words out. "She is marked for the sluagh."

Veronica's green eyes rounded. "Absolutely not. We promised them no one. Nor any power over either of you. That would be unthinkable."

"So what did you give them?" Ricky said.

"Access to Grace's building," I murmured. "It's a refuge for fae. You give them asylum there."

"Yes."

"And you allowed Olivia to move in?" Gabriel said. "You let her—"

"We granted access to the building for one manifested sluagh who had been injured and could not cross back to its own dimension."

"Manifested?" I said. "A high-ranking one, then. A powerful sluagh."

"Yes, but we only granted it five years of access, on the understanding that it would not provide us with a Gwynn until the *end* of those five years. We didn't want the sluagh in Cainsville after he was here. Of course, that didn't work out as we'd hoped, and you did not grow up here, Gabriel, but the sluagh was still gone before you were born."

"Except it left a door open," I said. "So it could come back."

Veronica let out a bitter laugh. "A mere child sees what we did not." She shook her head. "Sorry. I know you aren't a child, but compared to us, you are, and the fact you can see what they did is only all the more damning."

"But I have the hindsight of *knowing* it came back. I'm just making the logical connection."

"Still, we should have foreseen the possibility that we'd been tricked. They are sluagh, after all."

Ricky pushed his plate aside. "So you guys let it board at Grace's, and it kept the key when it left."

"You granted access once," Gabriel said, "which inadvertently granted it permanently."

"Yes and yes," Veronica said. "In order to allow a sluagh to stay at Grace's, I had to undo some of my wards. Of course, I reactivated them afterwards, but it seems that once it had been allowed in, the wards were no longer effective against that particular sluagh. It had the key, so to speak."

"Like vampire lore," Gabriel said. "Once they are invited in, you can't rescind the invitation and your wards are no longer effective."

"Looks like you finally get vampires," I said to him. "I know you've been waiting."

He sighed.

I turned to Veronica. "Okay, so you guys made a deal with the sluagh to get Gabriel. That deal granted the sluagh access to Cainsville. I know you're kicking yourselves for not foreseeing the trickery, but what's done is done, and neither of us was harmed by the sudden appearance of the scary sluagh, so presuming you can keep them out now, we're okay, right?"

"*Can* you keep them out?" Ricky said. "Is Liv safe here?"

"Yes, we need to know that," Gabriel said. "We also need to know what the sluagh meant when they said Olivia was theirs. The implication is that there *is* a mark. I looked for it on Olivia and—" He stopped short. "That is to say, I looked as best I could, on her arms and such, and I did not see it."

"Do you know what it looks like?" Ricky asked Veronica.

"I do."

"Can you check Liv?"

"Of course."

"You aren't marked," Veronica said as she finished her examination in my bedroom and I began redressing. "If I sound less relieved about that than you'd expect, it's only because the sluagh wouldn't dare take a Matilda."

"So they're bluffing?"

"No," Gabriel said from outside the closed door. "They simply don't mean it in that way."

"You can stop hovering and come in, Gabriel," Veronica called. "She's dressed. Though even if she wasn't, I don't think it's anything you haven't already seen."

I looked over at her sharply. She chuckled. "It's rather hard to miss the signs."

"Great," I muttered.

"The other elders aren't as astute at reading those signs. You can buy yourself some time yet. I won't spoil it." She turned to Gabriel as he walked in. "Yes, you're correct. If they said they have some hold over Liv, it means something other than the obvious."

"I'd say that's a relief," I said. "But I suspect whatever they *do* mean, I'm not going to like it a whole lot more."

"We will resolve this," Veronica said. "We owe you that."

CHAPTER TWENTY-FIVE

The elders were letting us leave town, on the understanding we'd return at night. The next step was to speak to Ioan about the sluagh. I now suspected the local Cŵn Annwn had more dealings with them than Ioan was letting on. And I suspected one of those "dealings" might be a bargain made twenty-three years ago, to see human killers punished and a broken Matilda healed.

Ricky was about to make that call when Gabriel got one from the state police contact I'd set on Greg Kirkman's trail. While Gabriel talked and jotted down dates and names, I typed them into a search engine.

"Greg Kirkman was being investigated for murder," I said when he hung up. "Multiple murders."

Ricky skimmed the articles on my screen. "He was a serial killer."

Gabriel cleared his throat.

"Sorry, counselor," Ricky said. "Kirkman was an *alleged* serial killer. Three missing teenage girls disappeared along rural roads. Two were discovered in shallow graves, raped and strangled. The third wasn't found, presumably because the killer learned to hide his victims better. Classic serial predator. And Kirkman fits the classic profile—the quiet white guy who lives alone. The last girl disappeared a month before he did. There were no more after that. Which suggests he was more than a suspect."

Gabriel conceded the point. "The police believed Kirkman was responsible and that he committed suicide somewhere in the forest, perhaps having gone for drinks to prepare himself. They continued to investigate the murders but found no other suspects. They did eventually locate and identify the third victim—her body was found buried a few miles from his home."

"Which was near Cainsville," Ricky said.

"That's not the only local connection." I enlarged another article. "The second victim disappeared during a summer visit to extended family, who lived . . ."

"Here," Ricky murmured as he read. "In Cainsville."

Ricky borrowed my car to take Lloergan to the Saints' clubhouse. He had work there, and our new "next step" wasn't something he could help with.

There were three people we could confront about Greg Kirkman. Four, if you included Seanna, but we had no idea where to find her. The question was which to choose. Which wasn't really a question at all.

An hour later, I was back where I'd first been stalled. And where I'd first known I was being thwarted but had gotten too caught up in the sluagh business to pursue it.

"Greg Kirkman," I said as Pamela took her seat across from me.

"I told you, Eden, I don't know—"

"Try again."

Pamela's lips tightened. "This woman—Seanna—is sending you on a wild-goose chase, and I can't believe you're allowing it. She's an idiot with just enough animal intelligence to know where to strike. Where it will hurt. For you, that's your father.

You need to guard your weaknesses more carefully, or your enemies will never stop using them against you." She sat back in her seat. "I see Gabriel isn't with you. I'm going to interpret that to mean he's tried to dissuade you from this path, knowing his mother and her schemes. As much as I hate to say it, he's right. Drop this, Eden."

"Can't. Not until I have answers."

She let out a hiss of frustration. "You're better than this. You have blind spots. You need to recognize them and—"

"Oh, but I do. I recognize them, and I work to overcome them. Sometimes I'm even successful, like when I finally realized I couldn't trust you to tell me the sky is blue. You fancy yourself a good mother, Pamela. Tough love. Preparing me for a harsh world. Like criticizing me when I'm making mistakes, when I'm not fulfilling my potential, not as clever as you expect."

"You *are* clever. That's the point. You aren't utilizing your intelligence—"

"Do you know what's worse than telling your kid that you're disappointed in her? Using that to manipulate her. Telling her she's made a stupid mistake, when in fact she hasn't—you're just trying to grind her self-confidence into the dust so she'll stop chasing questions you don't want answered."

Her face hardened. "I am trying to stop you from making a mistake, Olivia."

"Yep, you are. Except that 'mistake' isn't chasing a false lead. It's following it to a conclusion *you* don't want me reaching."

"You—"

"If you hate fae so much, stop acting like one. Stop manipulating and diverting and distracting. You don't know anything about Greg Kirkman? I'll refresh your memory. He killed three young women and then disappeared shortly before you went after the Tysons. All signs point to him as the guy who murdered those girls. One of his victims was from Cainsville. She had fae blood—I've confirmed that, which would make her killer a Cŵn Annwn target."

"What does that have to do with your father?"

"You made a deal with the Cŵn Annwn. That much is undisputed fact. But the details aren't entirely clear, like how you contacted them in the first place. It's not like you can look them up in the Yellow Pages. You know what Cainsville is now, but you didn't when you were growing up."

"How do you—?"

"I have visions, remember? I've seen you in them, as a child."

Her composure rippled. "You've seen—?"

"You only got the full picture once you made that deal. Maybe not even then. So how did you make contact?"

"I'd heard things, growing up. I figured out what Cainsville was."

"Bullshit."

"You asked, Olivia, so I answered—"

"With a lie, which comes as naturally to you as breathing, so I won't take it personally. I think my father knew his lineage. He knew what the Cŵn Annwn could do. So he told you. You realized that was my best hope. The problem was how to contact the Hunt. I mentioned those visions of mine. They give me all sorts of tidbits, pieces that seem random but eventually come in handy. Like this one I had of a guy trying to contact the Cŵn Annwn. He interrupted their hunt. He knew their target and waited for the Huntsmen. That's one method. A better one? Find someone who fits their criteria and do the job for them. Someone like Greg Kirkman. That's how you contacted the Cŵn Annwn, isn't it? You and my father killed him—"

"Not your father. Just me."

"Then why did Seanna visit him?"

"Because she's an idiot. How many times do I need to say that?"

I paused, then said, "You killed Greg Kirkman."

"Yes. I found him. I killed him to lure the Cŵn Annwn, while providing them with a gift and a sign of my willingness and ability to do more of the same."

"So you admit to this, yet when I accused you and Todd of killing the other four, you said you weren't responsible. You blamed him."

She flinched. "It wasn't like that."

"It was exactly like that, Pamela. You said my father did it. That he loved me so much he did that for me. You threw my father under the bus to save yourself."

"No, I said it because you love him."

I stared at her. "You accused him out of jealousy?"

"Of course not. You've always loved him more, and I never blamed either of you for that. He is easy to love. I am not. I accused him out of panic. Obviously, I didn't think it through, or I'd know you'd get to the truth eventually and hate me for the lie. All I thought at the time was that you loved him and so you would forgive him, as you would not forgive me. You would understand he did it out of love. With me? Nothing I can say will convince you I did it for you. You cannot forgive me."

"But I have."

A bitter laugh. "Ah, yes, I can tell."

"I forgive you for killing four people because they were killers. If their deaths let me walk? I'm okay with that. What I cannot forgive you for is James and Gabriel. The death of a man I loved. The attempt to ruin the life of a man I love."

"Love? Gabriel?" Her spine snapped straight. "I hope you're saying that to taunt me, Eden."

"I'm saying it to drive home exactly how much I hate you for doing that to him. You say I loved you less, Pamela? Maybe so.

But I did love you. I might still. Yet it'll never erase what you did and how much it hurt me." I got to my feet. "One last question. How did you find out about Greg Kirkman?"

She stared at the table, eyes unfocused, as if she heard my words but couldn't relate them to anything we'd been discussing.

"Greg Kirkman," I said. "How did you know he'd be a Cŵn Annwn target?"

"Because he killed a girl with fae blood. I heard talk in Cainsville." She settled in, finding her balance now. "The elders are careful, but once you know what they are, you understand more of what you overhear, as I'm sure you've realized. I knew there was a serial killer, and one of his victims was partly fae, which meant the Hunt would want him."

"But Kirkman wasn't charged with any crimes. The police had barely begun investigating him. How did you know *he* was the killer?"

"I heard the elders speculating. I did some digging and then confronted him and tricked him into a confession. I killed him, and the Cŵn Annwn came."

I sat in Gabriel's car, still parked in the prison visitors' lot. He'd been waiting in the hall. I hadn't said a word as we walked out, nor once we got into the car, and while I could feel his impatience strumming, there was too much going on in my head.

It felt like I was under a cliff, an avalanche rumbling above, and I was frantically trying to figure out what to do next, where to run, one eye on those trembling rocks and Gabriel standing in the distance, motioning that he needed to speak to me.

Wait. Just wait. Let me figure this out first.

Once I got my thoughts as ordered as I could, I turned to him and said, "Sorry. I'm just . . ."

"Busy."

I nodded.

"Did Pamela confirm your theory?" he asked.

"Yes."

"And . . ."

I said nothing, just stared out the window.

After a moment, he said, "Olivia?"

"I need to get another answer."

"One you don't want."

"Yes."

Silence. A squeak of the leather. A sigh, the softest exhale of frustration, not meant for me to hear.

"I'm sorry," I said.

"Don't be." A slight snap to the words. "Whatever it is, the prospect upsets you, and you don't want to discuss it until you know if there is cause for you to be upset. Do you wish to speak to Ricky? He's still at the clubhouse. I have business I could discuss with Don."

I shook my head. "No. I just want to get through this. As quickly as possible." I took out my phone and hit a recent addition to my speed-dial.

"Ioan," I said when he answered. "I need to talk to my father."

I braced for some lightly sarcastic comment to call attention to my lack of preamble. But Ioan wasn't Patrick. He could tell by my tone that I was upset.

"Are you being blocked again?" he said. "I thought I had that straightened out."

"No, I mean I need to see him in person. Face-to-face. In private, if possible."

He paused.

"I know you have access and contacts in the prison," I said. "I also know this isn't easy to arrange or I'd have asked sooner. This isn't me deciding I really need to hug my dad."

"I know if you're asking, it's important. You need something from him. An answer, I presume?"

"Yes."

A pause. A long one. Then, "Is it one I could give?"

"Yes, but I need it from him."

Another pause. Then his voice lowered, gentler. "Is it one he'd want to give you, Liv?"

"No, but I need it. Directly from him. And yes, that's cruel and he doesn't deserve cruelty, but I need all the answers and he needs to know I have them. No more secrets."

"I agree. All right. I can't promise this will be ready when you arrive, but I'll do my best."

Once I got off the phone, those rocks overhead stopped shaking and chattering. I knew they were still there. I hadn't averted disaster. I just had a moment to pause and reflect and say to myself, *What will I do if they come tumbling down?* Because they almost certainly would. That breathing room, though, was enough for me to turn to Gabriel and tell him my thoughts, my fears. To do it dry-eyed and steady-voiced.

When I finished, he said, "Thank you. For telling me." A moment of silence. Then, "Is there anything I can do to help?"

I tensed. I tried to hide it, but he'd already noticed.

"And the fact that I need to ask is indicative of the problem," he said, his hands tightening on the steering wheel.

"No, I—"

"Please don't lie to make this easier on me. It's about making it easier for you. I should know how to do that. Asking you is like watching someone drown and asking if I can help."

"I'd like to talk it out. *That* will help. Is my logic correct?"

"Yes." He glanced over. "Which is not what you want to hear. Your logic is correct. I'm less certain on your interpretation of the aftermath. But you're looking for the worst scenario. To brace yourself against it."

"Yes. Thank you."

When he didn't say anything more, I glanced up to see a look I knew well. He had more he had to say and wasn't sure he should.

"What is it?" I asked.

He hesitated.

"Gabriel . . ." I said.

He cleared his throat. "If you discover you are correct in the basic facts, it would only be discomforting. If you are right about the rest—which is your worst scenario rather than an honest fear—it will be difficult and upsetting. Yet . . ."

"Yes?"

"It isn't what you may discover that has you so upset. It's what you'll need to do to get those answers."

Tears prickled my eyelids, and I laid my head against him again to hide it, nodding instead.

"I do understand, Olivia," he said. "Just because I could do it myself without experiencing the same emotional response does not mean I can't place myself in your position."

"I know."

"You've made the right decision. I only wish you didn't need to do this."

I twisted to kiss his cheek. "Thank you."

CHAPTER TWENTY-SIX

I told Ioan I didn't want this meeting for something as fanciful as hugging my father. That was true. And yet that wish wasn't as fanciful as I liked to pretend. I had not hugged my father in twenty-three years. It didn't matter if, for most of those, I'd forgotten he even existed. Willfully forgotten, pushing aside the painful memories of a toddler who knew only that her beloved father had left her and so she banished him in punishment.

Now that I had Todd back, I felt every one of those years of separation. Seeing him through a Plexiglas barrier made me feel like a chained dog, going mad watching my goal only a few feet away, unattainable.

I had no idea what strings Ioan had to pull, but we'd been at the prison less than an hour before a guard came to take us through. A guard who I knew, instinctively, was not really a guard at all.

"Thank Ioan for me," I said as the man led us, wordlessly, down a hall. "And thank you."

The guard snorted. "You can thank me by getting Todd out of here. Which will get us both out. It's been a long twenty years."

"You've been here since—"

"It was the best way to help him. And I shouldn't complain. *I* get to go home every day."

"Does Todd know you're . . . ?"

"That wouldn't be safe for either of us." He opened a door and led us through. "He only knows I've been here a long time, and we get along well. With Todd, that isn't very difficult. I expected I'd have to use my powers to make the other guards go easy on him, but that's never been a problem. Which doesn't mean it's *been* easy on him." Anger laced his voice and he shoved the next door open a little harder. "All she had to do was confess. All she *still* has to do is confess."

"He wants her to have a chance."

"Too bad. This isn't about her. She made the deal. If you do that, you take responsibility for the outcome. You don't drag someone else along. He didn't deserve that."

One last door opened. We walked through and . . . he was there. My father. Standing right in front of me, nothing between us.

When I walked in, his face was tight, as if braced for an official to say there'd been a mistake and order him back to his cell before I arrived.

Even when he saw me, it took a moment. A pause. A blink. Then a blinding grin, and he stepped toward me, his arms wide.

The young guard accompanying him warned, "Todd. . ." and the Huntsman growled, "Don't be an ass, Porter."

And then Todd was hugging me. My father was hugging me.

No, not my father. My dad. His arms went around me, and it was as if every repressed memory broke free. The feel of his embrace, the rasp of his cheek against mine, the sound of his breathing, the smell of him—it was everything I'd been missing sitting on the other side of that Plexiglas. That full sense of the man I remembered, my little-girl's daddy.

When he pulled back and said, "It's so good to see you, sweetheart," even his voice was different, plucked straight from my memory, the one I'd heard through the speaker a poor reproduction.

And I cried. I hugged him, and I cried. Gabriel stayed behind me. The young guard stepped aside, taking a great interest in the decor, until the Huntsman guard said, "I've got this, Porter," and the younger man left without another word.

I moved back, and we walked to the chairs and sat, Todd pulling his chair around until we sat face to face, no table between us.

That's when I remembered why I was there. What I'd come to do. That little girl inside me screamed a tantrum shriek of a no. Not now. Not ever. Don't do this. Don't upset him. Don't ruin it.

But I am my mother's daughter, as much as I would like to deny it. I had a goal, and I needed to reach it, even if that might be cruel, might be painful.

No, it *was* cruel. It *would be* painful.

"Dad?" I said. "I need to ask you about someone."

"Sure, sweetheart. Who?"

"Greg Kirkman."

Did I want to see his brow furrow, lips purse, that look in his eyes that said he had no idea what I was talking about? Of course I did. But I knew better.

What did I expect to see? Fear. Fear of his secret being discovered.

Instead, he jerked back as if I'd struck him, and then his face flooded with pain and guilt, so raw that I flinched.

I looked up at Gabriel and said, "I can't. I just can't," and waited for the flash of disappointment, the tightening of his face as he told me I had to.

Instead, Gabriel just gave me a piercing look. Then he nodded and walked over and took my hand and said, "All right."

I panicked then, an explosion of panic, because I *wanted* him to say I had to do this. I needed his push, needed his strength and, yes, the ice-cold resolve I couldn't muster. He squeezed my hand and turned to Todd.

"I'm sorry," Gabriel said to him. Then he laid my hand on Todd's arm and asked, "What happened with Greg Kirkman?"

The prison room vanished, and I was slingshot through memory, lights and images and sounds whizzing past. I landed in the grass, on my back, the sun dancing in front of me. Then the sun became a daisy, petals falling on my face.

"What will my husband be?" It was Todd's voice, rhyming off choices as the petals fell. "Tinker, tailor, soldier, sailor, rich-man, poor-man, beggar-man, thief." When the daisy moved, I saw his face, even younger than I was now. "Looks like you get a thief, Eden. That's unfortunate."

He picked another daisy. I reached one chubby hand for the flower.

"Uh!" I said.

"Nope, gotta use your words, sweetheart."

"Uhhh!"

He smiled. "Louder doesn't count. Come on, now. You know the word. It's your favorite."

"Want!"

Another laugh. "And there it is."

"Want. Dada. Want."

He handed me the flower and picked another one, plucking petals onto me. "What will I be? Lady, baby, gypsy, queen." He paused. "Is that how it goes? Your mom's so much better at these."

"Sounds fine to me," a woman's voice said.

Todd sat up fast.

"What a pretty little girl. She has your hair and smile. Is Daddy babysitting today, honey?"

"No." A chill crept into Todd's voice. "I'm taking care of my child."

The woman laughed. "That's what I meant. Oh, she's so sweet." The woman bent beside me, but the sun blocked her face so all I could see was shadow. Her voice sounded vaguely familiar, but Todd didn't seem to know her.

"We should probably—" he began.

"This is such a lovely park. I'll have to bring my husband by."

Todd relaxed at the mention of a husband. He was a good-looking, doting young daddy. Biological catnip, and he was probably accustomed to ducking female attention. He picked me up, his hands under my armpits, and dandled me, my feet touching the ground. He let me dance the only way I could, supported where my legs failed. I shrieked and wriggled with excitement.

"Edie dance!" I crowed. "Edie dance!"

He chuckled. "Yes, Eden is an *awesome* dancer."

"She's such a sweetie," the woman said. "It's too bad about her legs."

He tensed, and I swore I felt a chilly comeback rise, but he swallowed it and said, "It's spina bifida."

"Such a shame. A beautiful, broken baby."

Todd scooped me up, ignoring my flailing protests as he held me against his chest, and rose to his feet.

"My daughter is dealing with a physical challenge," he said. "She is otherwise healthy and happy, and she will be fine, thank you very much."

"But she'll never live up to her potential. What if she *could* be a dancer? A prima ballerina? You think about that. I know you must."

Her voice faded as Todd grabbed the diaper bag and walked away. I tried to see her over his shoulder, but he held me too tight, shielding me.

"What if I said she could be fixed?" The woman's voice came clear again as she caught up. "What would you give to fix her?"

"I'm not interested in whatever you're selling."

"What I'm selling is hope."

He snorted, the sound rippling through him. "For a hundred bucks an ounce, I'm sure. Some cream to rub on her back. Some herbal drops for her to take each night. Is this what you do? Lurk around parks trying to drum up business with desperate parents? If my daughter wasn't here, I'd—"

"You'd let me know what you think of me." The woman chuckled. "You have a bit of a temper, don't you, Todd?"

He stiffened, still walking. "How do you know my—?"

"What do you know of the Wild Hunt, Todd?"

He picked up speed.

"You're familiar with the stories, aren't you?" she continued. "Because in your family, they aren't stories. They're history. Like having the phone number of a third cousin in the White House, who might be able to help if you really need it, but you have to really need it, or you don't dare call. The difference? You have no way of getting in touch with the Hunt. You know they exist. You know their blood runs in your veins. You know they have power—the power to do things like heal a broken baby."

Todd kept walking, but he had slowed, listening.

"What if I gave you that phone number?" she asked.

I felt Todd's heart beat faster. Then his arms tightened around me. "Sure. Just sign over the deed on my house, and you'll give me a number to a pay phone in Milwaukee."

"Don't be cynical, Todd. It doesn't suit you. I don't have an actual number. Even if I did, they'd never answer. You need to get their attention. I'm here to tell you how."

"And why would you do that?"

"Because the Huntsmen will appreciate me putting you in touch with them. I can say no more than that. They will be pleased, and they will owe me for the introduction. Speaking of introductions, I believe you know a man named Gregory Kirkman?"

"Who?"

A rustle of paper, and when I craned my neck, I saw the woman show Todd a photo.

"Sure. I worked a job with him, building cabinets for a house his crew was renovating."

"Good with a saw, I take it?"

"Huh?"

"He's good with a saw."

Another rustle of paper. Todd looked at whatever she held, and then staggered away, his hand going to the back of my head, nearly crushing my face to his chest.

"Jesus, what kind of sick—"

"Yes, that's the question. What kind of sick fuck does that?"

"Don't swear—"

"In front of Eden?" The woman laughed. "She's too young to understand, just as she's too young to comprehend that photograph. It *is* graphic. I should have warned you. But I wanted you to see what your friend Mr. Kirkman does in his spare time."

"He's not my friend. I worked one job with the guy."

"Sorry, I was being facetious, and this isn't the time."

"I don't know if this is some really sick prank or you are actually telling me Kirkman did . . . did that. If he did, I'm not the person you need to show it to. That goes to the police."

"Or the Wild Hunt."

"You want me to take that to them? But the point is that I can't make contact."

"They'd come if you killed him."

"*What?*"

"If you kill Greg Kirkman, following my instructions, the Hunt will come. He is on their list. They haven't been able to take him. If you do that for them, they will come and—"

"And what? Grant me a fucking wish?" Todd patted the back of my head, bouncing me, whispering, "Sorry, sorry." Then, to the woman, "I don't know what this is, but I'm walking away, and I would strongly suggest you don't follow me."

He set out.

She kept talking. "The proof is in this folder, Todd. The police files on two dead girls. There's a third victim the police haven't found. Three dead young women. Someone's daughters. Imagine if it was—"

He wheeled. "Don't say it. Don't you dare say it."

"I don't need to. I'm going to put this folder down right here. Take it. See the files. Read the proof I assembled. Conduct your own research—I don't expect you to execute a killer on a stranger's say-so. Draw your own conclusions. Then see the proof with your own eyes. I mentioned a third girl. He goes to visit her body every Friday. He can't help himself. That file shows where to find her. Go there, wait for him, confront him, and end his miserable life. If you do that, the Hunt will come."

Todd got as far as the parking lot. Then he sat me on the hood of the car and dangled a toy, whispering to me, "It's okay, it's okay. We'll go home. Mommy will be there and everything will be fine. Just . . ."

I whimpered, picking up on his anxiety.

His gaze swiveled to the park. A long pause. Then, with a kiss on my forehead, he scooped me up, strode back, and grabbed the folder.

CHAPTER TWENTY-SEVEN

That whirlwind hit again, memories whipping past. Then I was walking through a forest. It was night, and I had a flashlight in my pocket, but I didn't take it out. I could see well enough, even if it was only a quarter moon above. I could always see fine, and even when the clouds hid that moon, my feet instinctively stayed on the path.

A rustle sounded as I pulled something from my pocket, unwrapping it and popping it into my mouth. A mint, despite the fact my mouth already tasted of mint. My stomach twisted, and I chewed as I walked, knowing I should let the candy last, but I needed something to do, something to focus on. Swallow the mint. Unwrap another.

I remembered when I'd first gone to see Todd, making my way through a whole pack of spearmint gum, one stick after another, both to give me something to do and to calm my queasy stomach. This felt the same, anxiety making my stomach churn, breath coming hard.

"Stupid. Fucking stupid. I shouldn't be here."

I muttered the words, but the voice I heard was Todd's.

I should be at home, with Pam and Eden. No, I should be out with Pam. It's date night.

I'd had to make an excuse, and I'd seen the worry on Pam's face.

"If you want to go out for a drink with the guys, you can just tell me that," she'd said.

"No, course not. It's work."

She'd been quiet for a moment. Then, "You're happy, right?"

"What? Sure. Of course."

"I know it's tough on you, working two jobs, worrying about Eden, the medical bills, the mortgage. I worry . . ."

"You worry what? I'm going to get fed up and walk out? Jesus, Pam. If you can even think that, I'm doing something wrong."

"It's just . . . the last couple of weeks. You've seemed . . . stressed."

I'd hugged her and told her it was just a tough job—demanding client—and everything was fine.

I hated lying to her. Hated it. Sucked at it, too. But I'd been careful, setting up my alibi, going to the shop and doing some work before slipping out the back and riding my old bicycle the ten miles to the forest.

I finally reached the spot. I knew she was here—the third victim. I'd come out two days ago and found her hidden under a tree fall. I didn't check again. Didn't ever want to see that again. My stomach lurched, and I chewed another mint, wishing I'd brought antacids instead.

I should take this to the police. Take the file and my own research and anonymously submit it.

But that wouldn't help Eden.

Shit, did I really think *this* could help Eden?

I swallowed and hunkered down to wait. Twice I thought I heard a sound and jumped back into the shadows. But no one came. The third time, I almost didn't bother, chalking it up to paranoia. Then the sound turned into the clomping of boots.

A moment later, Kirkman appeared. Sweat poured off him, and he stank of booze. He swayed as he walked, grabbing trees for support.

"Shouldn't be out here," Kirkman muttered. "Shouldn't, shouldn't, shouldn't."

I stifled a humorless laugh. *Yeah, you and me both, asshole.*

Kirkman walked straight to the tree fall. He took a deep breath, shaking so hard I could see it. Then he pulled back a branch, and when he exhaled, it was almost orgasmic, and I pulled the hunting knife from its sheath without even realizing what I was doing, rage filling me, a rage that wasn't hot and blind but cold and focused, like nothing I'd ever felt before.

Up until this moment, I'd made excuses for him. Not for the murders—nothing could excuse those horrors. But I'd told myself it wasn't him. Despite all the evidence, it wasn't Kirkman, but just some fae trick.

I'd heard enough stories growing up to understand that fae weren't innocent little creatures with wings and pixie dust. They were amoral, unethical, cruel, sometimes even what we'd call evil in their complete disregard for others. This might be some fae's idea of a joke—promise me the one thing I wanted most and force me to kill an innocent man.

Even when Kirkman pulled back the branch, I still hoped. I knew him. Not well. Not at all well. But the idea that I could have met and worked alongside a monster, might have shown him pictures of Pam, of Eden . . .

I wanted to think if I ever met someone capable of doing this to another person, I'd see it in his eyes. But then I heard Kirkman's deep sigh of pleasure, and that rage filled me, and I started forward, gripping the knife.

A twig cracked behind me. I spun. So did Kirkman, stumbling, drunk, then falling and saying, "Who's there?" in a shrill voice.

I scanned the dark forest but saw no one. An animal, I supposed.

I turned back to Kirkman, still on the ground. I slid the knife into its sheath, my hand still on it, under my jacket. Then I eased forward.

"Greg," I said.

He blinked hard, struggling to focus. "T-Todd? You're . . . the carpentry guy, right? No." A sharp shake of his head. "Too much to drink. Too fucking much to drink."

"It's me, Greg. It's Todd. I know what's under that tree. I know about the other two. I know everything."

His jaw worked. Then his eyes rounded. "You. It was you. How—how—" He pushed to his feet and looked around. "Where is it?"

"Where's what?"

"The dog. The huge dog."

"You mean the hound?" I took a guess. "A big black hound with red eyes?"

He swallowed and nodded. "Every time I come in the forest, it's here. I *live* in the fucking forest. How am I supposed to stay out of it? But I did." A high-pitched giggle. "I figured out that the dog only follows me in here. So I stayed out."

I looked at the surrounding woods. "Yeah . . ."

He ran his tongue over his lips. "It's my day. My time to visit her. I thought maybe if I hung out with some guys, had a few drinks, I wouldn't need to come here. But I did."

"Why?" I asked, and I knew now the question was pointless. It was like asking the theoretical background to a quantum physics tenet when I'd barely gotten my high school diploma. No answer Kirkman could give would make any sense to me. It couldn't.

"Why not?"

That was what he said, and I blinked, sure I'd misheard.

"I mean that," I said, waving at the deadfall, not even able to look at the poor girl's body. "Why?"

"And that was my answer. Why not?" Kirkman rose, his sweat drying in the cold night air. "You've thought of it. I know you have. Everyone does. We just don't like to admit it. It isn't *right*." A derisive twist and lip curl to the last word.

I couldn't answer. I didn't even know the words to answer.

Kirkman leaned against a tree. "You think about it. In school, that pretty girl who let you put your hand up her shirt and then said no. The one on the street wearing the shirt that shows off her tits and then she scowls when she catches you staring. Even that pretty wife of yours, when she pisses you off. You think about it."

"Think about . . . what?"

I knew what he seemed to mean. But I thought I must be wrong. I glanced toward the deadfall, felt my stomach clench at the memory of what I'd seen in there.

"That?" I said, barely able to get the word out. "You honestly believe normal people think about . . ." I couldn't finish.

"Don't be coy, Todd. That's why you're here instead of calling the police. You're curious. You want validation. Someone to say it's okay if you feel the same way. If you want to do the same thing. If you look at her"—a chin jerk toward the deadfall—"and you like what you see."

"You sick *fuck*."

Kirkman's face hardened. "You're the one who came out here. Tell me you didn't like looking at her. Tell me it didn't excite you, just a little. Tell me you didn't, for one second, imagine your wife there."

Yes, I had. I'd seen that girl—what had once been a girl—and thought of her life. Thought of her family. Thought, *What if it was Pamela? What if it was Eden? How would I ever sleep again, when every time I closed my eyes, I'd think of what they'd suffered?*

"Yes," I said slowly, feeling that cold rage seep through my veins. "I thought of my wife under those branches. I thought of what I'd want to do to the man who put her there."

I saw the blade slash without even realizing I'd pulled it from its sheath. Saw blood spurt. Saw Kirkman fall backward. Then I fell on him. I stabbed him over and over until he stopped moving. Until he completely stopped moving.

I stood there, and I wasn't heaving breath, wasn't shaking, wasn't doing anything I *should* be doing. That rage slid away, and even to call it rage felt like an excuse. I'd known what I was doing. I'd done it intentionally, deliberately. Gregory Kirkman deserved to die, so I killed him.

When that ice in my gut thawed, I looked down at the bloody mess of his chest, the blood splattered over me, over the bushes, over everything. I saw that, and I pictured the body in the deadfall.

What makes me any different?

I threw up. Vomited, crouched on all fours, dry heaving when nothing more would come. I caught my breath, leaves crackled behind me, and I didn't jump up. Didn't even think to run.

I'd been caught. I deserved that. Whatever happened now, I deserved it.

But the woods fell silent again. Finally, I rose, wiping my mouth and looking down on the body of Gregory Kirkman.

I need to summon the Hunt.

I shook my head. I couldn't. Just couldn't.

Then what had I done this for? To stop him, yes, but I still needed to do what I came for, and if I'd made a mistake, I had to let the Hunt punish me and pray it would be an invisible death, that I would vanish and my daughter would never know what I'd done. Yes, that was cowardice, but it was all I could hope for. That if I deserved to die for this, Eden could keep her memories of her father untarnished.

I started following the instructions the woman had given me. Mark the body like this. Carve a tree like this. Draw a symbol in the dirt like this.

I hadn't even finished before I heard the thunder of hooves and baying of hounds. I backed away from the body and my vomit, and I sat on the path with my knees pulled up.

Then I stopped. Was I going to huddle on the ground in fear? No. I'd made a choice. There was no denying that.

I rose, and then I stood there and waited. Finally, through the trees, I saw the dark shapes of the hounds, the red glow of their eyes. The beasts stayed in the shadows. Waiting for their Huntsmen.

Hooves pounded, and horses snorted, and fire flickered through the trees. That was all I saw: dancing flames. Then a giant black stallion charged down the path. A stallion with red eyes and a flaming mane and burning hooves.

I stood my ground and waited for those hooves to trample me. To run me down where I stood. But at the last moment, the hooded rider yanked the reins and pulled the horse up short.

I couldn't see the man's eyes. Couldn't see his face at all. Just the hood and blackness below.

That hood turned from me to Gregory's body and back again. The Huntsman dismounted. He walked to the deadfall and reached to pull a branch aside.

"Don't—!" I began. Then I realized that was a stupid thing to say. These were men who'd seen such things before. But the Huntsman still recoiled and let out a snort, not unlike his horse's as the huge beast stamped the ground inches from Kirkman's head.

The Huntsman returned to the path. He looked at Kirkman's body and then at the symbol on the tree and the half-drawn one in the dirt. Finally, he looked at me, and while I still couldn't see his eyes, I could feel them boring into mine.

"Todd Larsen," he said.

"Y-yes, sir."

"You found and dispatched our prey. I presume those summoning symbols mean you wish something in return."

I told him what I wanted. Then I waited for him to laugh. To mock me. Scorn me. Or just turn and walk away.

Instead, he said, "Spina bifida . . ."

"Yes, sir. It's a condition—"

"I know what it is. A failure of completion. What is the name of the child's mother?"

I hesitated. I didn't want to tell him, but that was stupid—he could find out easily enough.

"Pamela."

"Family name?"

"Bowen."

He went still, and when he looked at me, I saw the shape of a face under that cowl. "Bowen? Where is her family from?"

"She grew up in Chicago, but her family is from a little town near here."

"Which town?"

"Cainsville."

The Huntsman exhaled. Silence. Then he nodded. "We can do this for you."

"Wh-what?"

"We can heal your daughter. There will, however, be a price. A blood price."

I looked at Kirkman's corpse.

"More than that, I'm afraid," the Huntsman said. "But I can assure you, they will all be equally deserving. The magic you need requires blood sacrifice. The exact nature of those sacrifices does not matter, so we will find you those whom we would take ourselves, had they committed crimes within our purview."

"*They* . . ." I swallowed, tasting vomit and bile and blood. "How many?"

Even as I said the words, my brain rebelled. Shouted that even one more was too much, that I could not do this again, could *not*.

The Huntsman didn't answer, and when I looked up, he was searching my face again.

"How many?" I repeated.

"I would need to make the proper inquiries and determine the sacrifice required. It will be more than one. Likely more than two."

I can't. I'm sorry, I just . . .

"It would not need to be like this," he said, his voice softer. "You were angry here. These would be fitting executions of killers who, like this man, cannot be allowed to live or they will continue killing."

I nodded. That's all I could manage. Nod, even as my brain screamed that I couldn't do it.

"Think on it," the Huntsman said. "While I conduct my investigations, you give it more thought. Meet me back here in a week, and we will discuss it further."

I nodded, and the Huntsman backed away, leaving me staring at Kirkman's bloodied corpse.

CHAPTER TWENTY-EIGHT

I rose from Todd's memories slowly, almost groggily. I could see light and moved toward it until the light became a room, and I was sitting in front of him, and he was staring at me, his eyes round with horror, my hand still on his arm.

"You . . . you saw . . ."

The scene flooded back. Everything he'd felt flooded back.

I yanked my hand away as my eyes filled with tears.

"Not quite as innocent as you thought," he said, with a smile that was more grimace, like he was trying not to throw up. He pushed his chair back. "Okay, I . . . I'll go . . ."

He got one step before I leapt up and took his arm.

"No. Please," I said. "I knew . . . I'd already figured out . . . I just had to see . . . I'm sorry. I should have just asked, but I had to know."

"You didn't do it," Gabriel said from his spot near the door. "I did."

I shook my head. "I planned to. I would have. It was wrong, and I knew that before I did it, which only makes it worse."

Todd returned to his chair. He lowered himself into it and rubbed his mouth.

"I'm really, really sorry," I said, tears threatening again.

"No, you were right. And Gabriel was right to help when you couldn't. You had to know the whole thing. See the whole thing. What I did. What I didn't do. Couldn't do. I should have . . ." He shook his head. "I think that makes it worse. That I started it and couldn't finish. I didn't have faith. Your mother did."

"No, my mother was just willing to take the chance. It isn't . . ." I sat again. "It wasn't the same for her. It didn't feel the same. Killing someone."

"They all deserved it."

He sat with his hands on the table, his gaze fixed on them.

"Can I ask . . . ?" I couldn't finish.

He lifted his gaze to mine and said, "Anything, Olivia. You've seen the worst. You can ask me anything."

"Did you talk to Pamela after that? Did she go to that meeting instead of you? Or did you go and *then* talk to her?"

He shook his head. "I didn't go. I never told her. She found out, somehow. They must have approached her. She once asked me . . ."

"What would you do to cure me," I said. "Whether you'd kill someone who deserved to die. I saw it in a vision. That's how I knew it was her, not you."

"Which should have told me that she knew about the deal. I never even considered that. I thought . . ." He shook his head. "I thought maybe I was talking in my sleep or . . . I don't even know. I didn't *want* to think about it. I missed that meeting, but I was still considering doing it, working up the nerve. Before I did, you started getting better, and I breathed a huge sigh of relief. It wasn't until we were arrested that I realized Pam had done it in my place. It never occurred to me that the Cŵn Annwn would approach her."

I snuck a look at the Huntsman guard, who shook his head.

"They didn't," I said. "Pamela went to them. She took that meeting in your place."

The guard nodded, confirming.

"I had another vision," I said. "Me, as a baby. She was meeting with them at the house. The Cŵn Annwn thought you knew about the deal and that she was handling the details in your place."

Todd glanced at the guard. "Is that true, Keating?" When the Huntsman blinked, Todd gave a wry smile. "I'm not that clueless. I know what you are. Otherwise, I'd hardly talk about this in front of you. Is Liv right?"

Keating nodded. "Pamela came to the meeting. She said you two had decided it was better if she handled all contact. You'd taken care of Kirkman, and you had a connection to him, so it was safer to remove you from the conversations. Also, if anything went wrong, the police would be less likely to suspect a woman. We dealt with her on the understanding you were involved. It wasn't until Olivia uncovered the truth that we realized we'd been tricked."

"But how . . ." Todd looked from me to the guard. "I never said a word to her."

"You heard someone in the woods that night," I said. "Several times. You thought you were being paranoid. You weren't. Pamela followed you. She was worried you were cheating on her, so she followed."

We lapsed into silence. Then Keating said, "Pamela needs to tell the truth. To let you out of here." He turned to Gabriel. "That will set him free, won't it? A confession from her?"

"It would add to the grounds for appeal, but . . ."

"It's not a get-out-of-jail-free card," Todd said. "Which is why we're avoiding that option until we've exhausted the others. After what Liv saw, I think everyone can understand why I'm refusing. I did kill someone. I'm no better than Pam. No less guilty."

"The crime is not the deaths," Keating said. "The crime was sacrificing your freedom. She took you from your daughter. She took you from your life. One word from her—"

"Pamela and I agreed never to turn on one another."

"The only honorable one here is you, Todd, for not condemning her. It was her duty to tell the truth—for you and for your daughter."

Todd shook his head.

Keating grumbled under his breath and said to us, "Pointless. Always pointless. He has too much of our blood, and he will do the right thing, even when it is the wrong thing."

Todd's lips twitched. "You realize that makes no sense."

"Yes, it does. Come on, then. Back to that cell you so obviously love."

I was quiet on the way out. When I looked over at Gabriel, he walked purposefully, his face set in that way that sent anyone in his path scurrying.

I wanted to say something, but I couldn't until we were in the parking lot, and then it was only, "We have things to do."

"Yes." The word came clipped, as if annoyed by the reminder of the obvious.

"I don't want to do them."

He looked at me then, gaze hidden behind his shades.

"We need to speak to Ioan about this and the sluagh," I said. "We need to figure out what Seanna knows about Kirkman and how to stop her from using that information. We need to get back to figuring out the meaning of that damned ritual I saw at the fun house, which has gotten completely lost in the crap with Seanna and the sluagh. And I don't want to do any of it. I just want to . . ."

"What?"

"The same damn thing I've been wanting since this started. A break."

"You're upset."

I wrapped my arms around myself. "I'm a lot of things. Frustrated, confused, angry. Scared." Hands back in pockets. "Ignore me. I'm being a brat."

"I need clothing," he said as we reached the car. "If we're going to stay in Cainsville for the foreseeable future, I need to pack a bag."

I managed a wan smile. "Add that to the list, then. We'll grab it after we speak to Ioan."

"We should do it now. It may take a while."

I realized then what he was saying. Not adding yet another task to the list, but giving me an excuse to rest someplace quiet.

When we were in the car, I said, "I like the way you push me."

He frowned, one hand on the ignition.

"Easy is, well, easy," I said. "It's someone who accepts me exactly the way I am, which seems great, no pressure, no expectations. But then it chafes. Makes me restless. I don't want someone constantly pointing out my flaws. That's toxic. But you get it right. What's the old saying? Have the serenity to accept the things you can't change, the courage to change what you can, and the wisdom to know the difference?"

His brow furrowed as if he was trying to figure out what the hell I was talking about.

"You do that," I said. "You accept what I can't change, and you push me to do the things I can."

"All right . . ."

"Don't ever stop doing that. Please. I want to be better. Be stronger. If I waver, don't fix things for me."

He gave a slow and careful nod. "I apologize. I realized I made a mistake as soon as I did it. I was trying to help, but that was the wrong way to go about it."

"Umm, this isn't about making a side trip to your apartment, is it?"

"You were talking about that?"

"And you weren't," I said.

"I was talking about putting your hand on Todd's arm. That wasn't my place."

"No, it was." I turned to him. "It absolutely was. I could have resisted if I disagreed. I'm only sorry you needed to push me."

"You were intruding on what is probably your father's worst memory, but you needed that information. Accessing memories is like reading omens or seeing visions. They provide what you need. What no one will—or can—give you."

"The truth."

"Yes. As for going to my apartment, I think we *both* need a break right now." He paused. "I would like one."

"Good."

CHAPTER TWENTY-NINE

As we were pulling into the condo garage, Detective Fahy called to remind Gabriel that his mother was still missing, presumed dead, and that she strongly considered him a person of interest. That was exactly what he needed right now.

On the elevator up, Gabriel seethed. He didn't say a word. Didn't even stab the buttons. That would be a loss of control. The angrier Gabriel gets, the more tightly he reins it in.

By the time that ride ended, I felt like I'd been locked with a keg of dynamite and a smoldering wick that sucked all the air from the tiny room. I wanted that keg to explode, blow the doors off, let me breathe. Because if Gabriel didn't vent his frustration, then slamming a door or cursing would make me seem selfish.

Look at me. I'm pissed off and I'm frustrated and I'm hurting. Pay attention to me. I'm the one who matters.

Gabriel unlocked his condo door so slowly I wanted to rip the key from his hand and do it myself. He was being deliberate, resisting the urge to throw the door open, stalk inside, and say, *Fuck this. Fuck all this.*

He'd gone about three steps when he seemed to forget why he was there. He stopped. I circled wide, careful not to startle him, in case he'd forgotten I was there. And he did seem to have, his eyes widening when I moved in front of him. Then he gave an abrupt nod.

"Yes. Packing. I need . . ."

He turned, and it was like his brain cut out, every ounce of energy spent keeping his temper reined. When his phone beeped, he tensed so fast I thought he'd throw it again.

He pulled it out and saw the damage from when he'd whipped it into the wall. Then he carefully and deliberately set it on the table, as if to say, *I won't do that again.*

I moved in front of him again, slowly, but he still jumped.

"Sorry," I said.

"No, I just . . ." He looked around, as if trying again to remember what he'd come here for.

I reached up, lacing my hands behind his neck, braced for him to tense. Instead, he closed his eyes, relaxing and leaning into my hands. I moved closer, my body brushing his, fingers moving up into his hair. He exhaled, the barest sigh. I could feel the tension strumming through him, and when his mouth lowered to mine, it moved carefully, restrained. But as soon as we touched, the restraints snapped, and he pulled me hard against him, his mouth coming down rough and urgent. Then he pulled back abruptly, holding me at arm's length. "I didn't mean—" he began.

I took a half step closer. "It's okay."

"It's not. I'm out of sorts and—"

"And that's fine," I said. "So am I."

I kissed him, pouring all my own frustration into it. And that really did snap off those restraints, and hell, oh, hell. Five seconds later, I was halfway over the back of the sofa, my legs around him, hearing the sound of a shirt ripping and not knowing whose it was and not really giving a damn. Then I was against the wall, his hands pinning my arms, kissing me hard enough that I tasted blood. He must have, too, and he stopped, blinking.

"Sorry, sorry," he mumbled, letting me go so fast I started falling to the floor before he caught me.

"It's okay."

He shook his head. "No. I didn't mean to hurt—"

"Gabriel?" I wrapped my hand in the front of his shirt. "I'm a big girl. I can tell you to stop, and I know you will. If you think I'm giving any indication that I want you to slow down?" I yanked him closer. "Then you are *really* lousy at reading the signs."

He let out a strained chuckle.

"You're angry. You're frustrated. Let's work on that." I pulled him closer and leaned into his ear. "If this is any indication of how you'd like to work on that, I am one hundred percent in."

He shivered against me.

I moved my mouth to his lip and nipped. "Pretty sure I can give as good as I get," I said. "And the same warning goes for you—if it's too much, say so. Is it too much?"

He answered by backing me against the wall hard enough to rattle the door. Then I was straddling him, pinned to the wall, his mouth crushing mine, and when his shirt came off, I suspected it wasn't going back on without some serious mending.

If asked before now whether I'd had rough sex, I'd have said yes. What I'd had, though, had been enthusiastic sex. In-too-big-a-hurry-to-be-gentle sex. There'd been some experimentation with BDSM, but very mild, because while I was intellectually curious, once I actually experimented, it didn't hold the appeal I expected.

I didn't like giving up control. Really didn't. As for the idea of *taking* control, I'd tried it, with a lover who wanted that, but there'd been no . . . thrill of victory? I'd already held the upper hand in the relationship, and dominating in sex only seemed to hammer that home, which really didn't do anything for me.

This wasn't BDSM. It was just rough sex. Really rough sex. Fingers grabbing hard. Nails digging in. Nips that drew blood.

Restraint and struggle mingled with hard kisses that lasted until they hurt. Then a moment to catch our breath, touching and caressing and gentle kisses and murmurs and whispers and sighs, and then right back into it, a stroke turning to a grasp, a caress to a light scratch, as if testing the boundaries.

Testing and reciprocating, the heat and fervor building again. Not sex as a battle but as a game, the upper hand changing constantly, both of us fighting for it and then, when the other achieved it, giving in because, yes, if Gabriel wanted that upper hand, there was no way in hell I could physically take it from him. But if I managed to get on top or pin him, he'd let me have that, which meant I'd won. A willingness to submit from a guy who did not ever submit? Delicious.

There was control in submitting, too. In knowing I could, with a word, stop him.

By the end, I honestly wasn't even sure who was on top. It was a hard, blinding, I-have-no-idea-where-I-am-and-I-don't-care climax. Probably more than one. Even when he stopped, I was still riding that wave, and once he realized that, he obliged, going until I collapsed—on him, apparently—exhausted, my whole body quivering. He turned me onto my side and kissed me, a long, sweet, gentle kiss. When it ended, he said, "Thank you."

"Oh, hell, no. Thank you," I said, and he chuckled, the sound vibrating between us. "That was . . . Wow." I lifted my head to look at him. "You want to know how to help me work off my angst? That'll do it."

He pulled me against him for another long kiss, our bodies entwined. I reached to touch his jaw, run my fingers over it, savoring the freedom to touch him. When I moved my arm, though, he caught my hand and frowned down at finger-shaped bruises rising on my forearm.

"I'm sor—"

I put my fingers to his lips. "I like the fact you've learned to apologize. But sometimes, you kinda overdo it."

"It wasn't so much an apology as an acknowledgment that I didn't realize I grabbed you hard enough to leave a mark. Which I suppose *is* an apology."

"Yep. It is. And if you apologize for that, then I have to apologize for this." I touched a scratch on his chest. "And this." A bruise on his bicep. "And I don't even want to see your back."

"It's fine." He rolled over and pulled me on top of him. "The acceptance of an apology would imply that one was required, which would imply that I would prefer no repeat of the circumstances that led to it. So I strongly reject any apology you might feel obliged to give."

"Ditto."

He relaxed and closed his eyes, and I touched his hair, still damp with sweat, and then tickled his neck, and he lay there, calm, eyes closed, lips curved as he enjoyed the attention.

Then my phone rang.

"It's too far for me to reach," I said. "Would you mind throwing that against the wall for me?"

He opened one eye. The phone continued to ring. Neither of us moved to get it, but when it stopped, I sighed and said, "I suppose we've had as much of a rest as we're going to get."

"It was a good rest. If not terribly restful."

I laughed. "Agreed."

Gabriel stretched under me. "I'm not intending to return Detective Fahy's call, but I do need to speak to Rose and Patrick, to see if Seanna has made contact. If you and Ricky want to handle Ioan, that might be a better division of efforts. I'll retrieve Pamela's file from the office and we can take that to Cainsville to discuss, in connection with your vision at the fun house."

"You have very kissable lips."

He laughed.

"Yes," I said. "You were talking. It was important. I shouldn't get distracted. But they're distracting. Have been for a while, which was very awkward. You'd be saying something important, and I'd be watching your lips and trying very hard not to think what it'd be like to stop you talking. For a minute. Or ten. So now I'm just going to randomly say that when the thought strikes."

He smiled and shook his head, in that way that said he suspected I was teasing him. "You do realize you're playing a dangerous game, stroking an ego that doesn't need the attention."

"Oh, I think it'll be fine." I slid my hands behind his head and leaned down to kiss him. His arms went around me and the kiss deepened, hands moving across bare skin, stroking, caressing, exploring.

"I'd better take it down a notch," I murmured between kisses. "I don't think you'll be up to . . . Oh, wait. Maybe? Mmm, yes. My mistake. Carry on."

PHONE ISSUES

When Gabriel's phone rang, he did not snarl at it. Did not need to fight the urge to hurl it into the wall. He simply opened one eye and waited for it to stop. When it did, he opened the other and looked down at Olivia, curled up in his arms.

He liked this. Liked it more than he would have imagined. The touching, the entwining, the closeness. The heat of her body, the smell of her skin, the soft whisper of her breathing, the pound of her heart. It made him feel . . . He wasn't sure what word fit best there. Secure? Comforted? Quieted? The choices all seemed odd, when applied to a lover. But he felt all that, curled up with her.

It was not dissimilar to the sense he used to get at the end of the day, when he closed the door and shut the world out and could just relax, be himself in his one safe spot. Something had been amiss, though, adding a restlessness and dissatisfaction that he'd never been able to pin down. Now he realized what it'd been. Loneliness. The sense that the only thing better than being alone would be to be with someone who made you feel as safe and comfortable as you did when you were alone.

He rose on his elbow to look down at Olivia. To savor the image of her in his bed. The realization of yet another fantasy he'd indulged in more times than he cared to recollect. It seemed an odd thing to fantasize about, compared to all the other, more active scenarios. But this was one of his, like seeing her wearing his shirt.

He'd had a taste of this particular fantasy already, letting her take his bed when she stayed the night. Again, he'd enjoyed that more than he ought to. There was a primitive quality to the fantasy, the idea that even if she'd been with Ricky, she'd been sleeping in *his* bed.

A little more proprietary than he should admit to. Not a sense of property, but a sense of place—that having Olivia in his bed said she held a spot in his life no one else could breach. She was important enough that he'd give up his most private sanctuary to her.

His phone started again. That did get a growl from him, less at the interruption than the reminder that it really was time to get up.

He eased Olivia aside, crawled from bed, and picked up his phone just before it went to voice mail. Only as he hit the Talk button did he see a number he didn't recognize and grunt, annoyed that he hadn't checked first. In that light, his greeting may have been even more curt than usual.

"Uh, sorry?" Ricky said. "Bad time?"

"No. I didn't recognize the number."

"Oh, right. Yeah. Phone issues. You know."

Gabriel did know. Or, rather, he did not know specifically, because he was not supposed to know specifics, only that, on his advice, at any time the Saints were doing particularly sensitive business, they switched to prepaid phones.

Ricky continued, "The new number might also explain why Liv didn't pick up. I've left messages. Is she okay?"

"We were visiting Todd earlier. She may have left her phone in the car."

Gabriel did not for a moment consider saying that Olivia was asleep in the middle of the day. That would have been cruel. Gabriel had seen Ricky's face when he spotted the discarded clothing in Olivia's parlor, and no matter how many times Ricky had assured him he'd be perfectly fine with whatever happened, his expression confirmed that "perfectly" was a gross exaggeration. Even "fine" might be overstating the matter.

"I presume you're calling to say you have business that won't allow you to speak to Ioan?" Gabriel said.

"Nah. That's all good. I'm just on call." Ricky paused. "Unless you'd rather speak to Ioan with Liv instead."

"No, I have other business to attend to. I can drop her off wherever you like. I'd only ask that you get her some lunch, before or after the meeting. She's had a busy day and hasn't eaten."

"I'll make sure she does. But who's going to make sure you do?"

"I'll be fine."

"Wrong answer." The sound of a door opening. "I'm in the city, running an errand for Wallace. How about I pick up lunch and swing by? You're at the office?"

"My apartment. I needed clothing because—"

"—the elders have grounded Liv. Right. I'll grab takeout and be there in thirty."

Thirty minutes did not allow both Gabriel and Olivia to shower and then dry their hair to erase the evidence that they'd bathed. Which led to Olivia making the perfectly rational suggestion that they share the shower. In her defense, she did seem to presume it would be uneventful, given the exertions of earlier. That was not the case, and Ricky was rapping at the door as she was finishing blow-drying her hair, his still wet. He towel-dried it as best he could before joining them in the dining room.

———

Lunch ended, and they were about to leave when Ricky said, "Shit," and "Can I talk to you a sec, Gabriel?"

"I'll get these dishes in the machine," Olivia said as she started clearing the table.

When she went into the kitchen, Ricky said, "I brought the bike. If you'd rather I picked up a car at my dad's—or you drive Liv to Ioan's—that's cool."

Gabriel understood the problem. As progressive as the Saints might be, they still held to the old traditions, one being that the woman riding on the back of a bike was sleeping with the guy on the front.

"That's fine with me," he said.

"You sure? I totally get it if you—"

"It's fine."

By the time Ricky and Olivia left, Gabriel was already on the phone, working through his own to-do list. Rose hadn't heard from Seanna. Neither had Patrick. Yet Gabriel could not be completely certain either was telling the truth, and he was considering what to do about this as he walked from his apartment and found two fae in his hallway. Two dryads, to be precise.

"We have solved the mystery," Alexios announced.

"Well, one of them," Helia said.

Gabriel closed the door behind him, his hand still on the knob. "While I'm glad to hear you've made progress, coming to my home is not the appropriate way to communicate it to me."

"How else were we supposed to tell you? Olivia forgot to leave us a phone number."

Gabriel suspected Olivia had not forgotten. She didn't trust them—understandable after their experiences with helpful fae. Nor did she quite seem to know what to make of them. They were far too flighty for Gabriel's tastes, but the Gwynn part of him understood that this was the way of dryads and accepted it with only minor exasperation, as if they were cousins he would not choose as friends but would grant respect and consideration.

Yet that did not mean he wanted them at his home.

"My office address is listed," he said.

"It's Saturday," Helia said. "No one's there. We went by."

"There is a message service."

"You have an answer for everything, don't you, Gw— Gabriel?"

"One would think you'd be pleased with our keen detective work," Alexios added. "Your home address is *not* listed. *Finding* it—and getting inside the building—wasn't easy."

"I will provide you with my cell phone number. Please use it."

"Next time. We have important news. We'll go inside and discuss it."

Helia nudged Alexios, subtly shook her head, and said, "That fancy car of yours is in the garage, right?"

"Yes, but—"

"We'll talk in there. While you drive."

"And where would I be driving?"

She grinned up at him. "To your mother, of course."

Gabriel did not blithely follow the dryads to his car. He and Olivia had been betrayed by two fae in the last few months, and both times he'd felt no more than the usual mistrust he did with 99.99 percent of the human population. He needed time to think this through and plan a safe course of action.

He told the dryads he had work to do at his office, and they could either wait for his call or accompany him. They seemed completely unperturbed by his lack of urgency regarding his mother. He suspected any urgency in their own lives was like that experienced by the average toddler—a sudden and burning need to have something right that moment . . . forgotten as soon as a distraction presented itself.

The dryads happily accompanied Gabriel to his office and then decided to play legal assistant while they waited, offering to file papers, answer e-mails, whatever task he might like to set them on. Again not unlike a small child who thinks household chores are great fun . . . for about five minutes. Gabriel put them to work tidying the supply closet. It seemed relatively harmless, and he wasn't about to turn down free labor.

On the drive over, he'd weighed his options. He did not consider refusing to follow up on the dryads' lead, no more than he or Olivia had ignored mysterious messages they had received, knowing they would almost certainly lead to a trap. It was rather like having an enemy invite you to tea—you know your Earl Grey will likely contain a lethal dose of arsenic, but if you refuse the invitation, he'll only find another method of attack, perhaps one you won't see coming.

The answer, then, was to take backup. The obvious and preferred choice was Olivia. Ricky ran a somewhat distant second. Yet both were off on an important task of their own, and Gabriel hated postponing a call to adventure. Which, perhaps, proved he shared more blood with the dryads than he cared to admit.

Gabriel weighed his choices. Then he made a call.

CHAPTER THIRTY

I hit the button on the remote for Ioan's gate, and we drove through. As I pulled off my helmet, Ricky looked at me and said, "You might want to pop your collar."

"Hey, if the biker doesn't pop his, I'm not popping mine. Also? We're thirty years past that fashion faux pas."

"Yeah, but it still comes in handy when you're sporting a hickey."

"What?" My hands flew to my neck, and I found the tender spot. "Shit. No, that's not— I burned it. My hair wasn't cooperating, so I dragged out the curling iron."

"Gabriel has a curling iron?"

"No, I meant— Damn it." I rooted through my bag for concealer. "I'm sorry. If I'd noticed, I'd have hidden it."

"I know." His lips twitched. "It is kinda funny, though, watching you guys scramble with excuses. Gabriel told me you weren't answering my calls because you forgot your phone in the car. Which is about as likely as you leaving your arm behind. He dried his hair so fast the back was sticking up. And then he scarfed down half the food I brought for lunch. I've never seen him eat like that." He smiled. "But I do appreciate he's being circumspect."

"He's not going to wave it in your face."

"No, but we are talking about Gabriel, who never goes out of his way to cushion anyone's feelings but yours. He's being very thoughtful. It's sweet. Just don't tell him I said that."

"I won't." I finished applying the concealer. "Better?"

"Yep." He leaned over for a better look and then stopped. "Is that a bite on your collarbone?"

"Shit! No. Damn it."

Ricky laughed as I frantically applied more makeup.

"I'm sorry. I'm really—"

"Stop. If it's not obvious, teasing you is my way of dealing with it. Honestly? I was afraid *that* part might be a disappointment for you. Because, well, it's Gabriel. In the four years he's been the Saints' lawyer, I've never known him to as much as date. But bad sex isn't going to make you come running back to me. It'd just make you less than totally happy with him. Happy is good. Hickeys are good. Even bite marks . . ." He shook his head. "Nope, not commenting on the bite mark. But at least now I know where that cut on his lip came from." He exhaled. "Can we change the conversation now?"

"Pretty sure I didn't start it. Or prolong it."

"Yeah, like I said, I'm trying to deal. But that's enough. Now, before we go in, let's take a minute, so you can tell me how you *really* feel about what your dad said."

Apparently, my makeup fix didn't hide the bruise enough to escape fae detection. Ioan's gaze went to it almost the second we were seated. He smiled. I was in his living room with Ricky, who'd been home from Miami less than twenty-four hours, and I show up bearing a sign that sex had been had. Obviously, we'd come to our senses and reconciled.

Fortunately, Ricky didn't notice. He was too busy giving Ioan shit for not telling me Todd had been the one to summon them.

As my Cŵn Annwn parent, though, Todd was their secondary champion, and Ioan had wanted to do nothing that might strain our relationship. I understood that.

Ricky told Ioan that if he wanted to win my favor, he should be a little more concerned with positioning himself as the side I could trust. And Ioan said nothing. Because Ricky was right. Even Brenin came in to watch, the alpha hound's gaze swiveling between Ioan and Ricky, watching and assessing.

Lloergan lay at Ricky's feet, giving Brenin a look that warned Ricky was hers. I smiled at that. There was no chance Brenin was considering a change of allegiance. He was just processing the fact that "his" alpha was listening to Ricky, which boosted the newcomer higher in the pack hierarchy.

After Ricky finished, I said to Ioan, "So who'd you make the deal with?" When Ioan didn't answer, I said, "The deal to cure me. You made it with the sluagh, didn't you?"

More silence.

Ricky looked at Ioan. "Did I just waste my breath? 'Cause I really feel like   "

"No, you didn't," Ioan said. "I'm framing my response in a way that explains, without seeming as if I'm attempting to dodge responsibility. Also, preferably, in a way that doesn't make me look like a complete idiot."

"You didn't know it was the sluagh," I said.

"In modern times, such deals are almost unheard-of. I had only been asked once before Todd, and in a situation I rejected without further investigation. Todd was different."

"When you heard I had spina bifida, you knew it was one of the possible side effects of fae blood. That's why you asked about my mother. You realized she was from a fae family in Cainsville. Add that to Todd's Cŵn Annwn blood and I fit the criteria for Matilda."

"I'd heard rumors that a Matilda had been born, disabled. Which meant if I could help, I would. While a physical disability would not prevent you from playing your role, it would be easier if you weren't dealing with that challenge on top of the others. You would be safer having the full use of your legs."

"So, to make the deal, you contacted . . . ?"

"That was the problem. Having never seriously considered such a deal, for me it was theoretical. Like a story passed down through generations. In that, I fear, I was little different from your father, who only knew he had our blood through family legend. These deals are typically made with what human folklore calls Celtic deities and the Christian invaders labeled demons. They're more aptly called forces of nature. The Cŵn Annwn work in their service—yet, like humans and their gods, it's a distant relationship of faith and service rather than a personal relationship."

"You can't just summon them for a chat."

"Exactly. If we wish to make contact, we must do so through a messenger. An ancient fae with a deep connection to the natural world—one so close to the end of life that he or she is already merging with nature and attuned to the will of those forces. I performed the ritual of contact. The next day, a fae answered my summons. I explained what I needed. She told me four sacrifices were required. She gave me their names, and when we visited them, we knew they would be righteous deaths."

"That's how you do it, then? How you determine guilt? It's a sense?"

"Not a sense, but a certainty. What's the saying? To see guilt written on a face? Sometimes we can access their memories, which is a power you seem to have inherited. Even when those memories are closed to us, guilt is as obvious as the color of their skin. In the case of the Tysons, we saw memories of their crime. With Hilton and Pasolini, we only knew they were guilty."

"Whatever they did, it's linked to the Tysons." I told him about the vision in the fun house. "Gabriel and I haven't had time to even *begin* investigating that. But it seems as if the Tysons, Hilton, and Pasolini were part of some group, some . . ."

"Cult?" Ricky said.

I made a face. "All the research I did into my parents' crimes taught me that ritual murderers and cultists are just idiots who've seen too many movies."

"Liv's right," Ioan said. "If these four thought they could summon dark forces with their sacrifices, it's just an excuse to exercise very dark and very twisted desires. They wanted to kill. Doing it in a ritual seemed more acceptable to them. A form of mob mentality, if you like."

"So Pamela was asked to execute four killers pursuing a single goal," I said. "The issue here, though, is who brought you that deal. The ancient fae. You presumed she was the messenger you'd summoned."

"Yes. I should have made certain."

His mistake was understandable. He put out a summons. Someone answered and gave him what he expected. Having never done such a deal, he'd have no way to test the messenger, no cause for doubt.

"So we're now thinking it was a sluagh in manifested form," I said. "Probably the same one who contacted my father, telling him how to summon you."

Ricky nodded. "A setup from the start. The sluagh prod Todd to ask for the deal. Then they intercept the message and negotiate the terms."

"Which gives them power over me," I said. "That's what the sluagh meant, isn't it? That it was the one who cured my spina bifida. That puts me in its debt. In its power."

"It shouldn't," Ioan said. "The price was paid. Four souls. The sluagh accepted its reward and should have no further claim on you."

"'Should' being the operative word."

BONDING

"Dryads," Patrick said when Gabriel met him in the parking lot. "Why does it have to be dryads?" When Gabriel didn't respond, Patrick said, "*Raiders of the Lost Ark*?"

"Is that a book?"

Patrick shook his head. "We have serious father–son bonding time to catch up on. We'll start with movie nights."

"This sort of bonding is perfectly adequate."

"This isn't bonding. It's me doing you a favor because I feel guilty."

"*That* is my idea of bonding. And it's not a favor—you're as curious as I am."

Patrick caught the exterior door before Gabriel could open it. "Dryads, though? They make me look like a stodgy old man. Flibbertigibbets. That's *Mary Poppins*. We'll get to it after the action flicks. But dryads? Really?"

"Yes, they're capricious."

"That's like saying the ocean is damp."

"They found Seanna."

"They *claim* to have found her."

"Which means either they are far less inept than they appear or far less innocent. Either makes them interesting."

269

Patrick sighed. "Of all the things you could inherit from me, curiosity is the one most likely to get you into trouble."

They walked into the office, where the dryads were trying to figure out the coffeemaker.

"I really don't think you guys need any of that," Patrick said.

The dryads turned, and Helia let out a teen-girl yelp. "Oh my gods, it's Patricia Rees!"

Patrick stopped mid-step.

Helia rushed over. "I love your books. *We* love them." She paused. "Well, except the last few."

Alexios nodded. "You do better with the gothics."

"I see . . ." Patrick said.

"Overall, the paranormal ones are okay," Alexios said. "The last one just went on way too long. Did you run out of time to edit?"

"Not . . . really."

Helia whispered to Alexios, "I don't think he wants to hear what's wrong with his book."

"I'm trying to help."

"The book is already out. He can't fix it now."

"But he'll know better for next time. Maybe he can hire a new editor."

She looked at Patrick. "It was good enough. Seven out of ten. It's just that you're usually a nine. Well, your paranormals are more of an eight, but you could get them up to a nine if you worked harder."

"Or just go back to the gothics," Alexios said. "They were much better. I couldn't get through this last book."

"He didn't even just skip ahead to read the sex scenes," Helia said. "Which is what he normally does with your paranormals."

Patrick turned to Gabriel. "This is your revenge, isn't it?"

"Helia and Alexios?" Gabriel said. "This is Patrick. He'll be accompanying us to Seanna."

"Oooh," Alexios said. "It's a family reunion."

"So you really *are* Gabriel's father?" Helia said. "That's what everyone says, but then we found Seanna and started thinking maybe the rumor was wrong, that you two couldn't have . . . you know. She seems kind of . . ." She wrinkled her nose. "Nasty."

"Maybe he likes nasty," Alexios said. "You've read his sex scenes."

"I'm not sure they're *meant* to be nasty."

"I believe it's time to go," Gabriel said, ushering them out.

"Well played," Patrick murmured as he passed. "Well played."

The Jag idled beside an abandoned three-story school. As soon as the car rolled to a stop, the dryads had hopped out with "We'll find her" and "We'll call."

Gabriel and Patrick watched them dart alongside the boarded-up building.

"Well, this looks sketchy," Patrick said. When Gabriel looked over, he added, "It means disreputable and suspicious. I'm a writer. I know all the lingo."

"I know what it means. I'm a defense attorney. And I have Olivia, who has used the term on occasion, along with others that aren't in my usual vocabulary." He surveyed the building. "Yes, it is disreputable and, in being disreputable, given the situation, suspicious."

"Sketchy."

"That is a vague term, used somewhat incorrectly, and therefore imprecise."

"You always use precisely the right words. Another trait inherited from your father."

"I read a chapter of the book you gave Olivia. I believe, wherever that trait came from, it was clearly an outside influence."

"Ouch." A moment of silence as they watched the dryads slip through a broken window. "So the book . . . Paranormal fiction isn't your kind of thing?"

"My tastes are eclectic. I would not dismiss a novel simply because I haven't read that genre before."

"Double ouch."

"That wasn't intended as an insult. I simply discovered that reading a book you'd written was not a properly immersive entertainment experience. I hear your voice, which hardly allows me to fall into the world of your female, human narrator."

"Okay. I'll take that." Patrick looked at the school. "So, the dryads are leading us into a trap. Unfortunately, being dryads, they've done a very poor—and obvious—job of it."

"Yes."

"You're not going to tell me it's actually a *good* thing we've seen the trap?"

"No."

Patrick grinned. "Because that makes it less of a challenge. See, this is why we work together so well. I was hoping you'd call me in when Liv was gone this fall."

"Call you in?"

"The last time Liv was away, you called me to help on a case."

"No, you *gave* me a case. And tried to insist we work it together."

"Same thing."

"Not even a little."

"You've been hanging with Liv too much. You're becoming a smart-ass."

"I always was. You just never had enough interaction with me to realize it. Now, are we going to sit here and talk until they have the trap set?"

"That'd be more fun."

Gabriel opened the car door and climbed out.

The dryads had entered through a window that, upon closer inspection, was not merely broken but boarded. The boards, however, were only partly nailed and could be swung aside. Once they were through, Gabriel took out his cell, turned on the light, looked around, and saw a problem. Possibly a significant one.

It looked as if some effort at reconstruction had been made years ago, the drywall torn out and the flooring removed, leaving wooden studded walls and bare underlay floor.

Wood. Lots of wood. Which dryads used for camouflage. As Gabriel recalled, though, it worked better in the forest, against uneven surfaces. He continued into the hall and then paused as light footfalls sounded overhead.

"Time to find a way up," Patrick whispered. "I vote . . ." He looked both ways. "Left."

"It's right," Gabriel said, and started walking.

"Are you just being contrary? Because—"

Gabriel pointed to the floor, where dusty footsteps led right. He followed them down two corridors to where stairs had been torn out, possibly to keep squatters from accessing the upper floors.

"That's inconvenient," Patrick said.

Gabriel ignored him. Presumably, dryads could not fly. Therefore they'd gone another way. He picked through the debris until he found the dryads' footprints, which led to a service elevator. The doors stood open, the car stopped eight feet off the ground.

When Gabriel looked around for more footprints, Patrick shook his head. "No, this is the way. Damn dryads are like monkeys. Give me a boost."

Gabriel did. Then he walked off as Patrick called, "Where are you going?"

"To find something to step on."

"You're a big guy. Haul your ass on up here."

"The fact that I'm a 'big guy' means that my 'ass' and the rest of me requires additional upper-body strength to lift."

"No, you just don't like to roll up your sleeves and get dirty. Why are you wearing a dress shirt anyway? It's Saturday. Wait . . ." Patrick peered down at him. "You aren't wearing a tie. I knew there was something different. No tie. Top button undone . . ."

"If I'm not wearing a tie, I'm hardly going to fasten my top button."

"I don't think I've ever seen you without a tie."

"You have. You just didn't notice."

Gabriel unbuttoned his cuffs and meticulously rolled his sleeves. It was not so much a matter of getting dirty as of permanently damaging an expensive shirt. He'd already lost one today, and while he did not regret the loss if he was going to damage shirts, he'd rather lose them in that manner.

Gabriel grabbed the bottom of the elevator car and hauled himself up, hoping the exertion might distract him from the memory of how he had lost that other shirt. It did not. When he pulled himself into the car, he stepped past Patrick and took out his phone.

"What are you doing now?" Patrick whispered.

"I need to check in with Olivia."

"This very moment?"

"Yes."

He checked his texts—none from Olivia—sent one, and then took another moment to fully distract himself.

"You're checking your stocks?" Patrick said, looking over his shoulder.

The market was slightly down, which had the proper effect, as did the disappointment of not having Olivia immediately text him back. He didn't expect her to—she was busy—but it successfully redirected his thoughts to the matter at hand.

"Oh, now we can leave?" Patrick said as Gabriel hefted himself out of the car onto the next floor. "Are you sure you don't want the weather report first?"

"Clear and cold," Gabriel said. "A chance of light snowfall tonight."

Patrick pulled himself from the elevator car. Gabriel continued tracking the dryad footprints down the hall. He was almost to the end when a sound made the hairs on his neck rise, and he stopped short, Patrick bumping into him.

"Time to check sports scores?" Patrick said. When Gabriel didn't respond, Patrick saw his expression and lowered his voice. "Gabriel?"

"Did you hear that?"

The sound came again. He couldn't quite place it. No, that was a lie. A shameful one, born of fear rather than uncertainty, like a child listening to thumps under the bed and telling himself he'd heard nothing.

Gabriel had spent twenty years building his defenses. Grow up, get in shape, learn to fight, and banish his fear of physical intimidation and abuse. Go to law school, work hard, invest wisely, and banish his fear of hunger and poverty. Learn to live alone, without attachments, and banish his fear of neglect and abandonment.

The last two were not ones he would ever acknowledge, but he had enough self-awareness to know they festered there, remnants of a very small boy who would light up when his mother was kind and then analyze his behavior to figure out what he'd done to please her. That child did not survive long—he quickly evolved into a boy who realized Seanna's kindness was as capricious as the moods of a dryad, untethered to his actions.

Gabriel had gone years without knowing true fear. That changed with Olivia. Allowing himself to form an attachment meant allowing himself to fear for another person. And, yes, to fear that person would leave him, would decide he was really too much trouble.

But the fear strumming through him now? The one that made him lie and insist he'd heard nothing? It was a fear he hadn't experienced since he'd been locked in that cubby, hearing the creaks and rattles of an old building and imagining all the terrifying creatures from his aunt Rose's wonderful and terrible books. It was, indeed, the fear of the child who dares not look under the bed.

Gabriel heard the beating of wings against glass.

He knew there was a rational explanation. Perhaps a bird had flown into a window. Or it was simply the wind. But it sounded like what he'd heard with Olivia in the vision, and therefore that was what came to mind, dragging with it the sheer and mindless fear he'd felt then, trapped between himself and Gwynn and some memory so deeply rooted it was part of both human and fae DNA.

The sluagh is coming. The unforgiven is coming. The darkness is coming.

"Gabriel?" Patrick prompted.

"Whatever it was, I don't hear it now," Gabriel said quickly. "I do hear the dryads, though. Coming this way."

Which was true. Their light footsteps pitter-pattered over the boards, like scampering woodland creatures. Gabriel stood his ground, and the dryads veered around the doorway and stopped short.

"You didn't wait," Helia said.

"You were supposed to wait," Alexios said.

"Yes," Gabriel said.

Alexios nudged Helia. "See? I told you he wouldn't. Gwynn does not follow the orders of mere semi-immortals." He looked at Gabriel. "I know you don't like that name. I just meant—"

"I understand what you meant. And no, if I do not wish to wait, I don't."

Alexios smiled. "Good. You shouldn't. You're king of the Fae. And if they"—he nodded to Patrick—"try to say otherwise, tell them where to shove it. You have the power to do that. Don't ever forget it."

Patrick's brows lifted.

"We were coming to get you," Helia said. "We just wanted to make sure Seanna's still here."

"It would be very embarrassing if she wasn't," Alexios said. "We also needed to make sure no one else had found her in the meantime. The mother of Gwynn is valuable. Others are looking. We've heard there is a reward for her capture."

"That would be mine," Patrick said.

"You only offered money," Helia said. "Others offer more."

"What others?"

"Those hunting wouldn't tell us. We tried insisting. We even threatened. But no one ever takes us seriously when we threaten."

"Not even when we scowl." Alexios looked at Gabriel. "You could make them talk. You have a good scowl."

"Where is Seanna?" Patrick said. "Every second you delay, *my* reward drops."

Alexios wrinkled his nose. "We don't want your money."

"Wouldn't take it," Helia said. "Money only causes trouble. We hope to win the goodwill of Olivia and Gabriel, but that is a hope, not a price for our help."

"Where is—?" Patrick began.

They turned and zoomed off.

Gabriel and Patrick followed. It was the only way to see what scheme the dryads were hatching.

As they walked, Gabriel's phone buzzed with an incoming text from Olivia.

All done. Meet up?

He sent back, *I'm in the middle of something. I'll call you within the hour.*

He hit three wrong keys typing that—his fingers were just too big for a phone keypad. Olivia would say that was a sign he should learn text-speak. Or at least allow himself to write sentence fragments. He would rather correct the mistakes.

He sent the message and then hesitated, his fingers still over the keys. Should he add more, now that their relationship had changed?

Miss you? It'd been two hours, and he did miss her, but it might make him seem needy.

Love you? If he hadn't said the words in person, he certainly shouldn't say them in a text, not in such a jaunty, offhand way. And if he did send that message, he suspected Olivia *would* come running, thinking someone had stolen his phone.

In the time he paused, she sent back, *Meet at office. Need to check a file.*

He still hesitated, his fingers ready to type back his usual *All right.*

"Put the phone away," Patrick whispered. "You'll see her soon enough."

Perfect. Gabriel texted, *See you soon*, and a moment later she sent back a smiley face. He allowed a hint of a smile himself and pushed the phone into his pocket.

The dryads scampered ahead, not even looking over their shoulders. When they reached the middle of the floor, they flanked a classroom doorway and said, "Ta-da!"

Gabriel let Patrick go first, reasoning that, as a fae, he might have more protection against whatever lay inside. Gabriel followed right at his heels, though, curiosity prodding him forward even as he tried to pace himself, ears attuned for a rear ambush.

Inside the room, they found . . . Seanna.

"She's bound," Patrick said.

"How else could we make sure she stayed put?" Alexios said.

"And gagged," Patrick said.

Helia looked at him. "You've met her. Can you blame us?"

Gabriel ignored Seanna's glowers. It was indeed much easier to deal with her—and ignore her—when she was in this particular state. He moved farther into the room and then realized the dryads still flanked the door. He waved them inside. They obeyed without hesitation.

It was a classroom, like all the others they'd passed. No windows. A flashlight propped up in one corner. A sleeping bag and nest of blankets. To one side, a duffel spilled clothing. Fast-food wrappers littered the floor.

Seanna must have been squatting here when the dryads found her. The sight of her "camp" brought back memories of Gabriel's own years on the street. Except he'd been unable to afford fast food. Or a sleeping bag.

"I'll need to question her," he said. "Then we'll take her to the police, to prove she is alive."

And after that? He hadn't thought of what he'd do with Seanna after that. He had ideas, most of which involved very deep holes, but they were only fleeting fancies. While Olivia would doubtless say he deserved to entertain those fancies, he wanted to rise above them.

The deep-hole fantasy wasn't about punishing Seanna; it was about protecting Olivia. Protecting Rose. Even protecting himself and the life he'd built. Put Seanna someplace she couldn't harm them.

Jail seemed the best solution. He was still working out the logistics for that. It might involve accusing her of a crime she had not committed. And no, he would not feel the slightest bit guilty for that.

"I will ask you to escort her out," Gabriel continued. "I have sedatives, if it proves necessary."

"You brought sedatives?" Patrick said.

"It seemed wise."

"You have sedatives just lying around your house?"

"It's an apartment. Seanna? If you don't wish to be sedated, I would suggest you accompany these two quietly. Remember, you can't escape if you're unconscious."

"I don't think you should give her ideas," Alexios whispered.

Patrick only shook his head. He knew Gabriel was advising her to stay alert because she had no actual chance of escape and sedation was merely inconvenient. Which was not entirely true. Gabriel was bluffing about the sedatives. He certainly didn't keep them on hand. If he did, there'd be far too much temptation to use them on far too many people.

The dryads started toward Seanna. Then they stopped, pursing their lips in unison as they looked about.

"Oh, let me guess," Patrick said. "You hear something. And we need to run and hide, leaving you . . ."

Patrick kept talking, but Gabriel no longer heard him. No longer heard anything except the softest beating of wings against glass.

The dryads had gone as still as trees. *They* heard it, too, that soft sound, slowly escalating—

"Down!" Gabriel shouted.

Dozens of windows shattered in one deafening crash. Gabriel ducked, arms over his head. He heard Helia shout "No!" as she ran toward him, Alexios following her. Patrick turned on them, his face contorted in a snarl, his glamour rippling, a flash of light keeping Gabriel from seeing what lay beneath.

The light arced and Helia fell back, knocked off her feet. Then came a tremendous crack, as boards were ripped from the walls. Black smoke rushed in. Patrick saw it, his eyes rounding. Gabriel lunged at him. The smoke hit Helia and the dryad screamed, and blood sprayed, and Alexios shrieked—an inhuman shriek of rage.

The floor shattered under Gabriel's feet, and he plummeted, one hand striking jagged wood, a flash fire of pain, yet still he dropped, so fast it wasn't even like jumping from the bridge, where he'd had a moment to think, to move, to position himself. The floor gave way and he fell, and then he hit the next floor so hard that he broke right through, another flash of pain.

Falling again, hitting again. Still plummeting through darkness.

He slammed down on a pile of debris, the wind knocked out of his lungs, leaving him flat on his back, gasping and wheezing, his brain screaming at him to get up—stop this nonsense, breathe, and get the *fuck* up, because the sluagh was here, and he was lying on his goddamned back—

"Gabriel?"

A hand touched his shoulder, and he twisted, snarling.

The fingers fell away and the voice became Patrick's, saying, "It's me."

Gabriel had to resist the urge to snap that he didn't give a damn. He was lying on his back in the darkness, and everything hurt, and the sluagh had attacked, and why the *hell* hadn't he told Olivia where he was?

At this moment, hers was the only voice he wanted to hear— the only person he trusted to help him out of this. That wish lasted only a heartbeat until he realized that, no, he very much did not wish Olivia was here with the sluagh attacking.

"Where are they?" he said as he started to push up.

"Don't move," Patrick said. "Let me check you—"

"I have this." When Patrick's hand touched Gabriel's arm, he yanked himself away, saying, "I said I have this. I know enough not to leap to my feet. Just step back, and let me get up."

"You don't need to be so damned self-sufficient, Gabriel . . ." Patrick's voice trailed off at the end, as if he realized what had made Gabriel that self-sufficient. "I'm sorry. I—"

"If I insisted on doing *everything* myself, you wouldn't be here. I simply would prefer to assess my own condition. Please step back and allow me to do so. If you can manage some form of light . . ."

Patrick turned on his cell phone. Gabriel rose slowly. He'd landed on the debris of the floors he'd crashed through, which kept him from hitting the concrete of the basement. He was only lucky he hadn't impaled himself on the broken wood.

It hurt to rise. Hurt to breathe. But nothing prevented him from doing either, meaning he had not sustained any mobility-threatening injuries.

Patrick cursed under his breath and said, "You've sliced open your arm."

As he remembered cutting his arm, he felt it, both the throbbing pain and the dripping blood. He glanced to see a gash about three inches long. While he'd had the forethought to roll up his sleeves, it hadn't saved his shirt. He sighed softly, and twisted his arm for a better look at the damage.

"You need to bind that," Patrick said. "I'll look for a rag."

"Anything you find down here will be filthy. I'd be safer bleeding. I can bind it with my shirt, which is already ruined. I've done this before."

Which might suggest he should start carrying a roll of bandages. Or buying cheaper shirts.

He pulled the shirt off, trying not to wince. While he didn't appear to have broken anything, it felt as if he'd broken *everything*. When he went to rip the fabric, the tensing muscles made his arm gush fresh blood.

"Give me that." Patrick took the shirt from Gabriel, tore a strip off the bottom, and said, "Now your arm," and seemed surprised when Gabriel complied. "There. Looks like you've got a few other scrapes, and you'll probably have—" He swore as he circled Gabriel, shining the light on him. "You've scratched up your back, too. They're shallow, though. They look more like . . . Um, unless the floor also nipped your collarbone, I'm guessing that's preexisting damage. Please tell me it was Liv."

"As opposed to . . . ?"

"Anyone else."

Gabriel gave him a look.

Patrick raised his hands. "Hey, I write romances. I know that old saw. Try to get a woman's attention by messing around with someone else, making her jealous and proving that other women find you irresistible."

Gabriel shrugged on the remains of his shirt. "I would hope it's obvious I have both the intelligence and the self-respect never to consider such a moronic stunt."

"Good. Wait. So . . . Liv? Yes? You're telling me that you and Olivia—"

"I'm telling you that we were just attacked by the sluagh and fell through three floors, and this may not be the time to discuss my love life."

"Love life. You said love life. Not sex life. Meaning it wasn't a heat-of-the-moment tryst followed by oh-no-we-really-shouldn't followed by another whoops—Yes, I write romances."

Gabriel ignored him and concentrated on the door, which naturally did not open. He shone the light from his miraculously-still-functioning cell phone at the gap, and when he turned the knob, he watched the latch retract. So there was no lock. Instead, dark horizontal strips on the other side suggested the door had been boarded shut.

The hinges indicated the door swung out. Gabriel heaved on it, and then hissed an involuntary gasp of pain.

"Here, let me," Patrick said, which Gabriel did, but it was clear that whatever gifts a bòcan might possess, extraordinary strength was not one of them.

Gabriel backed up to the hole in the ceiling and circled the perimeter. "You'll need to get on my shoulders," Gabriel said.

"Not in the shape you're in."

"Shall I climb on yours, then?" He didn't wait for an answer, just gave an impatient wave beckoning Patrick over. "The only exit is boarded over. Unless you can burrow under concrete, this is the answer."

Gabriel positioned himself beside the heap of debris, laced his hands, and gritted his teeth. Patrick started to lift his foot. Then he said, "Wait."

"We don't have time—"

"Just hold on."

Patrick closed his eyes and took a deep breath. As he exhaled, his glamour rippled, and Patrick's true form appeared.

"Yes," Patrick said. "It's not quite as conventional as others, so let's get this over with before anyone sees."

Patrick's bòcan form was indeed not conventionally human. Yet given the illustrations Gabriel had seen of hobgoblins, it wasn't nearly as bizarre as it could have been. The biggest difference was his skin. Which was green. A light green, but definitely that color. His hair was longer, wilder, and also green, a dark shade that appeared black until the light hit it. He was taller than his human height. Slighter of build, too, so lean he seemed all ropy sinew. That was why he'd shifted—it was a lighter form, easily boosted onto Gabriel's hands and then his shoulders.

Gabriel still felt the weight and winced at it, his battered body not quite up to this feat. But he gritted his teeth, and Patrick gripped the floor above and—

"No," Gabriel said, backing up so fast that Patrick let out a "*Cach*!" and grabbed the ceiling edge, hanging there.

"Some warning, please?" Patrick's glamour snapped back in place as he struggled to heave himself up. "At least give me a boost."

"Get down. Now."

"I'm almost—"

"I said get *down*."

Patrick glanced at Gabriel's expression and dropped to the floor. "What's—?"

Gabriel motioned him to silence. A moment later, footsteps sounded. That hadn't been what stopped him, though. No sound. No sight. Just a feeling, cold dread seeping through his veins.

They're coming. The darkness. The unforgiven.

"Probably one of those damned dryads," Patrick said.

"Helia was hurt."

"There's two of them."

"Alexios won't leave her if she's hurt."

"Unless that so-called injury was planned. This whole thing still smacks of a setup, Gabriel. Helia tried to attack you."

No, she'd tried to shield him, but Gabriel wasn't arguing with Patrick. Those footsteps were getting closer, and they sounded nothing like a dryad's scamper.

Gabriel strode to the door and threw his shoulder against it, ignoring the crack of pain.

"Come help me," he said, and Patrick did, without a word, both of them pushing—

"Are you trying to flee, Gwynn?" A voice floated down through the hole. "Hardly befitting the most famous king of the Fae. But you're not Gwynn, are you? Just a boy who thinks he's a man. Barely thirty years old. Yes, we know your birthdate, given our role in helping you enter this world. How is your mother, Gabriel?"

The voice gave him pause. It bore a note that plucked at his memory. But it was like hearing an actor who voiced a children's cartoon—those notes of similarity weren't enough to trace the thread back to the associated memory.

As she talked, Gabriel walked along the wall, shining his light and looking for a weak spot.

"Would you like to know how your mother fares?" she continued. "Or don't you care? I suppose you don't. Not much of a mother, was she? One cannot be a mother without a soul, without some trace of humanity. When you were a child, such a mother was a terror. Now, though, she's merely an inconvenience. Would you like us to rid you of that inconvenience, Gabriel? As a favor? We will. She has played her role, and it's time for her to come home."

Gabriel found a gap between wallboards and tried to pry one off, but it was nailed tight.

"Do you think you can escape?" she said. "Where would you go? There isn't a door that can stop us, Gabriel."

"What do you want with him?" Patrick said.

"Is that the bòcan? Like Seanna, you have played your role. You may be silent now. Your voice is but a reminder that we failed to ensure Gwynn had a more fitting sire. A half-bòcan Gwynn ap Nudd is terribly disappointing. There are so many more worthy types."

"Sticks and stones . . ." Patrick said. "If you'd like me to shut up, you'll need to tell me what you want with him. Otherwise, if there's one thing bòcans are very good at? It's *not* shutting up. What do you want—?"

"Nothing. Everything. It depends on him. But for now, like you and his mother, he is simply a means to an end."

And that end was Olivia.

Gabriel peered at the dark hole in the ceiling. Then, pushing against everything that shouted at him to stay clear, he cautiously approached it. When Patrick reached out, Gabriel ducked his reach and kept going.

Once under that hole, he looked up and saw nothing but darkness. Even when he lifted the light, the wall of black swallowed it.

The sluagh. The darkness.

"What do you want with Olivia?" he said.

"What we're owed."

"What are you owed?"

"Our fair share."

"Of what?"

"Of what indeed? Tell me, boy, what is Matilda's role?"

He hated giving the answer, feeling like a twelve-year-old being asked the sum of one plus one. When he didn't respond, Patrick moved past him.

"Matilda prolongs and improves the life of the local Tylwyth Teg or Cŵn Annwn," Patrick said. "She chooses between the two branches of fae."

"Does she?"

Patrick's voice sharpened. "If you want me to explain exactly how her presence cleanses the elements for her chosen side, I fear that answer is above my pay grade. Elemental forces of nature, blah, blah, blah."

"No, my dear bòcan. I want a correct answer, which I would have hoped I'd get from such an illustrious scholar. You said she chooses between the two branches of fae."

"Fine. You're arguing that the Huntsmen aren't fae. They are, but if you insist on mincing words—"

"No, I insist on *not* mincing words. The Cŵn Annwn *are* fae. But you say *two* branches. Is there not a third?"

"You mean the sluagh? That one is definitely debatable. The Cŵn Annwn and the Tylwyth Teg share a common ancestry. They were, at one point, the same species, and the Hunt was only a vocation within it. Then the Cŵn Annwn broke away, and like any group that severs ties, they eventually became a separate race, with characteristics—"

"I did not ask you for a history lesson, bòcan."

The snap in her voice made Gabriel flinch, but Patrick only said, "Mmm, anthropology really, with some biology. The point is that there's no evidence of a common ancestry with the sluagh. They are actually more human than Gabriel here, the majority of their ranks being comprised of human souls—"

"Do not lecture me." Her voice whipped around them, setting every hair on Gabriel's body rising. "I am as fae as you. I *am* the sluagh. The darkness. You call us the unforgiven. That is incorrect. Our melltithiwyd are the unforgiven. They are human souls that serve us. We are the sluagh, and we are fae, and we are tired of being forgotten. We want our share."

"Of Matilda," Patrick said.

"Yes."

"Fine. There's not a hope in the Otherworld she'd choose to keep you lot alive. But sure, why not. Join the fun. Sit at the table. Make your case. Just tell me where to send the invitation."

The room rocked, as if with sonic boom, setting the concrete under Gabriel's feet quivering.

"Do you think you are clever, bòcan? You are a fool. You have played your role, as has your *epil*. He plays it even now, graciously summoning Matilda for us."

Gabriel shook his head. "Whatever threat you plan to employ, you may save your breath. I won't summon her."

"But you already have." The voice slipped around him again. "Check your phone, Gabriel."

He glanced at it. The home screen showed no new messages, but when he clicked on his text conversation with Olivia, their exchange now continued past her smiley face.

Gabriel: *I could use your assistance if you aren't otherwise occupied.*

Olivia: *Just waiting 4 you. What's up?*

Gabriel: *I may have found my mother. It seems unwise to proceed without backup.*

Olivia: *Good call. Give me an addy & we're on our way.*

Their current address followed. Then,

Olivia: *Be there ASAP!*

Gabriel: *I'm inside. Text when you arrive.*

Olivia: *Yes, sir. :)*

Gabriel stabbed the button to call her back. Nothing happened. He checked his connection. No service. He typed a message anyway.

Stay where you are. I didn't call you. Do NOT come here.

The text appended at the end of the conversation, with the exclamation mark to show it hadn't sent. He flicked on the wi-fi and watched until it showed no service found.

"The next step is to raise it over your head," the voice said. "See if you can get signal that way. Then ask your father if his is working . . . Oh, I see he's already checking. I'll leave you both to that. I have a new arrival to greet."

CHAPTER THIRTY-ONE

I t took longer than expected to reach Gabriel's location. Snow was falling along with the temperature, which meant Ricky couldn't travel at his usual speed. He had an old car at his dad's but didn't put the bike away until he absolutely had to.

The address Gabriel texted led to an abandoned school. And the moment I saw that, my brain screamed, *Fae*.

The school looked as if it'd been empty for years. Nature had already reclaimed the playground, asphalt erupting with greenery, half covered in snow, an ancient swing set strangled by dead vines. Now, that greenery had begun its assault on the school itself, moss and vines tentatively cracking the foundation as they crept up the walls.

Seanna hadn't wandered here on her own. Someone had put her here. Someone fae. Set her up and waited for us to take the bait.

I called Gabriel as soon as I got my helmet off. When he didn't answer, I sent a text. Then I walked to his car, where the key fob in my purse automatically unlocked the doors.

"Someone was in the backseat." I held out a wrapper from candies Lydia kept in a jar. Ricky didn't suggest Gabriel had grabbed one and tossed the wrapper in the back. That was about as likely as him putting down the windows and cranking the tunes.

"And if there was a person in the back," Ricky said, "that means someone else occupied the passenger side."

I checked the front passenger side and found a pen wedged behind the cushions.

"A Montblanc refill in a cheap pen," I said.

"Champagne tastes on a Budweiser budget?"

"Not exactly. This particular someone can afford a drawer of Montblancs. He says they write like a dream and feel like a grade-school pencil. He buys more comfortable pens and sticks in the good ink." I looked up at the school. "So Gabriel came here with Patrick, which suggests he got a tip on Seanna and needed backup. He also brought someone else. Meaning he showed up with at least two other people . . . and then texts me to come help him?"

"Looks like you're getting false messages again. You guys need to come up with a secret code."

"No kidding." I surveyed the building. "But he is here. And he's not answering his phone." I typed in another number and listened while it rang. "Neither is Patrick."

"Whoever sent that message wants you here," he said. "Shall we accept the invitation?"

"We shall."

I could see where Gabriel and Patrick had gone in—there were footprints beneath a window. Inside, the dusty floor bore more prints. Gabriel's were obvious, given the size. I could guess at Patrick's by the sneaker tread. There were two other sets, smaller than Patrick's.

Ricky crouched and examined the footprints. When he touched the smallest, he said, "Fae," and then made a face. "Don't ask me how I know that."

"New power. Cool."

"Useful, at least." He rose. "You sent a couple of dryads to find Seanna, right?"

"I wouldn't say *sent* so much as allowed them to search. But yes, they're small, and they wear Docs, so the sizes and treads are about right. The dryads found Seanna—or told Gabriel they did. He knows it could be a trap. He needs backup. We're busy. Patrick joins Gabriel and the dryads at the office. They come here together and . . ."

I trailed off, frowning at the doorway leading deeper into the school.

Ricky said, "And the obvious answer is that the dryads sprung a trap, but you didn't get that sense from them."

"Which means nothing. Remember, I trusted Tristan *after* his partner tried to kill Gabriel and me. And then I trusted Melanie, who tried to kill me herself."

He gave me a hard look. We'd hashed through my guilt trips before. He would point out that Tristan's partner acted without his knowledge and even then, when Tristan lured me to the hospital, I knew it was a trap—I just went to see what he was up to. Melanie hadn't tried to hurt me until I uncovered her scheme. Still, I felt like an idiot—once burned, twice too-stupid-to-learn-her-lesson. Well, third time was the charm. I wasn't trusting the dryads, no matter what my gut said.

We followed the footprints. When we reached what had been a set of stairs, Gabriel's prints paced around it.

"Was he looking for a way up?" Ricky said.

"He was doing what we are—following footprints." I examined the traces more. "Patrick stopped here and scuffed around."

"Waiting for Gabriel to find the trail. So those two were tracking the dryads, who must have taken off on them."

"Which, being dryads, could mean they were fleeing . . . or just scampered ahead."

We followed the tracks down the hall. When I realized Ricky wasn't right behind me, I stopped to see him shining his light through a doorway.

"The windows are broken," he said. "And yeah, given that it's an abandoned building, that's no big shock, but the windows have been shattered very recently, pieces on the floor, no dust settled on them." He walked to the next door. "Same thing in every room we've passed."

"Olivia!" Gabriel's voice boomed from somewhere below. "Is that you?"

Ricky put his fingers on my arm. He knew I wouldn't run toward Gabriel's voice, but I would be tempted. I locked my knees and called back, "Where are you?"

"In the basement. We fell through the floor and seem to be trapped."

"What broke the windows?" I called.

"What?" Patrick answered.

"The windows. They're all broken. What happened?"

"We don't know," Patrick said. "A tremor? I thought it might be fae, but we didn't find any evidence of that. The building shook, and we heard glass breaking, and then the floor gave way."

I glanced at Ricky and then called, "Gabriel?"

"Hmm?"

"What did we have for lunch?"

"This isn't the time for games, Liv," Patrick said. "We're trapped in this basement, and the building keeps creaking and groaning. Gabriel fell three stories. He needs a doctor."

"We found a pen in the car, Patrick," I said. "One of your homemade jobs. What kind of ink do you use?"

Silence. Then a woman's voice said, "Oh, but you're clever, aren't you, Eden?"

It was the voice from Todd's memory. The one that plucked at my own memory but wove through Todd's until I wasn't sure if I'd really heard it elsewhere or just remembered it from him.

"Not so much clever as capable of learning," I said. "The fae like their tricks. Sluagh may not consider themselves fae, but they pull the same stunts. Where's Gabriel?"

"So *you* consider us fae? That will make this conversation so much easier."

"No, our conversation will be easier if Gabriel's standing beside me. It's the only way I'm talking to you."

"You have a high opinion of your worth, don't you, child? You think you're a player, but you are just a pawn. One we own."

"Because you're the ones who healed me. Yeah, I've figured that out. You set up the whole thing—giving Todd the idea, answering Ioan's summons, and then making the deal. Which you think means I owe you. It doesn't. My mother paid for my cure in full."

"Do you really think we'd go through all the trouble of arranging your cure simply to add a few mortal souls to our flock?"

"If you're trying to say I'm marked, I'm not. Nor did Ioan or Pamela bind me to you in any way."

"You're certain of that? Absolutely certain?"

"Certain that they weren't stupid enough to repeat some mystical incantation to bind me? Yeah. There was no part of those deaths . . ."

I trailed off as I remembered James's body, Gabriel turning him over for me to see what had been done.

"Liv?" Ricky moved up behind me.

"Oh, the mighty Arawn speaks. Of the three, you certainly got the worst of the deal, didn't you? The great lord of the Otherworld . . . reborn as a pretty biker. Even more a child than the others. Are you out of school yet, boy?"

Ricky ignored the voice and murmured to me, "You were thinking about something. What was it?"

"You always stand behind her, don't you, boy? Walk at her heels. Whisper your thoughts in her ear. The loyal hound, grateful for whatever scraps his huntress might offer."

"I want Gabriel," I said.

She gave a soft laugh. "Of course you do. And you say it right in front of poor Ricky. Thrown over again, Arawn. One might think you'd have the self-respect to walk away."

"I mean that I want you to return the guy you're holding hostage. Which is obviously not Ricky."

"Ignore her," Ricky said. "She thinks she can punch my buttons and I'll stalk off in a snit. Arawn might have. I am not Arawn. You heard Liv, bitch. If you want to speak to her, bring Gabriel."

"But we're already speaking. Her demands are mere bluster. You wish to see your beloved Gwynn, Matilda?"

She fell silent, and then a voice called, "Olivia? Olivia!"

"Not going to answer him?" the sluagh said.

"What'd we have for lunch?" I shouted.

A strained chuckle that sounded like Patrick. "That's an interesting greeting."

"She's making certain she's speaking to me," the other voice said. "Thai food, which I am regretting after falling three stories."

"What happened?"

"The sluagh, evidently. Which is why you need to get out of here. They've laid a trap—"

"She's already fallen in," the sluagh called back. "We've chatted. It was lovely. Now go rescue your lover, Matilda. He's right down the next hall. Well, down the hall *and* down two stories, but I believe he's already managed to crawl out of the hole."

"Olivia?" Gabriel called. "Go back out to the car. We're on our way."

"Mmm, no, Gwynn," the sluagh said. "You may have made it to the second floor, but that's like finding the jailer left your cell door unlocked for his own amusement. How fast can you run, Mr. Walsh? Not very fast, I bet. You aren't built for running. Nor are you dressed for it. But try. Please. See how far you get from that hole."

I pictured him hesitating, thinking he could run faster than the sluagh presumed, while knowing it was futile, that the sluagh just wanted to see him try.

"Give us a name," Patrick called.

"What?" the sluagh said.

"Your name. Your title of address. You seem determined to turn this into a long conversation, so at the very least supply us with a name to call you."

"So we can exchange pleasantries while you escape?" The voice snorted. "Poor play, bòcan. Poor play indeed."

A shriek rang out, an inhuman scream as the building itself shuddered. Gabriel shouted, "Get down, Olivia!" but Ricky was already knocking me to the floor.

A tornado of melltithiwyd whipped down the hall, their shrieks almost drowned out by the thunderous roar of their wings.

As Ricky lay over me, I felt the batter of those wings and bodies against his back. He hissed in pain, and I scrambled out to help him, but the swarm was still slamming into him, pecking at his back. By the time I got up, the throng was hurtling down the hall.

I saw something else down that hall. A spot where the floor seemed black. Where the floor was missing.

As one body, the melltithiwyd swooped down that hole, and I ran toward it screaming, "No!"

A curse from Patrick and then a snarling shout in Welsh. A crash. A thump.

I reached the hole, and I think if Ricky hadn't tackled me, I *might* have done something as stupid as leap right into it.

I struggled free and crawled to the hole.

The swarm of melltithiwyd flew straight at me. Their beaks opened, blood-red maws of tiny shark teeth. When one looked at me, its blank white eyes morphed into human ones, roiling with rage and anguish and hate.

That one melltithiwyd flew at me, beak wide. Ricky yanked me back, but the thing sunk its teeth into my cheek. It ripped and then swooped for a second bite, and Ricky smacked it so hard it flew into the hole, tumbling head over tail. Its brethren continued flying by, battering us with wings and bodies.

When they passed, I peered into the hole and saw Gabriel rising from a pile of debris, Patrick lying beside him. I started to call down, to ask if they were all right. Then the single melltithiwyd Ricky had knocked into the hole swooped up, shrieking, maw open, teeth flashing.

Ricky grabbed the thing. It wasn't any bigger than a swallow, and his hand engulfed it. The melltithiwyd went wild, pecking but unable to reach him. He squeezed. It started to scream, a scream of rage that turned almost human as it thrashed and pecked, its beak still spattered with my blood. Ricky kept crushing it, his fingers digging into the dark red feathers. The tiny body contorted, and the melltithiwyd snarled, white eyes turning human. Ricky squeezed until gore and black blood ran down his arm. That's when it stopped snarling, stopped screaming, stopped pecking, stopped struggling.

Ricky whipped the mangled thing at the departing flock. It hit one, and as the creature turned, it struck another, a chain reaction, the last few melltithiwyd pecking and shrieking as the rest of the flock swirled out of sight.

The dead melltithiwyd fell to the floor with a wet thwack,

and when the remaining ones heard that, they stopped in mid-peck and looked down at the corpse on the floor.

They swooped as one body, and all I could see was a red-black blur. But I heard more. I heard ripping and snapping and gulping, and when they finally stopped, there was nothing on the floor but a black stain of blood. The lingering melltithiwyd flew upward, bits of their dead brethren still hanging from their beaks as they flew to join the others.

I grabbed the edge of the hole. "Gabriel?"

"I'm fine," he said. "They only knocked us in. Which was not a pleasant reoccurrence, but we're unharmed. It was simply a message—telling us that we are not escaping until the sluagh allows it." He squinted up, holding his cell phone for light. "Is that blood?"

My hand clapped to the spot the melltithiwyd had attacked, and I felt a tiny divot of missing flesh. "I'm fine. Ricky . . ." I turned quickly. "Are you okay? Your back . . ." I moved behind him.

"A leather jacket is both symbolic and functional," he said as I saw the peck marks on the leather. "I'm good."

I reached to the rear of his neck, where blood dripped from his scalp.

"Yeah, I should have been wearing the helmet, too," he said. "But it's just pecks. Like oversized mosquitoes."

I wiped the blood and checked a couple of the spots, which really did look like bug bites, bloodied pocks like the one on my cheek.

"You do an excellent job of feigning concern," the sluagh said, her voice sliding around us. "Overreact to his injuries in hopes he won't notice you asked after Gwynn first."

"Shut the fuck up," Ricky said.

"Scraps of attention," she whispered. "Her dutiful hound—"

"No, really, shut the fuck up. You told Patrick his ploy was poor? Yours is poorer. I just crushed a fucking hell-bird. Obviously, I was fine, and obviously she's going to check the guy who fell through the damned floor again."

Ricky caught my shoulder as I crawled past and whispered, "Stop worrying. That's what she's really doing—trying to make you feel like you're neglecting me." When I didn't respond, he squeezed my shoulder and nodded toward my ankle tattoo. "You said you aren't getting rid of that, so I know where I stand. Stop fretting. We stick together, the three of us. That's how it works, right? The only way it works."

"Thank you," I murmured, and kissed his cheek.

"Hey, Gabriel?" Ricky called. "Liv just gave me a kiss on the cheek. I'm letting you know before this sluagh-bitch tries to make it sound like we're two seconds from screwing on the floor here."

Gabriel's snort of a laugh wafted up from the hole.

"You all think you're such clever children," the sluagh said.

"Just go," Gabriel called. "Both of you. We'll find a way out."

"He's right," Patrick added. "If you stay, that only means four of us need to escape this place. We're fine. We'll figure this out."

"So there's *that* option," the sluagh said. "It presumes we'll let anyone leave, which we won't, but you can certainly try. For amusement's sake, though *you* might not find it quite so entertaining."

"What do you want?" I asked.

"It's already told us that," Patrick called up. "The sluagh would like to throw their hat in the ring, as a suitor for your affections."

Ricky snorted a choking laugh. "Seriously?"

"He means with the fae and the Hunt," Gabriel said. "A third competitor."

"Still, doesn't that mean they need a champion?" Ricky said. "I definitely want to see their champion. I think you're in for some stiff competition there, Gabriel."

"We do not have a champion," the sluagh said. "We do not need one. Ours is not a campaign of subtle wooing and flowery promises. We convince. And we are doing exactly that, demonstrating that we can find you, anywhere, anytime, and threaten those you love. Kill those you love. Or do you require a more overt lesson in that?"

"Threats won't—" I began.

"—work. Oh, yes, I believe threats work much better than flattery and gifts and promises. The trick is to be very, very clear that those threats are not empty. So let's do that now. The cost of leaving is a life. Choose one, Olivia."

My gut chilled. "Don't you—"

"Not Gabriel. We'll remove him from the options, knowing he will never be the one you sacrifice. So choose between the other two. Arawn or the bòcan. Which may we have for letting Gabriel go free?"

"If you touch either, you will never win my favor."

"Is that a threat? Excellent. You do know how this works. Let me be generous, then. It doesn't help our cause to overplay our hand too soon. You don't need to choose. Not yet. In fact, we'll set them all free for you, Olivia. We'll even escort them out the door. But you . . ." Her voice circled me. "You stay. You find your own way out. And if they come back for you, they'll die."

Her voice turned to smoke, the black enveloping me even as I heard Ricky shout "No!" and lunge. His fingers brushed my arm, and then . . .

Darkness.

CHAPTER THIRTY-TWO

I woke facedown on a cold floor, my head throbbing. I rose to all fours and gagged as my stomach lurched. I felt like I'd swallowed that smoke, the most foul imaginable, like something from a crematorium. My stomach lurched again at the thought.

Less thinking. More doing.

I turned on my switchblade's penlight and looked around. Not surprisingly, I seemed to be in the same place Gabriel and Patrick had been—a basement room with a jagged hole in the ceiling. Also not surprisingly, I was alone.

The third "Nope, still no surprises" moment came when I tried the exit door, and it wouldn't budge. I figured if Gabriel couldn't open it, neither could I, but still I tried, again in case the sluagh decided to play pranks with my presumptions.

So the question became "How to escape?" I wasn't particularly concerned that I couldn't. I wouldn't be much use to the sluagh dead. Unless . . .

I thought of the melltithiwyd, and shuddered. I can't imagine Mallt-y-Nos would be very useful as a mindless hell-bird.

Gabriel and Patrick were able to climb out of this room, presumably by Gabriel standing on the pile of debris. Which is great, if you're six foot four. The obvious answer, then? Build a bigger pile.

That wasn't as simple as it sounded, given that I had to construct a pile stable enough to support me. I managed it. Then I heaved and hefted and hauled myself up through that hole . . . and in came the melltithiwyd, a swooping swarm of avian piranha. I instinctively let go and fell back into the damned basement.

Attempt number two. I did the exact same thing. And, shockingly, got the same result. When the melltithiwyd attacked, I squeezed my eyes shut and gritted my teeth and endured the pecks and the bites and the beating wings as I kept heaving myself up. Finally, I got out and rolled away from the hole. Then I crouched there, my head down, as the melltithiwyd battered me, and I lashed out as hard as I could.

That's what did it. Hitting them. I bashed a few into the wall, heard the thump as their bodies struck, the crack of bones, and then the shrieks of their comrades, diverting course to devour their brethren, not caring if they were dead or alive, only that they were momentarily dazed, weak, and vulnerable.

Whatever intelligence the melltithiwyd possessed, it was enough for them to see me hurting the others—and those others being devoured—and decide maybe they didn't want to torment me after all. Finally, with a scream that seemed to come from a thousand tiny throats, they tore off and I was left there, panting, blood dripping down my face.

"You're very pleased with yourself, aren't you?"

It was a woman's voice, which made me think of the sluagh, but this one was pitched lower, edged with anger rather than mockery.

When I didn't answer, she said, "Are you too good to speak to me, Miss Larsen? I bet you think you are."

A figure stepped into the doorway. I had a flash of instant recognition followed by . . . nothing. Just that flash that said, "I know you," but when I went to chase down a name, my memory had nothing to give.

She was my age, maybe a little younger, and she stood in that doorway, her blue eyes dark with hate. I'd seen that face. Seen it recently. Where . . . ?

"Does this help?" she said, and her jeans and blouse disappeared, and she stood there in her bra and panties. Dried blood smeared one bare thigh where I could make out part of a symbol carved into her flesh. Another symbol decorated her stomach above her panties, this one in blue paint, pierced by a twig. Blue woad. A mistletoe twig.

"Stacey Pasolini," I said.

"Very good. A shame you needed me to humiliate myself with that visual reminder." The clothing reappeared. "That's how it goes, isn't it? People remember the killers, not the victims."

"Except you were both," I said. "The world just doesn't know about the first part yet. Don't worry—they will soon, and I'm sure you'll get a fresh batch of news coverage."

She lunged, the edges of her body dissolving into black smoke, reconstituting when she stopped, looming above me. As she glowered, the blue seeped from her eyes and they went as white as the melltithiwyd's, and when she snarled, her teeth were razor-sharp.

I got to my feet. "Let me guess. You're one of the melltithiwyd now, and you're a little pissy about the whole thing. Can't say I blame you. It doesn't look like a lot of fun. Although I suppose there's always that option." I glanced at scattered feathers on the floor.

"Do you think it's really that easy?" she said. "Do you think that doesn't happen to at least one of us every day? It happens again and again, and we are reborn, again and again. Devoured and reborn, and constantly surrounded by those who cannot wait to do the devouring."

"Sounds like you have a group dynamics issue. I'd suggest team-building exercises."

She flew at me—literally flew—her arms becoming wings, her edges turning to smoke again, teeth bared, blank eyes fixed on mine, her face coming so close all I could see were those eyes.

"Our sluagh is right," she said. "You do think you are clever. You don't need to worry about becoming one of us, Miss Larsen. You have no soul to give. You are as empty as the bitch who whelped you."

"Right, yeah, because I don't feel sorry for you. Is that what this is supposed to be? A tableau to make me feel guilty about what my mother did?" I snorted and headed into the hall.

"Don't you walk away on me."

"You want to chat? Keep up. I have some escaping to do. As for making me feel bad, don't bother. First, I'm not my mother. Second, my soul is just fine because, third, I really don't give a shit about the terrible fate that befell someone who decided it'd be fun to slaughter innocent people with her boyfriend. That's not my idea of date night."

"You have it all figured out, haven't you? You know exactly what happened, just like your mother did. You don't care to dig deeper because then, if you decide I didn't deserve to die, well, that's a little bit uncomfortable. Much easier to tell yourself I deserved it."

I paused near the hole in the floor, considered edging around it, and then decided to take another route. As I walked, I said, "I'm sure you've convinced yourself—"

"I thought it was a performance. A game. A staged performance. That's what Eddie told me, and I was young and stupid and in love. Crazy in love with this guy who showed me a whole new world. A world where I didn't need to be the good girl anymore. Where I could be bad. And by bad, I mean having fun with dark-magic rituals. Don't pretend not to understand what I mean. The good girl from the rich family, running around abandoned schools with a switchblade and a biker."

"I definitely understand the power of a good adrenaline rush. I also understand that morals and ethics are luxuries we can't always afford. But this?" I waggled my switchblade. "This has never killed anyone. I could, in self-defense. What you did, though, was cold murder, and to call it a game only makes it even more loathsome."

"You are so smug, Eden Larsen. You aren't even listening to me, are you? I said I thought it was a performance. That's what they did to me—Eddie and Marty and Lisa and that bitch who brought us together, who promised us the moon if we did as she said. They told me we had to pretend to kill that boy in the fun house. But it wasn't real. They swore it wasn't real."

I stopped at the end of the hall, considered my options, and turned left. "Uh-huh. So you're telling me you were so drugged up—"

"I was naive—I wasn't stupid. After the fun house, I asked questions. I doubted. So when we had to make our kills, Eddie pumped me full of drugs. When I still said I didn't want to go, he beat the shit out of me. Knocked me out, and the next thing I know, I'm waking up in a forest beside the dead bodies of two street kids. Eddie's holding my hand and forcing me to make the cuts. We had to do it together. That's what the bitch said. Do it together, or it wouldn't work. I threw up. So he hit me, knocked me out again. That was my level of participation in those murders, Miss Larsen. A drugged-out, beat-up, half-conscious 'partner' who held a knife while her lover moved her hand to cut up the kids he'd killed."

"And what would you like me to do about that?"

Stacey swung in front of me, her eyes going from blue to blank white. "My God, there's nothing in there, is there? When I said you didn't have a soul, I—"

"You were goading me. Which is what you're doing now. You want me to feel bad for you. Maybe your story's true. Maybe it's not. Maybe you aren't even Stacey Pasolini, but a phantom conjured to wring a few pangs of sympathy from me."

I locked my gaze on hers. "I know there are innocents in that swarm of melltithiwyd. But unless you're here to tell me how I can help them, I don't see the point. If you didn't take a more active role in those murders, then you don't deserve this fate. But you aren't the only one. There are others more wronged than you in there. The only thing *that* tells me is that the sluagh don't deserve a moment of my consideration. The Cŵn Annwn might be a little bloodthirsty, overzealous in their pursuit of justice. The Tylwyth Teg might be conniving and amoral and completely self-absorbed. But the real monsters? That's the sluagh, and your story only confirms it."

She flew at me again, flew at me in a full rage, half woman, half bird, pecking and pounding and beating. I stabbed at her with the switchblade, but it was as if my knife passed through thin air.

I dodged past her and ran, and I was still running full out when someone shouted, "Olivia! Stop!"

Had it been anyone else, I wouldn't have listened. Even then, as soon as I put on the brakes, I cursed, certain I was hearing another mimicry. But I still skidded to a halt. My foot dropped, as if through the floor itself. Then there was a snap, and I was back in the original hall, inches from falling down that damned hole again. Gabriel stood on the other side, his hands out.

"Thai for lunch," he said. "Bacon and eggs for breakfast. The scratches on my back are not from the melltithiwyd."

I sputtered a laugh. "You're quick."

"I'm learning."

"You're also not supposed to be here."

"Yes, well, I am."

"Gabriel . . ."

"I'm not doubting you could have handled it. I'm not suggest-ing you require my assistance. But they aren't going to kill me, Olivia. I'm too valuable as a tool to control you."

"Ricky—"

"I may have incapacitated him. I may have left him in Patrick's care. He is not going to be pleased with me when I return, but I will return. The sluagh won't kill me. I could not guarantee the same for him." He looked behind me. "You were running. Was something chasing you?"

I glanced back to see the empty hall. "Stacey Pasolini mani-fested. She's one of the melltithiwyd now. She claimed she didn't kill anyone and then didn't like it when I failed to express the proper degree of sympathy."

"Whatever her situation, there's nothing you can do about it."

"That's what I said. I think she expected more." I squinted down the hall. "But I thought I was running along a different hall. Seems I'm caught in one of those mental mazes, like at the asylum and the villa."

"Hmm." He crouched and eyed the hole. Then he reached out to touch it, nodding when he discovered it was really there.

"Maybe I can . . ." I eased my foot along the six-inch strip of floor remaining between the wall and the hole. It crumbled on contact. "Nope. So, I wonder how my long jump is these days?"

"No, please. Go back down the hall and look for another way. I'll ask you to not go out of sight. And tell me what you see."

I walked down the corridor. "I see hall." I looked both ways. "Yep, hall."

"Are you sure?"

"Well, that's a little tough to answer when I haven't figured out how to see through a vision."

"No, but your foot felt the hole before you saw it. Do you see those windows?"

"Uh, right. Conveniently located first-floor windows, which I completely missed as an escape option. Duh."

"Perhaps not. They appear broken and boarded from here. Yes?"

I nodded. "This one's cleared of glass, though, and I bet I could break the boards." I went to put my hand out . . . and hit a solid wall. The illusion flickered and I *saw* the wall.

"No window," Gabriel said. "Now, take three steps forward, staying within my sight."

I did, and when he called, "Stop there," I did . . . and his voice came from in front of me.

"All right," he said. "You're back in this hall. You don't see me, do you?"

"No, but I hear you in front of me. Hold on."

I closed my eyes and ran my hand along the window, picturing wood instead. When I opened my eyes, that's what I saw—the original hallway, with the hole and Gabriel on the other side.

I returned to him. "Okay, so I'm caught in a vision maze. You're not."

"I have an idea," he said.

"Excellent." I grabbed the side of the hole and swung down into it.

He gave an alarmed, "Olivia!"

I dropped and then looked up. "Yes."

He sighed. "That was *not* my idea."

"Nope, it's mine. Now I just need to re-pile this stuff and come up on your side."

"Just climb what's there and reach."

I did, and he grabbed my wrists. We locked together, and he said, "On the count of—" and disappeared, me tumbling back as his hold vanished.

CHAPTER THIRTY-THREE

"Gabriel?" I peered through the hole to the dark first floor, no sign of him. "Well, that was too easy," I muttered, and started piling the debris. I was adding another piece when Gabriel appeared—the bottom half of him, at least, and then the rest as he jumped down into the hole with me.

"I don't think that helps," I said.

"Given the choice, I would rather be lost in the vision maze with you than stuck alone on the other side."

"That's really kind of sweet."

"It's practical."

"Also sweet. Own it. I won't tell anyone. Okay, so we'll both climb up on the other side and . . ."

He kept walking, heading for the exit door.

"That still doesn't open," I said.

He took hold of the knob and murmured something in Welsh. And it opened.

"Huh," I said. "So that's like an 'open sesame' for sluagh-locks?"

"Hmm."

I didn't ask how he thought of it—I suspected he didn't know, either, only that the urge sprang from deep in his Gwynn-memory bank.

Not surprisingly, the door led into another basement room. We continued past a furnace, shining the light this way and that until . . .

"Stairs," I said. "Which will lead right back to the hole again."

"Don't even say that."

We picked our way through basement crap until we reached the stairs. Halfway up them, the hairs on my neck rose, five seconds in advance of the damned voice that teased at my memory.

"Going somewhere, Eden?"

"You made your point," I called. "You're a badass. We need to take you seriously. We do. But keeping me locked in this building isn't actually going to accomplish anything. If you want to talk, let's talk. Otherwise, we really need to go."

"In a hurry, are you? For what, exactly? There's no fire to put out, Eden."

Those words snagged on a memory, the one that insisted I knew who this was, that I'd met her before.

Same voice. Different tenor. Different inflections.

There's no fire to put out.

No.

Hell, no. That wasn't possible. It just wasn't . . .

I took a deep breath and turned to Gabriel.

"Fire." That's all I said, seeing if he'd make the connection. In a heartbeat, he did, his lips forming a name.

I saw that name on his lips, and I tumbled through memory, images flashing. A house, nestled between two tall buildings. A woman, fleeing to a parking garage. Middle-aged with girlish barrettes and a girlish voice. A woman easily dismissed. A woman we *had* dismissed.

The young woman in the park who'd given Todd the file and set him on Greg Kirkman's path. I'd recognized her voice there, too, but couldn't connect it to the fragile whisper of the middle-aged woman with the silly pink barrettes.

There's one more connection that my mind makes as it tumbles through memories.

The fifth figure in the fun house. The person in charge, the one I couldn't see, couldn't even hear.

Just moments ago, Stacey Pasolini talked about "that bitch" who showed them what to do, made them promises for what the killings would bring them.

The same woman.

All the same woman.

Imogen Seale. The "witness" we'd been chasing for six months. An answer we'd been chasing for so much longer, though we never realized it.

Imogen Seale. A powerful sluagh in manifested form. The one the elders had admitted to Cainsville. The woman who'd given Todd a victim to get the Cŵn Annwn involved. When the Cŵn Annwn sought a deal with their "higher powers," she had answered and given Ioan the names of four killers. Killers *she'd* counseled to commit the crimes for which they would be executed.

Why so many levels of complication?

I knew.

The Tysons and Eddie Hilton each murdered a couple in the manner the sluagh prescribed. That allowed the sluagh to tell Ioan that my parents must kill in the exact same manner, to make the deaths seem like an extension of the original killings, supposedly done in some random and meaningless ritualistic manner.

Except it wasn't random. Wasn't meaningless.

It was a trick.

The ritual that Pamela conducted on her victims had bound me to the sluagh.

As Gabriel mouthed that name, the woman herself appeared. Imogen Seale.

"Do you know the problem with children who think they're terribly clever?" she said. "They're very quick to decide others are not. As you were with poor Imogen. A silly woman, unworthy of your time. That's how one sneaks past two like you. Stay beneath your notice."

She was right. We'd dismissed Imogen as a pitiful creature, clinging to her youth and her memories of Marty Tyson, her supposed lover. That's what the police had believed—that Imogen was his mistress. They'd found something in his belongings—a phone number, rendezvous times—and jumped to that conclusion. Then we tracked Imogen down with her "mother" and she "accidentally" revealed that Marty and Lisa were killers. She played us, and when we proved tiresome in our efforts to track her human identity, she staged the fire, victims and all.

"It's the ritual," I said. "The one my mother supposedly copied. You fed it to the Tysons."

"It binds Olivia in some way," Gabriel said. "But it does not mark her as yours. What exactly is the nature of her obligation to you?"

"Ah, the lawyer appears. Looking for a contract to weasel out of, counselor? You will need to wait until the papers are served, the obligation due."

"Bullshit," I said.

"Excuse me?" Imogen said.

"I call bullshit. You won't name the obligation because you want me to fear the worst. It's like telling a man you've cursed him, and then watching him fall into ruin because of his own superstitious fear. I'm not marked, as Gabriel said, so I'm not doomed to serve you. Nor am I forced to choose you over the Tylwyth Teg and Cŵn Annwn. If I was, you wouldn't bother trying to frighten me into choosing the sluagh. You invented a ritual so you can convince me that I'm bound to you. I'm not."

"Care to test that, Eden?"

"Olivia . . ." Gabriel moved up behind me.

"Listen to your lover, girl. He counsels caution."

I turned to Gabriel. "I'm a client, and I'm asking your professional advice. Do I call her on it?"

His lips compressed. The question wasn't fair because I knew the answer was yes, just as I knew there was no way in hell he could give me that advice.

"I'm calling your bluff," I said to Imogen.

"Are you certain?" she said, advancing on me. "Quite certain?"

Gabriel had gone quiet, and I took that to mean he was biting his tongue. When I started to speak, he shot forward, grabbing me from behind, his hand clapping over my mouth.

And Imogen—the sluagh—laughed. Laughed so hard the building trembled.

"I know the answer," Gabriel whispered in my ear. "Do not do it. Please, do not do it."

"Oh, but let her, Gwynn. Let her learn a lesson about brash arrogance. Go on, Eden. Call my bluff. Please."

As she said the words, her hand rose, a casual gesture. Pain ripped through my back and my knees gave way, and I fell back onto Gabriel so hard he stumbled. He caught me and held me as I gasped in pain.

"She said nothing," he snarled at the sluagh. "Undo it. Now."

"Is that an order, Gwynn?"

"*Fynd nawr.*"

"Oh, no, you don't want to banish me right at this moment. If you do, I can't reverse what I've done."

I struggled to make sense of her words as I gasped in agony. I was only dimly aware of Gabriel's arms around me, his grip supporting me.

I couldn't feel my legs. No, that's a lie. I felt the dead weight of them, memories of those early years flying back.

"Undo it!" Gabriel roared. "Now!"

"But I am. I'm undoing what I did. That's what your lover figured out, Eden. The question isn't what we can do, but what can we *undo*."

She lifted her hand again, that casual gesture, and I could sense my legs dangling as Gabriel held me aloft.

"Is that the threat, then?" I said, still wincing against the ebbing pain. "You'll undo the cure? Rob me of the use of my legs?"

"Oh, it's not just your legs, Olivia. Your condition was more severe than the doctors could bring themselves to tell your parents. By this age, you would have been in a wheelchair, unable to move the lower half of your body, unable to regulate your bladder and bowels. You would have lung issues. Loss of skin sensation. The list goes on."

"All right."

That echoing laugh again. "Ah, but with such arrogance comes a bit of actual strength, doesn't it? Right now, you're madly working through the worst case, whether you could deal with that. Which is why we didn't simply threaten it, Eden. Yes, we can reverse the cure. We can also ensure your father spends his life in prison for the murder of Gregory Kirkman. And we can take your lovers. Both of them. Notice that I do not say 'kill' them. I say take them. Which I think you will agree now is a far worse fate."

"Hey, *heb edifeirwch*, you done talking?" said a voice. A young voice, male. Then a female one, saying, "That's right. We called you by your Welsh name, *heb edifeirwch*. Because, being dryads, we're too stupid to be afraid of using it."

Helia and Alexios appeared. Helia's olive skin looked pale, and she limped, her mate staying close.

"You're done here, *heb edifeirwch*," Helia said. "You may send the Welsh fae running for cover, but there's no word for you in our language. So we don't have to be afraid of you."

"That is the most ridiculous logic I have ever heard," the sluagh said. "You really aren't that bright, are you?"

"Nope," Alexios said. "Definitely not bright enough to know that you are as bound to Nature as any other fae. Yet, unlike the others, you're not *part* of Nature. You have no affinity for her. And she has no affinity for you."

"Unnatural," Helia said. "If we had a word for you, that's what it would be. And Nature?" She lifted her hands, gesturing to the building. "She really doesn't like anyone messing with her world."

Helia closed her eyes and spoke words in Greek. Her fingers lengthened and twisted, her skin scaling like bark. Alexios did the same, beginning the metamorphosis to tree.

As they reached up, Nature reached back. Vines wound through the smashed windows and pushed through the ceiling, through the walls. I felt the energy of those vines, like straight alcohol driving into my veins, my mind swimming, heart pumping, the energy coursing through me, a raw and live thing.

The sluagh twisted, her edges turning to smoky wisps, as if she fought to maintain her form. Deep in the building, the melltithiwyd shrieked and screamed.

Gabriel grabbed my shoulders to pull me down, but as the melltithiwyd swooped past the stairwell, they reared up, in one body, turning sharply as if they'd seen a cyclone heading straight for them. They winged their way back at twice the speed, hitting one another, attacking one another, black blood and red feathers exploding in their panic to escape.

As the melltithiwyd flew up through the distant hole in the ceiling, Helia watched and said, "Huh. That went well."

"Swimmingly," Alexios said, and they giggled and I turned back to see that the sluagh had disappeared, and the dryads had resumed their humanlike form.

"And that is the advantage to our age," Helia said. "As we grow closer to death, we grow closer to Nature herself. Now, move quickly. Nature is full of bluster and blow, but she can't keep that thing at bay for long. Time to save ourselves."

CHAPTER THIRTY-FOUR

"We rescued your mother," Alexios said to Gabriel as we crawled out the side window.

"Even if you'd rather we hadn't." Helia smiled but then caught Gabriel's expression and said, "We will look after her for you, Gabriel, until you feel ready to deal with her. You only need to tell us what you'd like done."

"I would prefer not to answer that right now."

"Just—" I began, but Helia cut in, saying, "We'll speak to Patrick. She is his problem, not yours. A father chooses who mothers his child. The child has no voice in the selection of his parents."

In this case, neither was responsible, but I kept my mouth shut. Patrick could deal with it.

As Alexios helped Helia climb out the window, she winced and I said, "You're hurt, Helia. I noticed that earlier. I'm sorry I didn't ask—"

"We all had other concerns," she said with a soft smile. "I'll be fine. We heal quickly, even at our age."

Gabriel turned then, frowning, as if poked from his thoughts. "Yes. You were injured trying to protect me. Thank you."

"We have committed ourselves to the adventure," she said.

"Adventure comes with risk or it would hardly *feel* adventurous." She eyed him, the humor falling from her eyes. "I know something happened in there, and I will not pry now, Gabriel, but if you need our help, you have only to ask. I am not joking when I say we are committed. Fully committed."

"Taking care of my mother will be quite enough."

At the sound of running footsteps, the others went still, but I recognized them and hurried forward as Ricky ran around the corner, Patrick following at a more dignified quick walk.

Ricky caught me in a hug. "You're okay?"

I nodded.

Ricky released me and advanced on Gabriel. "I really do not appreciate—" He saw the look on Gabriel's face and stopped mid-sentence. "What happened?" he asked.

"Later," I whispered. "Patrick? Can I ask you to deal with Scanna? The dryads have offered to help."

Patrick nodded. "Of course."

"I'll go with them," Ricky said.

"Your bike isn't going to hold—" Patrick began.

A look from the dryads, Ricky, *and* me shut him up. He peered at Gabriel. "What happened in there?"

"We'll call," I said. "We just . . . We need to leave."

Gabriel's hand went to my back, and he steered me toward the car without another word.

Gabriel was driving. I didn't know where. I wasn't sure he did, either. When he reached an intersection on the city's outskirts, he stopped and his gaze traveled east, fingers tapping the wheel.

"You're thinking about the cottage you rented," I said softly. "Of going there."

"Anywhere," he said. "I want to go anywhere. Take you and drive as far as we can. Just drive until . . ."

He inhaled sharply. Silence for at least twenty seconds, and then he said, "Do you think it would help?" in a voice that was so quiet, I didn't dare reply, not when it wouldn't be the answer he wanted.

"It won't," he said, sounding more himself. "I know that. I just . . ." He ran a hand through his hair, setting it tumbling over. "I need a solution, Olivia. I must fix this, and the only thing I can come up with is running. Fleeing. Which I would do in a heartbeat if it would make any difference."

"We'll figure—"

"Do you know what I really want to do?" He turned to me, leather squeaking. "I want to say yes. Fine. All right. Let the sluagh be your choice. What does it matter to you? Really, what does it matter? There, the sluagh have your favor. Decision made. We're leaving now. Going as far as we can, and the fae and the Hunt and the sluagh can deal with the fallout after we're gone."

"It's not—"

"—not that easy. I know. It can't be. But what does it matter?" His gaze locked on mine. "No, really, what does it even *mean* to give one of them your favor? They talk and they talk, and they say nothing, and I'm so damned sick . . ." Another rake through his hair. "And I'm taking it out on you. You're the one they threaten, and how do I respond? Start shouting and cursing."

"Mmm, pretty sure shouting is louder. And cursing requires more than a single 'damned.' I can show you cursing if you'd like. I'm certainly in the mood."

"Which is my point. I'm making this about me. *I'm* upset. *I* had to leave. You needed to tag along and listen to me rant. I'm sorry."

"Given how rarely you rant, Gabriel, I'm fine with it. And honestly, right now, I just feel numb. You're ranting *for* me, and I'm okay with that, because I'm sitting here, doing exactly what the sluagh said I would. Trying to be logical. What if they undid my cure? How could I prepare myself for that? Except it's not just that—it's the threats against you and—"

"Not my primary concern at this moment."

"But it's mine. If they undid my cure, I could live with it—I'd have to. The rest?" I looked at him. "I can't. I just can't. That's where they have me, and yet you're right that I don't even know what they have me *for*, what exactly it means to give them my favor."

Another car came up behind us as we sat, still stopped at the intersection. The driver honked. Honked again. Then he jabbed his middle finger at us as he passed. Gabriel didn't even seem to notice. He sat motionless, staring straight ahead until he took out his phone.

"May I have Ioan's number?"

I gave it to him. When Ioan answered, Gabriel gave him instructions. Instructions that I knew would not go down easily.

"I understand your position," Gabriel said as Ioan argued. "And I do not care. This isn't about you. It's about cleaning up your mess, and if you want to do that, you will be there when we arrive."

He made his next call to Ida, with the same instructions, and presumably got the same response from her, followed by the same from him. Then he added a few additional demands.

"Absolutely not." Ida's voice came clear through the phone now. "We will accept responsibility for Seanna, but you are not bringing dryads into Cainsville. We're still suffering the fallout from your last refugee request."

"The only 'fallout' you are 'suffering' is that Veronica is fostering a damaged fae. It is Veronica's choice to continue that relationship. These dryads have been nothing but helpful, and I require their continued assistance."

"We can assign someone to watch your mother, Gabriel."

"I don't trust you."

"And you trust a couple of dryads?"

"More than I trust you. We will be there in an hour. Please have an apartment at Grace's complex prepared for Seanna and the dryads."

"Do you ski?" I asked as Gabriel took the exit for Cainsville. When he gave me a look, I said, "Yes, probably a stupid question, but I also presumed you didn't jog, and I learned my lesson from that. No presumptions. And . . . judging by that continued look, no skiing."

"As a form of physical activity, it would accomplish no more than jogging or swimming or weight lifting, all of which can be undertaken with little more expense than a gym membership and no more travel time than the two-block distance to the gym, which is still often too far to fit into my schedule."

"Skiing is also considered a form of recreation."

Another look.

I sighed. "Recreation, yes. It's a word we really need to incorporate into your vocabulary. I'm mentally planning a vacation for when this is done. 'Vacation' is another word you may not be familiar with. We'll go to work on that, too."

"So long as you intend to take one *with* me and not send me on it alone."

"I'll only send you alone if you get on my nerves. By doing things like rolling your eyes when I dare to ask if you ski."

"I did not roll—"

"So, no skiing. Gabriel's list of acceptable sports includes running, swimming, and weight lifting, none of which are something you center a vacation around. Unless your idea of a vacation is entering a triathlon."

"A triathlon involves bicycling."

"Which you don't do, either, I presume. And don't roll . . ." I sighed. "Too late. Okay. No triathlon vacation, which is fine by me. Do I even dare ask what you'd want to do?"

I didn't expect an answer and was about to continue when he said, "I'd like to see the ocean."

"You've never . . . ? Okay, first step, where *have* you traveled? I know you don't own a passport."

"I have visited neighboring states on business." He paused. "Nothing more."

"So, the ocean," I continued as quickly as I could, covering my surprise. "Sandy beaches or rocky surf?"

"Am I correct that sand attracts people?" he said. "Crowds of people?"

"Rocky surf it is. Any issue with flying?"

"I doubt it would be a concern."

In other words, he'd never even been on a plane. I'd semi-joked earlier about avoiding presumptions, and now I was making them all over the place.

"Maybe Oregon," I said. "I'm thinking oceanfront property. No neighbors within a half-mile radius. As close to the water as possible. And complete lack of cell service and Internet would be a plus."

"I'd say it's a necessity."

I smiled. "Agreed."

We could see Cainsville in the distance now. No signs announced it and certainly no high-rise buildings, but the distant dip in the tree line was enough.

"I need to speak to Seanna," he said. "Before we meet with Ioan and Ida. I'm going to ask you to allow me to do that alone." When I didn't answer, he glanced over. "I am more comfortable dealing with her when you are not there to draw her spite."

"I know. But I was going to ask the same—that you let *me* speak to her alone. There are a few theories I want to test out."

"Tell me what they are and I will do it. You've been through quite enough today. I do not want you having to endure her ridiculous and petty insults."

"Her insults don't bother me. I know they're ridiculous and petty. What bothers me, Gabriel, is how she treats you, and 'bothers me' is an extreme understatement. I just . . . I cannot . . ." I felt my temper spark and clenched my fists.

Gabriel pulled the car to the side of the road. "Let's take a moment."

I managed a smile for him. "Get past my imminent emotional outburst?"

"Yes."

He leaned over and kissed me. Just a long, sweet kiss, pulling me as close as we could get over the console. And that's what I needed, as much as I'd needed the sex earlier. A moment to reconnect.

"Now that's my idea of 'taking a moment,'" I said when we separated. "You might *say* you don't know how to deal with emotion, but you are one helluva fast learner."

He chuckled and put the car into gear. "Good. Now let's get the rest of this over with so that we may take *more* than a moment."

Gabriel agreed to let me speak to Seanna alone . . . with a raft of stipulations. While I did that, he'd grab a new shirt at my place and then talk to Patrick about the sluagh.

When I arrived at my old apartment building, Grace sat on the stoop, bundled up against the cold. As I approached, she said, "I don't like having her here."

"There's no place else—"

"I know that. But the shorter her visit, the better. She disturbs things. Her energy . . ." She made a face, as if talk of "energy" was for flightier fae. "She's soul-reft. That's what they used to say about changelings. People could tell they were fae because they lacked a soul."

"Which is true, isn't it?" I said as I climbed the steps. "You guys don't get an afterlife. Technically, then, you lack whatever we call a soul."

"Except we never had it," she said. "We aren't supposed to have it. Humans are."

I looked at the building. "You really think Seanna lacks . . . ?"

"She lacks something. I say soul-reft because she feels empty." Another face. "Whatever that means."

"Was she always like that?" I asked.

"She was never a pleasant child. She could be, if she got her way. She had a selfish streak a mile wide."

"Doesn't that go for all children?"

"Double for her. But Seanna had her good side, too. Then she grew up—and I don't know if it was the drugs or the booze or the men—but it's like she went looking for something, and it drained all the good from her. Made her queen of her own universe, where others exist only to benefit her."

"You mean she became more fae-like."

Grace wagged a bony finger at me. "You have as much fae as she does. Probably more." She settled back in the chair. "But yes, it made her like us. Except, again, we're supposed to be like this. We work around it to form attachments. Otherwise we'd never be able to live in this damned town together."

"And you wouldn't be running a home for aged fae."

She snorted. "That's not altruism. Don't go making that mistake, girl. None of us knows the real meaning of the word."

"But nor are you so self-absorbed that you destroy even useful relationships, the way Seanna does. If she had an ounce of sense, she'd at least feign remorse to wiggle into Gabriel's good graces and get at his money."

"She can't. Something in her is missing, and she cannot overcome it even to her own benefit. I know she needs to be here, but the sooner she's gone, the better."

"For everyone."

She nodded. "Now get in there and rescue poor Ricky. He's helping those dryads watch over Seanna, and she seems to have decided he's a very fine-looking young man."

CHAPTER THIRTY-FIVE

I was still climbing the stairs when Ricky opened the stairwell door.

"Thought I heard you," he said.

"You mean you were eagerly awaiting the arrival of anyone who might save you from another minute with Seanna Walsh."

He chuckled. "Maybe. Are we sure she's Gabriel's mom? She looks like him, but I'd demand a maternity test, because otherwise, I'm not seeing *anything* in common."

"He will take that as a compliment."

I fell in beside Ricky as we climbed. "Speaking of Gabriel, I know you weren't happy with him leaving you behind earlier, but he wasn't trying to play my white knight. His theory is that, given what the sluagh said, they wouldn't kill him."

"I'm more expendable."

"It's not—"

"Yeah, it is, and I'm okay with that. Part of making me more expendable is making me *feel* more expendable. Making me feel second-rate in hopes that'll turn me against you two. I need to watch my ego and not get prickly." He opened the door for me. "You *are* going to explain what happened with the sluagh, right?"

I tried to give a casual nod, but Ricky caught my arm and tugged me back into the stairwell.

"Liv . . . ?"

I took a deep breath. "I would love to take twenty minutes and go somewhere to tell you the whole story. But if I do, I won't be in any mood to take on Seanna."

"Okay." He pulled me into a hug and whispered, "We'll work it out."

"Thank you."

We reached the door and I said, "You don't have to stick around. I hear she's ogling."

"She keeps telling me I have a nice ass. I can't tell if she's hitting on me or dismissing me as a pretty boy. Hopefully the latter. As much as I hate being objectified, it's better than thinking she's actually coming on to me."

"She's just being honest. It's a very nice ass."

He laughed. "That's so much more welcome coming from you."

He pushed open the door and led the way down the apartment hall. When Seanna saw him, she gave him a slow once-over. Then she saw me and scowled.

"Is Gwynn joining us?" Alexios asked. When Helia elbowed him, he said, "I mean Gabriel. Sorry. Arawn said—Richard . . . Rick . . ."

"It's Ricky."

"So cute," Helia said.

"He is," Seanna murmured.

Helia rolled her eyes and said, "I mean the name. I like it. Much better than Arawn, which sounds like a dog's howl. Though that makes sense, all things considered."

"It does," Ricky said. "But yeah, I'll stick with Ricky."

"What are you talking about?" Seanna said.

"Nothing at all." Helia leaned toward us. "Muggles. So annoying."

I chuckled.

Seanna's scowl deepened. "I have no idea what you're talking about, but I want to know what's going on. I've been taken captive by a couple of . . ." She waved at the dryads. "Hipster street kids."

"That's offensive," Helia said. "We are not hipsters."

"I don't even own a fedora," Alexios said.

Seanna continued, "And then, after they hold me captive, Gabriel and . . . that . . . other man—"

"I think you know Patrick. Intimately." Alexios turned to Helia and whispered, "Old age. You forget everything."

"Unless you're us."

"True."

"That man is not Patrick," Seanna said. "I don't know what his game is, but there's no possible way—"

"He aged well," Alexios said.

"Very well," Helia added.

"Better than you."

"*Much* better."

"They're adorable," Ricky whispered in my ear.

"They have their moments," I murmured.

"That man is not Patrick," Seanna said. "And whatever happened in that place, with those birds and the earthquake and the floor—"

"Faeries," I said.

"What?"

"You asked what's going on. I'm answering. You like fae lore, right? That's what I heard. Well, there's your answer." I waved at Alexios and Helia. "Dryads." Then Ricky. "Arawn. Or the living incarnation of him. You know who that is, right? Lord of the Otherworld? Leader of the Cŵn Annwn? That's him. I get to play Matilda. Mallt-y-Nos, technically. And Gabriel? Well, that's kind of a funny story. You named him after the Wild Hunt—Gabriel's Hounds—but he's actually the star of the opposing team. Gwynn ap Nudd. King of the Fae."

Seanna stared at me. Blinked. Then she snapped, "I don't like being mocked, little girl. I don't know who you think you are—"

"Matilda," Helia said.

"Mallt-y-Nos," Alexios said, then whispered, "I don't think she's paying attention."

"Hearing loss," Helia said. "It happens when you get old."

"Unless you're us." Alexios cleared his throat. "Let's clear this up." He put out his hand, as his skin thickened to tree bark. "See? Dryad."

Seanna fell back. "Wh-what— What did you give me?"

Alexios reached to catch her, but his hands were still covered in bark, and she kept staggering away until she hit the couch and toppled onto it.

"Well, that was ill-advised, *agori mou*," Helia murmured. She walked over to Seanna and crouched beside her as the woman tried to rise from the sofa. "You've taken a lot of drugs in your life, Seanna. They've done things to your mind. You're prone to hallucinations. In fact, everything you've seen and heard today? It's all in your mind. It's very sad, but we found you like that and contacted your son, and he brought you here to Cainsville. Do you understand?"

I expected Seanna to tell her where to go. Instead, she nodded dumbly, her eyes wide.

"Compulsion?" I murmured to Alexios.

He nodded. "It works best when the recipient wants to believe, which Seanna obviously does. You said she was fond of fae lore, so I thought I was making the right move. Apparently not."

"Muggles," I said.

He smiled. "Half-bloods can be even worse. Either they want the answers, or they *really* don't. I misjudged."

"I started it." I looked at Helia, still calming Seanna, and lowered my voice further. "How is Helia? I know she said dryads heal fast, but I've caught her wincing."

"We . . ." His smile faltered. "We don't heal quite as quickly as we used to. Nature can be eager to reclaim her own when she feels their time is waning."

"You mean—?"

"Helia will be fine. Thank you for your concern, though. You are very kind, even if you fear you are not."

Ricky put an arm around me in a quick embrace and murmured, "If you want to talk to Seanna, now's the time. That compulsion seemed to work like a double shot of Valium."

He was right. Seanna was listening to Helia and nodding, paying full attention. For the first time, that animal glint in her eye had faded.

Even when I walked over, she only looked up, curious. Watching her, I got a glimpse of the woman she could have been. Grace said Seanna lacked something. She was right. Call it a soul. Call it a conscience.

My spina bifida was a failure of completion, a side effect of my fae blood. The bone and membranes around my spinal cord had failed to form fully because I had DNA that did not naturally assume a human shape. In others, fae blood manifested as a missing finger or rib or organ. In Seanna, it went deeper, and maybe that meant we should treat her lack of a conscience as we would a physical defect. But even if that was true, I could not excuse her for what she did to Gabriel. I just couldn't.

"I need to talk to you, Seanna," I said.

"You are . . . ?"

"A friend of your son."

She frowned at the word "son." That relationship—that obligation—was such a foreign concept that in this state, she didn't even seem to know what I meant by it.

"I know Gabriel," I said.

She nodded. "You're Gabriel's girl."

"Right." I bent before her. "Who told you to come back to Illinois?"

Across the room, Ricky frowned. Then he nodded, realizing I was playing a hunch.

"The woman," she said. "She wanted to get back at Gabriel for a case he defended. I didn't care what her reason was. I liked her plan. She promised if I followed it, I'd get all the money I need to retire. I'm getting old. It's time to retire. And Gabriel owes me. If it weren't for me, he wouldn't be where he is."

Even in her compliant state, she said that. Which meant she actually believed she'd played some role in Gabriel's success. Tempering steel through fire.

I took a deep breath. "Describe this woman."

Her description matched Imogen Seale.

"This woman gave you the scheme," I said. "And then . . . ?"

"She brought me to Chicago and sent me to his office. She told me what to say to him. What to say to you if you were there."

"What to say?"

"She said to tell you what I thought of you. And of Gabriel. Don't hold back. I had to make you both angry. If you got angry enough, you'd pay me to leave."

"Gabriel did try to pay you."

"It wasn't enough. She said you'd give more if I keep pushing."

"Yeah, that or kill you," Ricky murmured, too low for her to hear. When I turned, he said, "Sorry. I don't mean that. Just . . ." He shook his head. "It's a stupid plan."

"You did shoot her, didn't you?" Helia said to me.

"Not well enough," Alexios said. "You need to work on your aim."

I shook my head and started to return to Seanna. Then I paused. Thought. Thought a little more. Pushed that into the back of my mind for later and said, "Tell me about Greg Kirkman."

"Who?"

"The envelope you gave to the prison guard. For Todd Larsen."

She nodded. "I remember."

"The envelope contained a name. Greg Kirkman. Who is he?"

That blank look again.

"How'd you get the envelope?" Ricky asked.

"From the woman. She said it was very important."

"And you never opened it?" I asked.

"I didn't care what it was."

"Tell me about visiting Pamela Larsen. Why did you go there?"

"The woman told me to upset her—that would be another way to get your attention. She said you loved your mother and felt bad for her, and if I upset her, that would upset you."

I exchanged a look with Ricky and then asked Seanna, "Were you supposed to do the same thing with Todd if you got to see him? Upset him?"

"No, just give him the envelope."

I remembered what Pamela said, that Seanna had made small talk, poorly covering a segue to her true line of inquiry—about my relationship with Gabriel and my trust fund.

"Tell me more about your conversation with Pamela," I said. "Exactly what did you say?"

It was not what Pamela had claimed.

It was nothing like what Pamela claimed.

———

"Well, that was easy," Ricky said afterward, as we walked out together. "I don't suppose there's any way to keep her permanently under fae compulsion."

"No kidding."

"Can I walk you home?" he said as we neared the front door. "I'd like to talk, and these walls have ears."

As we stepped out, Grace said, "In this town, every building has ears."

"You do realize you should pretend otherwise," I said.

She snorted. "I don't care to. As for keeping Seanna Walsh under permanent compulsion, that's exactly what I've suggested. Feel free to tell Ida you support the idea."

"It's possible, then? To keep her like that?"

"How about giving her the wine?" Ricky asked. "Isn't that how you used to handle Muggles who stumbled into the fae world?"

"Muggles?" Grace said.

"It's from *Harry Potter*," I said. "It means—"

"I've read *Harry Potter*, thank you very much. I just don't think a biker should use the terminology. People might think he's semiliterate."

"I'm very literate," Ricky said. "I have a huge collection of comic books. I even know what most of the words mean."

"Name your favorite DC superhero."

"I'm really more of a Marvel guy."

"No, you're really full of shit. I'd be better off asking your favorite Faulkner character."

"Faulkner's not much for character. He's more style-driven. I identified better with the characters in *Harry Potter*. As for Marvel, I'd say Kitty Pryde, but if you ask me officially, I have to say Ghost Rider, because it's, you know"—he motioned at his Saints jacket—"obligatory."

Grace sighed. "You are a lousy biker."

"The worst. But I'm right about the wine, aren't I? That's the lore. You give fae wine to humans to send them into an endless fae party."

"Patrick says there's no party," I said. "Or they just don't invite him."

"That's possible," Grace murmured. "As for wine, we have several varieties. The correct one will induce a state of semipermanent pleasant hallucinations. Hence the fae-party lore. And, yes, that's what I've suggested for Seanna. Ida is resisting."

"Because it would send her to la-la land for good?" I said. "Yeah, I can see where that might be an issue."

"Only because it's better than she deserves."

"We'll figure out something. I'll make sure her stay here is as short as possible."

We headed out, and I told Ricky what the sluagh had said. What they'd done. I didn't want that last part to bother me. I know people live with spina bifida, so how dare I freak out as if it's the worst fate possible?

I can't fool Ricky, though. He stopped me mid-story, led me behind a row of hedges, and made me admit how completely freaked out I was.

"That won't happen," he said when I'd pulled myself together and we'd resumed walking. "They owe you. The fae and the Hunt. They owe it to you to make sure this never happens."

Ten minutes later, that was exactly what Gabriel was saying, as we sat in my parlor with Ioan and Ida. When I asked about Walter, Ida only made a dismissive gesture. Off running an errand for her, I presumed, relegated to the sidelines when things got serious.

Ioan told Ida what the sluagh had said and what I'd deduced about the ritual my mother had used.

"You set Pamela up with that ritual," Gabriel said to Ioan. "You brokered the deal. With the *sluagh.* You were careless with Olivia's future. You can blame inexperience and good intentions, but the truth is this: you are responsible."

"Yes," Ioan said.

That's all he said, but Ida couldn't resist chiming in with, "I'm glad you acknowledge the role you played—"

"As I hope you acknowledge the one *you* played," Gabriel said to her.

"We did nothing—"

"You made the initial deal with the sluagh to ensure my birth. Unlike Ioan, you knew full well who you were dealing with. You granted this sluagh access to Cainsville, which allowed her to return at least once. It's likely she's been monitoring Olivia since she first arrived. Did Grace mention the early incidents suggesting someone had been in her apartment?"

"We thought—"

"I don't care what you thought. Your deal set this all in motion. The sluagh has played both of you, and the one who will suffer for it is Olivia. That is unacceptable. You will find a way to ensure her cure is permanent and protect her from further repercussions. You will work together to accomplish this. If you do not, then there is no chance she will ever help either of you."

Ioan and Ida looked at one another. Then Ioan said, "We'll need more information. As much as you can give."

Gabriel nodded. "Patrick and Veronica will join us to add their expertise. Ioan? If you have someone who can help, the Tylwyth Teg will ensure he is welcome in Cainsville."

"When it comes to matters of policy, procedure, and history, as the eldest in our pack, I'm the expert."

Ida sniffed. "Which served you well—"

"No," Gabriel said. "Ioan is here to help. He is accepting responsibility and holding his tongue. I expect you to do the same. If you cannot, I'm sure we can manage discussions without you."

Ida glowered but only said, "Get Veronica and Patrick."

CHAPTER THIRTY-SIX

And so the strategy session convened. The best minds of the Cŵn Annwn and the Tylwyth Teg joining forces for a shared cause: to save their Matilda. Nearly three hours of talk, which amounted to . . . absolutely nothing.

Oh, they came up with plans. Or I think they did. I was already exhausted and frustrated, and three hours of discussing the finer points of fae lore—which would have fascinated me a few days earlier—put me to sleep. In the end, it pretty much came down to: We'll solve this.

We'll solve it. We'll protect you. Don't worry about a thing.

Which was not a plan. Certainly not one we were going to rely on. After they left, Gabriel said, "We'll figure something out. The three of us." Which was not a plan, either, but it was honestly the best we could do for now.

Rose brought dinner after that. She'd picked it up at the diner, saying something about burning a roast. We were too distracted to ask for details; she was too distracted to elaborate. It was only as she went to leave, as I asked if she'd join us to eat—and she just kept walking—that I realized what had happened.

"She's been to see Seanna," Gabriel murmured as the front door closed behind her. "Who is obviously no longer under the

338

dryads' influence and has upset her."

"I think she'd be more upset if she saw Seanna *under* that influence," I said.

Ricky nodded.

When Gabriel looked confused, I said, "It's Seanna without her edge. Without her venom. That's going to remind her of the girl she once knew."

There was a pause. Then Gabriel said, with obvious discomfort, "I should go after Rose, shouldn't I?"

"May I go instead?" I asked. "If you want to, that's fine, but I'd like to talk to her."

Gabriel exhaled with relief. "Certainly."

"You guys eat. Just save me a plate."

Rose's car was still in front of my house, and I was halfway to it before I realized she wasn't inside. I spotted her walking home, as if she'd forgotten she'd driven.

I jogged after her. When she heard footsteps, she tensed and turned. Seeing me, she relaxed.

"I thought it was Gabriel," she said.

"He wanted to come, but I convinced him to let me. We need to talk."

We started walking, and I said, "You went to see Seanna, I'm guessing?"

She nodded.

"Is she still under the dryads' spell?" I asked.

Another nod. Then, "That's easier. For everyone."

I shoved my hands in my pockets. "I'm not sure about that. I've been thinking I might want to ask them to undo it if Gabriel goes to visit. It could be harder on him. It was even rough on me, seeing her . . . vulnerable. I don't want her to be vulnerable. It makes it tougher to . . ."

"Hate her."

I nodded. "I know it might seem as if Gabriel needs to see that side of her, but he doesn't. I'm sorry. He just doesn't."

"I agree. He never saw that side growing up, and he doesn't need it now. It negates his own feelings." She walked a few more steps. "Yes, it is difficult, even for me."

"Maybe even *more* for you."

She made a face, rolling her shoulders, a reaction I knew only too well from her nephew. Physically sloughing off my concern. "I don't know about that. But yes, she . . . reminded me of the girl she was."

"The girl you lost."

She hesitated but didn't make that face again. Just said, "Yes."

We walked to the corner and she continued, "Seanna was never an easy child. There were hints of what you see. A self-centeredness that could be breathtaking, even for a Walsh. That worried her parents, but there was good, too, so we told ourselves if we were loving but firm, she would outgrow her selfishness."

"Instead, she outgrew the good."

"Too much of the love, not enough of the firm, I suppose. But it always worked with Walshes before. We are a naturally self-absorbed lot."

"The fae blood."

She nodded. "I realize that now. Growing up, we were just told it was an inheritance from our criminal ancestors."

"Kind of."

A brief smile. "True. Yes, caring about others doesn't come naturally, so we focus on caring for family, and with that combination of love and firmness we have avoided the worst of what we could be. So we were, perhaps, arrogant with Seanna. Overly confident that we could fix her."

"This is actually what I wanted to talk about," I said. "Her history. Is that okay? If it's a bad time, I understand."

"Actually, it's a perfect time." She paused, and then said, "Thank you."

I knew what she meant by that—she *wanted* to talk about Seanna. She'd just seen her niece in better shape than she'd been in thirty years, and she needed to talk about her.

Back at the house, Rose made tea and brought cookies, which we both agreed was a fine dinner substitute. She may also have added a generous dose of whiskey to our tea.

"Tell me about Seanna," I said as we settled in.

As a child, Seanna Walsh had been a brat. There was no other way to describe it. Spoiled. Selfish. Prone to tantrums when things didn't go her way. In other words, a kid with all the worst qualities of childhood amplified.

For most kids, outgrowing that self-centeredness is a normal part of development. We learn that the earth, sadly, does not revolve around us, that others have needs and emotions, too. For some, that connection never really clicks. The world is full of people with a degree of sociopathy, and I'll include myself in that.

I can remember, as a child, coveting another's toys, and needing to actively stop and imagine my parents' voices, explaining to me that the other child was just as attached to her toys—and just as deserving of them—as I was to mine. Even then, I think I refrained from stealing only because I didn't want to upset my parents.

I would love to say I've outgrown that. Just last month, though, I watched an elderly driver valiantly try to parallel park in the last street spot, and I'd had to recall my parents' voices to keep from ducking in with my little Maserati.

The Walshes had tried to instill that voice in Seanna. According to Rose, Seanna seemed to get it. She told the story of watching four-year-old Seanna at a town picnic, salivating over a chocolate gargoyle won by a cousin. When the cousin walked away from her prize, Seanna had realized no one seemed to be watching, and then, with some effort, had pulled herself away and run to join the other kids.

"It seemed as if she was learning," Rose said. "There were other indications, too, that convinced us she'd be fine. And then . . . she wasn't."

"Did she gradually get worse?" I asked. "Or did it seem sudden?"

Rose took a long drink of her spiked tea, looking exhausted. "I don't even know anymore. We thought it was sudden, and then we thought maybe we'd been fooling ourselves that she was improving, and then . . . after a while, it was like putting our fingers in dike holes. We were so busy stopping the flood that we had no time to wonder when or how it started."

"But if you were to give me a rough estimate," I prodded.

"Around puberty. We thought it was that—typical teen rebellion. She ran away shortly after, and then her parents died and—" Rose's voice hitched. "She didn't care. That was the last straw for everyone else. Her parents died in a car accident while searching for her, and she couldn't even bother coming to the funeral. The rest of the family gave up."

"Except you."

Rose reached for a cookie. She didn't eat it. Just stared down at it. "No, even I gave up. I think that's part of what happened, what went so wrong with Seanna. I . . . I had my own issues. My life just . . . imploded? Exploded? All I know is that I wasn't there for Seanna. I had my personal meltdown, ended up in prison. After I made parole, I came home for her."

"To be here for her."

A twist of Rose's lips. "Too little, too late. Next thing I knew, she had Gabriel, and when I saw her again, I barely recognized her. I kept telling myself that skipping her parents' funeral was a misunderstanding, that deep down she loved them too much to intentionally miss it. I was wrong. The Seanna I met after I came home was exactly the sort of person who'd do that. She'd . . ."

"Lost something."

"Lost everything. Everything that mattered."

I stopped by Veronica's next. The ponytailed young woman who opened the door looked like a teenager. She was lamia, a Greek subtype of fae that cannot age their glamours. For lamiae, there are only two forms: the teen girl and their true one, a snakelike human.

When Pepper saw it was me, she blinked, and her eyes reverted to slitted pupils. Past trauma had left her unable to hold her glamour, but under Veronica's care—and with the fae energy of Cainsville—she was making progress. When I'd first met her four months earlier, she couldn't speak. Now she greeted me with, "Hey, come on in. It's been a while."

"We've been—"

"Busy, I know. That wasn't an accusation, Matil— Liv. Sorry."

"You know you can call me that," I said as I walked in. "Only you, though."

"Which is why I try not to. It just slips."

The damage to Pepper had gone deeper than her ability to hold her shape. Not unlike Lloergan, she'd been psychically damaged. In her case, it caused mental impairment. That, too, had vastly improved, but if she stayed outside Cainsville too long, she started to revert. So she was here indefinitely, as a "Greek exchange student."

"If you're looking for Veronica, she's at another town meeting. I can let her know you're here. I'm sure she'd appreciate the excuse to leave early."

"Please."

Pepper texted Veronica.

"Give her five," she said. "Hot chocolate? No, you're a grown-up. I should offer you coffee."

I smiled. "Hot chocolate is fine."

Pepper loved her hot cocoa as much as I loved my mochas. In her case, "hot" was the biggest attraction. Her glamour issues meant that—like a snake—she was cold-blooded. That was improving, but the heat in the house was cranked to near eighty and she still wore a hoodie.

As she fixed the drinks, I looked at the papers and books spread over the kitchen table.

"That's our project," she said. "Mine and Veronica's. We're compiling a history of lamiae for her records. Patrick has lent us his books, which help bring back my memories—hereditary and personal."

"Sounds like a good project."

"Keeps me busy. Especially up here." She tapped her head and then handed me a steaming mug. "Patrick doesn't have a lot on Greek fae." She chewed her lip. "Which is an awkward . . . What's the word? When you switch topics?"

"Segue."

"Right. It's an awkward segue to something else. About Greek fae. Veronica says there are dryads in town."

"Does that worry you?"

She shook her head. "No, no. Dryads are cool. A little silly sometimes, but smarter than they seem. I thought maybe I could talk to them. I'd like to. I'm just not sure they'd want to talk to me. Dryads and lamiae might both be Greek, but we aren't exactly kissing cousins." Her face scrunched up. "Is that the term?"

"Close enough."

"They've probably also heard what Melanie did, which means they really aren't going to want to talk to me."

"You had nothing to do with that."

A wry smile. "Besides being the person she did it for? Murdered our own sister lamiae to get me into Cainsville? I still can't—" She sucked in breath. "Old song. Everyone's sick of it by now."

"It hurts. It's always going to hurt. But the dryads won't hold that against you, and I think meeting them would be fine. In fact, that's where I was going with Veronica. How about you text her back and tell her to meet us there?"

CHAPTER THIRTY-SEVEN

I left Pepper on the apartment stoop with Grace, ostensibly while I made sure Seanna was awake, but really to warn the dryads that Pepper was with me.

When I walked in, I found Alexios and Helia on the couch, huddled in urgent conversation, Alexios sounding upset, Helia trying to calm him.

I backed out quickly, but not before they saw me, Helia rising with, "Liv. Come in."

"I should have knocked. Sorry."

"No, we're fine," Helia said.

Alexios gave her a look that challenged that, and said, "Helia is tired. I'd like her to rest. You and I can speak."

Helia shook her head. "I want—"

"No."

She took her mate's arm and squeezed it, murmuring, "This is important to me."

His jaw worked, giving me a flash of the ancient fae behind his glamour, but he nodded and murmured, "I know, *agapi mou*."

"I don't actually need anything from you guys," I said. "I'm just bringing Veronica to see Seanna. We'll be fine, if she's still under your influence."

"She is," Helia said. "But there is something more, is there not?"

"It can wait."

"Might as well just tell her," Alexios said. "She's as stubborn as a mule, and she'll tire herself more pestering you."

"I brought someone who'd like to speak to you."

I started to explain, but Helia cut in with, "The little lamia. We know the story. I was going to ask if we could see her."

"I know you aren't exactly fond of lamiae . . ."

"We were being rude earlier. Fae have prejudices, just as humans do, and we must remind ourselves of that and speak with more care. Please bring her up. We'd be delighted to meet her. There are refreshments in the kitchen. I'll make her something."

"*I* will make her something," Alexios said firmly.

"A hot drink would be appreciated," I said. "She has difficulty holding her glamour and regulating her temperature."

"Poor thing," Helia said. "She's as damaged as the hound."

"Best not say that in front of her," Alexios said. "I think it would be rude."

She made a face at him, and he squeezed her shoulder, gently steering her back to the couch. "Sit and play hostess. I'll make hot tea for our guest."

By the time I got back to Pepper, Veronica had arrived. We all went upstairs, where Helia greeted Pepper with, "My mate is fixing tea, so we may play proper hosts. And, as proper hosts, I will invite you to leave your glamour at the door, along with your jacket, and make yourself comfortable."

Pepper smiled and thanked Helia, relaxing with obvious relief.

Veronica and I went into the bedroom, where Seanna was sleeping. I closed the door behind us. Then I told Veronica what I was looking for. At first she gave a start, and I think she was about to say that it wasn't possible. Then she thought for a moment and said, "Yes, I suppose we should."

Seanna was in a deep sleep and stayed that way as Veronica gently examined her. Three times Veronica said, "I'm not finding anything, Liv." Three times I urged her to keep looking, suggesting new places.

Finally, she stopped, holding aside a lock of Seanna's hair, and said, "Do you have—?" and I handed her the scissors I'd brought.

Veronica clipped a quarter-sized spot, trimming closer and closer, until only scalp remained. And there we saw what looked like a red birthmark. The mark of the sluagh.

We'd moved to an empty apartment now, Veronica and Grace and I, our voices lowered as we talked.

"You were right," I said to Grace after we explained. "Seanna is soul-reft."

Veronica shook her head. "Being marked doesn't mean they've taken what passes for a soul. It means they *will*, on her death."

"But they already have, in a way," I said. "An advance on payment. Rose says Seanna changed around the time she hit puberty. She was always self-centered. Always more fae than most. But there was humanity in her . . . and then there wasn't, and I bet if we lined up the exact date, it'd coincide with the time you guys made that deal with the sluagh."

Veronica's lips worked, silently calculating. Then she said, "Yes, it does."

"So that's how they got a mother for your Gwynn. Find a girl more fae than human. Mark her and take her nub of a conscience. Make her fully fae."

"I wouldn't say—" Grace began.

"Unruffle your feathers, old friend," Veronica said. "Liv is correct. The difference is that fae are accustomed to the lack of what one might call humanity. Seanna was not prepared for that. We failed to see what had happened and therefore failed to help her. We abandoned her, as much—and as unwittingly—as we did her son."

"I'm not laying blame," I said. "I'm saying this is what we have, and we need to deal with it. The sluagh marked Seanna and took her conscience, which left her vulnerable to their control. She became their marionette, fully open to their manipulation. They could set up her encounter with Patrick. They could convince her to get pregnant, claiming it was a way to blackmail him. They obviously have the power to make sure one time was enough to get her knocked up. They fulfilled their bargain with you by stealing one of your own."

"Stealing her from under our very noses," Grace muttered. "You were right, Veronica. We should never have made that deal. Damn Walter and Ida for talking me into it. If I had cast my vote with yours—"

"The motion would still have passed. As Liv says, this is not the time for blame. It's the time for fixing our mistakes. We're going to need to keep Seanna here longer. If she's marked—"

"Yes, yes, I know." Grace grumbled under her breath but said, "Letting her go wouldn't be right." She glared at me. "See? I do know right from wrong."

I was about to comment when my cell phone rang. It was Gabriel.

I answered and said, "Hey, yeah, sorry I haven't come home yet. I'm chasing down a few things."

"I presumed that, and I wouldn't bother you, but Ricky thought you should know this immediately." *Even if I don't agree*, his tone added. "Pamela has been taken to the hospital."

"What?" I shifted the phone to my other ear and moved into the next room. "Is she okay?"

His pause told me she wasn't.

"Is it serious?" I said. "Was she attacked again?"

"I don't know. She was found unconscious in the shower. When the prison medical staff couldn't revive her, she was rushed to the hospital, where they are still assessing her condition."

"Has she regained consciousness?"

"No. There's no outward sign of injury and no evidence of a stroke or heart attack. They're assessing. That's all we know at this point."

He paused. Waiting to see if I wanted to go to the hospital. He would never suggest it, because that might imply an obligation that he didn't believe I should feel.

"I should go see her," I said.

"The hospital has agreed to keep us informed. I will gladly take you, but if you mean you *should*, as in—"

"I'd like to," I said. "I'd rather get answers than wait for them."

"Understood. However, you should consider . . ." He trailed off.

"Should consider what, Gabriel?"

"Nothing. You're right. This is both efficient and productive. I'll pick you up as soon as you're ready."

I dreaded telling Gabriel about Seanna. Fortunately, I was able to avoid it for now—he was preoccupied, deciding whether he should tell *me* something. Finally, he said, "About the last time Pamela was injured . . ."

"When she was stabbed by another inmate."

"Yes." He cleared his throat. "After the fact, I conducted basic inquiries into the matter, which led me to believe . . . it may not have unfolded as she claimed."

"She wasn't actually attacked."

"No, it does seem she was."

"But she staged it, didn't she?"

"I believe so," he said. "Pamela has no history of altercations with other inmates, and she very deliberately provoked one known to be unstable and to possess a makeshift blade. She allowed the attack to progress just far enough to require hospitalization and then handily pinned the other woman."

"Damn."

"Pamela may not appear an intimidating adversary, but, unlike Todd, she has not avoided trouble in prison through the use of natural charm. She learned several forms of martial arts early in her incarceration."

"Oh, I didn't mean I'm surprised she could stop her attacker. I'm expressing admiration for one hell of a scheme. That takes some serious nerve."

"Yes, my mother could take lessons from yours, and I'll join you in unwilling but genuine admiration."

"And the reason you're telling me this now is that you think she's pulling the same stunt?"

He drove in silence for a minute before saying, carefully, "That seems the obvious answer. That instead of risking further injury, she's ingested something to cause the loss of consciousness."

"Something given to her by her fae sycophants."

"I hadn't thought of that, but it would explain why the doctors are baffled. What I don't understand is her goal. You two are, arguably, on the best terms you have ever been, with no recent altercations."

"She must want something else."

He shook his head. "There is an angle here, and it *does* involve you. I simply don't see it yet."

CHAPTER THIRTY-EIGHT

Gabriel did not suggest we cancel our visit to the hospital. As always, the only real way to learn an adversary's plans was to proceed as they expected and get a look at the trap close up.

At the hospital, we were directed to the proper floor, where the nurse told us Pamela's condition was critical and she wasn't allowed visitors.

"Critical?" I said. "We were supposed to get a call if her condition changed."

The nurse looked like a teenager. She couldn't be, obviously, but her expression was stereotypical teen, the one that said we were just a couple of adults making her life difficult and could we please move along and let her get back to texting with her friends?

"Please put down your cell phone while you're speaking to us," Gabriel said.

The nurse gave a start at that.

"Would you like me to speak slower?" he said. "Or perhaps text it to you?"

When she still didn't respond, he plucked the phone from her hand and placed it on the desk.

"Thank you," he said. "I appreciate having your full attention."

She looked around, but it was well past visiting hours and the hall was empty.

"We would like to see Pamela Larsen," Gabriel said. "We understand that she may not be permitted visitors. That is fine. Her daughter here simply wants to *see* her. I believe that's understandable."

"Mrs. Larsen is off-limits to anyone except medical personnel."

"Her daughter will look through a window if necessary. If she's allowed into the room, she will wear any protective garments required."

"The patient is off-limits to anyone except medical personnel."

"All right. Then may I request that you—as medical personnel—take your phone into her room and film a five-second video of the patient, to reassure her daughter. An unusual request, I'm sure, but Olivia is very concerned, and we would appreciate the effort."

A flick of his hand, and a hundred-dollar bill peeked from under her cell phone.

"I can't leave my post," she said.

"Call someone to relieve you for a restroom break."

"I can't leave—"

"Bullshit," I said. "If you're going to play the role of a twenty-year-old, you'd better act like one. No recent graduate is going to turn down an easy hundred bucks."

Her face screwed up. "What?"

"We've been through this before, and we're getting damned good at figuring out when the person blocking us is not a person at all. Do you think we've failed to notice there's no one else around? No one we can appeal to for help? Very convenient. Also? Very obvious. You fae need to get better at this game."

Gabriel nudged me. I looked to see a doctor watching us from a doorway. I thought Gabriel was telling me there *was* someone else around. Then I saw the total confusion on the nurse's face . . . and the faint smile on the doctor's before he retreated.

"Why can't we see my mother?" I said. "On whose orders?"

"One of the doctors. He said you'd be by. And he said you'd cause trouble, which is why you *can't* see her. At all. Or I lose my job, which is worth more to me than your hundred bucks."

"And that doctor's name?"

"Lang? Lee? I'm new here. I just know he said it was important to keep you away from your mother, and that's what I'm doing."

"I'm sure he was very compelling," I murmured as I stepped away from the desk.

"What was all that about?"

"Ms. Taylor-Jones mistook you for someone else," Gabriel said. "She's very distraught. Now, I appreciate that you're doing your job, but are you aware of the legal ramifications of keeping my client from her mother?"

"Client?"

Gabriel continued, smoothly holding the nurse's attention as I headed for the closed door. "Yes, client. Ms. Taylor-Jones is the de facto guardian for Pamela Larsen, who is a prisoner of the state, and under the provisions of the penal code . . ."

I tuned out whatever legalese fiction he was spinning and opened that door. Then I slipped through and found myself in an empty room. Across from me was another door, cracked open, which seemed a little too obvious. So I checked furniture instead—under a desk, inside a cabinet—and texted Gabriel.

Second door partly open. No sign he's hiding.

I hit Send and then typed: *I'll wait 4 U*, and imagined his exhale of relief as he got them, saving him from madly texting a warning.

I did wait. I also approached that door, though, slipping close enough to peer through and—

The hall door opened, and Gabriel walked through.

"The nurse is occupied," he said as he approached. "I put the fear of legal action into her and suggested she find the doctor who issued the order."

"Who I'm presuming is the one who went through that door. And is likely on the other side, listening to us. He could make this much easier by coming in here and joining the conversation."

I waited. Silence.

"And that's a no." I pushed open the door. It led into a back hall. An empty one, lined with doors. As we started along it, I called, "We get that you're luring us somewhere. It's kind of obvious."

"Then why are you following?" asked a voice.

We turned to see the so-called doctor, leaning in an open doorway.

"No, don't answer that," he said. "You're Tylwyth Teg. You can't help yourselves, poor things."

"Pretty sure you're more fae than we are."

"Fae, yes, technically. Tylwyth Teg?" He scrunched his nose. "No, I come from sturdier stock. Fae far less likely to allow blind curiosity to lead them into obvious traps."

"We love traps. They're like puzzles, only with higher stakes." I stepped toward him. "And for a fae who's so dismissive of his Welsh brethren, you're taking quite an interest in their affairs, playing sycophant to my mother."

"Sycophant?" He laughed. "Hardly. It's a mutual allegiance."

"Mmm, yeah. You just keep telling yourself that. Ask Tristan about my mother's idea of a mutual allegiance."

"Tristan was a *spriggan*. Inferior stock, again. I know what I'm doing."

I opened my mouth to dispute that, but Gabriel edged past me, saying, "Where is Pamela?"

"Ah, the great Gwynn speaks." The doctor mock-bowed. "Your highness. It is a pleasure."

Gabriel gave him a quick appraisal, those pale blue eyes taking his measure. Then he turned to me.

"He's stalling us. He has accomplished his mission—helping your mother escape undetected—and now his orders are simply to keep us from pursuit. She's gone exactly where I said she'd go. He's of no use to us."

Gabriel had not said anything about where Pamela would go, but I played along and turned to leave.

"I'm under no such orders," the doctor said as we walked away. "Your mother didn't expect you to show up. I only compelled that silly nurse to block anyone who asked after Pamela as a general precaution."

We kept going. A moment later, something flashed past us. Then he was there, in our path.

"You do not want to interfere with her," he said.

"Is that a threat?" Gabriel said, his voice a low rumble.

The fae opened his mouth, his expression saying he was about to make a jaunty response. Then he looked up into Gabriel's eyes and stopped.

"No," Gabriel said. "I thought not."

Gabriel shouldered the fae aside to give me room to pass. I did, and the fae popped in front of us again, far enough ahead to stay out of Gabriel's reach.

"It wasn't a threat," he said. "It was a warning. A . . ." A nervous glance at Gabriel. "A respectful warning. Whatever your mother has gone to do, Matilda, it is for you. It is always for you."

"Gone to do?" I slowed.

"Ignore him," Gabriel said. "His very phrasing makes it clear he doesn't know what she has in mind."

"But she has a purpose," I said. "Beyond simply escaping from prison."

The fae laughed, finding his arrogance again. "Escape? To what purpose? She can better protect you in jail than on the run from the police. No, Pamela will bide her time until she is legally freed. This is merely an excursion. The undertaking of a task. She'll be back before dawn, no one the wiser, and I would suggest you leave her to whatever she's doing."

"You have no idea what that is, do you?" I said.

"I don't require a reason. She was concerned for you, and she needed to leave briefly, so I manufactured an opportunity, putting her in my debt." A pleased smile. "Putting you in my debt, too, I'll wager."

I started to answer, but Gabriel's hand gripped my shoulder.

"Whether you have earned Olivia's regard—and mine—remains to be seen. You said Pamela was concerned for her daughter? Perhaps it's not what I thought it was. Is it something *we* should be worried about? A new threat?"

"Relatively recent," he said. "Not urgent, though. She contacted me two days ago, saying she feared a new threat against Matilda, and asking if it might be possible for me to orchestrate a temporary departure." That smug smile again. "She'd asked Tristan the same this spring, but he couldn't manage it. That's why he had to act for her. I provided, though. She asked, and I provided."

"She's going after Seanna," I said as we got into the car.

When Gabriel started the engine without answering, I said, "No, that's a wild guess, isn't it?" I took a deep breath. "Okay. Calm down. Talk it out. She said she's doing something for me, but that might not be true."

"It always is."

"It could be for Todd. Not breaking him out. Like that fae said, escape is pointless. It would mean life on the run, when they have a genuine shot at getting out legally."

"It's Seanna."

I looked over at him.

"Seanna is in Grace's building," he said, "with the dryads watching over her. Pamela can't simply slip in and kill her."

"But you agree that's what she's planning."

"It's the most obvious answer. Seanna visited her a few days ago, shortly before Pamela contacted that fae. Pamela's version of the conversation didn't match Seanna's. Seanna told you the sluagh provided a script for her side of that conversation, which amounted to thinly veiled threats against you."

"Seanna was supposed to upset Pamela, which supposedly would upset me."

"No. The real goal was to *anger* Pamela. The conversation was carefully orchestrated to convince Pamela that you are in danger from Seanna."

"Not just me," I said. "My father, too. That was the whole point of bringing up Kirkman. To threaten Todd. Either he'd read the note and tell my mother, or I'd get the note and ask her what it meant. The sluagh threatened me and Todd. Loading a double-barreled shotgun. Pointed squarely at Seanna."

"As the sluagh said, she's played her role. That means she has outlived her usefulness and is now more trouble than she's worth. A wild card, so to speak. She has only one final role to play: leverage against you. As far as Pamela knows, Seanna is the threat."

"We know better. Kill Seanna, and the sluagh still hold their ace on my father with Kirkman."

"Kill Seanna, and they gain another—a murder they can squarely pin on your mother. With that, they can guarantee that both your parents will remain in prison for life."

"Patrick," I said.

Gabriel's brows arched as he turned onto the highway.

"We need to tell someone in Cainsville. Someone who can help," I said. "He's the most obvious choice."

"Yes, but that also puts us in his debt, which is why I was going to suggest Veronica."

I shook my head. "Patrick owes us, and he's a much better match for my mother."

Gabriel paused and then nodded. I called Patrick and told him that Pamela was out of prison and going after Seanna.

"Ah," he said.

"Going after her to kill her," I said. "Not to invite her to tea. In case that wasn't obvious."

"No, it was. I suspect even a tea between them would end in bloodshed. Seanna's blood, shed."

"This isn't a public service announcement, Patrick. I'm asking you to do something about it. To watch over Seanna."

"Ah."

My hand gripped the phone tighter. "Fine. Obviously, Gabriel was right. I should notify Veronica—the one elder in Cainsville who actually gives a shit."

"We all give a shit, Liv, in our way. If I sound overly calm at the prospect of Seanna's death, well, you can hardly blame me."

"It's not just her death. If she dies—" I stopped myself and glanced at Gabriel as I thought of Seanna's mark. "Speak to Veronica or Grace, okay? There's more to this. But if you'd rather not get involved, I can call Veronica."

"No, Veronica has many talents, but I don't want her going toe-to-toe with your mother. I'm too fond of our Veronica. I'll head over and keep an eye on Seanna."

"And speak to Grace. Please."

SACRILEGE

If I were going to kill Seanna Walsh, how would I do it?

It was not a question Patrick had difficulty answering. He'd considered it many times, in fantasy and even in fiction, having written a few characters in whom one might recognize aspects of his son's mother, all of whom met terrible—and terribly satisfying—fictional demises.

But now, as he stood on the corner of Main Street, the question was not how he'd do it, but how Pamela Larsen would. Which was another matter altogether.

First there was the problem of finding Seanna. He doubted Seanna had provided contact information to Pamela.

Oh, and in case you decide to escape prison so we might take tea, I'm currently residing in Grace's building in Cainsville.

Patrick did have to smile at the image, so helpfully provided by Liv, of Seanna and Pamela at tea.

Oh, my dear, you must try the cookies. The lethal dose of arsenic adds a lovely almond flavor.

No, much too obvious.

I know, Seanna darling, at our age, it can be so difficult to get a good sleep, but I've found an incredible cure, a most remarkable tea, the perfect blend of nightshade and belladonna.

Nice, but poison was easily detected and not really Pamela's style.

Please, Seanna dearest, do try the chicken sandwiches. I deboned them myself. Well, mostly.

Yes, that was more Pamela's style. Still, he might be forgiven if he held quite another image in mind, a much more satisfying teatime pictorial of Pamela Larsen lunging across the scones and cucumber sandwiches, knife in hand, snarling, "Die, bitch!"

Crude but effective.

Yet there would be no tea. Simply murder.

So, how will you find her, Pamela? You won't leave that to chance. You wouldn't set foot outside your prison walls until every detail had been planned.

Patrick might not know Pamela Larsen, but he knew her daughter. Take Liv's more deliciously devious side, multiply it tenfold, and he'd have Pamela.

So it mattered, he supposed, not how she'd know where Seanna was, but simply acknowledging that she would.

Pamela Larsen was coming to Cainsville.

Coming to murder Seanna Walsh.

And Liv expected him to ruin such a perfect scene?

Sacrilege.

No, this wasn't about stopping Pamela. Not at all.

As he approached Rowan Street, he replayed exactly what Liv had said. She asked him to speak to Veronica or Grace first. Which seemed odd.

Patrick shook his head. His curiosity really could get the better of him sometimes.

As for why Liv wouldn't want him to let Pamela kill Seanna, well, that was no mystery at all. She had to say that, didn't she? Gabriel was sitting right next to her in the car, and while Patrick suspected Liv would kill Seanna herself if she could get away with it, she'd be much more circumspect in front of her new lover.

Gabriel *would* want Seanna dead. Yet he could not do it himself. Ergo, under other circumstances, Liv would happily turn a blind eye to Pamela's scheme. But Liv finally had Gabriel and was more nervous than became a young woman of her cunning and resolve.

Cunning . . .

Interesting word choice. And there, perhaps inadvertently, he had solved the mystery. Answered that niggling feeling that said such squeamishness did not become Olivia.

Patrick had misinterpreted the point of the call entirely. It wasn't to stop Pamela. It was to protect Gabriel. Call Patrick and tell him what was happening, and ask—*demand*—he do something about it, while knowing full well he wouldn't. Therefore, when Seanna died at Pamela's hands, Gabriel would suffer no guilt at having failed to stop it. Liv *had* tried to stop it. Gabriel had overheard her. Whatever happened after that . . . well, that was Patrick's fault, wasn't it? Not theirs at all.

Patrick smiled.

Clever, clever Liv. He should be furious, of course, at being played. But he admired her skill too much for that.

He appreciated the steps she took to protect his son, and he would reward her.

No, it's my fault, Gabriel. I told Liv I'd stop Pamela. I was very clear on that. She had no reason to doubt me.

There. A selfless act. Liv would be pleased. Moreover, *Matilda* would be pleased, and as much as Patrick liked to pretend otherwise, he was very aware of Matilda's importance. Currying her favor was to his benefit. She would owe him. Quid pro quo.

Now, time to give you what you want, Liv. What my son needs. For his mother to return to an unmarked grave and a cold-case file.

As Patrick walked behind Grace's building, he spotted a

middle-aged woman, her rounded figure further padded by a long down-filled jacket. A dark winter hat—pulled down as far as it would go—hid her hair and part of her face, the rest obscured by a thick scarf.

"Dressed for the occasion, I see," he said as he ambled over. "A cold night's dark endeavor."

The woman let out a laugh. "Well, it is cold. This will warm me up, though." She lifted a wine bag. "Just as soon as I get up to my friend's apartment."

Patrick stopped a few feet away, staying deep in shadow. "Who's your friend?" Before she could answer, he lifted a sheet of paper and unfolded it. "Ah, now, you really did come prepared. A map of the building and all. Very thorough."

The woman patted her pockets. "How—?"

"You dropped it," Patrick lied, flashing his teeth in a smile, and she finally turned to him.

Pamela Larsen. I see where your daughter gets that look of hers, the one that says she knows she's being conned but doesn't have enough evidence to convict.

He handed back the map. "That looks like Liv's floor."

Pamela smiled, a wonderfully guileless smile. "It is. I'll have to tell her I met you. Now, if you'll excuse me . . ." She reached for the door.

"Aren't you forgetting something?"

"Hmm?"

"My name. In order to tell Liv you met me, you'll need to know who I am first."

He stepped between her and the door, full under the light. Her eyes widened. Then they narrowed.

"You *do* remember me," he said. "It was such a brief encounter, and how long ago? Thirty years, at least. But you don't forget a fae face, do you?"

"I don't know what you mean," she said evenly. "If you'll excuse me—"

"I'm afraid you won't find Liv there. She moved into the old Carew house. Kids these days." He shook his head. "Communications options we only dreamed of—text, e-mail, voice mail. But they still don't talk with their parents nearly enough. Of course, in your case, I guess there's an excuse. You don't have Snapchat in prison, do you, Pamela?"

Pamela went still.

"Regretting the fact you can't kill me?" he said. "You *could*, but I haven't done anything to warrant it, and you need a good reason, don't you, Pamela? Well, maybe not *good*. You haven't quite sold me on your motivation for conspiring to kill James Morgan. I suspect a large part of that was just the opportunity to frame Gabriel. Which, between you and me?" He leaned closer. "Puts you squarely in my bad books. You'll understand that, though. Paternal instinct can be just as strong as maternal."

"Pater . . . ?" She trailed off and then curled her lip. "You're Gabriel's father." A contemptuous snort. "I knew there was more than a few drops of fae blood in him."

"Much more. Almost as much combined fae as is in your daughter, with her fae and Cŵn Annwn blood."

"The Cŵn Annwn are not fae."

"They are, too, but we won't debate that. I will only say that if you go after my son again, I will crush you."

"I won't. I've already promised Eden that."

He smiled. "Excellent. Liv looks out for Gabriel, as much as he looks out for her. He jumped off a bridge for her. You know that, don't you?"

"I know he fell off one, but I'm sure he's telling a very different story. And if he did jump? Well, her trust fund wouldn't have paid out if she died before her birthday."

"Pamela, Pamela, Pamela. You are a bright woman. As clever as your daughter and even more underhanded. Yet when you sing that particular song, you seem as foolish and thickheaded as the woman you've come to kill."

"I don't know what—"

"No time," he said. "Liv and Gabriel are coming to stop you, and having been in a car with my son, one cannot presume normal travel times. We must hurry. You're here to kill Seanna. But you'll never get to her without help. That's why I'm here. To make sure you can do it. And make sure you get away with it."

CHAPTER THIRTY-NINE

I burst through the front doors of the apartment building. Grace and Pepper stood just inside, deep in conversation.

"Where's Seanna?" I said.

"Right where you left her," Grace said. "What's the emergency-of-the-moment?"

"Didn't Patrick—?" I bit that off as I strode to the stairwell, Grace and Pepper following. "Patrick didn't talk to you, did he? Has he even been here? Damn him. If he's sitting on his ass, thinking I'm overreacting . . ."

"Where's Gwy—Gabriel?" Pepper asked as I pushed through the stairwell door.

"Parking." I'd also sent him on a bit of a wild-goose chase, giving him a few places to look for Pamela while I talked to Patrick. The truth was that the closer we'd gotten to Cainsville, the more I wondered if Patrick would actually do anything.

Which meant that Pamela might have already succeeded. If she had, then Gabriel shouldn't be there.

"Can you stall him?" I asked Pepper. "Please?"

"Gaze up adoringly at him," Grace said. "Like you did when you first arrived. Call him Gwynn, mighty king of the Fae. He loves that."

Pepper shot her the finger.

Grace cackled and said, "Just stall him, girl. He has a soft spot for you. Play up your disability. It's good for that, at least."

Another flashed middle finger as Pepper took off back down the stairs while we continued to climb.

"Any clue what this is about?" Grace said. "A summary will do."

"Pamela's free, and she's come to kill Seanna."

"*Cach.*"

"Exactly."

I yanked open the third-floor door to see Patrick lounging in the hall.

He straightened. "Liv. And Grace. Lovely. Come to keep me company in my murder-watch? No sign of Pamela yet, but I'm really hoping she'll show. I do hope to meet her."

"Where are Helia and Alexios?"

He pointed at the apartment door. "In there, of course. I decided I was more comfortable out here. They can be rather tiresome."

I started for the apartment.

Patrick caught my arm. "Before you go in there, I wanted to ask—"

I yanked away. "I need to see her."

He leaned in to my ear. "Don't worry—I'll help with any excuse you need. Just another minute and it'll be over, and we'll all be much happier."

"You— She's—"

I wrenched from his grip and lunged for the door. He tried to grab me, but Grace interceded, throwing him aside like a prizefighter with a toddler.

I opened the door and raced inside. Helia and Alexios lay on the sofa, curled up together, fast asleep, a bottle of wine on the coffee table. I tore into the bedroom. And there was my mother, with a pillow poised over Seanna's sleeping face.

I saw that, and I stopped. I just . . . I couldn't process. That sounds ridiculous. I knew what my mother was. I knew she'd killed four people to cure me. Murdered them in cold blood. But I ran through that doorway, and I saw her poised over Seanna, and a memory flashed, a woman leaning into my crib, brushing back my hair and kissing my forehead as she whispered, "I'm going to fix you, baby. Whatever it takes, I'm going to fix you."

"Mom?"

Pamela froze. Lifted her head, saw me, and backed away, pillow in one hand, a knife in the other.

"Stay away, Eden," she said.

"Or what?" I said. "You'll kill me, too?"

"*Never.* You know that. But this"—she waggled the knife—"will finish Seanna off much faster than this"—she lifted the pillow. "She's sound asleep. Drugged by the fae. If you want to show her mercy, allow me to do this the easy way."

"Let her finish, Liv," Patrick said. He appeared in the doorway, Grace holding his arm pinned behind his back.

"I can't—" I began.

"Fine, then. Grace? Release me, and I'll stop Liv so she *can't* stop Pamela, and we can get this over with, no one at fault but Pamela Larsen. Well, and me, but I'm fine with that."

"Are you all right with condemning Seanna to an afterlife as a melltithiwyd?" I said.

"What?"

"She's marked."

Patrick exhaled a curse. "All right. Maybe she doesn't deserve—"

"They didn't just mark her," I said. "They took a down payment on her debt. Borrowed her soul, her humanity, her conscience—whatever you want to call it. That's the only way they could guarantee she would do everything they needed. The fact that it meant Gabriel grew up with a soulless monster for a mother? Irrelevant. Or perhaps, as someone once told me, that's how you forge a good blade."

Patrick squeezed his eyes shut. "Does Gabriel know this?"

"No, and he's not going to. He . . ." I trailed off as Grace looked over her shoulder.

Gabriel stood behind her.

"I tried," Pepper said from the hall. "He tricked me."

"So Seanna is marked," he said. "The sluagh marked her and took her conscience, and this is the end result." He waved at the bed. "A room full of people debating whether she deserves to die."

"She doesn't," I said. "That gives the sluagh what they want." I looked at Pamela. "You've been set up. Both you and Seanna. The sluagh gave her that envelope with Greg Kirkman's name in it. Seanna had no idea what was even in it. Then they scripted her encounter with you, preying on your hatred of Gabriel and your drive to protect your family. Combine the two and you'd help the sluagh take out a pawn who's outlived her usefulness while providing a card to use against me—the sluagh can now accuse *both* my parents of new murders, with evidence. I was never in any danger from Seanna. Nor was Dad. You've been duped, Mom."

She hesitated, looking from Seanna to Gabriel.

"Yes," Gabriel said. "You can still kill her. You are in a position to do so. If you thought that would hurt me, I believe you can realize your mistake now. I don't care. Yes, she's marked. Yes, what she did to me isn't entirely her fault. Yet she still did it. I still had to live through it, and it was more than the lack of a soul. Seanna made choices. So while I would never take that pillow and finish the job, I do not particularly care if you do.

Nor does Patrick. Nor does Grace. There's only one person here who cares."

His gaze went to me, and Pamela's followed.

"Please," I said.

She laid down the knife and the pillow and walked out of the room.

CHAPTER FORTY

I went after Pamela, and I found her at the window, looking out.

"We need to get you back to the hospital," I said. "Before anyone finds out you escaped."

She nodded, holding the curtain, gazing into the night.

"Is there . . . is there anything you want first?" I said. "Before you go back?"

She turned, a smile playing on her lips. "Is that my reward, for doing as you asked, Eden? You'll take me out for ice cream before I go back to jail?"

"No, I just—"

"I'm teasing. You're distraught. I can see that. I hope I've made the right choice. I'm still not convinced I have. I didn't understand half of what you and Gabriel said in there, about marks and sluagh, and I fear you're *both* in over your head. That the fae have tricked you, and leaving Seanna alive was a mistake."

"It's not. I know it's not."

She opened her mouth to argue. Then she shut it. After a long moment, she said, "All right, then. You asked what I'd like to do. That fae—Gabriel's father—said you're living in a house now. The old Carew house. That's what I'd like for my reward. To see a sliver of my daughter's new life. Show me your home, Eden."

We didn't get out of the apartment building so quickly. When I turned around, Walter was there, talking to Grace and Patrick.

I tried to get Pamela to the door, but then the dryads woke up and, well, they were as pissed off as dryads can be, realizing Patrick had sprinkled fairy dust in the wine he brought.

"I'm going," I said as I dodged the mob of angry and indignant and unapologetic fae. "I really need to get Pamela back to the hospital before there's an APB out on her."

"Let me—" Patrick began.

"Yeah, no. Not now. Not ever."

"I'll meet you at the hospital, Pamela," Patrick said. "I'll smooth your re-entry."

Patrick left as Alexios went after him, still telling him off.

When I started to leave with Pamela, Walter tried to stop me. Gabriel blocked him.

"Olivia," Walter said. "Just one moment, please."

"She needs—" Gabriel began.

"We're going to relocate Seanna," Walter said. "Before the sluagh tries again."

"Is that necessary?" I shook my head. "Never mind. I'm sure Grace will be happy to see her gone. Just be careful."

"We'll go, too," Helia said. "To watch her."

"You're still injur—"

"We failed in our duty," she said softly. "Please allow us to do this."

"You didn't fail—"

"Please."

"All right, but don't let Alexios think I asked you. He's worried. Rest as much as you can."

Gabriel kept me moving, with one hand at my back, steering me out while holding off the fae. The door closed behind us and the chaos fell to silence, and I exhaled and leaned against him, saying, "Thank you. For everything."

A brush of his lips against the top of my head, and I started to straighten. Then I stopped.

"What you heard. About Seanna. I—"

"I know why." Another kiss, this one against the side of my head, as he bent to whisper, "Thank *you*. For everything."

At a noise, I turned to see Pamela, right there, watching.

"We'll go now," I said. "Gabriel's coming with us."

"I see that."

"Don't—"

"I won't. I have a limited amount of time, and I won't waste it registering my disapproval."

"It's been registered," I said, and headed for the stairs.

We drove to my place. It may only be a few blocks, but no matter how disguised Pamela was, I wasn't walking around Cainsville with my escaped-con mother.

When we arrived, Ricky flicked on the porch lights and opened the door, saying, "Hey, I was starting to wonder—" Then he saw the woman with me, and even with a scarf covering half her face, he said, "Pamela . . . ?"

"We broke her out of jail," I said as we walked in. "You know I hate playing Monopoly with only three people."

"Cool," he said. "But I still get the horseman."

Pamela unwound her scarf, and Gabriel took her coat, making her jump a little. Then she turned and said, "Ricky, I presume."

"Yep." He shook her hand. "Liv likes to keep me around. The only thing worse than playing Monopoly with three is playing it with two *and* against Gabriel."

Lloergan came out of the parlor and bumped my hand.

"Is that . . . ?" Pamela lowered herself to one knee and looked into Lloergan's eyes. "A *cŵn*. I haven't seen one in . . ." Her breath hitched. "A very long time."

I patted Lloergan, and Pamela tentatively did the same, then she said to Ricky, "It's yours?"

"She. Lloergan. One perk to being Arawn is getting my own *cŵn*. Slightly damaged." He ruffled the hound's shredded ear. "A starter *cŵn*."

Lloergan growled and he laughed, scratching behind her ears.

Pamela stepped away from the hound and looked around.

"Had you ever been here?" Ricky asked. "She'd have been your great-grandmother, right?"

"Granny Carew, yes. And yes, I spent . . . I spent many days here. Days and nights when I was little." She walked into the parlor and looked up. "The magpie frieze."

"One is for sorrow, two is for mirth," I said. "You taught me that."

"As she taught me. We used to—" She stopped, that hitch in her breathing again. She turned toward the window. "May I have a moment, Eden? I'm sure Ricky would appreciate an update, as patient as he's being."

We backed out. Gabriel went to start coffee, and I told Ricky what had happened.

"Holy shit," he whispered when I finished.

"I didn't want to call you in," I said. "After what she did to Gabriel, I couldn't take that chance."

He pulled me into a hug. "I get it. You didn't need to explain. How's Gabriel doing?"

"I can't tell right now. Everything feels like it's spinning a mile a minute, and there's no time to even stop and process what *I'm* thinking."

"Yeah."

"Felix?" Pamela said.

We startled out of our tête-à-tête and saw her standing at the base of the stairs, one hand on the polished banister, looking up at . . .

"Hey, TC," I said. "Yeah, that's my cat. TC."

"Short for 'the cat,'" Ricky said. "When Liv names animals, they're either dead simple or . . ." He waved at Lloergan. "Impossible to pronounce."

I stuck out my tongue at him. Then I noticed Pamela watching us, the way she'd been watching me with Gabriel. Analyzing. Processing. I stepped away, uncomfortable with the scrutiny.

TC chirped as he came down the stairs. He stopped three steps up, on eye level with Pamela. Then he chirped again.

"He looks like . . ." she began. She shook it off and stroked his head. He leaned into her hand and her fingers absently rubbed over his ear. Then she stopped, looked down, and touched a white spot behind his left ear. "No . . ."

TC chirped.

"You know him?" I said, walking to her.

"He's . . . was . . . Felix. My—" She cleared her throat. "My cat. Which should be impossible, but . . ."

"It's Cainsville," I said.

"There was a young woman. Hannah. She was friends with—" She glanced at Gabriel as he walked in with a tray of coffees. "Your aunt. Great-aunt."

"Rose," I said.

"Yes. Hannah said Felix was a *matagot*. I went to the library to look that up. I was concerned."

"That he was fae."

"He's not," she said emphatically. "It's French folklore, not Celtic. The book said he'd grant a gold coin a day. I asked

Hannah about that, and she laughed. She said there'd be no gold, but that he was special. That was all. He was special."

She bent and rubbed TC's neck as he purred.

"What happened to him?" Ricky asked, taking a coffee.

"It's what happened to me, I think. I grew up. I shouldn't say he was *my* cat. I didn't live in Cainsville. But he'd come around when I stayed over. Then I wasn't visiting very often, and he stopped coming around. I figured he gave up on me and found a family. A permanent home." She looked up the stairs. "And now he has."

"Well, I wouldn't say he's made it permanent yet, but he's with me for as long as he wants to be. Right, *matagot*?" I gave him a pat and he rewarded me with a chirp, and then headed into the parlor.

"Do you have time for the tour?" I asked Pamela. "Or just coffee?"

"Both if I can," she said. "Please."

I gave her the tour. She did not fail to notice Gabriel's shirt in my bedroom or Ricky's bag in the spare one. She didn't comment, though. Just assessed and looked around, and even told me a couple of quick stories about my great-great-grandmother.

I noticed Gabriel giving us increasingly concerned glances, falling just short of pointedly checking his watch. He didn't say anything. He knew that would only delay her more. I was keeping an eye on the time, though, and so was she, and finally she said, "I need to go."

"Okay, we'll drive—"

"I have a car."

"Then we'll follow—"

"Better that you don't, Eden. If anything goes wrong, you never saw me."

Gabriel nodded from down the hall, agreeing, and I said, "Okay, but while I'm not exactly happy with Patrick right now, if you do see him at the hospital, take whatever help he offers. He might be a bòcan, but this one will be a freebie. He owes me."

"Bòcan," she said, and then, "Hobgoblin. Well, that certainly explains—" She cut herself short and it was two long beats before she said, "It explains his troublemaking."

I knew that took effort, directing the barb away from Gabriel, but she made that effort and I murmured, "Thank you," as I walked her to the door.

We stepped outside, and she ran her hand over the brass knocker. "I remember this," she said. "Gran said it was a good . . ." She trailed off.

"Good marriage omen," I said. "I take it as a less specific omen, for a good household—whatever and whomever that household might include."

I knew that wasn't what she wanted to hear. She went still, her jaw working. Part of me wanted to change the subject. Avoid a confrontation. End this impossible visit on the best possible note. But I held my tongue, and after a moment she only nodded and said, "Yes, I suppose it means that, too."

We started down the steps. At the bottom, she said, "I'll walk myself back, Eden. I just . . ." She looked back at the house. "You know how I feel about you being in Cainsville, but this— the house, the cat—it does make it easier." She glanced at me. "You're happy?"

"Overlooking the absolute chaos of my life right now?" I said. "Yes. I'm happier than I ever thought I could be. There are still things I want settled, obviously. The appeal, for one. But Gabriel's on it, and it looks good. With any luck, Dad will be out by this time next year." I hurriedly added, "Both of you will be out."

"I know your father is your priority, Eden, as he should be. He deserves it far more than I do." She put her arms around my shoulders, an awkward embrace as she gave a wry chuckle and said, "I never was very good at this."

"Neither am I," I said, and hugged her back.

CHAPTER FORTY-ONE

I walked into the house, where Gabriel and Ricky were waiting in the hall.

"Did that just happen?" I said. "Did this entire night just happen? Or have I moved from visions to full-on hallucinations?"

"It happened," Ricky said. "Your mom broke out of jail to kill Gabriel's mom, and you stopped her, and then Gabriel made her coffee while she toured your new house. I'm still not sure what's the most unbelievable part of that."

"I believe the part where Olivia stopped Pamela from killing Seanna," Gabriel said.

I tensed. "I'm sorry. I know maybe you'd rather—"

"I was attempting to make light of the situation," Gabriel said. "I wasn't secretly hoping she'd do it." He thought for a moment. "No, that's incorrect. I didn't want Pamela to kill Seanna because *you* didn't want her to kill Seanna. The revelation of Seanna's mark merely makes her a pathetic figure, rather than a nefarious villain. I do not *wish* to see her dead."

"A pathetic figure," I said. "That's it exactly. I couldn't condemn her to an eternity of suffering for that."

"Of course not. I would neither expect nor wish you to do any different."

He stepped toward me and then glanced at Ricky, as if remembering we weren't alone.

"You know what?" Ricky said. "I'm suddenly very sleepy, and not at all in need of this." He produced a bottle of Scotch from behind his back. "You two enjoy. I'll go nap, and if Todd breaks out of prison to kill my father, please wake me up."

"Don't worry, I'd stop him," I said. "Now, if he went after *Gabriel's* father right now, that might be a whole other situation."

"One which I might very well condone under the circumstances," Gabriel said. "But no, presuming you aren't actually tired, Ricky, and are only attempting to politely extricate yourself from an intimate situation, I'll ask you to join us in the drink. I believe we could all use it."

We'd barely poured the Scotch when the doorbell rang.

"I would hope that was Patrick coming to tell us Pamela got back safely," I said. "But it's a little soon for that."

"Actually, he will text as soon as she does," Gabriel said. "I sent him a strongly worded message to that effect, as well as a warning that he may not wish to contact you directly for at least forty-eight hours."

"Good call."

The knocker banged. I winced and said, "Tell me we can ignore that."

"I don't hear a thing," Ricky said. "Lloergan? Get back here. You don't hear it, either."

Gabriel got to his feet. "I'll answer and tell the caller, in no uncertain terms, to go away."

Ricky grinned. "Dare you to say exactly that. Just open the door, give your best Gabriel stare, say 'Go away,' and shut it again. Better yet, slam it."

"I don't slam doors."

"You should start. It's very therapeutic."

I listened to Gabriel's footsteps. Then the click of the dead-bolt, the whoosh of the door, and a very eloquent sigh.

"Pepper," he said.

I went into the hall to see her standing in the doorway saying, "Gwy—I mean, Gabriel."

"You may call me Gwynn, Pepper. I have told you that."

He sounded deeply resigned, and I knew it wasn't so much the name as general exhaustion from the endless evening, but Pepper stumbled over herself to apologize.

Grace wasn't kidding about Pepper's near worship of Gabriel. If Pepper were actually as young as she looks, it'd be seriously creepy. But it has nothing to do with that. To her, he is Gwynn, legendary king of the Fae, and while she could flip Grace the finger at her teasing, it was a whole different story when she stood in front of Gabriel himself.

"Hey, Pepper," I said as I walked in, and I swear they both gave sighs of relief.

"Liv," Pepper said. "I know it's late. I know you guys must be tired. I wouldn't come by if it wasn't . . ."

She trailed off, and I said, "Important?" thinking she'd blanked on a word again, but she said, "Right, except I'm not sure it is. Maybe it's just me. I still get confused and . . ." She inhaled. "I should talk to Veronica first. I'm sorry. I didn't mean to bug you guys."

I caught her arm as she went to leave. "Just tell us."

She hesitated, then said, "I don't want to second-guess you, Liv. You might have totally known what you were doing, and if so, just tell me to shove off, but you seemed really distracted, so I started to think . . ." She looked up at me. "Are you sure you should have sent the dryads to watch over Seanna?"

"Ah," I said. "Come on in." I escorted her into the parlor. "You're right. That probably wasn't a good idea. Helia volunteered, and while I did try to stop her, I should have *insisted*." I looked at Gabriel and Ricky. "Maybe we should catch up and convince them they aren't needed. Helia really shouldn't be exerting herself."

"I can do it," Ricky said, pushing to his feet. "Lloe? You up to running beside the bike? Or should we take Liv's car?"

Pepper nodded. "Checking on them is a good idea. Helia wasn't in great shape, as hard as she tried to hide it. I don't think she was up to this kind of mission."

"Nor do I believe Seanna required extra guards," Gabriel said. "But we take your point. If they wanted to help Walter, they won't be swayed unless someone replaces them on their watch."

"Help Walter?" Pepper looked from me to Gabriel.

"With Seanna," I said.

"But I thought . . . I thought Liv sent them to *watch* Walter. Because she was suspicious."

"Of Walter?" I said with a laugh. "That makes a whole lot more sense now. That's definitely a mission I wouldn't send Helia on, given her condition. She just wanted to go and help him watch over Seanna."

"That's not . . ." She trailed off and looked from me to Gabriel again.

"Not what?" I said.

"I overheard Helia talking to Alexios. She said they were going to watch Walter, that him taking Seanna away seemed suspicious. I thought that meant you were suspicious of him, but it must have just meant she was. She told Alexios that they needed to see what he was up to."

"Walter?" I shook my head. "Then they're the ones who misunderstood. Ida wanted him to take Seanna someplace safe."

"Ida wasn't there."

"Sure she . . ." I thought. "Well, no, I didn't actually see her, but . . ." I looked at Gabriel.

"She wasn't there," he said. "I presumed she'd given Walter orders before he came over."

"Ida doesn't know," Pepper said. "Helia asked, and Walter said he hadn't told Ida about Pamela, that she was sleeping when he left and she needs her rest—everything that's going on is wearing her down. He wanted to handle this alone. Grace agreed. She grumbled about Ida always taking control, and she said if they could leave Ida out of it, that'd be easier for everyone. I ran after Helia and gave her my cell phone, because I remembered them saying they didn't have one."

"Good idea," Ricky said.

I was already on my phone, listening to the line ring . . . and ring. Then Pepper's voice mail picked up.

"Call Ida," Gabriel said.

I dialed.

CHAPTER FORTY-TWO

"Ida? It's Liv. I know it's late."

"Hmm? Yes."

I glanced at Gabriel, who was right beside me, listening in. "Ida? Are you all right?"

A pause, and then, with a little more of her characteristic snap, "Of course. I'm as fine as one could expect, being woken at . . . Where's the clock?" Something crashed to the floor, and she muttered a curse in Welsh. "Who put it so close to the edge? Give me a moment, Olivia. It seems . . ." Another curse, stronger. "What time *is* it? I can't seem to find where the clock fell."

My eyes met Gabriel's, and he nodded.

"Did you have anything to drink last night, Ida?" I asked.

"If you're implying that I'm inebriated, Olivia, let me remind you I am not human. Nor do I partake in such frivolities as alcohol. I drank nothing stronger than tea. I'm simply overtired, having been up late all week. Fae may not require as much sleep as humans, but we do require it."

"It's two a.m., Ida," Gabriel said. "In answer to your question."

"Gabriel? Wasn't I speaking to . . . ? Oh, it's one of those speakerphone things, isn't it? Human technology. You don't use it to end wars and famine, but rather to make even a simple telephone conversation confusing."

"Ida?" I said. "I need you to focus—"

"I am focused. As much as I can be at two in the morning."

"Something's happened."

"How shocking. I swear, you two should use that as your standard telephone greeting. Not 'Hello' but 'Something's gone horribly awry.'"

Pepper chuckled under her breath.

"My mother escaped from prison," I said. "She came to Cainsville and tried to murder Seanna Walsh."

Silence.

More silence.

"You're not dreaming, Ida," I said.

"Of course not," she snapped. "Fae don't dream. I didn't respond because I'm wondering if *you're* inebriated."

"Then so is Gabriel," Ricky said. "And me. And Pepper. Patrick, Grace, Walter . . ."

"Walter?" she said.

"He's not there with you, is he?" I said.

"We don't always share a bed, Olivia. After a certain age, one understands that there is comfort both in sleeping with someone *and* in sleeping alone. He must be in the other room."

"He's not," I said. "Go and check, but be careful walking. I think your tea was dosed."

"Dosed? As in drugged? Why can't you say that, then? Humans and their slang. It's understandable if you don't have a word for a thing, but why invent another one if you do? And yes, I'm walking while I'm speaking to you. I *am* focused, Olivia."

"Walter won't be there," Gabriel said. "We were with him less than an hour ago, and he was taking Seanna to a safer place. Do you know where that would be?"

"Walter?" she said.

"Yes, Walter," I said. "He insisted on moving Seanna. We don't know why, but I was too distracted at the time to argue. I'm calling to see where he took her."

Silence.

"Ida?"

"Yes, I'm sorry, Olivia. I was just checking the spare room, and you're quite correct that Walter is not there. Evidently, he's handling this situation by himself, which I am pleased to see."

"Do you know where—?"

"There's no need for you to worry, Olivia. We have this under control. You should all get some rest. If Gabriel wishes to see his mother in the morning, I'm sure that can be arranged. Until then, I'll ask that you stay in your house. You're all there, I presume?"

"Yes, but—"

"Excellent. Stay there until further notice, please. Now, if you'll excuse me, I'm going to get a little more sleep myself, and leave this in Walter's hands. Good night, Olivia. And you as well, Gabriel."

She hung up. I stood there, holding the phone.

"She's been drugged, hasn't she?" Pepper said. "She wasn't understanding what you're saying."

"Oh, she got it," Ricky said. "She's not going back to bed. She's going to find out what the hell Walter is up to."

"And if she finds out," I said, "we can't trust her to ever tell us the truth. We need to get to him first."

It didn't matter that Helia still wasn't picking up. We could find her using the phone. When we'd bought it for Pepper, I'd suggested adding the same tracking app Ricky put in ours. With Pepper's condition, that had seemed wise.

We took Pepper back to Veronica's and asked her to tell Veronica everything. Then we set off tracking Pepper's phone.

That wasn't as easy as it should have been. The coordinates kept jumping around, as if bouncing off cell towers. But we had the basic direction, so we headed that way, with Gabriel driving, Ricky in the passenger seat, me in the back, cursing at my phone. Lloergan had her head on my knee, her jowls quivering in a deep sigh at every curse.

"Do we think Grace is in on it, whatever *it* is?" Ricky asked. "She didn't want Ida involved, either."

"I can see her agreeing just to keep Ida out of her hair," I said. "But that doesn't mean I'd confide in her right now, either."

"When it all went down at the apartment, someone contacted Walter. I hate to say it was Grace, but I don't know who else. Not the dryads, if they're suspicious of him. Not Patrick, if he was busy trying to *help* Pamela."

"Grace didn't know what was going on until we arrived. She didn't have time to contact him. I'm not sure anyone did."

"No one needed to," Gabriel said. "If Walter drugged Ida's tea, then he knew what was happening well in advance. Presumably Pamela's fae accomplice was motivated by more than hopes of currying favor with her."

"The sluagh orchestrated it, right down to the minutiae, and when it went wrong, she had Walter there to spirit Seanna off."

"Why not just kill Seanna, then?" Ricky said. "Or is that what Walter's doing?"

"By this point, I'm beyond guessing."

A few miles in silence. Then Ricky glanced over the seat at me. "Are we sure we're right about all this? There's more than one solution to this equation. Maybe Walter really did just decide to step up and handle something for Ida."

I showed him my cell phone, finally displaying Pepper's phone coordinates on a map.

He zoomed in on the map and then said, "Shit."

"Exactly."

Back where we began.

Not the absolute start—I wasn't even sure where that was. The moment I discovered the Larsens were my parents? The moment I stepped into Cainsville? The moment I first heard the Matilda myth?

No. For me, this was where it all really began. Ricky and me and Gabriel, fighting a common foe, our first taste of what life as Arawn and Matilda and Gwynn would be like. Endless traps and tricks and betrayals.

Twice I'd stood in this spot. Twice I'd looked at this collection of buildings. The first time was the beginning. The second had seemed like an ending. An ending to so many things.

Gabriel stood beside me, gazing on the same scene, his haunted expression telling me I wasn't the only one remembering. When I touched his arm, he flinched.

"You did come," I said. "The last time. You got my message, and you came."

I leaned against his side, and he put his arm around me, and we stood there, staring at the distant buildings of the abandoned asylum.

When we heard Lloergan's panting, we turned to see Ricky jogging over, the hound at his side.

"You guys actually stayed where I put you," he said. "I'm impressed."

"How does it look?" I asked.

"Clear. Lloe's not picking up anything, either. We're safe here until—"

Lloergan whined. Her ears shot forward as she stared toward the road.

"You can join them if you want, girl," Ricky said.

She huffed as if offended, and leaned against his leg. The sound of hooves followed. Quiet hoofbeats, not the usual thunder of them. No baying of hounds, either. When I caught a glimpse of the riders, they were nearly impossible to see, dark figures against the night, no fiery hooves and glowing eyes.

"Go talk to him," Gabriel murmured to me. "We'll wait."

Ioan was dressed like a guy out on a modern-day foxhunt, in jeans and a jacket and boots. He swung off his horse as he motioned for the others to join Ricky.

"I'm glad you called," Ioan said.

"I need help," I said. "And I trust you a lot more than I trust the Tylwyth Teg right now."

"Whatever's happening, they would never all betray you. This is one or two fae acting alone."

I managed a smile. "You give them the benefit of the doubt, even knowing they'd never do the same for you."

"It's the right thing to do."

I chuckled. "They got the names wrong, you know. You guys are the fair folk. The Tylwyth Teg . . ."

"They are fae. Pure-blooded fae. With good examples and bad. The Cŵn Annwn are no different. You've seen our bad side. My mistakes with Edgar Chandler and the sluagh. Our own capacity to turn out examples of evil, like the rogue who abused Lloergan."

I looked toward the hospital. "I have no idea what's going on here."

"I wish I could enlighten you, but I can only guess. Fortunately, we may be able to get answers to those questions." He nudged Brenin at his feet and then nodded up at a raven winging past. "Let's see what they can tell us."

Ioan turned to Ricky. "I'd like to take Liv with me. You'll go with the rest of the pack, splitting up to survey the terrain. Liv and I will ride closer and see what Brenin and Lludw"—the raven swooped, as if recognizing its name—"can tell us, while I keep Liv safe."

Gabriel cleared his throat. "As you have failed to include me in those plans, I assume it's implied that I travel with Olivia."

Ioan hesitated. Gabriel knew that wasn't what he had in mind, but he only stood there, his cool blue eyes leveled at the Cŵn Annwn leader.

"I can't take two passengers," Ioan said. "I meant for you to stay with Ricky. You're right, though, I should consult you as well. I apologize."

"Accepted, but I am not certain I approve of any plan that sees Olivia separated from both Ricky and myself."

Ricky shifted, and I could tell he wanted to leap to Ioan's defense, but he kept quiet as Gabriel continued. "We're questioning the allegiance of several Tylwyth Teg elders. I agreed with Olivia about seeking your help, but I'm not convinced I want to also entrust you with her safety."

Ioan looked toward the buildings.

"Yes," Gabriel said. "There's a problem to be resolved there, and I'm stalling. But I'm stalling with valid concerns. What proof do I have that you aren't involved in this? Beyond simply, 'I'm Cŵn Annwn; trust me.'"

Ioan gave a wry smile. "That's usually enough." He took a deep breath and then turned to the other Huntsmen. "I'm giving my solemn oath not to harm Olivia in any way. If I break that oath, my life is forfeit. I will have harmed someone with fae blood, and the punishment for that is clear. *Anyone* who harms her tonight— in any way—is subject to your retribution. If that someone is me, so be it. You have your orders. Will you carry them out?"

A chorus of ayes and solemn nods. Then Ioan turned to Gabriel with that same wry smile. "It's not a perfect solution. You can still argue that they are *my* Huntsmen. But Ricky understands. I have given an order that must be obeyed regardless of their personal feelings on the matter. If I defended myself against Liv while she was possessed by a vision, they would still be bound to hunt and destroy me. We are executioners, not judge or jury."

"Quickly, then, please," Gabriel said. "I'd rather we weren't separated any longer than necessary."

I wasn't sold on the idea of splitting up. Wasn't sold on the point of it, either. How would I oversee Ioan's results if he was the one communicating with his canine and avian spies?

That was ultimately why I went: to see what Ioan was up to.

Ioan helped me onto the back of his horse, said a few last words to his men, and then we took off.

The first time I rode Ricky's motorcycle, I'd found what I'd been searching for in every roller coaster and sports car, a need I'd never been able to fill until then. Except even that had only been as near an approximation as I could manage. Now, on the back of that horse, I found what my blood had been seeking, what Ricky and his father sought, too, their own love for motorcycles arising from this hunger they couldn't otherwise satisfy, couldn't even identify.

Now I found that, as Ioan's steed ran so fast the scenery blurred, and all I could do was hold on, my eyes slitted, hair streaming back, laugh bubbling up each time the horse leapt over some obstacle I couldn't even see.

This was in my blood. And feeling it, for the first time, I understood that aspect of Matilda. Matilda of the Hunt. Matilda, who even in the human lore had been unable to give this up for her bridegroom.

Even after we stopped, and Ioan dismounted, I stayed astride, my hands against the horse's quivering back. With a sigh, I slid down.

"I need to change," he said. "It will only take a moment. Then we'll ride again."

I must have grinned at that, wide enough to make him chuckle.

"We'll have to get you a horse," he said. "It's better from the front seat. And a hunt is better still. That's what—" He stopped himself.

"That's what . . . ?" I prompted as he started walking away.

He shook his head. "I was about to start what would sound like a sales pitch, and this really isn't the time."

"That's what Matilda does," I said. "If she chooses the Cŵn Annwn. She rides with you. Like in the legend."

"Yes." He paused. "Which does not mean you couldn't if you chose the fae. But I suppose I shouldn't say that." A shake of his head. "I'll change. That will make it easier to get close. But it's still me. Don't be alarmed."

I didn't quite know what he meant by that until he led his horse behind an outbuilding, and when he returned, I didn't see Ioan—I truly saw the Hunt.

I'd seen Ioan as a Huntsman in Todd's memory. Ioan would have been the one who talked to him, but even if I'd logically made the connection, I hadn't viscerally made it. Now Ioan rode from behind that building and I took a step back, an ancient fear igniting in my gut, one I hadn't felt seeing Huntsmen in visions. There, I'd known they were visions. I'd known I was safe.

The beautiful roan stallion was gone. Instead, Ioan rode a creature woven from dream and nightmare, jet-black, with flame licking through its fetlocks and mane. Its eyes were red-hot coals.

Ioan himself was a hooded figure atop that creature, his polished boots gleaming in the moonlight, dark jodhpurs blending with the black of his horse. A dark green cape concealed the rest of him, even his face lost in the darkness of the hood, leaving only the glow of red eyes.

When I stepped away, he leaned over the horse's back and reached out one gloved hand.

"It's still me, Liv," he said, yet his voice had changed, too, a sonorous tone that came from impossibly deep within his hood.

As I took another slow step back, I tried to stop myself, knowing I was being foolish, but everything in my gut said to run, run now—the Hunt was here, and if you saw it, you would die.

"What have you done?" he asked.

That gave me pause. "What?"

"Exactly. *What?* You only need fear the Hunt if you've done something that deserves judgment. What have you done?"

I wanted to say, "Nothing," but it was like when I was a kid and my father would say, "Livy, I need to speak to you," and every bad thing I'd ever done flashed to mind. That was exactly what happened now.

"No," Ioan said. "No, and no, and no and . . ." He sputtered a laugh. "Definitely not."

I stopped mentally chronicling my past transgressions—fast—and Ioan chuckled.

"That's my point, Liv. You have done nothing to remotely deserve your fear. It's ingrained. That's all. Now climb up behind me. If you enjoyed the ride before . . ." His eyes glittered and I swore I saw his teeth glitter, deep in that darkness. "You ain't seen nothing yet."

CHAPTER FORTY-THREE

As unnerving at it was to have the leader of the Wild Hunt quote rock lyrics—even classic rock lyrics—Ioan was right. When the horse took off again, we flew. Not actual flight—that would have been almost disappointing. This was rocketing at speeds so fast we seemed to burst out of our world entirely, flashing through other dimensions like an old-time casino dealer shuffling cards too fast for the eye to follow.

I saw lights unlike any I'd seen before. I heard sounds I shouldn't hear, sounds I couldn't recognize, sounds that made me strain for more, and sounds that made me burrow against Ioan's back, my shoulders hunching as if they could stopper my ears. I caught the smell of fire and then fire-that-was-not-fire, if that makes any sense. Smells I wanted to hold on to forever and smells I wanted to cast out in a sneeze.

Then the horse stopped, and I clung to Ioan's cape, part of me wanting him to keep going, to please keep going, and yet part of me saying that was enough, thank you very much. Enough for now. Not enough for forever. Sensory overload that my brain needed to detangle or I might find myself in a place very much like the one towering in front of me.

The abandoned asylum.

Hello, my old friend.

My old enemy.

We dismounted in the overgrown cemetery. A hidden cemetery, a convenient burial ground for inconvenient patients, those who died without family to pay for a proper gravestone. Tucked away in this plot, markers nestled into the earth, allowed to submerge beneath the weeds and vines, probably before the place even shut down.

Shut down . . .

I flashed to a memory of Pamela's, of being brought here to see the woman I now realized was my great great-aunt, a figure who'd haunted my visions and nightmares. Unable to deal with her own fae powers, she'd wound up incarcerated here, clawing out her own eyes and cutting out her own tongue.

Pamela had somehow understood what had happened to her great-aunt. That was my mother's gift—her curse. She could recognize fae, even when she hadn't understood what they were. All she'd known was that they were not human and that her aunt had done these horrible things to herself, and it had something to do with these creatures.

Can I blame my mother for hating the fae? For growing up harboring a hatred so deep it poisoned everything?

I can blame her for what she did to Gabriel. That was a choice. But can I blame her for seeing him—the living representative of their legendary king—and being unable to overcome her loathing?

My mother is, in her way, not unlike Seanna Walsh. We can hold them accountable for the choices they ultimately made, while still understanding that something inside them made those choices far easier than they should have been.

I walked to the gravestone I'd cleared the last time. My great-great-aunt's. Vines had already wriggled across it, and I was pushing them away when Ioan walked over, back to his usual self now, with Brenin at his side.

"It's a relative," I said. "My great-great-aunt . . ."

I trailed off as I read the name. *Charles L. Manners.*

"Interesting name for an aunt," Ioan said.

"The last time I was here, I cleared it and saw her name, and then fell through into a vision."

"Then I would suggest her name was part of your vision. This appears to be what we would have called a pauper's grave, for those without family. I can hardly imagine your people would have abandoned her here."

"You're right."

I kept looking at the stone, and in my mind I did see her name. Then I saw her again, my last vision of her, following me through the halls of the asylum, urging me to kill myself, telling me it was the only way out.

That image still haunts me. I'd like to think it was a projection of whatever dark magic worked in this place, but part of me fears it really was her, that she really did think that was the only solution.

"Liv?" Ioan said softly.

I straightened. "Okay, so this is the part where you send the beast-spies in to see what the sluagh have in mind. How does it work?"

"Well, first, I need your hand."

I started to reach out. Then I stopped. Since the moment his horse first took flight, I'd forgotten what I'd really come with him for: to see what Ioan was up to.

When I hesitated, he arched his brows. Then he nodded and said, "You think I have a trick up my sleeve. I do. But you're going to have to give me your hand to see it."

A smile played on his lips. Naturally charming. Naturally charismatic. That's what Cŵn Annwn were. Yet I saw his smile and it was like being back on the horse, all my doubts melting. I gave Ioan my hand, and he laid it on Brenin's head.

"Close your eyes," he said.

I did.

"Now I'm going to take your other hand. Feel it?"

I nodded as his fingers encircled mine.

"All right, then." *Brenin, go!*

Ioan's last two words resounded in my head, and I flew off my feet. I hit the ground, knees and feet and hands smacking against it, and all I could see was the black blur of Brenin's fur as he dragged me through the cemetery.

I tried to let go, screamed for Brenin to stop, but the hound ignored me. My hand seemed grafted to him, as if he were a kelpie, dragging me to my doom.

I'd been tricked.

Of course I'd been tricked. Fae lied. The Cŵn Annwn were just better at hiding it.

Ioan claimed he didn't know he'd been dealing with the sluagh. More lies. He'd set me up from the start, and I'd been stupid enough—

A wall loomed up in my path. A solid brick wall. Brenin swerved around it, and I headed right for it and . . .

And nothing. I passed through the wall without even a bump.

That's when I realized I really wasn't feeling *anything*. I was apparently being dragged by a hound running full out, and I felt the speed and the turns and the leaps as he bounded over obstacles, but it was like riding a sleek new steel roller coaster, without so much as a jerked neck, much less the skin-peeling I'd have gotten if I really was being dragged over the ground.

I managed to look back and caught a very distant glimpse of . . . myself. Crouched beside Ioan, our hands extended, as if resting on a hound that was no longer there.

Brenin leapt again. I felt the jerk of it and twisted and saw another wall coming straight for my head. I shut my eyes and—

I slammed into the wall. I felt the blow this time, yet it wasn't the blow of physically hitting a brick wall, but a jolt, like being thrown against my seat belt, and with that jolt, the wild ride smoothed out even more.

I opened one eye . . . and saw a darkened corridor. The scene bobbed, as it had when I'd seen the world through Lloergan's eyes. Then Brenin stopped. He let out a low growl and my field of vision swung left and then right.

To my left, I heard distant voices. My nose lifted, nostrils flaring, and a scent wafted in, one that made my hackles rise as I stifled another growl.

I was *inside* Brenin now. Seeing through his eyes. That's what Ioan had done. Not a trap, but a surprise. Showing me what the Cŵn Annwn saw, watching through the eyes of their spies.

Would have been a lot easier if he'd just said that.

Easier, perhaps, but not nearly as entertaining. Ioan's voice, in the hound with me.

I ignored him. I was seeing through Brenin's eyes, inside the hospital, and that was worth my full attention.

Now that I knew what was happening, I realized it wasn't exactly like witnessing it myself, but rather like looking through narrow glasses, a sphere of perfect clear vision surrounded by a blurred perimeter. At that periphery, I kept catching glimpses of colors and flashes of motion, but even when Brenin swiveled his head in the right direction, I saw nothing but a wall.

He padded along a corridor filled with debris, leaping over it absently as he trotted, his attention focused on senses other than sight. Tracking those voices. Every now and then one would echo in just the right way for me to catch a word or two, and he'd pause to lift his head.

Liv?

At Ioan's prompt, I understood Brenin was pausing to give me time to identify the voices.

"One is Walter," I said. "I don't recognize . . ." I trailed off, something poking at the back of my memory, and I amended to, "I don't *think* I recognize the other."

Brenin continued down the corridor. When a pile of debris blocked his path, he nosed it, pushing aside a plank to see that, beyond the blockage, the ceiling had caved in. He snorted in annoyance and headed the other way, faster now, retracing his steps. We passed where we'd come in and hit another block.

This time, nosing aside broken wood let him wriggle through a spot that seemed improbable even for a beast half his size. Then he took a slow look around, assessing his options. Ioan spoke to him in Welsh, his voice low, seeming more to soothe the *cŵn*'s frustrations than give him directions.

Brenin set out more slowly as he moved along the passage. He stepped into a room, his big head swinging from side to side. Something flickered in the corner, an image that wouldn't quite take hold. He ignored that and looked instead at a far door. He padded through the room for a closer look. The door was closed, knob long gone. Brenin tilted his head, listening, and I picked up voices again. Walter and . . .

I recognized the second voice then. Grace's cousin, Jack, who'd been the one to refer me to Grace's building. Who'd sent me on my way to Cainsville.

Then, from behind us, a whisper.

"Find the darkness. Need to find the darkness."

Brenin ignored the voice, but the phrase "the darkness" gave me a mental start. The hound seemed to sense that, and he turned, and there was the flicker I'd noticed. It was a man, crouched in the corner. He wore pajamas and there was something in his hand, moving fast, as he hunched over, almost like he was playing a violin, drawing the bow back and forth in a frantic accelerando.

No, Brenin, Ioan said, and the hound snorted, as if he'd already come to that conclusion, and as he turned away, I saw blood dripping down the man's wrists as he sawed at them with what looked like a butter knife. I let out a soft *Oh* and Ioan said, *Yes, you didn't need to see that.*

What am *I seeing? Ghosts? Trapped spirits?*

No, simply impressions. Tragedies that have imprinted themselves on this place. Fae-related.

I tried to look back at the man, but Brenin kept his gaze forward as he nudged at the door. I could still hear the man whispering that he needed to find the darkness.

He has—had—fae blood? I asked.

Yes, but that wasn't the cause of his madness. In this case, his fae blood is why you see the impression, but his madness came from other sources. Sometimes the mind simply cannot cope. In his case, the blame lay with war. When he closed his eyes, that's all he saw. He wanted to sleep.

That was what he meant—he wanted to find sleep. Eternal sleep, if necessary. My brain was overly attuned to the word "darkness," reading something into it that wasn't there.

Brenin snorted, and I saw the door swing open as he'd managed to get his nails under the bottom and pull. He walked through into yet another corridor. After maybe twenty feet, he stopped, and I couldn't hear or smell anything, but the hairs on his back prickled, and a growl rippled through his flanks.

Do you feel that? Ioan asked.

Feel what? I said.

Concentrate.

I did, but picked up nothing. *What is it?*

We don't know. It's . . .

Ioan trailed off and then urged Brenin forward. The hound took it slow, no longer sniffing or pricking his ears but still straining for something, his deeper senses attuned for it as he took careful step after careful step. When his paw touched down on air, he jerked back. I saw broken floorboards. Intentionally broken, it seemed, pieces lying to the side as if someone had pried them off.

Brenin lowered his snout to the hole, his nose working, nostrils flared as he detected something that I couldn't catch. He inched closer, his muzzle dipping into the hole.

The voices came again, from deep in the building. I strained to listen. When I couldn't make out words, I let out a mental curse, and Brenin's head jerked up, startled. His one paw slid over the edge. He scrabbled to get his balance. A crack, as a floorboard gave way. His other front paw slid and then he fell, tumbling through. He didn't flail, didn't panic, just let out a snarl of annoyance before landing on solid ground, his legs bent to absorb the impact.

I'm sorry, I said. *I'm really—*

Brenin cut me short with a grunt, further annoyance, and I whispered another apology, but Ioan said, *He's fine. Angry with himself for being startled and then for tumbling. But he's all right. A hound can take more damage than your human canines. And he's quite capable of finding his way out of this predicament.*

Brenin chuffed in response. As he looked around, at first I saw only blackness. Then he blinked a few times, and with each blink the scene lightened, as if his receptors could use any pinprick of light.

We stood in a room. Seeing rough-hewn wooden walls, I couldn't suppress a mental shiver, my mind flying back to the vision of the cabin, Gabriel and I racing to shut it up against the melltithiwyd.

Brenin's gaze swung up to the hole in the ceiling. He circled and then hunkered down, muscles bunching, seeming to consider the likelihood he could reach the floor above.

I kept trying to see more of the room, until Ioan said, *Brenin? Pause here, please. Liv would like to take a look around before you go.*

No, I said. *We aren't here to sightsee. I'm bad for that.*

You aren't sightseeing. You sense something. Brenin? Look, please.

Brenin had already risen from his crouch and was walking to the wall. He sniffed at it. Old wood, rotting and ripe with some smell I couldn't quite catch. He did catch it, backing up quickly before turning away. Another wall zipped past as he swung his head. A wall like the first but—

Brenin stopped. There was something on this wall. Dark marks against that dark and rotted wood. He moved closer. Sniffed. Ioan gave a low *Hmmm.*

What is it? I asked.

Brenin backed away, and those marks came clear. It was writing on the wood. Three words, written over and over.

Beware the darkness.

I stiffened. Brenin gave a questioning grunt, and Ioan said, *No, as much as I might like to leave it at that, I don't think we can. Liv? Please prepare yourself. Brenin was attempting to shield you from something, but I'm going to ask him to turn around now.*

The hound did, and as he moved, I caught the smell he'd picked up earlier, enough that I realized what it was, and that prepared me, as he turned toward a corpse. A corpse ringed by melted candles.

CHAPTER FORTY-FOUR

The man lay in the fetal position in a circle of candles, all melted to puddles on the dirt floor. My first thought was *ritual*. A sacrifice of some kind. But then I saw the matches lying by his hand. Brenin gingerly stepped over the wax puddles and looked down.

It was a matchbox, rather than a book of matches. I would expect that, given how old the body appeared to be. Leathery skin stretched over a skull topped with dark blond hair, the rest of him seeming no more than a bag of bones encased in clothing.

Then I got a closer look at that matchbox. A perfectly preserved wooden one, with a painted logo for an adventure supply store with a website address.

Brenin moved closer to the body and lowered his head to examine it, starting at the top. It was exactly as I'd thought from farther back—skin stretched tight over bone. But here I could see lesions, like pockmarks, dotting the cheeks.

Definitely male, a young man with stubble and hair a little longer than Ricky's, drawn into a topknot. A modern hairstyle. Modern clothing, too, from a multi-pocketed khaki jacket to hiking boots to a T-shirt announcing that he'd survived whitewater rafting in the Devil's Gorge. He didn't survive this, though. Whatever *this* was.

When Brenin backed up, I spotted two items, half hidden under the young man's corpse. A cell phone and an open notebook. Brenin used his nails to tug out the notebook. The ink had smeared too much to read, but words covered the pages, as if the guy had been scribbling notes right up until . . . well, whatever happened.

Another step back. Off to the side lay a backpack with a crowbar and flashlight. I remembered the hole above, the boards looking as if they'd been pried off.

Urban-explorer dude came into this room. Specifically into this room, tearing through the boards to get to it. Then he wrote that on the wall—

He didn't write it. Ioan had been quiet, and his mental voice startled me.

The blood isn't his, he continued.

Blood? Oh, it's written in . . .

Yes. We can smell it, and Brenin can tell it's not the same as that from the body. It's also older. Significantly older. And from multiple sources.

Multiple . . . ? Oh.

The writing was what this guy had come to see. He'd somehow known this room was down here and broken in to get a look at it.

And then surrounded himself with candles?

Beware the darkness.

He'd brought the candles. He'd come prepared.

He did, a voice said. *Yet he didn't listen. Wouldn't listen.*

It took a moment to realize that wasn't Ioan's voice. I looked over to see a man writing on the wall. Brenin moved closer, and I saw the man's finger . . . the end bloodied and raw, bone poking through as he wrote in blood.

I gave a start, and Ioan said, *Liv? What do you see?*

You don't? I asked.

No.

The man turned. He wasn't much older than me, dressed in old-fashioned pajamas and a bathrobe, cinched tight. He tucked his hand into his pocket.

"My apologies. That was rude. Nasty to look at, I'm sure. But I had to do something. We all did. We had to warn the others. Not that it ever worked. One can't hide from the darkness. Which never stops us from trying, does it?"

"You're talking to me, right?"

He looked around. "I don't see anyone else."

His gaze was fixed above the hound's head, where my face would be if I were standing there. The ghost was addressing what he must have seen and heard as another person.

"Tell me about the darkness," I said.

A brief, wry smile. "I don't need to, and that would waste our time, wouldn't it? The darkness is here. It is always here. It waits, and it feeds. Now it just waits. For you, apparently."

"Who am I?"

The man chuckled. "If you don't know that, I can't help you. If you're testing me again, it's a waste of time. I know only that you are the one they've been waiting for." He pursed his lips and tilted his head, as if listening. "Though apparently, you are unfashionably early."

"Bad habit. Why are *you* here?"

"Can't leave. Well, I could, but I avoided that particular fate." He shuddered. "The red birds. You know of them?"

"Melltithiwyd."

"*Gesundheit.*" He smiled. "If that's what they're called, I'll stick with calling them red birds."

"You escaped them? Does that mean you were supposed to be taken by them?"

"Everyone is, if they're brought down here. Along with everyone who comes down here voluntarily." He nodded at the young man's corpse. "My job is to warn them. My self-appointed task. Most, sadly, paid me no heed. When you're mad, it's hard to put much stake in the words of a ghost telling you to run for your life. One hears such things too often to be taken seriously. Some, though, had a chance. Like him. But he wouldn't listen. Couldn't seem to hear me, which is a shame, because he came here quite determined to see ghosts. I glimpsed his journal there. He followed some tale about this place. Perhaps a story told by someone I did save? He came quite prepared against the darkness. But not against the *darkness*, if you know what I mean."

"Candles don't hold off *that* darkness. Not for long."

"I really did hope to save him. I even wrote on the wall for him, and he could see that and became quite excited. Started taking pictures with his device." The ghost sighed. "Mortal terror would have been so much more helpful."

"You said others were brought down here?"

"Food for the darkness. Souls for the . . . slooy-ah, is it? I heard some say that word, before they died. A couple of the old ones, talking in their old language."

I nodded. "The sluagh. You were food for the sluagh that lived here."

"For their bird things. We fed the birds and then became them—the others did, at least. Not quite certain how I escaped, but I'm grateful for it. One might argue that I deserved such a fate. I would disagree. Wasn't in my right mind. Murder is a mortal sin, but when your child is . . ." He shook his head. "I went too far in my vengeance. I know that. Something snapped in my head, and I am certain I will pay the price with my immortal soul, but for whatever reason, I did not pay it by becoming one of *them*."

"Were the other victims all like you? Here for some crime?"

"*There* for some crime." He pointed above, at the hospital. "And then *here* for it." He pointed into the room. "Spirited down to await the devouring darkness. Which is not why you're here at all, though, is it?"

"Why *am* I here?"

He chuckled again. "I'm hoping that's another of your tests, and *you* know the answer. They want you. They've been waiting for you. They need you. I don't know why. The trick, I presume, is not to give them what they want and, with that, to free me and the tormented souls in their flock." He peered at me. "That is your plan, correct? You don't *wish* to join them?"

"I'm not really for jumping on the bandwagon of evil. It's never as much fun as it seems."

He grinned. "Excellent. I would agree, which is perhaps why I managed to abstain. You'll defeat them, then?"

"I'm guessing if I ask for tips, I'll only get a hearty good luck and fare thee well?"

"Oh, no. I've been here a very long time. I cannot physically help you. But I have made observations that could come in handy."

"Thank you."

CHAPTER FORTY-FIVE

I got what I could from the ghost, and then Brenin tried leaping back up through the hole, and I had no idea what the ghost saw, but it made him laugh.

"You'll want to go that way." He pointed with his mutilated finger and then quickly switched to the other hand with a murmured apology. "That's the way I sent them. Tried to, at least. Just push up the boards."

I directed Brenin. We found a large board at the base, hanging by one nail. When Brenin nosed it up, it left a space barely big enough for *me* to squeeze through, but the hound managed it, wriggling.

"It'll close behind you," the ghost said. "Quite clever, if I do say so myself. I convinced one of the unfortunate souls that God wanted him to pry that off. Couldn't convince him that God actually wanted him to escape. The mad are quite difficult to reason with."

His sigh fluttered behind us as the board swung shut. "Good luck, and fare thee well. Though, I hope you realize, they mean the same thing. But I suppose an extra dose of good wishes can't hurt. Particularly under the circumstances."

———

The ghost's secret escape route was some kind of tunnel. I had no idea what it'd been used for, though the underlying smell suggested sewage. It was dry now, and Brenin was able to creep along until it joined a larger passage, allowing him to do an odd waddle-crawl, his occasional huffs suggesting he wasn't convinced this was the way out.

You didn't see another route, did you? I said.

He huffed again.

We only caught one side of that conversation, Ioan said. *Care to fill me in while poor Brenin labors through?*

I was telling him what the ghost had said when Brenin stopped and growled. I strained to pick up whatever he did. Again, I heard nothing, smelled nothing, saw nothing.

Ioan? I said.

I don't know. There's something, but . . . it's muted. Muffled. Weaker than before, and yet stronger. Which makes no sense, I know.

You detect something with a sixth sense.

If you call it that, yes. Though in honesty, we have sixth senses, seventh senses, and possibly eighth. One can help us find prey; another can warn us against danger, not unlike Gabriel's rather embryonic ability. Which I suppose suggests he may also have—

Brenin snorted, cutting Ioan off.

Is he telling you to stop digressing? I said. *Or just objecting to the idea that the current Gwynn could have Cŵn Annwn blood?*

Ioan chuckled. *Either is equally likely. As I was saying, we have senses for both prey and threat. This is . . . neither? Both? I cannot tell. Brenin? You decide whether to continue.*

Brenin growled, more of a vibration than actual sound, and he twisted, as if testing the likelihood of turning around, but while it seemed possible, he decided to continue forward.

When a familiar smell hit, he snorted it out.

Seems one of the ghost's success stories wasn't so successful, I said.

Yes, I'm afraid so. That might be what we detected. Brenin?

The hound chuffed, as if in agreement.

I believe we're also picking up residual senses of the melltithiwyd, Ioan said. *Which would be, in their way, both prey and threat to us.*

Prey if they become a threat?

Precisely.

I spotted a body ahead. Brenin crept up on it, careful, sniffing and testing the air. Soon we were close enough for Ioan to say, *It seems they devoured this poor soul, trapped in her escape.*

It was an older woman, wearing a nightgown that looked like it came from the last years of the hospital. A cave-in had halted her progress. Dirt covered her hands and forearms, her fingers bloodied, nails ripped ragged as she'd tried to dig her way out. The saddest part was that she'd almost succeeded, clearing a hole nearly big enough to squeeze through before the melltithiwyd struck.

Like the urban explorer, she lay on her side, even more tightly wrapped in that fetal position, her dirty hands around knees drawn up tight, head tucked down as if she could avoid the pecks of the demonic birds. With the explorer, the melltithiwyd seemed to have almost sucked him dry. Here, the piranha birds had done their job more thoroughly, only tatters of flesh remaining on her extremities, the rest devoured down to bone.

Can I free them? I asked Ioan. *Is that ghost right? That people like this, taken by the melltithiwyd, can be freed if I defeat the sluagh?*

He hesitated.

That's a no, I take it.

It's an "I don't know."

So either the ghost has insight or just a lot of hope, and I won't know the answer until I defeat the sluagh. All right. Brenin, can you make it through that hole she cleared?

The hound grunted. Then he stepped onto the body to get to the hole, and he did so gingerly, as if trying to be as respectful as possible. He had his rear legs planted on either side as he pushed his forelegs and head through the hole. Then he lifted one back leg and felt around for better footing. When his paw landed on the woman, she moved.

I jumped. Brenin just went still, considering, and likely concluding that he'd shifted her corpse. He started to lift his paw . . . and something struck the bottom of it.

Brenin scrambled off the corpse. Then he stood behind her, huffing. Another huff, as if annoyed by his reaction. He nosed her feet. Nothing. Her legs were bone, and he surveyed those in a glance before his gaze rose to her midriff, covered in a thin nightgown.

He reached out one tentative paw and touched her torso. Nothing happened.

Brenin chuffed, and I could hear Ioan's murmurs, too low for me to make out words. Another chuff, and Brenin's teeth grabbed the corpse by one foot to get her out of the way. He gave a tug. A chittering sound followed. He went still, his nose working frantically. I inhaled but smelled only the stink of the long-dead corpse and the damp earth.

He tugged again. Something knocked against the woman's nightgown, rising and then falling like a cartoon heartbeat.

Go, I said. *If you can get through that hole, just go. Now.*

Brenin considered. Then his hind paws dug into the earthy floor as he steadied himself. Muscles bunched, he crouched, still holding the corpse by the leg. Then, with a tremendous yank, he jerked the body back. As he leapt over the corpse, it exploded, and it felt like a dozen fists slamming him square in the stomach.

As he fell, I saw the melltithiwyd bursting from the woman's rib cage, tearing through her nightgown, shrieking as they flew at the hound. And Brenin flew right back at them. Grabbed one, chomped, threw it aside. Grabbed another, chomped.

The rest attacked in a frenzy, truly like piranha, swarming, biting and ripping both the hound and their fallen comrades. Ioan shouted for Brenin to retreat, just retreat. The hound clamped down on another and threw it into the wall, and I felt the force of that throw, his head whipping, the bird flying free . . . and me flying with it, flying and hitting the wall, the world shattering into darkness.

I passed out for only a moment, coming to as my body executed what felt like a barrel-roll dive. I opened my eyes to see exactly that—the earth spinning toward me. I braced for impact, but my body changed course, as if on a bungee cord, the air whistling past as I flew upward.

I opened one eye. I was upright now, flying on a roller-coaster course, hearing the sharp flap of air hitting wings.

Melltithiwyd.

I was a melltithiwyd.

My gut seized, every fiber in me exploding in sheer panic.

Turned into a melltithiwyd. My soul consumed as I became one of the sluagh's bird slaves.

My first impulse was to kill myself. To rush at the nearest tree and splatter my brains. The very thought stopped my heart cold with its suddenness, its ferocity. I've never even contemplated suicide, and here it was, bursting into my brain as the most obvious course of action, the *only* course.

Except even that wouldn't work. I remembered Stacey

Pasolini's words, that the melltithiwyd died over and over, only to come back. Trapped in a hell that could not be escaped.

Panic flared again, and I flailed, my limbs sailing out as I expected to fall in another spiraling plunge toward the earth. But I just kept going. Calmly flying, surveying the earth below.

If I'd become a melltithiwyd, wouldn't I be able to control my body?

What if I was simply inside one, like I'd been inside Brenin?

At the thought of Brenin, my gut seized again. Had I just been thrown from him? Or had something happened?

Had he died? That's what I meant, of course, though I flinched at the word.

The bird dropped again, and this was more of a swoop, skimming along the roadway before winging back up for an aerial view. I closed my eyes and focused on returning to my body.

Take me back. Take me home.

Nothing happened, and panic licked again. What if I couldn't escape? The one thing worse than becoming a melltithiwyd? Being trapped inside one forever, unable to even control it. What if—?

The bird dropped onto the roof of a building. It wrapped its claws around the edge, and when it looked down, I saw talons. They were bigger than I expected. And black. The melltithiwyd's feet were white. I could see feathers as black as those talons, not soot-red like the demon-birds'.

The creature let out a croak, and I melted in relief.

A raven. I'd been flung into a raven.

Can you hear me?

No response.

Allwch chi fy nghlywed, bran? I asked.

While I suspected my Welsh wasn't quite correct, the raven should know what I meant.

But it only looked around. Then it tilted its head, and I thought maybe it heard me, so I tried again, louder, but it only launched and winged across the road. It flew to a gap between two buildings before landing on a twisted tree.

Below, I saw two figures. The raven peered down and I peered along with it, and the darkness lifted enough for me to recognize Helia and Alexios. I let out a mental sigh of relief. They seemed fine. They were crouched in that alley-like gap, Alexios peering around the corner and whispering to his mate.

Then the dryads went still, and the raven's head shot up. Footsteps sounded from the empty field behind the buildings. Alexios gave a quick look around, and the two dryads darted to the tree the raven was perched in. They pressed against it and melded with the bark until the dryads looked like two extra lumps in an already twisted trunk.

The raven took flight and sailed down that alley toward the field. It flew straight to four shadowy figures making their way through the field. Four cloaked figures. Four Huntsmen, it seemed. Then the raven dove between them and, under two of the hoods, I spotted faces. Very familiar faces.

DEATH BY HELL-BIRD

"**I** think she likes you," Ricky said, moving up beside Gabriel as the raven swooped past him twice, cawing.

Gabriel barely gave a distracted "Hmm," his gaze fixed on the bird.

"Trouble?" Ricky whispered as he patted Lloergan's head.

Gabriel gave his head a sharp shake and pulled his attention from the raven. "That's theirs, I presume."

Ricky was about to answer, but Meic—one of their Huntsman escorts—beat him to it, saying, "She is."

"Can we ask what she's seen?" Ricky said.

"She's roaming free. Ioan will be linked with Brenin. I cannot communicate directly with her, but she seems calm, and she's suggesting we walk down that passage. I'll take her word for it."

Ricky glanced at Gabriel, who was trying to hide his impatience and doing a shitty job of it. They'd been scouting for the last hour now, finding absolutely nothing.

At one point, Gabriel had said, "Is this necessary?" and Ricky knew he wasn't just asking about the surveillance. He meant the whole expedition. If Walter had taken Seanna to kill her, she was almost certainly dead. And if she wasn't? Well, Gabriel wasn't particularly concerned about that, and only mildly more concerned about the dryads. But Liv was concerned, and that's why Gabriel was here, keeping his mouth shut as well as he could manage, letting out only that one complaint before setting his jaw and resuming the search.

They walked into the passage between two brick buildings. It was a densely overgrown passage, and they had to pick their way through the undergrowth as Gabriel watched the raven, perched on a tree, watching him back.

Gabriel turned to Meic. "Do we know where Ioan is? I'm familiar with the area, and I really don't feel I'm assisting here at all. I would prefer to find Ioan and see what his hound has found. I accept all responsibility for any danger incurred in doing so."

"Olivia is fine," Meic said.

Gabriel made a noise under his breath, a soft growl of annoyance, not at the answer but at how transparent his true motive had been. Then Gabriel checked his cell phone.

"They haven't started working again in the last sixty seconds," Ricky murmured.

He got a glower for that, but it was true—the phones had lost service shortly after Liv left, and Gabriel had been doing sixty-second checks ever since.

"Satellite radios," Ricky said. "We need to invest in satellite radios."

"Or we could just not split up. Wasn't that the plan? Stick together no matter—" Gabriel broke off and rubbed the back of his neck. "I don't like this. Which I realize is stating the obvious."

"Kinda, yeah. Are you getting a sense she's in danger?"

A pause.

"That's a no," Ricky said. "If you did, you'd have said something."

"There was a moment, roughly ten minutes ago, where I did have the sense something was wrong."

"Which passed too quickly for you to even remark—"

"Ricky," a woman's voice said.

There was that split second where he thought it was Liv, which only proved how much he too was hoping to hear her. This voice, light and girlish, sounded nothing like Liv's. When Ricky looked around, seeing nothing, Lloergan sighed. Deeply. Then an old tree beside him rippled, the trunk seeming to separate.

Ricky gave a start, but Gabriel only said, "Helia. Good. We've found you."

The dryad stepped from the tree, her skin still brown bark. Alexios followed from the other side.

"Are you all right?" Ricky asked. "Liv was worried."

"Yes," Gabriel said. "She was very worried. But you are apparently fine, so we may leave." He turned to Meic. "Could you tell that raven to fetch Ioan? We have the dryads. It's time to go."

"I think Liv still wants to find out what happened to your mother," Ricky said.

"With any luck, the dryads can tell us. Yes?"

Helia nodded. "She's alive. They—"

"Excellent. Now fetch Ioan. Or, better yet, if that raven can lead me to him, I'll tell him myself and we'll be off."

"Your mother is alive," Meic said.

"And he really doesn't give a shit," Ricky said. "But, yeah, Gabriel, let's slow down a little here. Alexios? Tell us what's going on. Helia. Sit and rest."

"Yes, sir," she said, and promptly slumped at the base of the tree, her skin starting to meld with it.

Alexios watched her, frowning.

"I'm obeying orders," she said.

"Yes, that's why I'm concerned."

She stuck out her tongue, and Alexios smiled for her, but Ricky sensed genuine worry strumming from the dryad. When Helia moved her arm, she found it fused to the tree and seemed surprised. Alexios glanced over sharply, and Helia pulled away fast—Ricky had a feeling that spontaneously merging with flora wasn't a good sign for a dryad.

"Just tell us what you know," Ricky said. "And then you can go back to Cainsville. In fact, we'll insist on it. We have the Cŵn Annwn, as you can see. Hounds, ravens, horses—the full Hunt. Not to be rude, but . . ."

"We don't need you," Gabriel said. "Ricky is right. Tell us what you know and then leave. That is an order. From me." He paused, then added, "From Gwynn."

Alexios mouthed a silent thanks. Then he explained that the sluagh were here. A group of lesser sluagh in service to one elder—the one who took the form of Imogen Seale.

Ricky suspected this was a base camp, which would explain why Liv kept being drawn back. That suggested that Tristan hadn't been acting quite as independently as he'd claimed. Or not as independently as he'd believed.

According to the dryads, Walter had brought Seanna here to the sluagh, who were, frankly, pissed about that. He'd had one job: make sure Seanna died. If the plot with Pamela failed—which they were also kinda pissed about—then the very least he could have done was kill her and frame Pamela.

Walter's excuse? He wasn't a murderer, and he hadn't signed up for any actual killing. So he'd brought Seanna to them.

"And inadvertently brought *us* to them," Ricky said.

"Do they realize that?" Gabriel asked the dryads. "Walter knows *you're* here. He must presume that's a link directly back to us."

"Actually, he didn't know we came along."

"We were tricksy," Helia piped up.

"Very tricksy," Alexios said, with an affectionate smile for his mate. "We played spy to find out what he was up to. Then we planned to call and see what Liv wanted us to do. But the phone?" He took it from his pocket. "As useful as a rock."

"Technology," Helia said. "Humans are so fascinated by it, but when you need it, what happens? Beep-beep-beep. *Your call cannot be completed.*"

"It was working well enough to get us here," Ricky said. "If the sluagh don't know Walter was followed, then I'm going to agree with Gabriel—it's time to grab Liv and retreat. I'm sorry about Seanna, but I'm guessing she's not going to survive long enough to be rescued."

"Was she still alive when you left?" Meic asked.

Helia nodded. "They'd put her in a room. She hasn't woken."

"Instead of simply killing her." Gabriel turned to Ricky. "The sluagh may not know the dryads followed Walter, but they know we'll come. That means Seanna is useful again. We need to get Liv out of there. Now."

The raven, now huddled in the tree above, croaked as if in agreement. It launched from the tree and began circling back toward the main building as Meic called after it, in rapid-fire Welsh.

"She'll find Ioan," he said as the raven winged off. "He'll understand the message. We should retreat and wait . . ."

Meic trailed off and Ricky followed his gaze to a dark dot, dropping from the sky. Then another one fell, and another, a line of them falling, plummeting toward—

"Down!" Gabriel shouted.

The first melltithiwyd hit the raven. Then the flock enveloped the bird, which let out one terrible shriek. And then blood. A burst of blood, and the melltithiwyd winged away, leaving nothing but blood raining down and Gabriel lunging, shouting, "No!"

Ricky grabbed his arm, but Gabriel had already recovered, with a snarl and a shake of his head, as if not knowing why he'd care about a bird, terrible though its death had been.

Then he wheeled, grabbing Ricky by the shoulders and yelling, "Down," while not giving him even a second to actually get down, pitching him to the ground and dropping over him as Lloergan did the same.

Ricky appreciated the sentiment. Really did. He'd have figured Gabriel's idea of thoughtfulness would be *not* throwing Ricky to the melltithiwyd as he ran. But—not to sound ungrateful—the combined weight of Gabriel and Lloergan's bodies threatened to trade death by hell-bird for death by suffocation.

Before he could say anything, though, Gabriel rose off him. The melltithiwyd had only swooped past and continued on. As Ricky got up, he saw that Gabriel's attention was focused on a blob of viscera, presumably from the raven.

"You okay?" Ricky whispered.

Gabriel shook it off. "Yes, of course."

"We should take shelter," Meic said. "In case they come again."

"No," Gabriel said. "We need to get to Ioan and Olivia."

"They won't hurt Liv," Ricky said. "Counterproductive."

"And Ioan? Would that not be a coup—killing the leader of the Cŵn Annwn?"

Ricky recognized this for what it was—manipulation rather than an actual display of concern—but it worked. The other Huntsman—Wmffre—said, "I'd hope they wouldn't dare, but yes, perhaps we ought not take that chance."

Wmffre scanned the sky, looking ready to hit the ground himself. Ricky presumed they'd never encountered melltithiwyd, and he was about to give a couple of pointers when he caught a blur of dark red against the gray night.

"Incoming!" he shouted.

Gabriel hit him. Ricky supposed it was meant to be a protective blow, but it felt more like a *Shut the fuck up* . . . in the most productive way.

"Everyone take cover against the wall," Helia said. "We know how to fight them."

Ricky got to the side, Llocrgan pressing against his legs, shielding his lower half. Gabriel stayed where he was, watching that dark streak.

"Gabriel . . ." Ricky said.

The melltithiwyd swooped, and Gabriel shouted, not a warning this time, but a string of booming Welsh. The hell-birds changed course, shrieking.

Ricky grabbed Gabriel's arm. "Great, but you can do the shouting thing from over here."

He yanked Gabriel closer to the wall. Gabriel didn't fight. Didn't seem to notice, either, his gaze fixed on the swarm, which was coming around again.

"Let them come, Gwynn," Alexios said. "We have this."

"We really do," Helia said.

The melltithiwyd swooped toward the alley again, and Ricky gripped Gabriel's arm tighter. He felt the other man tense, his gaze riveted to the swarm, and for a split second Ricky caught a glimpse of an older man, blond hair and beard streaked with gray, bright blue eyes the only part that said, *This is Gabriel, in a way.*

The two forms shimmered, Gabriel and Gwynn, both of them focused on those hell-birds as he moved back against Ricky, shielding him along with the hound.

The melltithiwyd swooped, and Gabriel went board-stiff, and Ricky could feel the shout build, held in by only the greatest of effort, ready to explode as soon as whatever the dryads planned failed.

Then the ground erupted beneath his feet, toppling Ricky off balance. The dryads had betrayed them. Ricky lunged, but now Gabriel was the one grabbing *his* arm, holding him steady. He looked down to see that the ground *had* erupted . . . in a way.

Every tiny shoot of undergrowth shot up, every tendril of ivy burst from the brick, like something out of a time-lapse video. The flora exploded, filling the passage, leaving only empty pockets where they stood.

The melltithiwyd hit the impenetrable mass of greenery and soared up again, screaming in frustration. Ricky squinted to see their red-black bodies through the vines as they took off into the night.

"They'll be back," Meic said from deep in the foliage.

"They will indeed," Alexios called. "And we'll be waiting."

"With an even bigger surprise," Helia said.

"Are you all right?" Ricky called to the dryads.

"We're fine," she said.

"Hold on," Alexios said. "They're coming back."

"And trust us," Helia said. "We do have this, however unlikely it may seem."

The melltithiwyd struck again. This time, they didn't just hit the green barrier and fly off. They landed on it and began wriggling through gaps.

"Wait for it," Helia shouted.

Beside him, Gabriel pulsed between himself and Gwynn, drawing in breath, ready for that shout. The melltithiwyd wriggled into the barrier, snipping off vines and burrowing through as Helia urged patience.

Ricky tensed, Lloergan, too, all of them beginning to suspect that whatever the dryads were doing, it wasn't working.

"And…" Alexios called.

"Now!" Helia shouted.

The greenery rustled. That's all it seemed to do. It gave a shiver and a shake, and Ricky was ready to grab a melltithiwyd that had appeared right in front of them. Then the vines snapped like bowstrings, drawing tight.

The melltithiwyd shrieked, and a burst of black blood hit Ricky's face. He wiped it away to see the melltithiwyd impaled on long thorns. Off to the left, another had been boa-constricted with thick vine. Yet another had been neatly guillotined by a thinner one.

"Torn between kinda gross and totally cool," he called to the dryads.

"We'll take both!" Helia called back.

The vines retracted, slowly, having not caught every hell-bird in their deadly trap. Lloergan and the other two cŵns chomped the ones that came free. Gabriel looked off to the side just as one bird beelined for his head. Ricky grabbed and crushed it, black blood running down his arm.

"More gross than cool?" he said as Gabriel glanced over.

Gabriel shook his head. When another came at him, he swatted it and brought down one big shoe on its dazed body, not a stomp but a simple step, as if it just happened to be underfoot.

"Not nearly as cool," Ricky said.

"Not nearly as messy."

Ricky wiped off the melltithiwyd's blood on nearby leaves, as the plant life retreated. They walked to the dryads, camouflaged again against the twisted tree.

"Thank you," Ricky said to the dryads as they pulled from the tree. "Now, I don't suppose you have any idea where Liv is?"

"I can find her," Gabriel said. The confidence in that twisted at Ricky, just a little. There was no arrogance in the declaration, no one-upmanship, but Ricky still felt the knife-sharp reminder that he'd lost her. That he'd tried his best and lost her to someone who understood her better, connected to her better. Which should have made it easier. But his ego still felt the bruise—the sense that he'd done his best and it hadn't been enough.

Gabriel knew where to find Liv; Ricky did not, and that proved, yet again, where she belonged.

Where she'd always belonged.

Gabriel's eyes narrowed, a studying look that asked if Ricky was all right, even if he would never actually say the words.

Ricky squeezed his arm and said, "Let's go get her," and if his tone was a little too bright, he only got another searching look before Wmffre said, "We'll head this way."

They picked their way along the alley, past the bloodied melltithiwyd. Wmffre was talking to the *cŵn*s, in Welsh, and when he lifted his arm, the two hounds took off to scout ahead.

Lloergan looked up at Ricky.

"Go on," he said.

She leaned against his leg, like a kid clutching her father's leg as the others took off to play. Ricky crouched.

"They're your pack. Go with them. I'll be fine."

She still hesitated, but he gave her a gentle push, feeling like that dad, struggling between the impulse to keep her safe and knowing she had to separate, stand on her own, join her peers.

A sigh from Lloergan, one that made him smile, and then she took off, his hand skimming her back as he tried to give her a final pat.

"Be home before dark," he called after her.

Meic chuckled. "She'll be fine. She's doing very well. It helps, being with you. It's a tremendous boost to her confidence, being chosen by Arawn's representative. You're good to her."

"She deserves a little good."

The Huntsman dipped his chin. "Very true. Now, I believe if

we go this way, we can keep an eye on the hounds. Let them scout and find Ioan and Olivia while—"

Meic stopped with a near-convulsive jerk, his head shooting up. Gabriel had gone still, too. "No!" Gabriel whispered, and then, "Everyone! Cover! Now!"

Ricky felt it. Felt it before he saw it, only a split second after Meic and Gabriel must have sensed the same thing.

Something's coming.

No, not something. The darkness. The sluagh.

Gabriel was pushing him toward a door, and Ricky wanted to say no, it was just the sluagh, just that woman, and they'd dealt with her before, but even as he thought that, something in his brain screamed, *Not the same. Not the same at all!*

Gabriel shoved him toward the door, muttering, "Get inside. Need to get inside," a note in his voice making the hairs on Ricky's neck rise, as if he wasn't hearing Gabriel, wasn't hearing Gwynn, was hearing something older, something deeper.

Gabriel grabbed the doorknob, twisted, and yanked. When it didn't give way, he wrenched, frantically, as if in panic.

"Here, let—" Ricky began.

Gabriel inhaled deeply, and came back with, "No, I have this," sounding himself again as he pulled picks from his pocket.

That's when Meic said, "No!" and Ricky turned and saw the sluagh—the *true* sluagh, the darkness—a black funnel cloud shooting for the hounds.

Meic shouted something in Welsh and Ricky started to run, seeing Lloergan out there, the sluagh heading straight for her, and thinking, *I need to be there.*

And then he was. He slammed inside his hound. There was not even a split second of darkness. Ricky was running for Lloergan and then he *was* Lloergan, racing behind the other *cûn*s, the earth pounding under her paws.

The sluagh struck. It hit the lead hound, and the poor beast somersaulted backward, and all he could hear—all Lloergan could hear—was the cracking of bone. The hound flew into the air, body limp and lifeless, and then blood, as if in afterthought, burst from the beast's stomach, blood and viscera, as the sluagh slammed through the hound like a fist.

Lloergan saw it—saw her pack brother ripped apart, the sluagh bursting through—and she let out a stifled yelp, as if she couldn't even find breath.

Another scene flashed through her mind. A forest. A *cûn* being ripped apart by something Lloergan couldn't see, a blur of black against a night equally dark.

In the memory, Lloergan leapt to save another pack brother, but she couldn't find anything to grab, her jaws passing through shadow and fog. The thing hit her. Glanced across her face, barely seeming to strike it while leaving fire in its wake, red-hot pain in her eye, her ear, blood spraying as she howled in pain and rage.

She twisted, fighting half blind. The fog caught her by the leg, sending her up, flying through the air, the only thought in her head that she had to save the others, save her brothers and sister and protect her Huntsman.

She would hit the ground and bounce back. She had to bounce back, fight with everything—

She hit the ground, and the world went dark.

Lloergan snapped from the memory. Ricky knew what it was—the terrible fight that had crippled her. She'd woken in that forest to find her pack dead, and she'd slunk off in shame, to self-imposed exile, never understanding what had happened, what enemy they'd fought.

Now she knew. She saw her new pack brother ripped apart, and she understood.

This was what she had faced before. This was what had crippled her. Defeated her. And now it was here, again, doing the same thing, and terror filled her—complete and absolute terror. She saw the sluagh coming. Saw her pack sister rise up, snarling, ready to fight and . . .

And Lloergan ran. Turned tail and ran.

THE DARKNESS

Gabriel heard Meic scream. Not a shout in Welsh for the hounds, but an honest scream of grief and rage, then shouting, "Derwyn!" as he started running, Wmffre lunging to pull him back.

Gabriel paid them no mind. He had quite enough to deal with. The sluagh were coming, and he'd finally gotten the damned door unlocked, only to have Ricky collapse. Collapse unconscious, beyond waking, it seemed, leaving Gabriel to drag him into the ruined building and then, when that proved unreasonably difficult, heave Ricky up over his shoulder.

This task more than fully occupied Gabriel, leaving no time to worry about the Huntsmen and whatever battle was unfolding there. He did look up sharply, for the dryads, calling, "Helia? Alexios?" They raced through, presuming he needed help, and he let them think as much, not that he'd felt a spark of worry.

He got Ricky inside, and the dryads cleared a spot in the vine-choked debris. As Gabriel lowered him, Helia checked Ricky's pulse and declared it strong, and Gabriel said, "Good," not caring if it was obvious that he was concerned.

The Huntsmen came in then, and Wmffre nodded at Meic and said, "The sluagh took his hound, Derwyn."

Gabriel paused, feeling the Huntsman was waiting for a response, and then finding it with, "I'm sorry," which he was—sorry for the fact that Meic had come to their aid and paid for it with a beloved companion. For Gabriel, though, the news only made him think of that raven, torn apart by the melltithiwyd.

He couldn't stop thinking about that damnable bird. Of seeing it explode in blood and feeling his heart seize, a flood of fear and pain. For a bird? Of course, he understood that it was not merely a bird, but these things did happen. Casualties of war.

But that raven . . .

Another thought rammed forward, taking precedence, and his head shot up as he said, "Lloergan?"

"She was there. That's all we saw."

Gabriel's gaze shot to the door, and he had to squelch the urge to go after the hound. The urge itself gave him pause, but he rationalized it easily enough. Olivia and Ricky cared for the beast, and he did not want to see them hurt by its death.

He nodded toward Ricky. "Is that what's happened? He's bonded with his hound?"

"Perhaps." Wmffre checked Ricky's pulse. "He seems all right."

"What if—?" Gabriel was about to ask what happened if Lloergan perished with Ricky bonded to her. The answer seemed suddenly paramount, not only for Ricky but for . . .

For what? He didn't know. He kept seeing that raven. Yet before he could get the question out, a blast of icy terror seized him, his head shooting up, one thought taking over.

"They're coming. Now. The sluagh. Close the—" He was about to tell them to close the shutters, but enough of himself remained to realize that was ridiculous in a half-ruined building. "Farther," he said. "Get in farther. Look for a room without windows. Hurry."

"We'll stop the sluagh," Helia said. "You take cover. Let us—"

"No."

"We can—"

He wheeled on the dryad. "No, Helia. You cannot. You will not. You'll stay with us. This isn't the melltithiwyd. It's the sluagh."

He expected her to argue, but that was the problem with her human glamour—it was easy to forget he *wasn't* speaking to an impulsive youth. She studied his expression and then nodded and hurried away with her mate to find a windowless room. Gabriel strode off to do the same, gesturing at Ricky, wordlessly telling the Huntsmen to watch him.

And what exactly is the point of this, Gabriel? Gwynn's voice asked in his head as he jogged through the building, hunting for the right spot.

He didn't answer.

You're safe. The sluagh won't hurt you. You mean too much to her.

It isn't about me.

No?

No.

Good.

He didn't ask what that meant.

He needed to get everyone someplace safe. Part of him knew it was a fool's errand—nowhere was safe from the sluagh. But he had to try. Buy some time until he figured out what to do next, how to help them, how to save them.

Any advice you have would, at this moment, be appreciated, he said to Gwynn.

Silence.

He growled a curse, pulled open a door, and saw an empty and windowless room.

"Here!" he called.

The sluagh struck the building like a fist, shaking it to the foundation, plaster raining down.

Gabriel ran back to the front room, where Meic and Wmffre were lifting Ricky.

"Back there!" Gabriel shouted to be heard as every unbroken pane of glass exploded.

Wmffre handed him Ricky's arm, and Gabriel took it without question, helping Meic haul the unconscious young man across a floor littered with glass.

"The room is right back here," he said, then shouted, "Helia! Alexios!"

They answered from somewhere in the building. Outside, all had gone silent, which was worse, so much worse, as if the sluagh waited, biding its time, knowing it had them.

They turned a corner, and Gabriel realized Wmffre wasn't following.

Gabriel shouted the Huntsman's name—or the best approximation he could manage. "Get in here! Now!"

"He's standing watch," Meic said.

"Then he's a fool. Tell him to get—" Gabriel bit it off and stalked back around the corner. "You! Get back here—"

The door exploded. Shards of wood flew like needles, impaling Wmffre and throwing him back. Gabriel ran for the Huntsman as he staggered, blood dripping, pierced by hundreds of needle-like shards, but still alive, still moving, reaching for Gabriel—

Wmffre exploded, darkness plowing through his stomach and bursting out the other side, coming straight for Gabriel. Hands closed around both Gabriel's arms, yanking him back, two voices spitting words in Greek. Every vine in the room shot up to shield Gabriel as the dryads dragged him away. He twisted, getting his footing and then shoving them, saying, "Go!" and pushing them ahead to where Meic was hauling Ricky into the room. He grabbed Ricky's legs and pushed him inside, nearly tripping Meic.

The dryads slammed the door behind them and started shouting in Greek, calling on the forces of Nature. The first words had hardly left their lips before the door was ripped from its hinges, Alexios still gripping the handle, disappearing as the door flew. Helia screamed and ran for him, and before Gabriel could react, she truly screamed, a terrible shriek of agony, and Gabriel dove, falling on Ricky, shielding him, Meic doing the same, both of them barely touching down before the sluagh hurtled into the room, darkness filling it, and then—

Nothing.

CHAPTER FORTY-SIX

When the melltithiwyd attacked the raven, it happened so fast that all I felt was pain. One second of unbelievable agony, as my entire body was ripped apart, and for that split second I was still conscious enough to feel it happen.

I hoped that was just me, my consciousness operating on a brief delay, and that the raven itself hadn't experienced that.

There wasn't enough time between the strike and death for me to process the fact that it wasn't actually *me* being ripped apart. I saw myself die. I felt myself die. I had that one moment of knowing I was dead. And it was the most horrific thing I could imagine.

When I came to, lying in that overgrown cemetery, my brain just gave up, as if my very psyche had gone into shock. I lay there, and while some part of me knew I was alive, I couldn't process the fact. Even when true consciousness returned, it felt like the ebb and flow of a tide, a lapping awareness that I lived, followed by a mental and physical and emotional blank.

I don't know how long it took me to raise my head from the ground. When I did, I saw Ioan, sitting beside me, upright, cross-legged, his eyes shut, as if meditating, and all I could do was stare at him and think, *Who is this?*

My brain skated around possibilities, traversing my mental landscape, touching on every man who'd made an impact in my life, from my earliest memories of Todd to my adopted dad to James to Gabriel to Ricky. No, this wasn't any of them, so who . . .

A fiery flare. Hooves pounding. A hound baying. A hooded figure. A laugh. A smile. A voice.

Ioan. Huntsman. Cŵn Annwn.

Cŵn. Hound. Brenin.

Ghost. Corpse. Melltithiwyd.

It all came back in a rush. I scrambled up and grabbed Ioan's shoulder. He wouldn't wake. His vitals were strong, and his eyes moved beneath the lids, as if he was dreaming. Did that mean Brenin had survived? I hoped so. I remembered the raven and the flock of melltithiwyd, and my stomach lurched.

When the raven died, I'd returned to my body. Ioan was still gone. Therefore, Brenin was alive. That was the logic I would use until proven wrong.

I rose and looked around. Still night. Still quiet.

I'd seen Ricky and Gabriel through the raven's eyes. They'd been with Lloergan and the dryads. Everyone had been fine.

And then the melltithiwyd attacked.

Don't think about that part. Just don't.

They'd fought the demonic birds before. Fought and won. They would be fine. My job was to get to them, and thanks to that poor raven, I knew exactly where to go.

The sluagh was here. It knew we were, too. So subterfuge was a must. I slipped past the nearest buildings, and was just about to dart across the road when fingers tapped my shoulder. I jumped a mile high and spun to see . . .

Imogen.

"Looking for your lost lovers, Eden?" she said, smiling.

I didn't get a chance to even open my mouth. She leaned in, her fingers wrapping around my arm as she said, "Here, let me help," and blackness enveloped me.

I came to in the belfry tower. I was lying on the floor, the sluagh beside me, nudging me with her toe.

"Come, come, Eden. No time for sleeping. Your lovers await rather anxiously."

I rose, rubbing my eyes, feeling like I'd taken a double dose of sleeping pills. I swore I heard Gabriel's voice in my ear.

You've been drugged. It's likely magical in nature. Be aware of that, and proceed with caution.

Yes, sir.

"Where are—?" I began.

"Over here," the sluagh said.

She stood across the room, pointing down. As I walked, I saw broken, rotted boards, from when Ricky and Gabriel had been up here months ago.

The sluagh pointed through the hole. I crouched beside it. At first I saw nothing but darkness below. Then it was as if a peephole opened, drilling all the way down, level after level, until I could, improbably, see two rooms with a wall between them. And in the rooms, two men, action-figure size. I knew who they were, though. I would always know.

"They're fine," she said. "Before you ask."

I wasn't going to. I knew in a glance that they were all right, my anxiety instantly settling.

"Now comes the part—" she began.

"Don't bother."

Her lips tightened, that smug composure rippling.

"I know what comes next," I said. "This is the part where you tell me to choose. We've done this dance before. I remember the steps. You insist. I refuse. You threaten. I continue to refuse."

"The last time—"

"You backed down. Now you'll warn me that won't happen again. I've had time to think about my choice. Here's my decision: take away my cure."

"That isn't one of the options, Eden."

"Why not? You don't need me. You never did." I rose and faced her. "I finally figured it out. There's always that piece that doesn't quite fit, and the temptation is to play two-year-old, smash it in and say good enough. But if you're not two years old, you know it doesn't fit, and that keeps plucking at you, whispering you've missed something. That means you need to re-evaluate. Throw the puzzle in the air and start over."

I took a step toward her. "You say you want me to choose the sluagh. But why? Your reasons are bullshit. No side can force me to choose it. The Cŵn Annwn know that. Even the Tylwyth Teg reluctantly admit it. They woo me. You threaten and punish, and you say it'll achieve the same goal, but it won't. Because you don't *have* the same goal."

I walked to the hole and looked down at Gabriel and Ricky. "The Cŵn Annwn and the Tylwyth Teg want Matilda, whatever form she may take. Gabriel and Ricky want *me*. That's not arrogance. It's confidence. They want to be with me. They love me for who I am—the good, the bad, and the incredibly annoying. Then there was James. He wanted me symbolically. He wanted me for the role I would play in his life. I was, to him, the perfect wife—smart but not a genius, attractive but not gorgeous, cultured but a little bit wicked, too. When I left, he couldn't handle that. Not the loss of me, but the loss of the *idea* of me. He felt as if he'd lost me to Gabriel and to Ricky. He was like a child watching two other boys argue over a toy and wanting it, too—not because he gives a damn about the toy, but because *they* want it."

"I'm presuming there's a point to all this reflection?"

"You're that third little boy, watching the other two fight over the toy. You don't actually want me. You just want to take me away from them. You want to win. And then, presumably, use me as leverage to gain whatever it is you really want, which I suspect is nothing more than power."

"Nothing *more*? What is there if not power?"

"Not a single thing that you'd understand. You are the darkness. You are the unforgiven. You are the end point, the conclusion to all things. There is nothing more. You take life. You consume it. And you do nothing with it except add to your ranks, increase your power. Power for the sole purpose of gaining more. That's all I am to you. A source of power."

"Do you honestly believe you mean more to the others?"

"In my way, I do. The Cŵn Annwn were with Gabriel earlier, and they protected him. Ricky has been in and out of Cainsville for months, and the Tylwyth Teg has made no attempt on his life. That would hurt me, which would be counterproductive. You don't give a shit. Your only goal is to break me. Break me. Claim me. Use me. So go ahead. Take my cure. As for making me choose between Gabriel and Ricky? That's the other thing I learned. We need to stick together. If you want them, you have to take them, which will only make me all the more determined to see that you never win."

"Pretty speech, Eden, but I don't actually need you for this part. You're about to have a front-row seat to the conclusion of this silly romantic drama."

I opened my mouth to respond . . . and she disappeared in a swirl of shadow.

FINALLY

The walls appeared to be solid. While Gabriel was not the one subject to visions—nor even the out-of-body experiences Ricky had with the hound—he was taking nothing at face value. He'd circled the room twice now, methodically searching for a hidden door. That was not merely a desperate and foolish hope, but a very real likelihood, because otherwise, the room had no exit. Which didn't make sense. There seemed little point in constructing a room without a door. Which was exactly what it looked like, solid walls with no hint of a depression where a door had been plastered over.

He'd tried breaking through the plaster, with both fist and elbow. That had won him nothing more than throbbing pain. Which was vexing, both the pain and the fact he'd been unable to break through. Proper plaster should give under the right amount of pressure.

He considered his options, positioned himself, and drew his foot back for a kick—

The only thing you're going to break is your foot.

Gabriel grumbled at the sound of Gwynn's voice.

I couldn't help earlier. Anything I know, you know.

Gabriel tapped at the plaster, looking for a weak spot.

This isn't your battle, Gabriel. Your war, yes. Your battle? No. This is hers. You know that.

Yes, he did understand that, because of the simple fact he'd been placed in this damn room. The knight had been moved off the chessboard. Set aside while the real showdown began.

Or, perhaps, not so much a knight as a pawn.

Yes, almost certainly a pawn. Not swept clear of the board but moved to where he could be useful. Useful to the sluagh. A captive pawn.

He kept tapping.

Gwynn's sigh rippled through his mind. Gabriel ignored it.

You can't help her. You know that.

More tapping. Was that spot . . . ? No.

Do you trust her, Gabriel?

Absolutely.

Then trust she'll get you out of here. Trust she'll win her battle. In the meantime, take this. If nothing else, it might calm you down.

Something slid through him, almost like a warm breeze. Then it *was* a warm breeze, and he was kneeling on a blanket in a meadow.

No, not him. Gwynn. He realized that as soon as he saw Matilda crouched beside him, taking cheese from a basket, as she laid out a picnic.

They were alone in the meadow, the sun blazing, a soft breeze tickling past, a hummingbird chasing the smell of spring wildflowers.

Matilda set out the last slice. She pulled back, as if to grab something else from the basket, and he reached for some of that cheese, not because he was particularly hungry, but because it would make her laugh. She would laugh and swat his hand and tell him to wait, her eyes dancing—

Matilda changed course, reaching for the plate at the same moment he did. They nearly collided. Both stopped short. He stared at her, just inches away. Close enough that he could lean in and . . .

Kiss her. That's what he could do. What he should do. What he'd been trying to do on each of these damned picnics, so many picnics that by now he was surprised she hadn't said, "Can't we do something else, Gwynn?"

But this was the one activity Arawn wouldn't join. Terrifically dull. He never asked to join their picnics, and Matilda never offered to invite him.

It was just the two of them, and each time, Gwynn vowed he would kiss her. He'd devised a hundred ways to do it, a hundred ways that would allow him to brush it off if she pulled back in shock.

Too much wine, too much fresh air, whoops, how did my lips end up *there*?

Yet each time he screwed up the courage, he panicked. What if he offended her? Upset her? Angered her? And then there was Arawn, and he tried not to think of that, tried to relegate their promise to the foolish vow of children. It wasn't as if Arawn hadn't taken a dozen lovers since. He seemed to have no feelings for Matilda beyond the fraternal. No, Arawn was not an obstacle. The obstacle was Gwynn's fear.

But there she was, her face in front of his, lingering there, and yes, yes, this was it, the perfect moment. All he had to do was lean in and—

Matilda kissed him.

Gwynn never saw it coming. Possibly because his own eyes weren't quite open at the time. They opened fast, though, as her lips pressed against his, and he looked to see her kissing him, absolutely, beyond any doubt, kissing him.

Then she wasn't. She was pulling back, blushing, but her eyes still danced, and in those eyes he saw challenge.

Well, Gwynn, aren't you going to—

He did. He covered that distance between them, his hand going behind her head, mouth moving to hers and—

"Wakey-wakey, Gabriel. This is hardly the time for napping."

He snapped from the memory-vision to see Imogen Seale. She wagged her finger at him.

"Is it confidence that lets you snooze? That legendary Gabriel Walsh arrogance. You know what's happening, and yet you think you have nothing to fear."

"Nothing . . . ?" he began, still dazed from the memory. A sharp shake of his head. "The choice," he said. "You're making her choose. Between me and Ricky. Yes?"

"Running a little slow today, Gabriel. And with a tad less than your usual confidence in your conclusions."

He straightened. "I have full confidence in my conclusion. I am here, waiting. Ricky will be nearby, waiting. Olivia will be asked to choose. It is, you believe, the worst thing you can do to her, and so you will do it, for nothing but the satisfaction of sadism."

"Ouch."

"You are sluagh. You enjoy inflicting pain. In this case, it also serves a purpose. Break her by forcing her to choose."

"Ah, there's that confidence surging. Bolstered, I'm sure, by the certainty she will pick you. She already has, after all. Chosen Gwynn; overthrown Arawn. Such a fickle girl, our Matilda."

"Not fickle at all. Ricky was what she needed when I was not."

"Such arrogance." The sluagh moved closer and whispered. "What if I said that I do not expect Eden to choose you? In fact, I'm quite certain she won't. You are her favorite, but she still loves him, cannot quit him, cannot sacrifice him. Part is guilt. Part, too, is pure and cold logic. Ricky is strong; you are stronger. He is resourceful; you are more resourceful. You have a deviousness and a cleverness and a gift for manipulation that our young biker lacks. You are better suited to escaping whatever fate I attempt to inflict on you, and that is why she'll choose him."

Gabriel said nothing.

"You know that, don't you?" She moved closer, lips rising to his ear. "And deep inside, it pisses you off. You can't get rid of him. You tried, so long ago, to push Arawn from her life, and what happened? She ran to him. Could not quit him. Still loves him. You give her everything, and she still climbs on the back of his motorcycle, puts her arms around him, her cheek against his back, and she smiles. She tells you she loves you, but he's always there. He will always be there. And there's only one thing you can do. The one thing you have failed to do, despite multiple opportunities."

"Kill him."

She smiled and stepped back. "There. That was easier than I dared hope. You are indeed the smart one, the rational one, and this is the smart and rational answer. I will let you kill him, and I will tell Eden that he attacked you. He heard of the choice and attacked you, and you were forced to kill him. Not only will he be dead, but she'll hate him in memoriam for what he tried to do. Problem solved."

"No."

"I beg your—"

"You heard me. I was not offering to kill Ricky. I was merely hurrying you to the suggestion obviously forthcoming. The answer is no. I agree that if you do force Olivia to choose, it is entirely possible she may pick Ricky, both from guilt at having hurt him and from reasoning that I am, as you say, better equipped to escape whatever trap you set. Therefore, I will take this further. You do not need to make Olivia choose. I'll do it for her. I volunteer."

"Because you presume you can get out of it."

He pursed his lips. "Hope, certainly. Presumption is a dangerous thing. But yes, I'm not actually throwing myself on the pyre.

More like agreeing to face *your* champion. That's fair, I believe."
He peered at her. "You do have a champion, don't you?"

Her form rippled, the edges blurring to shadow, her eyes deepening to pits, and in those pits he saw the death of self, the death of soul, the death of everything. Which should, he reasoned, fill him with terror. Certainly, even the sense of the sluagh had done so earlier. But now, he looked into those pits and felt only a sort of odd satisfaction.

I see all that you can do. There's nothing more you can frighten me with.

"Oh, but you're wrong about that, Gabriel Walsh. Take your time. Think about our offer."

"I don't need to."

And that was, strangely, not bravado at all, but the truth. He did not want Olivia to choose him over Ricky. Where would that lead? Right back where they started, only with a different two surviving in guilt and pain and blame.

No, this was the answer. This had always been the answer.

Stay together.

No matter what.

"You have *my* offer," he said. "I volunteer. Now bring me your champion."

The sluagh snarled . . . and disappeared.

You learned, Gwynn whispered. *You aren't just paying it lip service. You finally learned.*

No, *we* did. About time, too.

Gwynn chuckled. *It is indeed. This isn't over—but you know that. So while you wait, let me return you to this . . .*

Sunlight pierced the dark room, and a breeze brought the scent of wildflowers and of Matilda, right there in front of him, still blushing, eyes open as Gwynn leaned forward and kissed her.

THE PACT

Ricky paced around the tiny room, some sort of magical cage with no exits. Every now and then he'd bang the walls and shout, "Hey! I wanna talk to someone!" Which was probably as effective as a convict clanging his cup along the bars, but at the very least, he might get their attention.

And he did. He was opening his mouth to shout again when she appeared—the woman who was the manifested format of the elder sluagh.

"Where's Liv?" he said. "Where's everyone? Gabriel, Lloergan—"

"Yes, yes, you came with many people. Some of them more important to you than others, but you will ask about every one of them. That is the weakness of the Cŵn Annwn, the fault of a life spent in service to others. You might play the rebel biker, but you are as bound by your sense of honor as your Huntsmen."

"I want—"

"You want many things, Arawn. But you don't get them, do you? Or if you do, it's only temporary. Gwynn has always been just that little bit better. In the beginning, he was the kind one, the thoughtful one. Uncommonly considerate for a fae prince. But you drove that out of him. Taught him a lesson. And what happens? He comes back now, having fully assimilated your lesson, a true king of the Fae, more manipulative and head-strong and selfish than you ever were. And somehow, despite all that, he still wins. He's still better."

"Yep, I lose. So where—"

"You say that so cavalierly. But you don't *feel* it cavalierly, do you?" She waved her hand and a mirror appeared on the wall. "Look at yourself. A perfect specimen of young human man-hood. Beautiful face and physique, with the brains to match. Add in charm and wit and compassion, and you should be the unbeatable suitor. So how does she choose . . ."

Another wave and the mirror turned into a window. On the other side, Gabriel sat on the floor, knees drawn up, head against the wall, eyes shut.

Asleep? Really? He was fucking asleep at a time—

Ricky squelched the indignation. If Gabriel appeared to be napping, he was unconscious. Or deep in thought.

"Or actually asleep," the sluagh said. "Resting confident in the knowledge that Matilda will choose as Matilda always chooses."

"Choose?" He turned to the sluagh.

"Shocked? Perhaps that's why she picked him. You aren't quite as quick on the uptake."

"No, maybe I just thought you wouldn't beat that dead horse again. So you're making Liv choose between us."

"Yes. Gabriel already knows. And as you can see, he's terri-bly concerned."

That jolt of indignation again. Damn it, yes, he wasn't quite as cavalier about this as he should be. As he wanted to be.

She's playing you.

He knew that, and yet as he watched Gabriel, he kept bristling, kept thinking . . .

"She chose him," the sluagh whispered. "She will always choose him. He is better. No matter what you do, what you accomplish, he will always be better. That pretty face of yours? Merely genetics. That brain? His works a tiny bit faster. Your success? An MBA on the fast track to leader of a motorcycle gang?" She laughed. "Not exactly Eden's idea of a life partner. Whatever Gabriel's reputation, *he* has a legitimate career. He has the success and the stock portfolio to show for it. You might be able to make a decent down payment on a condo . . . half as good as the one he bought outright when he wasn't much older than you. But all of that isn't nearly as important to Olivia as sheer strength of character. And that is where he beats you, hands down. He rose from nothing. Endured neglect and abuse and abandonment. And you? Your mommy left you, too . . . and let your adoring daddy take you, while she remained part of your life. As childhood traumas go? Negligible compared to his."

The sluagh leaned into his ear as he watched Gabriel. "Don't you just want to wipe that arrogance off his face? Wouldn't you like to see how confident he looks when he realizes he's lost? All those years ago, he took her from you. Stole her. He allowed her to die rather than let her even remain friends with you. He doesn't deserve her. You do."

Ricky kept staring. He thought of all the times Gabriel had betrayed Liv. All the times he'd hurt her. Ricky had never done that.

Arawn had never done that, either. It'd been Gwynn. Gwynn broke his vow and wooed Matilda and then made another vow, that if she went to Arawn, he could have her.

So arrogant. So cocky. So sure of his success. Just like Gabriel.

"Exactly," the sluagh whispered. "That is exactly right."

No, it's not, a voice whispered, deep in his mind.

The scene blurred. A smell wafted past, out of place here, and Ricky inhaled. Horse? He sniffed deeper, not trusting his senses. Horse and hay and dung.

He heard a *skritch-skritch*, and when his vision cleared, he was grooming a coal-black stallion, brushing it a little too hard, the beast's ears twitching in complaint.

"Sorry isn't enough," said a voice behind him. "Sorry can never be enough. I realize that."

He kept brushing.

"I made a vow," the voice continued. "It doesn't matter if I thought you weren't interested in her—"

"Not interested?"

He dropped the brush and spun to face the speaker, a young man, mid-twenties, fair-haired and blue-eyed. Even if Ricky didn't recognize Gabriel in that face—particularly the expression, gaze downcast, contrite, even cowed—he knew it was Gwynn.

When Gwynn spoke, it was with great care, as if not wanting to defend himself but feeling the need to say, "You've never given any sign. And you've taken many lovers, seeming happy with them . . ."

Because Arawn wanted Matilda to see that other girls fancied him. Other girls chased him. And he earned their interest—he was an attentive and skilled lover. Matilda would notice that and wonder what all the fuss was about and, perhaps, see him in a new light.

Or realize she was jealous. See Arawn with them and think, "Why not me?" and join the competition for his affections.

No, that last part put a distasteful angle on Arawn's ploy. He'd only been trying to position himself as a potential lover.

All that, and whom did she choose? Gwynn. Who had never taken a lover, never even cast a longing glance at a woman or a man. Because all his glances were for Matilda. And all hers for him. Both of them, since they were old enough to feel that longing, since Arawn first realized their connection and went to Gwynn . . .

"Gwynn, I need to talk to you about Mati."

"Hmm?"

"I don't think we should woo her. Either of us. In fact, I think we should make a pact that we'll never do so."

"I don't under—"

"I don't want you to get hurt. I'm afraid you would get hurt if I wooed her. I don't want that."

"Oh. Yes, I suppose—"

"So, it's a pact, then. We won't woo Mati. Either of us. But we can't tell her that. She'd kill us both. Now, let's go find her and race to . . ."

Arawn shook off the memory. He *did* have Gwynn's best interests in mind at the time. He hadn't wanted his friend to be hurt.

And then Arawn had proceeded to woo Mati in his own way. Through temptation and jealousy.

No, it wasn't like that. If Mati had come to him, he'd have told Gwynn. Been forthright and up-front. Told him the pact was over before he took Matilda. But he'd still have taken her. Still would have snatched her from under Gwynn's nose, knowing how Gwynn felt.

Just like Ricky with Liv. He'd seen how Gabriel felt. Sensed how Liv felt. Too bad, so sad. You snooze, you lose.

Arawn's thoughts pushed Ricky's aside.

Yes, maybe he'd acted less than honorably, but he'd never have gone as far as Gwynn had, all the way to the brink of marriage before admitting he'd been wooing Mati, kissing Mati, bedding Mati . . .

Arawn looked at Gwynn, standing there with the sheer gall to apologize, hanging his head like a misbehaving puppy.

"You broke our pact," Arawn said.

"I know. And if there's any way we can get past this, still be friends, all of us—"

"Oh, is that your offer? You'll let me still be friends with your wife? How generous."

"Friends with *our* friend. Our Mati. Neither of you needs my permission for that."

"You broke our pact. That comes with a penalty, Gwynn. You know it does."

"All right. Punish me—"

"Oh, I intend to." Brush clutched in one hand, Arawn stepped toward Gwynn. "If Mati comes to me the night before your wedding, she is mine."

"What? You intend to seduce—?"

"She only needs to come to me. To hunt with me. If she chooses me on that night, she chooses me forever. That is the new pact."

Now Gwynn's temper flashed as he stepped back, his jaw setting in a way Ricky *did* recognize as Gabriel's. "I will never agree—"

"Too late. You broke a pact. As the wronged party, I can claim a new one. I just did. It stands. A pact and a curse. Now run home, Gwynn, and see if you can keep your bride by your side for a single night."

Ricky ricocheted from the vision, blinking hard. The sluagh stood there, her mouth open as if frozen in time.

"No." He rubbed his face. "No. We were told it was *their* pact. That Gwynn and Arawn made it together."

"They did, in a way," a voice said.

Ricky looked to see an older man, fair hair shot with gray. Despite the age, he knew the face as the one he'd seen only moments ago. "Gwynn."

"I did not disagree the first time," Gwynn said, "so the pact was sealed. By breaking it, I gave Arawn the right to set a second pact."

"I had *no* right."

Ricky looked toward the new speaker, a man he'd seen once before, a man he now realized was the older Arawn.

"What you just saw?" Arawn said. "That is the truth. Gwynn might take the blame, but the lion's share was never his."

"I wouldn't say—" Gwynn began.

"Stop," Arawn said. "Really. Stop. Martyrdom does not become you, old friend. No more than petty vengeance became me." Arawn turned to Ricky. "I'd rather you didn't remember that scene. Much easier on the ego to think we were the more wronged party. But I had to show it to you. Gwynn never stole Mati from us. No more than Gabriel steals Liv now."

"I know. I just—" Ricky ran a hand through his hair and looked at the frozen sluagh. "Bitch."

"Agreed," Arawn said. "But remember that, and trust Liv and Gabriel. *Always* trust them. It's when you don't that you get yourself in trouble, a firestorm of outrage and jealousy that ultimately consumes even you."

"Got it. So the answer is . . ." He moved in front of the sluagh. "Go fuck yourself."

The sluagh snapped out of it. "What did you—?"

"You heard me. Go fuck yourself. And while you do?" Ricky took a step back and lowered himself against the wall. "I'll be right here."

CHAPTER FORTY-SEVEN

"They told you no," I said to Imogen as she returned.

As I rose from the floor, she flung her arm out, pointing at me. Down I went, my legs giving out, pain ripping through my back as she undid my cure.

I took a deep breath, trying not to panic, as a voice in my head screamed for me not to antagonize her. To remember she could do this.

Yes, she could. And if she did? That was my choice. This was what I'd offered in trade. I'd meant it. I would sacrifice my cure before I'd sacrifice Ricky or Gabriel.

As for antagonizing her, I had to silence the primal fear that screamed at me to stop. I *had* to antagonize her. Push, push, and push some more, no matter how far that took me. Be prepared for it to take me all the way.

That's what the ghost had counseled, if not in those exact words. He'd warned that this was a battle I could not physically win. I was the puny human against the ancient dragon. Whatever meager powers I possessed, they weren't going to help me here.

One way to win.

A million ways to die trying.

Not the best odds, but I'd never been all that good at math.

I sat there, my teeth gritted against the pain until I could speak, and then I said, "You tried to set them against one another. Gave them the chance to take out the competition and win the fair maiden. Well, actually, you offered the chance to survive *themselves*, but the other version sounds much more romantic."

She glanced toward the stairs, as if expecting to see an ally who'd turned on her.

"No one told me your plan," I said. "It's the obvious one. That's the inherent weakness in triangles. You only need to get one side to buckle, and the whole thing collapses. But it didn't, did it? So now you're taking me up on my own offer. Withdrawing my cure."

A flick of her hand and feeling returned to my legs, the pain in my back ebbing.

"Thanks." I got to my feet. "That'll make this part easier."

I walked toward the belfry balcony. Part of the railing had been ripped away. I touched the broken and jagged edges.

"Did you see this?" I said. "It should have reminded you not to bother going after Gabriel. Tristan already tried that. He was working with you, right? Tristan. Like Walter and Jack."

"No one works with—"

"Bad turn of phrase. They were your lackeys, though they may have thought themselves partners. In Tristan's case, he probably didn't even realize who he was working with. I bet you impersonated some fae confederate. A lackey of his own."

Her lips rose in a faint smile. "Tristan was a fool. As arrogant a fae as any. At least Walter had some sense of his true place. Not surprising, given how firmly Ida kept him in it."

A board creaked deep in the building, and I turned, but the sluagh said, "No, that's not Walter. Did you fail to notice the past tense to my phrasing? He served his purpose." The sluagh stepped toward me. "You've made your point about Gabriel. He rescued

Ricky at that balcony, when he could have let him fall. I thought he might have grown a spine since then. Realized exactly how annoying it was, always having Ricky buzzing about."

"I'm not standing over here to rub your face in your mistake. I'm admitting that my aunt was right. Well, my great-great-aunt. I've seen her here in the asylum. Or I thought I did. Was that her? Or you, playing mind games? Doesn't matter. Either way, she was right."

I stepped closer to the edge of the broken balcony. "There's only one way out of this. That's all there's ever been. One way out. One way to stop being a pawn. To take control of my life. Or my death, as the case may be."

I jumped. I didn't hesitate, and that wasn't conviction so much as gut-wrenching terror. I jumped before I could fully process what I was doing.

I dropped, and it was like falling off the bridge, where the moment I hit free fall, I stopped thinking, *Oh my God, I'm plummeting to my doom*. There was a split second of something like clarity. *Yep, I'm falling. Should probably be concerned. Deathly concerned, ha-ha.* But I wasn't.

The sluagh let out a shriek, like a human scream, the sort that should have been coming from *my* throat. A scream of fear. Then a snarl of rage that set the very air vibrating. A swarm of melltithiwyd slammed into me, shrieking themselves, as if enraged by being called to do something other than rend me limb from limb.

They pecked, and they clawed, but they lifted me, too, still attacking, unable to keep from venting their frustration as they deposited me in the belfry.

"Huh," I said. "That didn't end the way I expected."

Which was, of course, a lie. Yet if one is going to threaten self-annihilation for a cause, one has to actually seem willing to do it.

I got to my feet, swatting off the last few melltithiwyd, who couldn't resist one final peck. Then I strode to the balcony.

"If at first you don't succeed—"

My legs buckled, and I pitched to the floor, arms flying out barely in time to catch myself. That now-familiar pain twisted through me, and I closed my eyes, pushing it back and reminding myself it was temporary—the pain, that is. The reversal I *did* need to accept—that I might survive this but not actually walk away from it. The pain was just my body dealing with the renewed trauma, which would ease, leaving me with the rest. I could live with the rest. People did. I could. I'd have to, wouldn't I? The alternative was . . .

Well, the alternative was exactly what I needed to attempt, yet again. I dragged myself along the floor, muscle memory returning, back to those infant days when I'd done exactly this.

"Do you really think that will help?" the sluagh spat.

"I don't see how it can't. If I'm removed from play, you three groups have nothing to fight over."

"If you do this, Eden, we will take revenge. You know we will. We'll take your soul. Make you one of them." She swatted a melltithiwyd, still fluttering about. Hit it so hard it exploded in a spray of black blood.

"Yeah, sorry," I said, still dragging myself. "I'm not marked, and I've done nothing to deserve the punishment. I haven't taken part in anything that deserves it. I haven't been found guilty of anything that deserves it. So I won't be joining your flock."

"Then they will. Your lovers. I'll kill them and take their souls."

"Again, same issue. There isn't even a loophole you can exploit with us. We might not be the nicest people around, but we've done nothing that can make us one of the unforgiven."

I moved up onto the balcony, wiggling across it.

She strode into my path. "I can still kill them."

"For revenge? Sure, but once you do, the fae and the Hunt will exact their revenge. They'll join forces to do whatever they can to you, and maybe it won't be much, but will it be worth the few moments of vengeance against me? A dead woman, who'll never know what you've done?"

"Do you really think I'll let you jump?"

I looked up at her, towering over me. "Does it matter? I can find a way to do it. You have no power over me. Take my cure. Take my Arawn. Take my Gwynn. That only means I would never, ever stop trying to do this, and that you will be left with nothing."

"She's right," said a voice as steps crossed the belfry floor. "She's won, *heb edifeirwch*. In giving up, she wins. That's the hardest thing to do, but it's the one thing you can't fight."

Ida stepped into the moonlight.

"So you're suggesting we cut our losses?" the sluagh said.

"No," Ida said. "I'm insisting on it."

The sluagh laughed. Ida's aged form disappeared, as she struck the sluagh in a flash of light that doubled me over, hands to my eyes. I heard them fighting, and I tried to get to them, pulling myself along, blinded, using the snarls and yowls and curses of their battle to find them.

As I moved, I caught pulses of light, felt the air rippling, smelled a stink as fetid as the grave. But I saw nothing. Then the thumps and grunts of battle stopped for a moment, and the sluagh said, "You know you can't survive this fight, old one."

"True, but neither can you."

More sounds of battle, and as the air vibrated anew, I felt the beating of melltithiwyd wings, and I pulled myself along faster, swatting and grabbing at the ones that passed, trying to fling them away from Ida, but soon I could see enough to realize the melltithiwyd were circling. Not attacking. Just circling.

The thumps of battle stopped, and I squinted hard against the light until I could make out two figures on the floor.

"Do you want to live?" Ida said.

The sluagh snarled.

"I have you," Ida said. "I can destroy you. I *will* destroy you. But I can set you free, too. Just do the same for her. For Matilda. For Olivia. Return her cure."

More snarling, the sound not even vaguely human now, and when I drew up alongside them, the thing that had been Imogen Seale had blackened and twisted, not unlike the corpses pulled from the burning house.

Ida had her hands around the sluagh's neck, and light pulsed from her fingers, each flash weakening the sluagh.

"Fix her," Ida said.

One black and wizened arm rose and then fell, and the pain in my back evaporated. I rose, tentatively, my vision still blurred.

"I suppose you want me to promise to leave her alone, too," the sluagh said, its voice thick, garbled.

"No, that won't be necessary." Ida began whispering under her breath, her hands still around the sluagh's neck.

The creature began to fight, wildly, rasping, "You promised!"

"I'm fae," Ida said. "We lie."

Ida lit up, her entire body, a live wire that whipped through the air, her hands squeezing the sluagh's neck as it screamed and the melltithiwyd screamed, and I dove out of the way of that lashing rope of energy, feeling it ignite the very air.

The melltithiwyd flapped, frantic, and the sluagh screamed, thrashing itself into a frenzy of shadow, the stench of the long-dead filling the air. The sluagh bucked up under Ida's hands. And then it exploded in sizzling ash.

I ran over to Ida. She crouched on all fours, light pulsing under her translucent skin, the light beginning to fade as she panted for breath, dark hair hanging over her face.

I pushed her hair gently aside and said, "Tell me what I can do."

"There's nothing to be done. She was right. This is the price." Ida lifted her eyes to mine, bright, impossibly violet eyes. "Thank you."

I choked on a half laugh, half sob. "I didn't do anything except get my ass rescued."

Her hand closed around mine, that energy still pulsing. "You did everything," she said. "You pissed it off."

"That's not exactly—"

"You weakened it. I'd never have been able to kill it otherwise. You won. You just needed a fae to make the killing blow. Before I pass, though, I need to ask you for something."

"What?"

She gripped my hand tighter. "Don't turn your back on the fae."

I smiled, my eyes welling up. "Can't stop lobbying for them even now."

"Especially now."

I leaned down and whispered in her ear, and she smiled as her light faded. Then she fell to the floor.

Something struck the floor beside me. I jumped to see a melltithiwyd drop. Another and another, and as they fell, I heard their voices, the trapped souls whispering as they winged past, invisible now, invisible and free, their bodies littering the floor, where I knew they would finally stay, rising no more.

I was crouched there, gripping Ida's hand, blinking back tears, when claws sounded on the steps. I jumped up, thinking, *Shit, it's not over.*

Lloergan burst through the doorway with another *cŵn* behind her, both of them bloodied from battle. Brenin and Ioan followed, other Huntsmen behind them, rushing in and stopping short as they saw Ida on the floor, atop that pile of ashes, surrounded by the dead melltithiwyd.

"Is that . . . the sluagh?" Ioan said, gaze on the ash.

"It was," I said. "Now we need to find Gabriel and Ricky."

"Done," said a whispery voice, so weak it was barely audible.

Helia appeared in the doorway, supported by Alexios. Her skin was bark, fingers tapering to twigs.

"We found them," Alexios said. "She insisted."

He lifted Helia in his arms, ignoring her weak protests and Meic's insistence that the Huntsmen could carry his mate. "She's mine. I have her. Now let's get the others. We don't have much time, and we have a favor to ask, before it's too late."

CHAPTER FORTY-EIGHT

Helia's favor.

We were home, at my house in Cainsville. Gabriel was with me in the yard, bundled up against the cold dawn. Ricky hung back with Lloergan at the pond, both giving us space as he treated the hound's injuries. Lloergan had fled when the throng of minor sluagh attacked—she'd remembered the first time she'd met its kind, the attack that took so much from her. But she hadn't run far before she circled back and fought, saving her pack sister and making the minor sluagh decide they had better things to do than battle a couple of *cŵn*.

As for Helia . . .

When Helia and Alexios asked me for a favor, I'd waited for something momentous, like Ida's request. They deserved it, after all, for everything they'd done. But what they asked for . . .

Gabriel and I stood in the back corner of my yard, in a particularly untended patch, one that had been empty of everything but brambles and weeds. Now there was a tree, a strong young linden. Alexios crouched at its base, his hands against it, whispering to it. Then he rose and turned to us.

"That was Helia's request," he said. "To root here in her death. Now I'll make mine. I'm asking for the same. To root here, with her."

"Absolutely," I said. "Whenever you think the end is close—"

"I'm not waiting for the end. I'm bringing it to me." A faint smile. "Which is why I didn't dare ask while she lived. We'd have argued. We hated it when we argued. But if she's done, so am I. There's no place in this world that won't remind me of her, and I don't want to be anyplace that she isn't. May I go now? Here?"

I opened my mouth to protest. I *had* to protest, had to try to talk him out of it, but Gabriel said, "Of course," and Alexios nodded, and he stood, one hand on the linden tree, leaning toward it and whispering as we walked away to give him privacy.

When we came back, I had two lindens in my yard, one straight and true, the other leaning toward it, a branch wrapped around its trunk. And I cried. I'd managed to stifle my tears with Ida, but now I cried—for Ida, for the dryads, for everyone we'd lost, everyone who'd given themselves in that final battle.

I stood in that yard with Gabriel's arms around me, holding me against him as I cried.

I was back inside the house. Ricky had gone to help Ioan deal with the loss of a Huntsman and hound. Gabriel and I were with Rose in my parlor. Veronica, Grace, and Patrick were there, too. I'd never seen any of them quite as somber as they were that morning. Ida was dead. Walter was also dead, a traitor whose true story would never fully be known.

I thought about that. Mostly, I thought about it in relation to Ida. I remembered those noises on the stairs to the belfry when the sluagh had been talking about Walter's betrayal and his death. That had been Ida, I realized, listening to confirmation of her mate's treachery and his murder. What had that been like for her? He was her lover, her consort, her partner for centuries, and he'd turned on her and on Cainsville, and she would never know why. She died not knowing why.

I think that makes her more "human" to me than anything. It makes me grieve more, and I wonder if her sacrifice was in part to rectify the damage he'd done but also because, like Alexios, she'd lost her life partner. For her sake, I hope that, in those final moments, she was able to tell herself he'd done it for Cainsville—that, in a twisted way, he'd still done it for them.

But we weren't talking about Ida or Walter or what would happen in Cainsville now that they were gone. We were talking about Seanna. We'd found her, sleeping as soundly as when my mother had been poised over her with a knife. All that drama, and she'd never woken. She still hadn't, deep in her fae-induced sleep. Now we had to decide what was to be done with her.

"So what happens with her mark?" I said. "The elder sluagh is dead, but it's still there."

"As it will be, unfortunately," Veronica said. "The death of the sluagh only means that one specifically cannot take her soul. She'll still be collected, by other elder sluagh. However, now that the one who marked her is gone, I can remove it."

"And removing it means she won't be taken?"

Veronica glanced at Patrick. There was a long moment of silence.

"It doesn't mean that?" I said.

"It does," Patrick said. "But if you take away the mark, you give her back what they stole. Give her back her humanity."

"Then that's a no-brainer, right?" I glanced at Gabriel, sitting beside me on the sofa. "Sorry. I shouldn't be the one talking. In fact, I probably shouldn't even be part of this discussion."

Gabriel's hand reached for mine. "No, you should. What happens to her affects you, should she somehow regain her humanity and still decide to hurt you."

"She wouldn't," Veronica said.

"But it does affect you, Liv," Rose said. "If it affects Gabriel . . ."

She let that one hang, but we all knew what she meant. If this decision affected him, it would affect me. And it definitely affected him.

Gabriel said, "I believe, then, it is, as Olivia called it, a no-brainer. To restore her humanity—and annihilate that part that might seek to harm Olivia, either for petty pleasure or for profit—seems only positive. But the fact you haven't merely told us you're doing so suggests it isn't that simple. I certainly hope you aren't asking because you think I would *want* her marked, as punishment for what she's done to me."

"No," Veronica said. "We know you wouldn't. The problem . . ."

When she trailed off, Rose said, "Memories."

I looked over at Rose, seated on a chair, hands wrapped in her lap. She straightened and said, "The problem is memory. If they return her humanity, I'm guessing that means she'll remember everything. How she treated her parents, her family, her friends. All of that would be bad enough. But what she did to her own son . . . ?" She shook her head. "It will break her."

I looked from Veronica to Patrick. "Is she right?"

"About the memories, yes," Patrick said. "About breaking her . . . I didn't know Seanna as a child. It'll be hard on her, yes, but—"

"It will break her," Rose said firmly.

"Rose is right," Veronica said. "If we restore her soul, we break her mind."

"What kind of a choice is that?" I said. "How the hell is anyone supposed to decide—?"

Gabriel's hand squeezed mine, cutting me short, and he said, evenly, "Is there another option? And, yes, I suppose we could take her mark and then give her a merciful death, but I don't believe we could ever agree to that. Is there another choice?"

"We can take the mark and make her comfortable," Veronica said. "Use fae compulsions and such to let her rest and dream pleasant dreams. She'd have periods of lucidity, where she would be calm, but she would never be about to live a normal life. It would be, I fear, a form of institutionalization."

"She'd stay in my building," Grace said. "We'd look after her, Veronica and I. You'd be free to visit if you wanted, but that would be up to you."

"No," Rose said. "She's my kin. My responsibility. If Gabriel agrees to this, I would look after her. In my home."

Grace shook her head. "Our compulsions will work better in my building. She'll be happier there."

"But—"

"If you wish to be her caregiver, I won't stop you," Veronica said. "Yet Grace is correct Scanna will stay in the apartment building. Under your care, but living there."

Gabriel shook his head. "You did nothing to cause this, Rose. You shouldn't feel obligated—"

"I don't. I want to do this." She met his gaze. "I'm asking you to let me do this, Gabriel."

He nodded, and silence fell.

Two days of holing up in my house with Gabriel. Taking the time I needed to recover.

I hadn't been injured—not physically—but I felt more exhausted than the times I'd actually been shot or stabbed. It wasn't even a melancholy exhaustion, but more one of relief. I'd made my choice with the Tylwyth Teg and Cŵn Annwn. I had yet to tell anyone other than Gabriel, but it was made, and all I wanted to do now was hole up in my house with him, feel the

ground finally steady beneath my feet before I had to finish this.
Commit to a choice I'd rather not make.

I had other obligations as well, and after those two days I was
ready for one. Time to see Pamela. She was out of the hospital
now, having recovered from her mysterious ailment, with no
one ever realizing she'd left her hospital bed.

I had something to tell her, something important, but I would
have postponed it longer if she hadn't summoned me.

I took my usual place, and she'd barely sat in hers before she
said, "I'm confessing."

"What?"

"I'm telling the court it was me. You're getting your father
back, Eden. That's what you want. That's what I owe you. What
I owe both of you."

I stared at her. "You're offering . . ."

"Yes, and please don't ask if I have an ulterior motive. There
are no strings on this gift, Eden. I want you to be happy, and
this is the one thing you lack. So I offer it. No, I *give* it. Freely."
She started to rise. "I've already asked to speak to someone. It'll
be done today. That won't get your father released instantly, but
I have evidence. He'll be out as soon as it can be done. I would
like to speak to Gabriel about that."

She walked toward the door, and I looked at her, speechless.

Then, as the guard was about to take her, I said, "Mom?"

She stopped. Just stopped, as if not sure she'd heard right.

"You don't need to do that, Mom," I said. "You have the
appeal. I was coming to tell you that. You and Dad. Gabriel was
notified yesterday. The appeal has been granted, and it's strong.
It's really strong."

She turned and looked at me, her expression unreadable.
Then she shook her head. "I don't want strong. I want guaranteed. For him. I'm going to do this, Eden. Please let me—"

"No."

"I'm asking—"

"No. I can't stop you, but *I'm* asking. Let this go to court. Please. If you can get out . . ." I took a deep breath. "I'd like you out."

Silence. Such a long silence. I could feel her gaze on me, assessing. Then she said, "And how will Gabriel feel about that? He may prefer my option, given what I did to him."

"He's never cared. I'm the one you hurt."

She flinched at that, but I didn't regret it. It had to be said.

"Let him get you out," I said.

"All right," she said finally. "But if it doesn't work, I will confess."

I got up and hugged her. "Thank you."

CHAPTER FORTY-NINE

I was outside the prison, looking for Gabriel. He'd had business at the office but was coming to pick me up. Then I heard the familiar sound of a very different motor as Ricky pulled up.

"Hey," he said, taking off his helmet. "Change of chauffeur. Gabriel got held up at the office."

"He could have just texted. I'd have been fine taking a cab." I caught Ricky's look. "Ah, he's not really held up, is he? And you're not taking me back to the office. We're going to see Ioan."

"You need to do it. Rip the bandage off before the sliver starts festering." A pause. "Yep, that analogy totally didn't work. But you know what I mean."

I smiled. "I always do. And yes, I get it. Is Ioan waiting?"

"He is."

I took a deep breath. "All right, then. Off we go." I looked at the bike and hesitated. "Maybe . . . I should probably stop riding . . ."

A look passed over his face, eyes beginning to shutter. Then he stopped. Waited a beat and said, evenly, "Okay. If you'd prefer that."

"Not at all. But I don't know what's right, and I don't want to keep doing something that might put you in a bad position—"

His finger pressed to my lips and he said, "No." Then he looked at me. "You have a spot on the back of my bike for as long as you want it. The only question is whether you want it."

I grabbed the helmet, swung my leg over the back seat, and climbed on behind him.

"Have you told them?" a voice asked behind me.

I looked up from petting Lloergan, both of us sitting in front of the roaring fire. I rose, along with Brenin, as Ioan walked in.

The Cŵn Annwn leader stopped to pat the hound's head. "Have you?" he asked.

I shook my head. "I wanted to talk to you."

"Ah." He tried for a smile. "Inform the losing party first. Best they hear about it directly, and not through the crowing of the winners." He shook his head and lowered himself to a chair. "No, that's unkind. The Tylwyth Teg won't crow. This isn't that kind of battle. It may have been once, but it is no longer."

When I sat on the sofa, he said, "If you're going to apologize, don't, Liv. You couldn't make any other choice after what Ida did. I'd love to claim she snuck in and stole the banner after we'd won the war, but that, too, is unkind. We assisted. We did not win. We never could have won against that thing. She did."

"She asked me to choose the Tylwyth Teg. Those were her final words."

A sharp laugh. "Of course they were. While I'd like to fault her for that, I can honestly only say that I hope you agreed in time for her to hear it. She did deserve that."

"I told her I wouldn't turn my back on them. But I'm not turning my back on the Cŵn Annwn, either, Ioan. I can't."

He looked over at me, frowning. "You have to choose, Liv."

"So I've heard. I've also heard that the Persephone solution isn't an option. Too bad—I'm making it one. And yes, I know what that means—that neither of you gets the golden key to survival. If I split myself between you both, I split whatever power I have. The sum may not even equal the whole. Patrick has explained it. But that's my choice. Live in Cainsville; hunt with the Cŵn Annwn. Give enough power to both sides to buy you time while you figure out your own survival plan. Because I'm not it. I won't be it. Stick together—that was the lesson Gwynn and Arawn and Matilda taught us. That's what I'm applying here. Matilda divided her time between the fae and the Hunt. That's how it was. How it should have been. And how it will be. Even if it's not what either side really wants."

He rose and walked over, motioning for me to get up, and I braced for a lecture on how I had to choose.

"This *is* a choice," I said. "It's my choice."

He reached out and pulled me into a tight embrace. "Then it's the right one."

My first Solstice in Cainsville. First of many, I hoped. I'd bought the house. There had never really been any question that I would. It was, as the little girl in my visions had said, mine before I was born. I belonged there, as much as I belonged in Cainsville, as much as I belonged with the Hunt. Some things are not choices. We tell ourselves they are, but they aren't—not if we want to be happy.

The Solstice celebrations had ended an hour ago, the streets empty, bonfires still smoldering. Gabriel and I had escaped the festivities earlier—staying for as long as he could stand being sociable, before I suggested we celebrate in our own way at home.

But we'd come out after the music and the laughter died down, after people headed home. Our night wasn't over. Gabriel had promised to show me the last gargoyle, the one he'd found twenty years ago on a night like this.

We walked, bundled up against the cold, snow crunching underfoot, more falling while we headed along the empty street.

As we neared the town hall, Gabriel steered me into the park instead. In the bushes behind the bank, he found a conveniently placed metal hook—too conveniently placed, suggesting he'd put it there earlier. With the hook, he tugged down the fire escape. Then he motioned for me to climb up.

"Seriously?" I said. "You're voluntarily climbing something?"

"For you. I would only ask—"

"That I go up first and don't watch you, lest it requires serious effort."

"It's been a while since I've done this."

I smiled and went on ahead. Once I reached the top, he directed me to the ledge that let me climb onto the roof. I crawled to the top and sat, legs dangling as I looked out at the town hall bell tower. A few minutes later, Gabriel joined me, still catching his breath.

"Not as easy as you remember?" I said.

"Definitely not. But this is the best vantage point. Do you see it?"

I grinned at him. "I do."

The gargoyle was right across the road, leaning from its tower, its grin as wide as mine.

"Do you think it's actually there all year?" I said. "Hidden from sight? Or does it fly in on Solstice?"

"No idea. But you can ask the elders now. You're entitled to answers, if you want them. Or you can savor the mystery."

"Or figure it out myself?"

He smiled. "Or that."

"We'll figure it out for ourselves. Far more exciting."

"Agreed."

He put his arm around me, and I snuggled in against his side, and we sat there, watching the gargoyle in the falling snow, making plans for our future. So many plans. So much future.

When I started shivering, he said, "We should go back down."

"I don't want to."

"No? I thought you wanted to find all the gargoyles."

"I just did, right? That was the last one."

His lips twitched in a smile, pale blue eyes warming. "No, I don't believe it is. You asked to see one more, for your Solstice gift."

"*Yours*. You're actually going to show me— Where—" I jumped up so fast, I nearly tumbled off the roof.

Gabriel grabbed me as he chuckled. "Slow down."

"Uh-uh. If I wait, the rest of that mulled cider will wear off, and you'll never show me. Where is it?"

"I said you'd need to find it."

"No, don't you dare—"

"But, being your last one, you are entitled to a hint."

He caught my chin in his bare hand, fingers warm against my cold skin as he turned me to face the rear of the building. Toward the park.

I started scrambling toward the ledge, and he grabbed me again, murmuring, "Slow down."

I did. Kind of. I was off the roof a good five minutes before him, already scouring the park when he came up beside me.

"Clue?" I said.

He smiled and said, "It's there all the time."

"So it's hidden. Well hidden."

I surveyed my options. Beyond the park fence there were a few trees, but none wide enough to hide a gargoyle. Which left one option.

I raced to the fence surrounding the play area. Along it were bushes tangled with ivy that wound over the wrought-iron fence. I went around back and pushed aside branches, checking each spot until—

I found it.

Gabriel's gargoyle, hidden by branches and so much ivy that I had to untangle vines to see it, and when I did, I couldn't stop smiling.

It was Gabriel as a very young boy, not more than a pre-schooler. He crouched in that tangle of bush and vine and looked straight at me, one hand extended, a baby rabbit on his palm.

"Yes, I have no idea why they put me in that pose," he said. "It looks nothing like me."

I saw that statue, and I remembered my vision of Gwynn, crouched beside a hole, showing Matilda a baby rabbit. My eyes filled with tears and I managed to say, "I think it's a perfect likeness." Then I threw my arms around his neck and kissed him.

KELLEY ARMSTRONG is the internationally bestselling author of the thirteen-book Women of the Otherworld series, the Nadia Stafford crime novels and this series set in the fictional town of Cainsville, Illinois, which also includes the novels *Omens, Visions, Deceptions* and *Betrayals*. She is also the author of the hit crime novels *City of the Lost* and *A Darkness Absolute*, three bestselling young adult trilogies, and the stand-alone YA suspense thriller, *The Masked Truth*. Her Otherworld characters also inspired the hit TV series *Bitten*. She lives in rural Ontario.